About th

Tom Ward is an author and features writer, writing for publications including *Wired*, *Esquire* and *National Geographic*.

He has won the GQ Norman Mailer Award, the PPA New Consumer Magazine Journalist of the Year Award and has been shortlisted for The People's Book Prize. He is also a graduate of the Faber Academy.

Tom lives with his dog, Ralphie.

About the Author

The Lion and the Unicorn

Tom Ward

unbound

This edition first published in 2021

Unbound
TC Group, Level 1, Devonshire House,
One Mayfair Place, London W1J 8AJ
www.unbound.com

This book is a work of fiction and, except in the case of historical fact, any
resemblance to actual persons, living or dead, is purely coincidental.

ISBN (eBook): 978-1-78965-154-6
ISBN (Paperback): 978-1-78965-153-9

Cover design by Mecob

Printed and bound in Great Britain by Clays Ltd, Elcograf S.p.A.

For Maureen Isbister and Myrtle Ward,
my grandmothers

Super Patrons

Maffew Albridge
Singh Alexia
Katie Allen
Enrique Alvarez
Matt Blake
Jenna Marie Booth
Denise Brown
Darryl Camp
Stacey Camp
Naomi Cauchi
Fong Chau
Jamie Chipperfield
Tom Colvin
Jude Cook
Dan Dalton
Toby Darling
Ali Dean
Samuel Dodson
Eric Down
Sheila Dunn
Joel Edwards
Scarlet Emanuelle Faro
Amelia Farhang
Piers Farhang
Reza Farhang
Scarlett Farhang
Felix Fisher
Andrea(s) Flisi
Sophie Fourçans
Richard Furniss

Tom Gillespie
Christopher Greenland
Georgina Gregory
Roboute Guilliman
Robyn Gunn
Simon Haslam
Connor Isbister
Michael Jacobs
Ashley Jarman
Dean Jones
John-Paris Kent
Lance Kidney
Jasmin Kirk
Josh Kirk
Maximilian Kücking
Jeremy Liebman
Michael Markle Jr
Sophia McKeever
Michael Mclennan
Tom Morgan
Jessica Morris
Hannah Newey
Audrey Niven
Mark O'Neill
Jeanette Page
Billie Parker
Tony Parsons
Alan Partridge
Mae Physioc
Ben Read

Pablo Ridler
Ellie Rose
Frederic Rukes
Outi Ruokolainen
Charlie Scott
Ste Sharp
Ali Siam
Jamie Smith
Max Smith
Vanessa Smith
Henry Stansall
Rosalind Stern
Jarek Szenher
Kirsteen Tait
Sarah Thomson
Juvy Torio-Ward
David G Tubby

Jake Tyler
Marlene Ulschmid
Hugo W
Eliah Ward
Ralphie Ward
Sue Ward
Tom Ward
Lottie Warren
Charlie Wheeler
Lucy White
Hayley Whittaker
Suzie Wilde
Aaron Williams
Ross Williams
Matty Williamson
Harriet Wilson

A Witness Statement

We were never ones to get things wrong, police officers. I should know; I was one for the best part of my life. And, while no official account was ever recorded, I know for a fact that it has been two years and fifty-four days since what happened started to happen, at the cold, tail end of my fifteenth year on the force. For almost all of those years I truly believed we were making a difference. The following events changed all of that in almost every way. A lot of people died. I killed some of them.

Forgive me if my handwriting is shaky. I'm writing this on the train as it rattles north through tiny provincial towns, shuttered windows and empty cafes staring back at me from the stations. I thought it best to set this down before I arrive. I want to get my thoughts in order. Although I don't seem to be thinking as clearly as I once did. Every day now, I can feel my mind beginning to break open. Like an egg shell.

As we race through empty fields, trees standing bare at their edges, one thought comes to mind; as a child I remember visiting the giraffes, the lions, the hyenas, at the zoo in Regent's Park. I remember eating candy floss and riding on the carousel. Later, when I'd grown out of these visits, when the

Reformation was at its height and the nights were filled with smoke and broken glass, the animals disappeared. Set free by persons unknown, they escaped their cages, into the wild. Into urban myth. Ask anyone with a long enough memory and they'll tell you about the jaguar that still roams Epping Forest, its black coat part of every shadow. But my story doesn't start with those smoke-filled nights. It starts fifteen years later, in 2054, when the animals, freed from their cages, had long since grown wild.

H. – Somewhere north of London. 8 January 2057

1

The Unicorn

It used to be that we called murders 'Bag Jobs' after the black morticians' bags the recently deceased were taken away in once we'd taken our pictures, and our hair samples, and set out our small flags denoting anything of interest around the body. Like a shell casing. Or a bone fragment.

For the most part, a Bag Job is easy to spot from the off, arriving, as they often are, drenched in the aftermath of violence. It was clear from the beginning that, lying face down in a trashed flat with his hair matted and syrupy, a hole in the back of his head large enough to fit my fist in, Caleb Jennings was a Bag Job.

'Vigilante Hit,' a kid in uniform said, pointing to where the body lay sprawled on its front by the window, one arm reaching as though crawling towards an escape, even in death.

'VH. Any money. Case closed,' the kid said, looking pretty smug.

'Don't count on it yet,' I told him, making a sign with my

thumb that he should go and re-join his partner on the landing outside.

'Maybe the kid's on to something,' Mercer said, peering down at the body while the crime scene geeks moved around in their white space suits, snapping this and collecting that. Somewhere in her fifties, DSU Judith Mercer – my superior – looked like she could do with a healthy spell at The Farm. To put it politely, she looked absolutely flattened.

The crime scene geeks pushed past. The flat was small; a standard high-rise unit with a kitchen off the lounge and a bedroom and bathroom off a corridor that led out onto the landing.

'Looks like our boy's a star,' Mercer said, pointing to the television with a gloved hand.

The victim had one of the old, eighty-inch 8K TV units mounted on the wall. On the screen was a video of one of the pre-Reformation talent shows playing on a loop. Judging by the glitches on the image it had been much watched in the fifteen years since such material was deemed illegal. Thankfully, the sound was muted.

The boy singing on stage – 5'8", late teens, brown ponytail – bore an uncanny resemblance to the man in the framed photographs beside the television. It didn't take a genius to work out that once we turned the deceased over onto his back we might be looking at the same star, only a decade and a half older, and no longer shining as brightly.

'This, too,' Mercer said, handing me a glossy sheet of A5 paper. 'A whole stack of them in the other room.'

I took the photograph and saw the same man staring back from his professional headshot. His hair was short but tousled and his lips were set in a grim pout presumably meant to portray mystery, and possibly danger. The cheekbones were sharp and would have been startling were it not for the eyes –

each one a different colour – that seemed to follow you about the room like the Mona Lisa. He wasn't alive in the photo, either. Something in the corner of the eyes, the edge of the smile, seemed about to give way at any moment. It was a look I was seeing more and more those days.

Across the picture he'd written his name in a flowing hand.

'Caleb Jennings,' I read out loud. The name rang the very slightest of bells. Before the Reformation, televised singing contests had been considered the height of entertainment. After the Reformation, Britain was supposed to have been 'refocused' into an enlightened and socially conscious nation with lofty ideals of cultural and moral perfection. Of course, Britain was supposed to have been like that all along, it turned out we just needed a revolution to remind ourselves of the fact.

In order to ensure the need for another revolution never arose, the post-Reformation government had put a premium on high-brow culture. Such material, the official line went, would improve our minds, and make us the best citizens we could be. Remove meaningless distractions, make highbrow, thought-provoking art the only art available, and we would all become more engaged and intelligent citizens, talking our problems through instead of hiding our heads in the sand until the country's problems blew up in our faces, as they had fifteen years earlier. Do this, and we might just avoid another revolution. So far it seemed to have worked.

In line with this thinking, low-brow 'entertainments' like reality TV, along with particular books, films, artworks, certain styles of clothing, alcohol, cigarettes, other unhealthy habits, and anything else that might sow dissent and division, were banned. In other words, for the past decade and a half, Low Culture had been deemed Bad Taste. And Bad Taste was illegal.

As I examined his professional headshot, a brief recollection came back to me. Caleb Jennings had had his fifteen minutes of fame as a child star just before the curtain came down; there had been the TV appearance, then a single hit song before he disappeared back into obscurity, his chosen career soon to be outlawed before it had even really begun.

It certainly fit the bill; I'd been called to the flat because of a noise complaint, nothing to do with a dead body. Over the last few weeks neighbours had reported a man busking around the flats, belting out old pop songs popularised by the pre-Reformation TV talent shows. It was a serious allegation, and in violation of Section A4000204, the so-called 'Bad Taste' law. Which just so happened to be my unit's purview.

Unfortunately, uniform hadn't been able to catch anyone in the act. Then, tonight, a call came through complaining of the same tunes coming from this flat. The old woman who had made the call directed me along the corridor. I arrived to find the door open, the body on the floor, and suddenly the situation evolved from an investigation into Bad Taste infringements to a murder.

I put Caleb's photograph down and examined the coffee table. An ashtray held two cigarette butts. One burned down to the filter, one half-smoked but stubbed out, as though he had got up to get a drink, or answer the door, in the middle of it. The best part of a bottle of Vinosynth had been polished off, too. The cork was still twisted onto a corkscrew beside a half-full glass. A bag of Health Chips had been scattered over the table, along with a few cheap silver rings, a pack of guitar strings and a guitar pick. It was a mess, but it looked of his own making, rather than collateral damage from the ransacking that had occurred. The entire living space had taken a thrashing. Chairs had been overturned. Ornaments knocked off shelves. Scuff marks on the floor. On first inspection, it didn't look like

4

the place had been turned over, only that the struggle had been animated.

'Cat piss,' Mercer said, tapping the bottle of Vinosynth with her pen. 'He should have gone for a '48.' She turned to the body, tapping her pen against her teeth. 'Look like a VH to you?'

I held up Caleb's photograph. 'He's reliving his glory days, trying to get a singing career off the ground again, someone finds out, decides to do their civic duty, shows up pretending to be a fan, he lets them in, a struggle ensues, bad move, he ends up dead, killer flees the scene?' I said.

'Could be,' Mercer shrugged. 'Either that or he killed himself and tried to make it look like a frame job. Or, you know, a bit of police work might reveal a third option…'

'Just might,' I said, crouching by the body.

There's always a smell, like burned bits of bolognese that have stuck to the pan, around gunshot victims. And this boy was burning, all right. Judging by the spray against the far wall, he'd twisted around after he'd been shot, on his way to the ground. Death would have been instantaneous. Any notion that the hand stretched towards the window was searching for help – or a weapon – was simply romantic. The death was clear-cut. What concerned us was what came before. The pink, grazed flesh of his knuckles and the bruising on the part of his cheek that was visible told us that what had preceded death had not been pretty.

'Excuse me,' a crime geek said, crouching beside me as he sprayed a fine misted powder over the body. It was a new form of cadaver varnish they were using, designed to keep everything fresh until they got the body to the morgue. There, the fun could start without any evidence deteriorating or becoming contaminated en route. It smelled like pine needles and childhood sick days.

I stood up and got out of the way. I let myself into the bathroom. It was small, and neither clean nor dirty, with coffee table art books piled beside the toilet, a scented candle, and a two-in-one shower and bath with a polka dot shower curtain pulled neatly back. A collection of different coloured shampoo and soap bottles stood in a corner beneath the shower head, and a damp bath mat lay on the floor. The mirror on the front of the medicine cabinet had been polished clean. Standing in front of it, I saw a framed photograph on the wall behind me. I only had to turn and lean slightly to bring my face up close to it. It was a framed snapshot of the victim on stage. Expensively done, but old and sun-damaged.

The cabinet itself would be where anything of interest was to be found. Pulling the edge of my coat over my fingers, I popped it open, expecting a crime scene geek to run in at any moment, chastising me and brandishing a spare pair of blue plastic gloves. When none came, I took out my pen and started rummaging around, moving the bottles about so I could read the labels. All the usual suspects were there: Wellness Pills, multivitamins, anti-pollutants, omega 3s, magnesium, zinc, B-vitamins for hair, calcium caps, melatonin pills, omega 1250s, moisturiser, charcoal tablets, three loose condoms, a packet of teeth whitening acids, a tube of Beroccas, and not much else. I closed the cupboard and headed through to the bedroom.

This too was small, with a single bed pushed up against the wall under the window. The curtain was pulled back, revealing the lights of the opposite tower block. There was a cheap, tasselled green rug on the floor, a flimsy-looking desk with a lamp, a small, ceramic Alsatian, and some books (the usuals here, too: Dostoyevsky, Bulgakov, Vonnegut, Shakespeare – none of which looked like they'd been opened recently). The cupboard was open and hung with t-shirts, a few jackets and the odd pair of trousers. A few pairs of socks were on the floor, pushed under the bed beside a sweater, and an old plate. The posters on the wall fit the bill as well. There was a David Shrigley print, an Edwina Sandys of a couple in the bath and beside it, Georgia O'Keeffe's *Abstraction Blue*. Next to that was an A1 print of Bowie's last album cover. You could purchase all of these from the shop at the Tate Modern, and I wouldn't have been surprised to find any of them in any bedroom in the country.

I didn't buy it.

I listened to the geeks moving about in the corridor then crossed to the Bowie poster. It was pristine and unwrinkled, except for one frayed corner. I took hold of the corner and pulled. The whole thing came down, folding in on itself with a noise like tearing paper.

'What's going on?' one of the geeks said, sticking his head around the door.

I shrugged. 'It just came down.'

The geek muttered something and stormed out. I let Bowie lie on the floor. In the space where he had been was a smaller poster, depicting one of the old boy bands. Four members, leaning forward on stools as they sang into microphones, their gelled hair sticking up like radio antenna.

I whistled. The poster and what it represented was certainly Bad Taste. The crime scene boys would photograph it, bag it up, and when the case was stamped 'closed', it would go off to the kilns north of Islington to be incinerated. It was evidence of a crime, but whether it played into his murder was still to be uncovered.

I walked back through to the lounge. Mercer was chewing on her pen, clearly itching to get outside for a vape.

'Contraband,' I said, indicating the bedroom.

'A flat like this, I'm sure we'll find more than our share,' she said. 'In the meantime, uniform are out canvassing the tower block. These walls are thin. Someone heard what went on here.'

Outside the window the streetlights hummed against the night. I scratched my cheek, trying to stifle the yawn that was coming.

'You and Bagby go and check his Video Disk file against the banned list, see what you can dig up.'

I nodded. The body was still lying there. It hadn't moved.

'Just where is Bagby?' Mercer asked, enquiring after my wayward partner.

I moved towards the door. 'He comes and goes.'

Just then the smart-arse uniform kid came back in, a look of excitement on his face.

'Have you cracked it?' I asked.

'Ma'am, there's been an incident,' he said, ignoring me.

'Another one?' Mercer sighed.

'We're getting reports of gunfire at the Diamond Club, in Soho. A police officer was involved, Detective Chief Inspector Bagby.'

I can't remember if I grabbed the kid by the collar, but I do remember Mercer shouting at me for something.

'Bagby, is he all right?'

The kid dropped his act. 'The report said he's fine, sir. Just a bit shook up and erm…' his eyes darted to Mercer, 'very inebriated.'

'Go get him,' Mercer said. 'For god's sake, we can do without Bagby causing us more trouble, especially tonight.'

There was not much I could say, so I headed towards the door. Something made me pick up the dead man's photograph and fold it into my pocket. There was no need to take a final glance at the body; that image would be coming with me, in one form or another.

Mercer called after me as I stepped outside. I'd almost gotten away with it, but nothing escaped her. Even after fifteen years.

'Don't think I've forgotten,' she shouted. 'Happy birthday. Now go rein in your partner.'

Outside, London was all bright lights and drizzle. I'd almost forgotten myself.

2

The Minotaur

It wasn't the first time I'd had to pick Bagby up from the Diamond Club. But the scattered tables, broken glasses and torn length of awning outside were new additions to the decor. The four uniformed police officers pretending to be busy were new, too. The nearest one looked up as I approached. I didn't like doing it to junior officers, but I pulled out my badge and gave them a flash.

'Scram,' I said, completing the effect.

'Sir...' one of them began, about to pour his heart out to me.

'I'm aware of the situation,' I said.

A gentleman's club in the Soho-meets-Singapore model, the Diamond Club occupied an easily overlooked nook down an alleyway off Tottenham Court Road. Apart from the collection of tables and chairs that made up the patio area, the casual passer-by would have been forgiven for thinking the place was empty – if they noticed the building at all. To those in the know (a handful of lonely husbands, certain elements of the criminal underworld, a few high-ranking police officers, and its owner, Luca Macelleria) it was a place to come and take stock in the presence of 'average to moderately attractive' dancers of all descriptions, and many that defied categorisation. Or so Bagby told me.

A businessman walking down the street stopped to take in the commotion outside. There were no Observation Units in the area due to an agreement with the management, but if the uniformed officers didn't move along there would soon be cameras of another kind. Violence among citizens had become so rare that the mess outside the club was a big enough draw without the fuzz hanging about too.

'Tell that man to move on. And confiscate his phone.'

The officer blinked at me for a moment, then shouted at the others to make a move. Their vape break was over. Too bad. I watched them leave, doing my best to exert an air of calm. Four officers meant they knew who was inside, and tales of nightclub hysteria would not do well for anyone's morale back at the station. After all, the LDNPD worked hard to uphold its reputation.

My partner had certainly made a mess. Shell casings shone among the cobbles. Some 9mm, and a few larger ones from Bagby's Smith & Wesson. After many decades of resisting American influence in our ways of life, the British authorities had finally caved in and allowed its detectives to carry firearms. (The rank and file could whistle.) With so much of our new, highbrow, cultural intake imported from the States, it made sense to adopt this policy, too. Bagby's Smith & Wesson wasn't strictly regulation equipment. But then, neither was the Colt .45 he had given me when I joined the unit. The gun took bullets as wide as my little finger and had never been fired. But, still, I felt it hanging heavily in my shoulder holster every time I set out on official police business. Knowing it was there did not bring me any reassurance. Especially considering the criminal classes had seen coppers carrying guns as an invitation to arm themselves as fast as humanly possible.

There was a sizeable crack in the window by the door of the club, either from Bagby's gun or one of the others firing at close range. Another bullet had embedded itself in the brick column separating the club from the next building. I eased it out with the tip of my pen. The calibre marked it as one of Bagby's. I knew that he wasn't one to fire warning shots, which probably meant he'd become sloppy in his cups.

I headed inside to get the bastard.

'Hey!' one of the dancers, Cindy, cried as I slipped through the velvet curtain. She flung her arms around me and kissed me on the neck. She was Black, and trans, and beautiful. Delicately, I detached her body from mine. A bamboo plant towered overhead, its leaves drooping to tickle the back of my neck. I brushed them away. Smiling, Cindy took me by the hand and led me through to the main room. Her outfit was something like a fish scale bikini and winked gold light back at me.

'He's in here,' she said, opening a sliding door. 'Be nice to him; he saved us from a lot of trouble with you-know-who. And thanks for getting rid of the Law.'

She meant the uniforms outside. Bagby was a patron first and foremost, and as the person who turned up to get him out of the occasional bit of trouble, Cindy and the others seemed to consider me on the level, too.

If this went any further, though, Bagby would have a lot to answer for. Extra attention from both the club's owner and the police spelled bad news for Cindy. The club was not strictly Good Taste, but it was allowed to continue as long as it didn't cause any problems for anyone involved. Sex work – even the low level form of entertainment practised here – was deemed low culture. But, by operating his establishments under the radar and not causing any issues for the police department, Macelleria was able to keep everyone happy and still turn a profit.

For the time being, Bagby looked like he was feeling pretty sorry for himself. He was sitting at the only table left standing, his head in his right hand, his back to the stage. His pistol dangled from the fingers of his left hand under the table. The other tables had been scattered, overturned chairs lying among them like bodies, drinks bleeding out on the floor. The scent of cordite hung in the air. Ukrainian jazz played softly over the speaker system.

The dancers – whom Macelleria referred to as the 'Diamond Dogs', regardless of whether they were male, female, or other – were doing their best to add to it with the fumes from their cigarettes. Putting your health at risk through cigarettes – like non-synth alcohol – was Bad Taste, of course, but after the shock they'd had, I thought it wouldn't do them any harm. I raised a hand in greeting, picked up the chair nearest Bagby, and sat down.

Once, Bagby had been dedicated, diligent and brave. Now, in his mid-sixties and without any chance of retirement in his near future, he seemed to be prematurely breaking down a little bit more each day. The worrying part was that he seemed to care less and less about concealing it. Taking up drinking again didn't help tip the balance in his favour, either.

'Evening, partner,' I said, reaching under the table for his gun. He pulled back. He lifted his head slowly, saw that it was me and let me take the weapon. I put it on the table then pushed it away from us. A ripped sleeve, torn shirt, and bloody forehead aside, I was relieved to see that he had made it through the evening relatively unscathed.

'Tell me about it,' I said.

He waved a hand dismissively. 'Just a pair of young upstarts getting lippy.'

His eyes were rimmed red and his grey-flecked jowls seemed to hang heavier than ever, as though they'd soaked up more than their fair share of booze. He looked around, as though only just remembering where he was. Then, in a sudden panic, he began smoothing down his shirt. As he did so, the Score Projector lit up over the stage, activated unwittingly by the CashPlant™ in Bagby's arm. Translucent, digital stacks of currency shimmered beneath floating names, denoting which punter had donated the most to the dancers' travel funds. By the looks of it, it had been a quiet night.

'Didn't win a private dance?'

No reaction.

'Want a drink, lovelies?' Cindy called, rummaging among the bottles behind the bar. 'We've got, erm… Vodkasynth?'

'Make it two,' I said. Then, 'Wait, he'd better have the real thing.'

'I'm sure we have a bottle lying about somewhere,' Cindy replied, playing the game.

She brought the drinks over, setting them down with a flash of her fish scale outfit. I picked up my glass of fake alcohol and sniffed it. No one except the old timers drank anymore, but it still smelled like the real thing. I moved my chair closer to Bagby's. The dancers took the hint and started making noises about having to get home and relieve their babysitters / wake up their partners / get ready for their day jobs.

'Who were they?' I asked Bagby.

A shrug. 'I've never seen them before,' he said, speaking into his glass. 'But they said something about gambling money.'

'Who?' I asked again. I had thought that Bagby had kicked the gambling. And the booze. But, friend that I am, I'd memorised a list of his former creditors just in case he ever found himself in trouble again. I ran through it in my head now.

'Anyone we know? I can help, if you've gotten into something serious?'

Bagby waved the question away. 'No. Just some lightweight who thinks he can send his goons around.' He took a drink and pursed his lips in approval. 'Don't worry, I'm sure he'll consider the debt paid, with any extra credit due to the ladies here, for the damages.'

'Forgive my concern, partner,' I said, gesturing around at the destruction, 'but this isn't exactly an everyday occurrence.'

Bagby shrugged. 'I'm not an everyday kind of guy.'

I had little hope of getting anything useful out of him in this condition. All I could do was try to ensure the night's events wouldn't come back to haunt him. I looked around the room. There might have been something I'd missed. 'Do we need to worry about any bodies turning up with your bullets wedged in them as souvenirs?'

'No. It was just a friendly tussle. A bit of a flirtation. They came in, wanted me to "go for a walk". Can you believe that? I know we're limited in our cultural intake these days, but you'd think the youth would possess a bit of originality.'

'What happened next?'

'Well, I told them I didn't want to miss the show, but I could meet them outside in a few hours if they didn't mind waiting. Then they started getting rude. Cindy got up on stage with the shotgun, but I think they knew it wasn't real. My guess is ex-army kids.'

'Narrows it down,' I said.

'Christ, I wish it did. Anyway, they wanted me to think they were tough, so one of them pulled out a knife and started waving it about. We had a bit of a scrap, and just as they were being sent on their way, the other kid pulled out a pistol and started letting it off willy-nilly. If you ask me, he was new to the whole thing and his nerves got the better of him. The other one, though…'

'Did you hit either of them?'

'Just the one with the knife,' Bagby said, clinking his glass against mine in a toast. 'Aaaah. That was the strange thing,' he said. 'This kid just grinned the whole time, even after I plugged him in the arm. He wasn't dressed like the others, either. Like everyone else. He had on these white tennis shoes, white jeans and a white sports t-shirt. Skinny little thing, with a shaved head. He'll soon have a sling to match his outfit, too. Should be easy to recognise if I ever come across him again.'

People had still dressed like that when I was a teenager, but I hadn't seen anything like it in over twenty years. It didn't match any cultural youth uniform I knew of. 'Sounds like a renaissance man. Don't worry, we'll get him. And the other one?'

'Nothing special,' he said. 'Now, leave it alone. I've dealt with it, and that's the last of it. No need for you to get involved.' He pushed his chair back and stood up, swaying slightly.

'I'm already involved,' I said to deaf ears.

Bagby weaved across the floor, navigating fallen tables and potted plants.

'All right, all right. Let's forget about it. Come on, I'll take you home,' I called as he re-adjusted his course towards the exit.

'I can manage,' he called. 'I'm sixty-four, not ninety-four.'

He staggered towards the cloakroom. I pocketed his gun and went to wait by the door. He re-emerged, swearing as he struggled to get his coat on.

'Here, luvvie,' Cindy said, helping him as he tried to insert his right arm into his left pocket.

He was too tired to resist. When he was sorted, he dug about in his pocket and pulled out a collection of old, crinkled bank notes. 'For the damage.'

Cindy met my eyes and smiled. 'Oh, darling, that's OK. You boys help us out enough as it is.' She looked at the money again and let out a short, high laugh. I don't think she could help it. She clasped a hand to her mouth. 'Sorry! It's just I didn't know they still made paper money.'

She chucked Bagby on the arm. 'That's why we love you, Bagby. They don't make them like you any more, either.'

'Thanks, Cindy,' I said. 'And sorry.'

She pressed the cash into my palm as I led Bagby away. I pocketed it alongside the gun. Then, at the door, I took Cindy's wrist and pressed mine against hers, transferring her the damage through my own CashPlant^{TM}. Bagby hadn't noticed.

'You're a one off,' Cindy said, and she seemed like she meant it.

Bagby had bought his flat high up in the Barbican back when that was still something people did. Over the years he'd dug in as best he could, collecting books and records and paintings and piling them up like someone trying to build a physical barrier to block out the outside world. The usual titles were there. All taken from the official 'Approved List' taught in schools, colleges, and universities across the country. But sprinkled among the Camus and Burgess and Ishiguro were rare copies and ancient editions of Baldwin and Harari, Barker and Angelou, Carter, Morrison, and more. Most had long since been taken out of circulation, and by inviting me to visit his flat-cum-archive as often as I could, over the years Bagby had given me an invaluable education. Nor did he ever try to hide the fact that these musty rooms contained many of the very same materials we sent people to prison for possessing. Should anyone but myself ever stop by his flat, Bagby might have been in trouble for possessing so much contraband. It was lucky, then, that I was his only visitor.

So brazen was Bagby in displaying this illegal collection that the first time he invited me to gaze upon his treasures, shortly after he had seen me promoted to the unit, I had been sure it was a test. 'Post-Reformation thinking goes that if we consume Low Culture, we emulate that low standard in every aspect of our lives,' he'd said, orating from the middle of the cramped living room, at this point still firmly on the sauce. 'But, tell me, does unfortunate cultural taste make for a lesser person, with less strident morals? Let's pretend that, pre-Reformation, most of the country enjoyed murder mysteries, sci-fi, and romantic fiction, and wanted the same from their cinema. Let's pretend they loved tabloid newspapers and reality shows and the exploits of talentless "personalities". Would such a cultural malaise really be enough to distract us from the fact that the country was slowly sliding down the toilet?' He paused professorially, a finger in the air, a thumb capping a vodka bottle. 'Was the dire state of the nation pre-Reformation really due to the average person's indifference? Or, do you think that top-down policies promoting deeply ingrained nation-wide inequality, nasty nationalistic strategies, hate crimes passing unpunished, endless austerity, medical professionals and school children forced to resort to food banks, tax breaks for the top ten per cent, crooked media, the deaths of innocent ethnic minorities, not to mention the millions of preventable deaths and the government's utter indifference to this during the HAF pandemic are a more likely cause? The boot stamping on the collective face. The communal kick in the nads. If that were the case, perhaps it's even plausible that, post-Reformation, those who managed to cling to power simply pointed the finger back at the people, blaming them for taking their eyes off the ball, instead of shouldering the blame themselves? Now, by keeping us all watching what we're all watching and reading – according to their objective cultural shit list – are they in fact hoping to make us forget the real reason the people rose up and demanded change? Change that, arguably, is yet to materialise? What sort of sense does this list make anyway?' he asked, picking up a James Kelman book and tossing it across the room. 'Does it make any sense to you that Unsworth and Lochhead are banned but James and Armitage are A-OK?'

He paused, eyes trying to focus on me, clearly expecting an answer. I shook my head, pretending I knew half of the people he was talking about.

'What I'm trying to say,' he said, 'is that there's a difference between the job we're asked to do, and how people actually live their lives. This new unit is supposed to care about all of this. But does it actually make a difference what books people read?'

All I could do was nod along as my partner denounced our unit's entire raison d'être, half-certain that the walls were bugged and that the slightest sign of acquiescence would find me whisked off to the detention centres in the North. Only later did I learn that the real test was Bagby having to keep a straight face as we arrested people for possessing *White Teeth* or *Honky Château*.

While he went drunkenly on I thought about my father, about how he'd never put much emphasis on books and music, especially not after my mother died. About how he was a dyed-in-the-wool copper and would have called in reinforcements to turn over Bagby's flat as soon as he'd walked through the door and found it full of illegal paraphernalia. Or would have, had the HAF virus not carried him off, delivering his last breath in the crowded corridors of St Thomas' at the age of sixty-three just two weeks earlier.

I was half-thinking I should take after the old man and turn my superior officer in. I could even hear the old man's voice in my head urging me to do just that.

That's when I saw it, her one and only record, the worn spine standing out among Bagby's collection. According to the rules this too was banned. When I first saw it on the prohibited list I was half-flattered that anyone had remembered it, then half-ashamed because my father had blamed music for her death. Section A4000204 would have suited him to a T, had he lived to see it. He certainly hadn't kept any copies of my mother's music about the house. Or even much to remember her by, almost pretending she'd never existed, acting as though her death was a cautionary tale we would both benefit from remembering.

I decided then that while against the rules, Bagby's point of view was essentially harmless, as long as it didn't interfere with out professional relationship.

Besides, I reasoned, ever since the day we first met Bagby and I had been bound together by a secret that could ruin both of us. So, dobbing him in would surely be the end of us both.

Truthfully, while I'd come to appreciate Bagby's private archive over the next fifteen years, working to uphold the Culture Laws for a decade and a half didn't particularly bother me one way or the other. The Reformation was finally over and done with and these were the terms we'd all agreed to live under. There was nothing I could do to change that, even if I'd wanted to.

'It's a real bottle,' Bagby said now, brandishing a bottle of Armagnac as he came back into the living room where I was crouched, flicking through his bookshelves. He was still a little woozy from his ordeal at the Diamond and his feet threaded uncertainly toward the sofa, like those of a punch-drunk boxer.

It was still night and, with the throws covering the windows and only the light of a single lamp seeping into the room, the flat felt cocooned from the outside world. A bouquet of white lilies stood in a jar on the coffee table. I leaned over and sniffed them but couldn't smell anything. A mantelpiece above a faux fireplace held old album inserts and photographs of a young Bagby in uniform, alongside others of him with people I didn't know, gathered around a table in some smokey den. Pinned to the wall above this were odd newspaper cuttings covering certain cases that he and I had a hand in bringing to an end over the past fifteen years.

'This is the one,' Bagby said, pulling out a record from his collection: Billie Holiday. 'Here, have a drink.'

I held a hand over my glass. 'Just water.'

'You can't trust that,' he said, sitting down on the sofa opposite me. 'Not in London. You new breed have got it backwards.' He reached under the sofa and pulled out a rectangular object wrapped in brown paper. 'Besides,' he said, tossing the package to me, 'it is your birthday, after all. You don't turn thirty-three every day.'

I sat back on the sofa. 'How did you know?'

'Because I'm a detective. And it's the same day every year. Open it.'

I pulled the paper apart. It was a book. A hardback edition of *The Ministry of Fear* by Graham Greene. It must have been over a hundred years old.

'This is too much…'

'Have a drink and say thank you,' Bagby said, filling my glass.

I tasted the brandy then knocked off the rest of the glass and helped myself to another. With the warmth climbing from my stomach I settled back to listen to the music.

'We've got a murder,' I said. 'A man. Could be a VH.'

'Tomorrow,' Bagby said, waving his hand. 'There'll always be work to do tomorrow.'

The record ended. He sat among the silence for a moment, starring past me. Then he got up and put something else on, something I didn't recognise, something slow and mournful played on an organ.

Bagby sat down again, picked up the bottle and drank straight from it. In all of those years he never once played my mother's record. Never once mentioned it or indicated he knew who the woman smiling on the cover was. Since I was six years old, that's all she'd been to me; a half-remembered face on the front of a record cover. For a while, before the Reformation, her song was played a lot. Much to my father's distaste. But then Section A4000204 came in and suddenly her voice was gone from the radio, from television shows and record stores. And from my life.

The brandy and the record Bagby had selected were working on me in a way I didn't like. I decided to change the subject and focus on the night's events.

'Who were those guys, really?' I asked, knowing I was chancing my luck. Bagby might have been slipping, but everything he did remained a calculated play – he couldn't maintain such a collection of contraband otherwise. Gambling didn't fit his MO. It involved too much risk. Most of his creditors had long since disappeared, too. And I knew for a fact that he'd been going easy on the drink for the past year – despite him brushing off this achievement every time I'd tried to mention it. Everything that had happened tonight signalled a dramatic change of direction, an adjusting of the sails against a new and unexpected wind.

"'*Everything has been figured out, except how to live,*'" he said, lying back on the sofa, quoting Sartre.

He was one of few people I knew who recited quotes for the pure admiration of words and the people that had written them. Not like the taxi drivers hoping for a better tip. Or the politicians reminding you that their education had cost more than yours.

'You know I can help you with anything you've fallen into,' I said.

'Ha!' Bagby laughed sharply. He put the bottle down and eyed me narrowly. 'I haven't "fallen into" anything. Just let it alone, for god's sake!'

He stood up and headed towards the kitchen. The empty bottle teetered on the edge of the table. I caught it just as it fell. The alcohol I'd drunk rushed to my head and the tip of my nose pulsed. I followed Bagby through to the kitchen for some water. Whatever they put in it, it was still cleaner than French brandy.

I found Bagby leaning against a counter. 'They couldn't leave her alone!' he shouted to no one in particular.

'I don't think Cindy really minded,' I said. 'No real damage done. No injuries.'

Bagby mumbled something I didn't catch.

The clock said 3am. I didn't want to commit to another night of Bagby lamenting the state of the nation until dawn. Time to be going.

'Well, I've got to get off. Killers to find, and all that.'

'All right,' Bagby said, his head resting against a cupboard.

'Thanks again, for the book.'

I went back into the lounge and turned the record player off, then sat, thinking for a moment. I picked up my jacket and put the book in the pocket. After a while, I heard Bagby move down the corridor to bed.

I was temped to reach for my mother's record and play her song one last time. I didn't need to, though, it was permanently stuck in my head, a part of my DNA. That voice, like Etta James doing the Righteous Brothers. On the few occasions I thought of my mother, I thought of that voice wrapping me up like a duvet, her arms around me. For some reason that slow, famous chorus always made me think of a ship coming into a dark harbour in the middle of the night.

'*On oceans we float, away from it all*
And birds they soar,
like my heart at your door'

I gave it two minutes, letting those thoughts sink away, then went into the kitchen and pulled out the ball of bank notes Bagby had given to Cindy and pushed them into an empty mug by the kettle. I emptied the bullets from Bagby's gun onto the counter. Only two shells out of six were unspent. I scooped them all up and put them into the mug with the money. I hid the gun in the empty fridge in case Bagby got the urge to use it somehow in the night, then let myself out.

3

The Boy

It was raining by the time I got home. Despite the hour I couldn't sleep. Instead, I lay there thinking about Bagby and how we'd first met. It was fifteen years ago, after the Black Week of rioting when the nation's grievances finally came to a head all across the country. While Manchester, Sheffield, Milton Keynes and the rest burned, it was my job to protect the lives and property of the blameless bystanders caught up in it all. I was eighteen and had been in uniform just three weeks – pushed into the family business with my father's hand firmly on my back – when the guillotine came down on London; part of the latest batch of foot soldiers they rushed through training to put down the uprising.

We were deployed, newbies alongside professionals, to guard the streets around parliament and Westminster while rioters broke windows along Pall Mall and down in Brixton and up in Camden and east in Dalston. Even with the sudden influx of new police officers, and the army reserves driving their tanks down Wardour Street, there was a nervous recognition that we were well and truly outnumbered. To make matters worse, the HAF virus, the most deadly pandemic since smallpox, was then rampaging freely through the population, claiming more lives than any revolution could. While the protestors were driven by their belief in the need for a new social order, among us police officers it was clear that we would all rather have been elsewhere, preferably with those family members struggling through their final hours.

The HAF virus and the government's reaction to it was a particular cause of ire for the protestors. But it wasn't the only reason they claimed they were taking to the streets. Rather, they argued, the poor response to the HAF virus was the final insult in a long litany of transgressions carried out by our government. It was true that riots about austerity and our immigration policy and institutionalised racism had been commonplace for as long as I could remember. Now, a perfect storm of all of this, plus a bungled response to a global pandemic and the recent deaths in police custody of Aarav Kahn in Birmingham and Daniel Adebayo in Liverpool had brought the nation to boiling point. The only thing needed to turn the nation-wide protests into a revolution had been a leader.

And, sure enough, a messianic figurehead had emerged in the form of 'RZ', a former stand-up comedian-cum-light-entertainer who experienced an epiphany when he realised that achieving fame and fortune for his own ends didn't actually bring him happiness, and that the throwaway television programmes he was involved in were but a temporary salve against the brutality of everyday life in Great Britain. Instead of distracting ourselves with dumb TV shows, we needed to wake up and demand action, he argued. This crisis of conscience had seen him become increasingly politically outspoken until, under pressure from the crowds gathering behind him, he accepted the role of revolutionary figurehead, taking to television and the internet to campaign for a better life for all.

At the time, I'd viewed all of this through my father's distorted lens, but even I had to admit there was something about RZ that brought people together, the disenfranchised and the dispossessed, the immigrants living in poverty.

I remembered watching him on television when I was about sixteen. It had been a political debate programme. RZ was dressed up like George Harrison in full Hare Krishna mode, calmly asking the exasperated presenter over and over again 'But why can't we have a country that treats everyone fairly?'

'Tosser,' my father had said, switching off the TV.

Naively, I assumed I was on the right side of history because my father was out there every day, policing the streets as he had done all of his life. And if he was against what would become the Reformation, and if he'd spent his whole life studying what was right and what was wrong, surely his opinion on the uprising was right. Looking back, I'm not so sure I would play it the same way if I had my time again.

Before I joined the police – when I could still pass unnoticed in such places – the chatter in pubs, in coffee shops and book shops across London was almost unanimously in support of radical change. And I'll admit, even at that age, I was beginning to feel that something had to be done. There was a point when I might have landed in either camp, but with or without my father's influence, a violent faction involved in the protests made my decision for me. The bombings, the kidnappings and the arson were a step too far in any protest. And there was no end in sight, despite RZ appearing on television, pleading with his followers to stop the violence and continue the fight peacefully.

Which brought us to Parliament Square, standing shoulder to shoulder with the august buildings at the height of the Black

Week, the defining event in what would soon become known as the Reformation.

From where I stood I could clearly see a procession of rioters advancing towards us along Whitehall, their shape and number becoming more defined as they neared. I was surprised to see a figure resembling RZ at their head. Dressed in a long grey kaftan, a microphone in hand, he looked so much like he did on television – long dark beard, hair pulled back in a ponytail, sunglasses – that for a moment I didn't believe he was real.

'Brothers, sisters, *people*,' he said, in the cultivated RP that he used on screen. 'We march now peacefully, despite the violence this government has done to us, and continues to do to us. We demand a fairer system for all, and by our words and our toil, we shall achieve it!'

In hindsight, what happened was inevitable. Even as RZ orated his message of unity, some among the crowd were brandishing sticks and throwing stones. It must have been clear to everyone except RZ that there would be nothing peaceful about this demonstration. This was, of course, before most of us carried guns, and I'll admit that I didn't much fancy my chances against the crowd with only a stab vest and truncheon for protection.

In the end, it didn't much matter. Before the rioters could reach us, a tank fired over our heads and blew a hole in their front ranks.

I saw RZ duck. The microphone dropped to the ground and he seemed to be being dragged away. That's when the rest of the army officers appeared from behind the Abbey and set up positions for their .50 calibre guns. They started firing into the crowd, their mortars whistling overhead, their rifles answering with a rhythmic tapping, all of this punctuated by the apocalyptic crack and boom of the tank firing again and again. A few coppers turned and ran away. A few simply took off their helmets and stared as smoke filled the square. All the while the protestors kept coming, as months of tension broke into a bloody wave of bodies intent on expressing their anger in any way possible.

The protestors scattered and spread out, pushing forward, ducking this way and that behind cars abandoned by their owners, carrying little more than lengths of pipe and the occasional improvised petrol bomb. The soldiers pushed forward to meet them and the square became a cacophony of gunfire and injured cries.

A shout shook me out of it. I turned to see two police officers running along the street towards Millbank and Lambeth Bridge. At first I thought the army might shoot them as deserters. Then I realised they were running towards a group of five protestors coming up behind us from the bridge. I ran to assist. I glanced across the river as I reached the parliamentary gardens, seeing columns of smoke. Something hot and fizzing shot past my ear. I tripped and, winded, looked up in time to see a rocket explode against parliament in sparkling greens and reds. A firework. The protestors were just children, three boys and two girls, none of them older than twelve. They'd come to join in, firing rockets from two lengths of scaffolding pipe in imitation of rocket launchers. Just kids having fun. Just kids in the wrong place at the wrong time.

'Get out of here!' I shouted at them, waving my hand as the ground shook with tank fire.

Four of the kids dropped their ammunition and ran to the cover of nearby buildings. A police officer gave chase. The last child, a boy, took off along Millbank towards Lambeth Bridge. The other officers would have reported me had I let him go, so I sprinted after him, across the bridge, eyes focused on the child's running back as smoke continued to rise over the city. On the far side of the bridge the boy turned left, ran down the steps, then doubled back under the underpass. Hurrying to catch him, I turned too sharply and slipped, sliding on the wet pavement. I looked up as the kid made the other side of the tunnel. Then, a police officer I didn't recognise appeared and slapped the kid across the face, sending him sprawling back against the wall. I could hear the crack his head made from where I knelt. I could also see that the kid wasn't moving. The officer seemed either furious or scared out of his wits as he straddled the body and began pummelling his lifeless face.

By now I'd dragged myself to my feet and was running towards them. I shouted a warning, then pulled the officer away from the kid. He turned and hit me with his truncheon, knocking me down once more. He stood over me, ready to swing again, when a gunshot sounded, echoing along the empty tunnel. The officer looked like he was trying to focus on something for a moment, then dropped the truncheon and slumped to the ground.

I shielded my face with my arm. When nothing happened I put it down again. A broad-shouldered man with close-cropped brown hair was standing just inside the tunnel, a small revolver still raised. His face was blank, as though the whole thing had been confusing to him as well. He looked at me and for a moment I was certain that my life had come to its end after all. Instead of shooting me, he turned and threw the gun into the river, took a last look at the dead child, then hurried away down the street. I sat on the ground, breathing heavily for a moment or two, then went over to the kid and felt for a pulse. He was just a boy. An innocent child caught up in it all. I tried CPR for I don't know how long, then held my hand to the child's cheek before closing his eyes, the sounds of the tanks rattling across the river all the while.

Forty-seven people died that day in London alone, including fifteen police officers. Two days later, RZ agreed to meet with the government in an attempt to bring the uprising to a peaceful resolution. The government seemed to listen to him. There were resignations across the board. The new government was formed of a permanent coalition and offered promises of change. Promises of open forums with the people. Promises of a time of great healing for Britain. The new Prime Minister took RZ's message that we mustn't let ourselves be distracted by meaningless entertainment and apathy again, and ran with it. RZ was never seen publicly again. A cure was found for the HAF virus and, slowly, over the next few years people moved on with their lives. All but my father, who had contracted the virus on that day of bloody riots, and died equally bloodily in hospital a week later.

Of course they found the dead police officer under the bridge, and of course he received a posthumous medal for bravery. He was one of six new recruits to have died that day. No one asked who had shot him. And no one mentioned the dead boy.

But the issue wasn't finished. The dead boy was there when I closed my eyes. He kept me awake. I went to St Thomas' Hospital and tried to speak to my father about it in the middle of the night but he was beyond conversation. Instead, I prepared a statement, not caring if my career or freedom was on the line. I was determined to hand it in the next day.

Then, the next morning, I was summoned before my sergeant. I was certain it was all over. But when I walked into his office there was the same tall, broad-shouldered man from under the bridge standing beside the desk. A badge on his belt identified him as a detective. So, he had come to deliver judgement on me for not being able to save the boy.

'Congratulations,' the sergeant said, before I could speak. My single page police file was open on his desk. 'DCI Bagby here has personally commended you for bravery during the Black

Week riots,' the sergeant continued. 'He is requesting that you join him in the detectives' squad. A new unit is being formed which will have a vital role in maintaining order and stability now the nasty business of the "Reformation" is coming to an end. Apparently, DCI Bagby witnessed you putting your life at risk in order to disarm a rioter. Well done.' He smiled briefly. 'I shouldn't get used to it, though. No doubt you'll be back here with us, when all of this dies down.'

Bagby raised his eyebrows in greeting, then stepped from behind the desk. He took my prepared statement from my hands, scanned it then scrunched up the paper and slipped it into his pocket. His eyes briefly met mine before looking away.

'Come on, kid,' he said. 'We've got work to do.'

For better or worse, the dead child under the bridge was our shared secret, and one that would bind our fates together.

4

Police Work

The dream was always the same, and always as vivid – filled with tanks and broken glass and a broken young boy. The sound of a ringing phone woke me. I answered. It was Mercer.

'About time. That was two rings too many. I need you to come see me first thing. We've found Caleb Jennings' mother. She's a Professor at University College. And there's a sister. A twin. I want you to find her and see what she knows.'

I ended the call. There was a square of white paper on the bedroom floor, glowing in the moonlight. I got out of bed and picked it up. But it was only the photograph of the victim, Caleb Jennings, which must have fallen from my coat pocket. I stared at it, standing by the window. A spark like electricity jumped from the paper. But it was only static. And Caleb was still gone.

After Queen Mary and Imperial College closed they transferred all of the students over to UCL, near Euston Road. Apparently, there was just enough demand to keep the place going. The quads and the grand portico, at any rate, looked deserted.

'Are you here to collect a student?' the receptionist asked, squinting up from his computer.

'No. I want to see Professor Jennings. Where is she?'

The receptionist rested his head in his hand and smiled up at me. 'I'm sorry, there's no one here by that name.'

'Professor Jennings. Head of Biological Science.'

'Ah, you mean Professor *Faron*.'

From what Mercer had told me it didn't look like Caleb Jennings had been a stage name. A divorce was the most likely explanation for the Professor's name change from Jennings to Faron.

'That's right. Where is she?'

I flashed the badge. The receptionist peered at the unit insignia for a few seconds then clacked away at his keyboard without any further encouragement.

'Professor Rachael Faron is currently giving an undergraduate lecture. In the Harrison building. She'll be finished in forty minutes if you'd like to wait here.'

'Thanks. I'll manage.'

I left him and followed signs to the lecture theatre. I peered though a window in the door. Twenty or so students were pretending to listen to a cardiganed woman standing at the front of the room. I sat outside and waited. Half an hour later the students filed out, followed some moments later by the Professor.

A student had waited for her chance to speak to the Professor. I let her skip the queue, hoping it wouldn't take long.

'Professor?' the student asked. 'Sorry to accost you like this.' Her eyes shot to me and I moved a further two steps away, letting them have their privacy. In the quiet corridor it was difficult not to overhear their conversation. 'I wondered,' the student continued, 'if you were able to explain what you meant about Hamilton's theory of inclusive fitness in birds? That they naturally help other birds with which they share DNA, even down to nephews and nieces?'

The Professor turned to her, and smiled. 'Well, Susan, I think that can best be summed up by "Family First". Got it?'

Before the student could ask a follow-up question, the Professor turned and continued on her way, shooting me a quizzical eye as she spotted me standing there.

'Yes?' she asked as she drew level with me.

She was a tall, efficient-looking woman in her late fifties with shoulder-length blonde hair just turning to grey. She and Caleb looked nothing alike.

'You don't have his eyes,' I said, without meaning to.

Each was a dove grey, unlike Caleb's green and brown irises. The Professor narrowed hers at me now.

'Would you mind telling me who you are, and what you want, before I have security remove you?'

I stood and produced my badge. 'Don't worry, I'm not here to ask you about the familial habits of birds. Do you have an office? Somewhere we can talk?' A group of students lingered nearby, excited to see their lecturer conversing with the law. 'It might be better.'

'A police officer,' she said, with an expression I couldn't read. Exhaustion, maybe. She looked back at the group of lingering students. 'Follow me, if you must.'

She took me inside a different building and up a flight of stairs. I hurried behind. We stopped in front of a door with another name, poorly scraped away, still visible beneath hers. She let me in without comment. The room was small with a circular window on the far wall. A desk stood in front of it. There was a rug and a chair and metal shelves filled with books; mostly scientific journals alongside battered copies of Mukherjee's *The Gene* and Roberts' *The Incredible Unlikeliness of Being*. The desk, I noticed, was bare except for a pen with a silver cap, and a single white lily standing in an old milk bottle.

'So,' the Professor said, sitting down in the only chair. 'What do you want?'

'I'm sorry to be the one to tell you this,' I began, 'but I'm afraid your son was found murdered last night.'

People react differently to news of a sudden death, from immediate and all-consuming grief to denial to anger. The Professor laughed. She stood and turned to the window. The winter sun lit her hair.

'I don't have a son.'

I hesitated a moment, wondering if she was in shock.

'Forgive me. I understand you have two children? I'm afraid Caleb was found dead last night. At his home. His body was found at 10.37pm, to be precise.'

'As I said, I don't have a son. But I saw my daughter this morning.'

The Professor turned away from the window. This time it was definitely exhaustion on her face. Whatever she had presumed to be the reason for my visit, it wasn't this. She sat down again.

'I'm sorry,' I said. 'Can I contact anyone for you?'

She put her head in her hands and spoke from between her fingers. 'No. It's OK. Caleb... Caleb wasn't my son.'

'I beg your pardon?'

'Ask them to let you read the whole file next time,' she said. 'Or is it above your pay grade? Kate *Faron* is my adoptive daughter, and my only child. Caleb Jennings is her brother. But he and Kate were adopted separately, fifteen years ago. To the best of my knowledge, they never knew about each other.'

'Right… I see. And why was that?' I asked, trying to pretend I hadn't been outmanoeuvred by yet another redacted file.

'They never knew about each other because it was a painful time in our lives,' the Professor said. 'My husband and I were having… difficulties and we thought a child would help. Kate and her brother had been in the system separately for fifteen years – their birth mother died in childbirth. The father was unknown, and they had no other family. We adopted Kate, and only found out about Caleb later. But one teenager was enough for us, without the challenge of introducing her to a brother she never knew existed.'

'My apologies. Our files must need updating,' I said, envisioning myself repeating the same conversation with a new set of parents. Presumably Mercer had been able to dig out information from the adoption agency that Caleb and Kate were siblings, and that Kate had gone to the Professor, with no mention of Caleb.

'Did you have any contact with Caleb's adoptive parents?'

'I'm afraid not.'

Something caught in my mind. 'You mentioned you and your husband had difficulties. What sort of difficulties?' I asked.

'I'm not sure how this is relevant,' she said, 'but Edward and I had professional difficulties. We worked together, on a… research project. We had our own lab. Although I'm sure you know all about that, too. Unless that file is above your salary as well.'

'And where is your husband now?'

The Professor laughed. Her eyes locked onto mine. 'My husband is dead. So I'm not sure he'll be of much help to you. You really don't know the first thing about me, do you? And yet you've come here to try and tell me my son is dead.'

My control of the conversation was slowly sliding off a cliff edge. 'You're right,' I said. 'I apologise. Your file is very thin.

Caleb's is thinner. I rushed here without being able to do as much research as I would have liked because I believe time is of the essence. We don't yet know exactly how or why Caleb was killed. But there's a slim possibility that your daughter, Kate, might also be in danger.'

The Professor sat down again and leaned forward. She stretched her arms across the desk, her hands palm-down, as though working out a kink in her shoulders. If she'd wanted to, she could have reached out and struck me without too much effort. In the small room there was nowhere for me to retreat to.

'Let me guess, perhaps it's a case of mistaken identity and somehow my daughter was the intended target?' the Professor said. 'Not very likely, though, is it?'

My only response was 'That's about it. It's a slim chance, but we have to follow through on it. Policy.' I smiled. 'I have Kate's place of work down as the V&A Museum – although I had thought it had all but shut down?'

The Professor leaned back. New air seemed to surge into the room. 'Yes, that's where she works. And you're right, they are in the process of closing it down. They have but two months remaining. Kate is in charge of finalising the itinerary for the move to the new Government Museum by the Embankment.'

'And is she at work now?'

'There's no reason to bring her into this,' she said. 'I'm sorry Caleb died, but as I said Kate had no knowledge of him, and this will only hurt her.'

'Then I imagine you might want to speak to her first,' I said, turning towards the door. 'But, afterwards, please, have your daughter come in and see me as soon as she can. It might be that she knows something important. Perhaps she's seen something unusual or noticed someone hanging around. She can ask for me, or my partner, DCI Bagby.'

The Professor laughed as though I'd just suggested she send her daughter to the Moon. 'Do you really want to protect people that much, detective? In that case, take a look out of the window and tell me what you see.'

I paused. Then, deciding it couldn't do any harm to humour her, went around the desk and looked out of the window. It was almost lunchtime and a handful of students were milling about outside eating fruit, others doing stretches on the grass.

'Students,' I said.

'What do you notice about them?'

I looked again and thought I knew where this was going. 'They're mostly women. And nearly all caucasian.'

'Top marks,' the Professor said.

I crossed the room again and stood by the door.

'Immigration is "Bad Taste", yes?' she asked. 'That's what counts as "Bad Taste" now, right? Anything that could be controversial? Such a huge issue of contention for both sides, better to ban it all together. No more angry, mistreated immigrants wanting to blow us up because we can't stand their funny scarves. Thanks to our sagacious government, we've eliminated the risk of foreigners wishing to do us harm. But that still leaves a lot of home-grown angry young men and women in need of an outlet.' She tapped the chair arm and I had a sudden sympathy for errant students facing her across a desk. 'Tell me, do you know how many wars this country has been involved in since the Reformation?'

'I have an idea,' I lied.

'We're officially at war with six different countries on two continents,' she said. 'That's a lot of young men and women off the streets, practising their rifle drills in foreign fields. Tell me,' she continued, 'do you think it's right that the only immigrants we let into this country are the ones who've served at least five years in our military, with an additional year required for every family member they want to ship over? Despite any academic promise they might show? Or, you know, the fact that they're human beings like the rest of us?'

'That's just the way it is,' I said. 'I haven't considered it.'

'That's the way it is because for the past fifteen years a permanent government coalition has supposedly been working to ensure that everyone's interests are always represented, for now and for evermore. To ensure we always have parity and equality.'

'It's a fair system.'

'Where's the democracy in bowing down to unelected leaders? And where's the democracy in your department enforcing its syllabus of snobbery? Why are our enlightened leaders afraid of encouraging education and independent thought? Why kill off all of my students in endless wars?'

The Professor was on the verge of going too far. It would be unfortunate to have to arrest her after delivering bad news.

'I'm sorry,' I said, smiling as widely as I could. 'This is really over my head. I only wanted to speak to you about your son. I'm sorry if our meeting has been a distressing experience.'

Before she could respond, I took a card from my pocket and placed it on her desk. On it was the department's logo in blue and gold, with my name and desk number in small black lettering.

'Ask Kate to get in touch. And please do let me know if you've seen anything unusual yourself,' I said. 'Anything at all. Thank you for your time, Professor.'

She called after me as my hand touched the door handle. 'Detective... Kate will be at the museum this evening, after closing time.'

I turned back. The Professor was staring out of the window, looking down at her students. 'Find those responsible, detective.'

On the way out I tried to think of the last case that had gone to trial, but my memory didn't reach that far back. Should we find a suitable suspect, it was much better to quietly shut them away somewhere outside the M25, never to be seen again, rather than risk upsetting the public mood with a court case. Whoever had killed Caleb would be all but certain to receive the same treatment.

The evening was a long time to wait. In the meantime, there was a chance I might catch Kate at home. The house was set back from the road in the centre of a row of identical Edwardian builds. Pre-Reformation, fitness personalities, hereditary millionaires, marketing gurus, and personal chefs had all called the area home. The uprising put paid to that. It was less a social cleansing, more a relocation. London's rich and famous seemed much happier in the new sky-apartments in the east, after all. Without its former occupants, Kensington was slowly sinking back down into the black sludge of the Thames, from whence it had risen. Paint peeled, walls streaked, gardens overgrew. It was here that I was hoping to find the sister of a murdered man.

I pressed the bell again. It rang long and emptily inside the large house. I pressed it a third time and waited. There wasn't so much as a single twitching curtain, there or anywhere along the road. If Kate was home, it seemed she didn't want to speak to me. I walked down the steps, then looked back at the house, imagining the flicker of a ghost in an empty window.

5

Acquaintances

The Met Police headquarters had moved sometime in the last decade to the old Japanese embassy on Hyde Park corner. The embassy (or new embassy) had been relocated to the International Zone, with all the others. I waited while the guard checked my ID card and thumb print at the door. Office workers were walking hand in hand through the park, jackets draped over their arms. The grass was turning brown with the November heat and patches of dry soil were being blown about in the breeze.

Eventually, I was let inside. At one time the embassy had been a grand, ornate building full of carved wooden chairs, tasteful artwork and brimming book shelves. Now, it was crammed wall to wall with small desks where harried detectives worked hunched over, dictating notes to their computers, their voices forming a constant clamour like the clack-clack-clacking of the typewriters of old.

Our department was in the subbasement, two floors down. There were, of course, no windows but the strip lights were bright and the walls had been painted white to maximise the effect. Potted plants formed green pathways amongst the desks to make us all feel better about seeing no natural light for nine hours a day – an idea passed straight down from the top brass. Mercer's office ran across the back wall, fronted by planes of frosted glass. I knocked and was shouted in.

Mercer was behind her desk, chain-smoking. It wasn't strictly allowed, neither here in the building, nor anywhere at all. No matter; a fan whirred above her head sucking the smoke out as fast as she could breathe it in. The desk was a mess, littered with files – as were the shelves, the floor, the chair. Bagby aside, Mercer was the only person I knew who still used actual paper. A kettlebell stood on the floor in the corner alongside a cricket bat. Behind Mercer's desk was a large black and white map of London marked with red splodges of felt-tipped pen. Framed photos of Mercer in military fatigues hung beside it on the wall. The photos had been taken before the explosion that took her left arm. Before the prosthetic replacement was painfully fitted in a dingy Eastern European field hospital. But, unless you'd already seen the photographs, it was impossible to decipher what was hidden beneath their veil of dust. The AutoArm^{TM}, however, was currently on full display, Mercer's shirt sleeves rolled up to the tarnished metal of the elbow, the robotic fingers reaching for another cigarette.

'Well, come on, sit down,' she said, gesturing with her cigarette.

I hesitated. She looked at me, rolled her eyes then stubbed out the cigarette. 'Better?'

Her metallic hand tapped the table automatically. Had she been called up to serve post-revolution, when things *really* started kicking off, they would have fitted her with one of the new, mass-produced enhancements of the type they still made replacement parts for. As it was, production of Mercer's outdated model had long since ceased and should it break down, become damaged, or simply rust away, replacing it would be akin to trying to rustle up spare parts for other outdated tech, like a VR headset or an electric car.

'Did the girl say anything?' Mercer asked, dragging my attention back to the dingy office.

'She wasn't there. I spoke to her mother,' I said, sitting down. 'But I don't know if the girl will be of much use. They were separated at birth. They've never met. The Professor has never met Caleb, either. We had the wrong parents.'

Mercer sat back. 'Well we'd better find the right ones. Higher up wants this solved, which means you'll be staying on it for the time being. While murder isn't our unit's purview, Chief Superintendent Ormsby believes the singer-songwriter connection may be important. So you're on it.'

I nodded. Police work was police work. Nothing Bagby and I couldn't handle.

'It's unlikely the sister is at risk, but she could still tell us something,' Mercer continued. 'Maybe there's some obsessive fan who mistook her for Caleb once, from a distance. You never know.' She let her false arm fall to the table with a thud.

'Now, on to more pressing matters. Do you want to tell me why Bagby thought it necessary to shoot up Mr Macelleria's sordid sex den last night?'

'It's a burlesque club,' I said. 'They don't do that.'

'I don't give a fuck,' Mercer said, reaching for her cigarette packet then scrunching it up with annoyance as she realised it was empty. I ducked as she threw it at my head. 'The point is it is a disturbance we do not need. You know the drill. We leave Macelleria alone and he agrees not to cause us undue trouble. I can't tolerate any alteration to that agreement, especially not where Bagby is concerned.'

Macelleria was the closet thing London had to a criminal

underworld. Or at least, the closest we came to acknowledging one. Post-Reformation, it was easier to trust one guy to run the entire ship, keeping things quiet to the benefit of both parties. In short, post-Reformation, organised crime had been franchised. The Diamond Club was one of fifteen that Macelleria owned across the city. The jewel of which was The Cat's Eye in Stockwell.

'It was a minor incident. Bagby was attacked. The dancers understand.'

'That might be the case,' Mercer said, hunching over her desk like she did when someone was about to get a dressing down. Like a panther preparing to pounce. 'But Bagby has stepped beyond his remit too many times. Not only is it becoming embarrassing, it's making me lose sleep. And not because I care about the bastard, because CS Ormsby keeps calling me at 4am to tear my ear off.'

'I can see how that might be irritating,' I said.

'I don't give a monkey's arsehole what you can see might be irritating. The fact of the matter is Bagby is suspended until further notice.'

'Ma'am,' I said, sitting up straight.

'Don't "Ma'am" me, or you'll join him. Now, back to the Jennings case. Because murder isn't our specialty, Ormsby has seconded one of his best and brightest to work with you.' She smiled, grimly. 'See it as a sort of inter-departmental team building exercise. You'll find your new partner waiting for you downstairs. In the shooting range.'

'But I've worked with Bagby for fifteen years. Surely he should be in on this?'

'I've had bunions for longer that have proved more productive than you two. It's not up for debate. Get down there and introduce yourself to your new partner, or leave your badge here and go sunbathe in the park. Either way, get out of my office.'

I left her stewing over my wayward partner and headed back to the lift. On the way I noticed a folded square of paper tucked under the lamp on my desk. Only one police officer I knew left memos. I slipped it into my pocket.

Sounds of gunfire echoed up from the depths as the lift sank further underground. Post-Reformation, the motion to equip police officers with firearms was quickly passed with only token resistance from a minor party. Since then, violent crime rates had, for the most part, levelled off to an almost manageable plateau. Even though they too packed more heat than they previously had, today's scallies knew that a run in with the law might well mean a bullet in the stomach.

The range was much like any other firing range; a long row of booths with mechanised targets, frazzled police officers plugging away at them. The only difference was that the old, human-shaped targets had been replaced with spinning concentric circles, like a mechanised version of Duchamp's Rotorrelief. Because, of course, while guns were mandatory, killing humans remained Bad Taste.

'How many rounds?' a clerk enquired as I stepped out of the lift. I waved him away and started along the range.

It was coming up to lunch and the booths were filling up. Mercer hadn't given me a name so it was unlikely my temporary partner was anyone I knew. No one looked up as I passed, or waited with a bunch of flowers. At the very end booth was a plainclothes policeman of around twenty-seven, dressed in black trousers with a black shirt with the sleeves rolled up. His face was all angles, with cheekbones leading to a tight undercut, the hair on top scraped back. I watched as he worked slowly through the remaining shots in his Sig Sauer, firing with neat precision, grouping his shots in the centre of the spinning circles with rhythmic *thud-thud-thuds*. The electronic card flashed over his target with every shot, announcing scores of nine or ten out of ten.

He finished the clip. I coughed. He slid the magazine out and checked the chamber. I coughed again.

'I'm DI Stohl. I've been assigned to work with you, on secondment from my usual unit,' he said, still without looking at me. He inserted a new magazine and drew the breech back. 'It wasn't my choice to join your unit. But there's no reason why we can't finish this quickly and get a good result for everyone involved.'

'Except Caleb,' I nearly said.

Stohl had seemed about to fire again. He lowered the gun instead and said: 'I read your file. And your father's, also. Pretty unremarkable. Him, not you. I hope this case will bring out the best in both of us.'

I was trying to work out if I'd actually heard him correctly, and to formulate a response when my new partner continued: 'I like to start early,' he said. 'How about I meet you at 7am tomorrow?'

'I'll meet you here,' I said, wincing as someone fired a shotgun behind me, somewhat missing the point of a shooting range. 'But there's plenty we can do now.'

'I agree. Which is why I'm going to speak to Jennings' father this afternoon. Uniform dug out his information and informed him of his son's death this morning. By all accounts he was quite upset.'

'Right,' I replied. Better to let him get on with whatever he wanted to do, and conduct my own, efficient investigation into the murder unimpeded. 'You do that,' I said. 'I've a few things to check on here.'

He glanced at me for the first time. There was a gleam of something smug and knowing in his eyes.

'Ah yes, the sister,' he said, toying with the safety catch. 'You don't think that finding her would be a waste of time? They never met, never so much as heard about the other in thirty years. The dead man will mean as much to her as a dead stranger. Because he is a dead stranger.' He raised the gun at a fresh paper target. 'I doubt she can tell us anything.'

Apparently deciding the conversation was over, DI Stohl nodded to me, then turned and resumed shooting with the same regular efficiency.

Bagby was waiting in the park, under his favourite oak tree. Men and women in office-wear sat about here and there, drinking their smoothies. Bagby was a small, squat shadow under the browning leaves.

'Got the note, I see.'

'Very romantic,' I said. 'But meeting here won't make any difference; you know they've got cameras in the trees now, too?'

'Let them see,' Bagby said. 'After forty years they think they can suspend me because a pair of hoodlums got hurt trying their luck?'

The hangover looked to be in full effect. If I didn't know him better I'd say he had been crying. His eyes were red and watery, his face slowly collapsing with each word. He looked like he'd crawled out of a vat of vinegar. And smelled like it too.

'You'll be back,' I said. 'Mercer knows you're too good an officer to stay on the sidelines. And we need good police officers, now more than ever. First the bombings, now this…'

Bagby bristled at the mention of the explosions. 'Bombings aren't our remit. Spitalfields. The docks. No one was hurt.'

'You know what they're saying it might be?'

'Don't believe everything you hear them say,' Bagby snapped. 'We've already had one revolution. Every few years or so some idiot thinks he's the new RZ. But there was only ever one RZ, and they've got him locked away for good in that mental hospital. You can't wind back the clock.'

'Look, I'm not here to talk about bored kids getting bomb-making books in their Christmas stockings,' he continued. 'I'm here to warn you about your new partner.'

'You're too late. I've met him.'

'Yeah, you've met him. But you don't know the first thing about him.' He looked up as a couple walked past, arm in arm, a woman's face pressed into her lover's shoulder. When they'd gone, Bagby continued, his tone lowered conspiratorially. 'Your new partner is under secondment from the Unit. You know the sort of things they do over there.'

I nodded. 'I imagine they're very busy at the moment.'

Bagby punched me on the arm. It wasn't my favourite habit of his. 'Exactly. So why move him over here for this case? There's plenty of officers from our unit you could have been paired with.'

'So what... You think they're watching me?'

'I think they're watching the case, to see what happens.'

'And why is he the wonder-kid that gets the job?' I asked.

'You tell me. Seems like overkill to assign him to a case no one cares about. Unless he's really here to keep an eye on something or someone else. What I'm saying is, be careful; he isn't someone you can take the piss out of. DI Alvan Stohl is twenty-eight years old, and two years out of the military, where his records say he was the best marksman this side of Helsinki. Deployments across Europe and the Near East. You know the drill. Plus – and I had to dig deep for this – his uncle happens to be Elliot Wallace, CEO, founder and general big-shot behind Vangelis. You know, the company that makes everything from traffic lights to rocket fuel? Wallace brought him up ever since his parents died in a plane crash twenty years ago. His mum was Wallace's sister. Apparently brother and sister never spoke, but still. You can imagine how pleased Wallace was to take his estranged nephew in. But, the word is that over the years they've grown as close as can be. In summary: our over-qualified, crackshot whizz-kid has access to the craziest technology around and most likely a chip on his shoulder the size of the crater in Spitalfields Market.'

'All of which is very interesting,' I said. 'But how do you know all of this?'

Bagby glanced around, as though expecting to see a man in a trilby peering over the top of a newspaper on the next park bench. 'They're not the only ones with their cameras everywhere,' he said. Then, 'Look, that's enough to be getting on with. Just keep an eye out. Look after yourself first. I have to go, but I'll be in touch.'

'Go where?'

He looked back and his eyes seemed to be watering again. 'Don't worry,' he said. 'I'll see you again.'

He hurried off among the trees, hands thrust into his pockets, head down like the office workers rushing back to their offices after lunch. I didn't know then that I wouldn't see him again for what felt like a very long time.

I spent the afternoon going through the Observation Unit tapes in a dark little office on the fourth floor. It wasn't a difficult job, after inputting Caleb's details, to follow the tapes and watch how his last day on earth had unfolded. Even in fast forward it was uninspiring stuff. Rising around 10am, he left his flat and took part in a two-hour fitness class in the park. Then he went for coffee on his own, reading a romance novel by Heinz Helle before leaving two hours later and wandering in and out of clothes shops without buying anything. After that he returned to his flat where he would stay for the rest of his life.

When we canvassed the building the neighbours reported hearing loud, strangled sounds throughout the early evening. He was singing. Practising along with his old audition tape, which he had downloaded only once – fifteen years ago. Then, just before midnight, the singing stopped but the Video Disk download continued on repeat. It would stay that way until I responded to the noise complaint, found him lying there and hit the mute button out of respect.

None of the neighbours, including the old woman who had first called it in, had seen anything of interest.

Alone in the cramped, dark room lit by the flickering light of outdated television monitors, I rubbed my eyes and blew stale breath between my fingers. I checked and double checked. Then triple checked. Not once during the day did Caleb speak to another person. Not once did a passerby pay him any attention. No trench-coated figure followed him home, creeping from one frame to another.

I'd managed to get hold of his actual file from the adoption agency. It confirmed that his mother (and Kate's) had died in childbirth – as the Professor had said. Fifteen years in care homes across London followed and then he was marked down as adopted. Stohl would know more after he spoke to the adoptive father in the morning. But at that moment, it seemed that there was nothing to mark Caleb Jennings out as special or unique in any way. A day had passed and I was no closer to finding out what had happened to the murdered man.

After a while, I switched tactics and searched for the nearest Observation Unit to the Diamond Club. Part of our policy of appeasement with Macelleria meant we didn't keep too close a tab on him so I had to start a few streets out and work my way in. For an hour all I got was empty streets and businessmen hurrying along in the drizzle. Then, I caught a flash of white, disappearing around a corner on the grainy screen. I stopped, went back and enhanced the image. I checked the map, found out what the next street was, and there he was; a tall, skinny kid dressed all in white, hurrying along with his head down. The image was rough but I zoomed in and snapshotted the top of his head. I hit a few buttons and fed the image through the database. The computer came back with no matches. I hit a few more buttons and got the same answer. I hit play again and watched as another, badly dressed man stepped out of the shadows and tried to shake the kid's hand. The kid kept his hands in his pockets. The second man seemed to shrug, then they set off towards the club, and out of sight.

I hit fast forward and caught them twenty minutes later, hurrying away in the opposite direction. Both had their backs to the camera, but the kid was unmistakably grasping his left arm just above the elbow, exactly where Bagby said he'd hit him. I downloaded the file, saved it under a codename, then sent it to myself. I had no idea who the kid was, but his partner was Vasily Popov, a middle-aged draft dodger who hung around Tottenham Court Road and the International Zone off Commercial Road getting into all sorts of minor quibbles. Tomorrow I would pay him a visit. Now it was time to take a trip to the museum.

6

Empty Corridors

Knightsbridge was all towering, glittering glass showrooms. The screens along the side of Harrods flashed adverts for antique Japanese tables, Inuit furs, Korean sportswear. Tourists from the provincial towns took their pictures and blocked the footpaths as packs of cyclists slipped past. Further on, towards South Kensington, the pavements outside the museums were near-deserted, with only the odd local hurrying along. I always liked taking in the grand old buildings. It was a shame, what happened to the Natural History Museum. Now, after almost two hundred years, the V&A was apparently going the same way.

I badged the security guard at the side gate. He grumbled something beneath his breath then pulled his collar up and shrunk away as though I carried something contagious. A side door gave me access to the building. Away from the eyes of the public the back-corridor arteries of the museum were falling apart. The red carpet was threadbare and damp stains marked the panelled walls. There was no one about. I reached the end of the corridor. The automatic door wouldn't open. I retraced my steps. An old woman pushing a vacuum cleaner smiled at me as I passed.

'I'm looking for Kate Faron,' I said. But the woman just smiled at me, nodded, and continued on her way.

'Can I help you?' a voice asked. A tall, thin man in a V&A jacket was advancing along the corridor towards me.

'I hope so. I'm a police officer. I'm looking for Kate Faron. I believe she works here?'

'May I ask what this is regarding?'

'You may not.'

He took the badge from me, studied it for a moment as though trying to discern some flaw in its design then gave it back. 'Follow me.'

I did. He took me along the corridor to a staircase leading downwards.

'She's down there?'

He nodded. 'Somewhere among the boxes.'

Before I could thank him he turned on his heel and retraced his steps along the corridor. I made my way downstairs, emerging into a cavernous store room, wooden crates of all sizes stacked haphazardly throughout. A corona of light illuminated the far corner of the room. I headed towards it, shouting hellos. I rounded a box and came face to face with a woman dressed in overalls, a hammer in hand, a nail pinched between her lips. My brain hovered above us both for a moment before it realised who she was. The resemblance to her brother was minimal, but not invisible; Kate Faron was around thirty with black, shoulder length hair, one eye hazel and the other green, like her brother's. Her cheeks, however, were higher, her jaw sharper, her brow harder.

'Hello,' I began, taking a step back, 'I'm...'

'You're the police officer who's come to talk to me about

my dead brother,' she said, taking the nail from her mouth but holding on to the hammer. 'Tea?' She indicated a camping table behind her, lit by lights standing on tripods. A thermos flask stood among a collection of smaller wooden crates and what I took to be a number of museum pieces.

'No, thank you. I'm sorry, I didn't mean to surprise you in the middle of your work,' I said. 'Ms Faron…'

'You can call me Kate. And it's no surprise. My mother told me you'd be coming to see me.' There was something of a challenge in her eyes. Something similar to what the Professor had carried in her own stare. Both were a long way from the abandoned gaze of Caleb's professional headshot.

'Kate, then. I'm very sorry for your loss. This whole day must seem surreal to you…'

Kate shrugged. 'Being told that I had a twin brother, and that he's been murdered? Yes, I've had less confusing days. But maybe you also mean the fact that my mother hadn't told me about him before must have come as a surprise, too? We've had easier conversations, I'll admit.' She shrugged.

'Well, yes,' I said. 'Still, I'm sorry.'

She poured herself a tea from the thermos and took a short, quick sip. 'Finding out that anyone has died isn't pleasant, is it? And of course I've been wondering all afternoon what it might be like to have had a brother. But now I'll never know.'

She put the cup down. 'Though we're used to death now, after the HAF virus, aren't we? So long ago, but we don't seem to have recovered. My mother doesn't like to talk about that either. Anyway, as you can see, I have a lot to get on with, detective. You may have heard that we're about to be shut down. Actually, I'm certain you have as you represent the people who deem this museum a waste of funding. Now the entire contents of this museum have to be catalogued and stored away. And guess whose job that is?'

'I'm only here to talk to you about your brother. I think it's a shame the museum has to close,' I said. 'Of course, I won't take up much more of your time. I just wanted to ask you...'

'If I'd noticed any strange people following me lately? If I'd be woken by noises in the night, or had any strange premonitions? No, detective. I'm afraid that until my mother called me this afternoon my life has been completely untouched by anything out of the ordinary.' She was telling the truth, but the way she tapped her foot as she spoke suggested she was more touched by her brother's death than she was letting on.

'I see,' I said. 'Then I'll leave you to it.'

She turned back to her work. A lined wooden crate stood on the table. Beside it was a baroque sculpture roughly twelve inches tall. I looked at it again; it was a skeleton hunched forward with its knees under its chin, an Assyrian-style hat on its head, jewels studding its silver armour.

'Just out of interest, does this fall under the banned list or not?' I asked.

Kate saw where I was looking. 'I thought you were supposed to be the one to tell me that. Until recently it was considered art of the first order. It's a Carolein Smit, 2011. Part of our 'Myth and Mortality' exhibition. You're one of the last people who will ever see this,' she said, placing the piece into the empty box then fitting a lid. 'Which is pretty sad, whether you value it or not.'

She picked up the hammer and nails and looked at me expectantly. 'Well, now that you know I'm alive, and not at risk... if you aren't going to help I'd appreciate it if you could leave me to it,' she said.

'Of course. I'm sorry for taking up your time. Here's my card, in case anything comes to mind. Or you do happen to experience any strange premonitions.'

She smiled sarcastically. 'Of course. Well, goodbye.'

I retraced my steps through the maze of boxes. I hadn't gone far when she called after me, her voice softer now, like the light rubbing up against the shadows. 'Detective... I always knew I had a sibling. I felt it – that connection that twins are supposed to have – and then, last night, I felt it just drop away without any warning... Find him for me, whoever's behind this. Whoever took him away.'

'I will,' I called back. I made for the stairs, leaving her there among her boxes of treasure.

7

Evasion Techniques

Lying there pale and naked on the marble slab, Caleb was a macabre opposite of his sister. The small round hole in the centre of his forehead, however, was unique to him. He'd been shot by a professional, neatly and without fuss.

Kavinksy, the police force's chief mortician, lingered by the body, his own body bent and pale from all the time spent hunched in his sterile underground workshop, opening up the city's dead and probing their insides in order to reconstruct their last moments of life.

'What can you tell me?' I asked.

'What do you want me to tell you?' he replied, scrubbing his hands in a pristine white sink against the wall. 'Same thing happened that happened to all the other Bag Jobs.' He indicated the rows of bodies lying naked or covered by dark blue sheets around him, awaiting his attention. 'He pissed someone off. One assailant. Specifically, he was shot in the head with a 9mm pistol. The most common calibre there is, used by our armed forces and the large majority of our detectives.' He turned from the sink, his hands and wrists dripping pink foam, and peered towards me as though trying to see through my jacket with x-ray vision to determine what sort of gun I carried.

'How long did he fight for?' I asked, looking at the purple bruise spread along Caleb's arm.

Kavinsky sighed. He shook his hands dry then closed his eyes and began reciting his litany of the man's injuries, like a bored and clever child told to run through a list of all of the kings and queens of England in front of the class.

'I would say some time; he has abrasions on both wrists, his right elbow, thighs, knees, the back of his neck. His right hand has two broken fingers and he was hit across the mouth, resulting in the split lip. There are no signs of sexual assault, you'll be pleased to hear, and we haven't been able to find any of the attacker's DNA. Best guess is he, or she – or *they* – wore gloves. The deceased opens the door, the assailant hits him across the mouth and forces their way inside, there's a fight, the assailant gets the upper hand, pulls their pistol, and wham! End of story.'

The theory sounded right, and the gloves were a near-certainty. The lack of the assailant's DNA, though – not even skin scrapings beneath the finger nails – was unexpected.

'Can I help you with anything else?' Kavinsky asked, making it clear that he had bodies to process.

I took a last look at Caleb. There was a faint mark on the inside of his right elbow, at the centre of which was a tiny blue dot. 'What's that?' I asked. 'It looks like someone injected him with something.'

'Impossible,' Kavinsky said. 'We tested his blood for toxins and found nothing. Maybe he gave blood to the war effort.'

'Not on his last day alive,' I said, remembering the tapes. 'Run the toxin analysis again. Check for everything – not just the category A toxins.'

Kavinsky actually gasped. 'I have a room full of customers! I do not have time to test this man again. He is dead. He was shot. That is your answer.'

I reached into my jacket. Kazinsky flinched. I pulled out my badge and tapped the unit insignia with my index finger. 'This says you should do it again.'

'Those tests cost too much,' Kavinsky protested. 'And need I remind you that without written permission from your superior officer, another test is highly illegal too.' He sighed then scratched his right ear theatrically. 'He was only a washed up television star, anyway,' he said, with extra emphasis on the words 'television star' to show his disdain.

'Mercer will authorise it,' I said. 'But I suggest you don't make her have to ask.'

'All right,' Kavinsky said, drawing the words between his teeth. 'It will take some time. Twenty-four hours. At least.' He gestured to the stiffs lying dead-eyed around us. 'I have other departments to please as well. Some of them even more important than yours.'

'Thanks,' I said, on my way out of the door.

Vasily Popov wasn't known to rear his head in the Wyndham pub on Commercial Road until early evening so I had some time to ponder things. Stohl had set up a desk opposite mine, and, when I stepped into the office, I was relieved to find that he wasn't there. Going to see Kavinsky had made me late for our 7am meeting. I assumed Stohl had grown tired of waiting and made a start on the day's distractions without me. I'd just sat down when Mercer called my name then jabbed a finger towards the ceiling, indicating there was something for me to see in the video room upstairs. I took the stairs and found Stohl in there, bent over the monitors, his shirt sleeves rolled up, his badge and gun arranged neatly on the table top beside him.

'You won't find anything,' I said from the doorway. 'I checked yesterday while you were out. There's nothing out of the ordinary in Caleb Jennings' last day on earth.'

He registered no surprise at hearing my voice, and didn't turn around to greet me. I watched the back of his head as he answered. 'On the contrary, I think there's something very significant that has been under your nose all this time.'

I looked at the screen. He wasn't surveying Caleb Jennings' last movements at all. The figure frozen and flickering on screen was Bagby.

'What are you doing?'

Stohl's fingers hovered over the keyboard. 'Your partner is reported drunk at an "adult entertainment club" on the night a young man with a predilection for performance is found murdered less than five miles away. In the absence of other clues, I feel this is an avenue of enquiry that must be pursued.'

'You bastard,' I said, grabbing the back of his chair and spinning him around. 'Bagby had nothing to do with this.'

Stohl looked calmly up at me. 'I hope we can prove that to be the case. But until then we have to explore all angles…'

I clenched my fist. I could tell him about the Kid in White, about Vasily Popov, but Bagby was right, Stohl was not to be trusted. Far from venerating Bagby, if Stohl was determined to find him at fault, any information about Bagby's extra-curricular endeavours, innocent as they were, could prove dangerous.

'*You* had him suspended,' I said instead, the picture suddenly becoming clear. 'You little…'

'What's all this shouting about?' Mercer asked, elbowing me aside as she leaned into the room. I hadn't heard her approach. 'For god's sake you two, play nicely. There are people trying to work in this building and I don't want to have to take the stairs up here every time you two spit your dummies out. Now, Stohl, you're wanted downstairs. Your uncle is on the phone, apparently.'

He tried to hide it, but the flicker at the corner of his mouth suggested that the last person Stohl wanted to speak to was his uncle.

'Thank you, ma'am,' he said. He stood up, rolled his sleeves down, collected his badge and gun, then slid past me without a word.

'Watch yourself,' Mercer said when Stohl was out of earshot. 'There's only so much I can do to protect you if you insist on rubbing up against him. His master keeps him on a very short lead, but he's our problem for the foreseeable. Find the boy's killer, then perhaps Bagby can come back.'

Mercer left me alone with the blinking monitor screens and Stohl's cold mug of Earl Grey. I sat down. There was only one way to prove Bagby was guilty, and one way to prove he was innocent, so I rewound the tapes and started from the beginning.

The day of the killing had been Bagby's day off. The Observation Unit across the street from his flat showed that he had risen early, at one in the afternoon, to go buy a bottle of whisky. After that, he'd pottered down to the local library, where the OUs showed him arguing animatedly with the librarian over whichever literary classic they, in their wisdom, had chosen not to stock. Then he went to the park. The OUs caught him walking about, then the unit in the bandstand showed him feeding the ducks and sipping casually from the bottle in his pocket as joggers ran past.

Stohl had already threaded together this much of Bagby's day, and judging by the time signatures on each part of the tape, there hadn't been any foul play with how he'd spliced it together. The next part, however, was down to me to work out. After half an hour of searching OUs for Bagby, I found him again on a unit close to the underground. And sure enough, there he was three minutes later on the Victoria Line, heading home. Fifteen minutes after that he opened his flat door, then immediately came out again, stuffing a narrow envelope into his pocket and glancing up and down the street. Even in such paranoid times this was unusual behaviour for Bagby.

I watched him for a long time, cutting back and forth between various Observation Units as he walked and walked, doubling back on himself, getting on buses then getting off three stops later and walking back in the same direction, going into cafes and leaving by a different exit. It was classic evasion technique. Luckily, it was Bagby who had taught me everything I knew about such tactics.

I thought of his two attackers – Vasily Popov and the Kid in White. So far there had been no sign of them, but I hoped they might be able to fill in some blanks. I picked up the phone and dialled the uniformed officers downstairs. I gave them my name and told them to go pick up Vasily Popov, explaining where they'd find him. Popov, I was confident, would be able to shed some light on who his associate was and what they were both after.

'But, sir,' the officer on the other end of the phone said, 'Vasily Popov is already here.'

'OK. Good, I'll be down to speak to him in a minute. Put him in the last interrogation room on the left. The one without any windows.'

'But, sir,' the officer said again. 'I don't think that would do any good. We dredged him out of the Thames this morning. He'd had his throat cut.'

I put the phone down, wondering how long it would take until the Kid in White turned up in the same state.

I'd accidentally leaned on the keyboard while I used the phone, and the on-screen Bagby hurried about in fast forward like a microscopic man inhabiting his own little world inside the console. If Popov had been murdered it was even more important that I put my efforts into laying out Bagby's movements before the attack.

I slowed the footage as Bagby turned off a side street, heading towards what looked like an antiques shop at the bottom of a lane with old windows obscured by thick, dark curtains. I watched as he paused outside the door, knocked once, then hurried inside. He came out twenty minutes later then, after half a mile, he pulled out his phone, took a call and collapsed against the wall. I checked the time: 9.22pm – exactly an hour and a quarter before Caleb Jennings had been found dead.

After a minute, Bagby pulled himself to his feet and flagged down a taxi. I followed the taxi through the night-time traffic, watching as it drew up close to the Diamond Club. I checked the same cameras I'd seen the two thugs on yesterday and there was Bagby on his way to drink through the repercussions of whatever news he had just received.

So that was that. It was enough to prove Bagby had never been near Caleb, but not much more. I was about to hit 'delete' on the day's record when something struck me. I rewound and went back to the antiques shop. Bagby was a fan of old books and records but it wasn't like him to spend money on bric-a-brac. The name above the shop door said 'Harrington & Sons'. I checked the database; Harrington didn't exist. It was a trade name, that was all. But Leslie Jennings, fifty-eight years of age, did. He'd been the proprietor of the antiques shop for almost exactly fifteen years and what's more, he was listed as Caleb Jennings' adoptive father.

I printed off Jennings' file. The photograph was small, but I was sure. That wasn't Leslie Jennings, or at least, Leslie wasn't his real first name. I'd seen him before, among the dusty photo-frames in Bagby's flat, in a photograph of the two of them together, thirty or more years ago, arms around each other in a bar room, a snooker table in the foreground.

'Jennings,' Bagby had said. 'He was a good friend, once.'

I typed 'Jennings' into the database, setting the age range at fifty-five to sixty-five. Four hundred men came back matching the description in London alone. I thought back to the photograph in Bagby's flat. There was a Badger's Arms crest in the background of the photograph. I re-set the search criteria to include men who had lived near the pub at that time. Fifteen names came up. Only one file was redacted. I typed in Mercer's passcode. And there he was, Harold Jennings, at one time one of the most wanted revolutionaries in the country. Two names jumped out from his 'known associates' section. A photograph attached to the file confirmed it. It showed a protest march outside Buckingham Palace. Jennings standing in the front row, his mouth frozen in anger. Beside him stood Professor Faron. Beside her stood RZ, the revolutionary who started it all. And beside *him* stood Bagby, dressed almost identically to the day I had seen him shoot a policeman dead while trying to save a young boy's life.

I closed the file then wiped the video record of Bagby's afternoon, cutting it off at the point when Bagby returned home. Let Stohl fill in the hours between then and the club shoot-out himself. He might be on Bagby's trail, but I would work out what all of this was about long before he even got close to the truth. It was the least I owed my partner.

8

Criminal Elements

It was almost dark by the time I reached the International Zone. I parked the car in the police compound, a rough, concrete building standing between two wire fences. On one side stood Commercial Road. On the other, the collected human detritus of war-torn nations near and far – all safely locked away in a permanent refugee community that few police officers and zero civilians ever ventured into.

An officer on the roof swivelled her machine gun to follow me as I approached the gate.

The officer in the sentry booth sat up and scratched his chin. 'Look into the screen please, sir.'

I did as I was asked. There was a buzz as the small, rectangular screen scanned my retinas, then with a ping, it announced that I was allowed to pass.

'You're not going in there alone?' the officer in the booth asked.

'Why not?'

'They've been unsettled today. They won't be pleased to see you.'

'They need hosing down!' the officer on the roof shouted, standing now with her leg cocked beside the barrel of the machine gun.

Exhausted-looking immigrants hung to the fence at a safe distance from the checkpoint. They were the newly arrived from down-at-heel nations; men, women and families dragged out of the surf at Whitstable, Brighton, Margate. They watched me without emotion, just vacant eyes observing the facts.

'Don't worry about me,' I said. 'I'm only here for a quiet word.'

'Your funeral,' the officer in the booth said as he pressed the button to open the gate. Gears whirred and the gate slid slowly back. I knew that behind me the officer on the roof would have her machine gun trained on the temporary gap in case anyone tried to rush through. She needn't have bothered. The gateway to the rest of London seemed to hold little interest to the families clinging to the wire.

'Enjoy,' the sentry called as the gate closed behind me.

The streets were busy for November, with men and women, old and young standing about enjoying the unseasonable heat. A few fires had been lit in old metal bins for light and used furniture was piled high here and there against the buildings as though shoring up the walls. Faded murals of RZ were just about recognisable beneath the 'missing' posters that had been plastered over them, his black beard and benevolent eyes looking down on the minutiae of immigrant life.

Some of the Zone's occupants stood with their hands in pockets, eyeing me as I passed. Others took no notice, joining in the songs started by their neighbours, voices mixing in Urdu, Cantonese, and Moldovan, hymns that made little sense to British ears, or what we still told ourselves British ears should be. Further along the street fruit sellers were selling kumquat, tamarind, and carambola from their storefronts, holding up their produce to entice passers-by, or sitting smoking in the warm night air.

The door I wanted was further down the street, in a building that had once been an old bookshop – a chain store outlet disguised as an independent shop that still bore the faint marks of the scraped-off name on the glass door. There was a brass buzzer beside it, a round black disk that looked like an old coin stuck to the wall.

I pressed the buzzer.

'This won't take long,' I said.

A sigh came from the other end. The door opened and I pushed through.

Families hung about the stairs, laughing and murmuring quietly. Old women in headscarves shared a flask of soup, two old men argued over a rusted harmonica that they snatched between them. If any of them knew who I was they didn't show it. From a door on the next landing came a plume of steam, bringing with it the stomach-swelling aroma of gyoza. It had been a long time since I had enjoyed Japanese cuisine but the risk, if I was discovered, was too great to consider. A large Middle Eastern woman and an Eastern European man stood with arms folded in their black hooded sweaters, blocking my ascent. There was no point reaching for my badge – they knew who I was.

'It's all right, Ahava,' a voice called from the top of the stairs. Reluctantly, the two security guards stood aside to let me pass.

'Thanks.'

'Well, if it isn't our favourite policeman!' the woman at the top of the stairs said, as I climbed up to meet her.

'Sid.' I bent to shake her hand. Even with her heeled boots

she only came up to my stomach. It was something to do with the chemicals they used in the bombs they dropped on whichever country she'd been born in. But she didn't complain. Most of her was unaffected and her tailored trouser suit did a good job of hiding what she didn't want you to see.

I followed her through a heavy, lead-lined door. 'What have you got for me today?'

'Oh, lots of crap. The usual,' she said.

In the next room young men and women dressed only in their underwear and rubber marigolds stood by long rows of tables, sorting through the products there. As we passed through I glimpsed waistcoats of vermillion satin, gilets with the stuffing coming out at the breast, corduroy trousers in viridian, square-toed brogues, bootcut jeans. Each and every item was a Category Two infringement under section A4000204 of the Culture Laws. Like Cindy's bottles of authentic alcohol, it wasn't strictly down to Bagby and me to enforce sartorial rulings but we could make sure the right people looked the wrong way – as long as Sid and her people kept us supplied with information about any serious infringements coming into the country.

'Come through to my office,' Sid said, holding a curtain aside.

The room was all bare wood and tiny, as though built for a woman of her proportions and constructed in a hurry. Sid sat on a low desk and I leaned against the wall. She indicated a cafetière of what looked like fresh coffee. I shook my head.

'Hard to believe anyone ever wore that stuff,' I said.

'Not in our lifetimes,' Sid said. 'Or, at least, I've wiped it from my memory if we ever did.'

'You're a wise person.'

'It's been said. Now, tell me, what can I do for you today, officer?'

'Vasily Popov,' I said. 'Low level runner. Thieving. Robbery. Makes extra money selling luxury items like tinned fruit and bandages to the population of the Zone. I know you know him, so save us both some time and tell me where it was you saw him last.'

Sid leaned back, tapping a finger against her teeth. 'Vasily Popov... Vasily Popov.'

'Sid.'

'OK, I remember. Vasily Popov? Oh, yeah. I think I saw him two nights ago, early. He was drinking down by the social club on Effra Road. He'd just come in to collect some funds. Usually he sticks around, but he seemed to be in a bit of a hurry. Said he had some business in the West End.'

'Did he say who with?'

'I mean, I didn't speak to him myself, I'm just recounting what a friend told me. But with Vasily, it was always someone important. I think that's exactly what he said. He had a job on for some rich guy. Some big shot.'

'Is that all you heard?'

'Afraid so. Any use to you? What's he done now anyway? He in trouble?'

'Not any more, he's dead.'

'Fuck.' Sid blinked a few times then leaned her head back and whistled at the ceiling. 'Popov's dead? I never thought I'd see the day.'

'If you hear anything, you'll let me know, right?'

'Of course, of course,' she said, jumping to the floor as I turned to leave. We passed through the workshop, back to the main entrance. A thought occurred to me.

'You don't have any business with legitimate antiques guys, do you?'

Sid shrugged. 'Antiques? Not really. The people I deal with only buy clothes, and they don't like to call them antiques.

Puts the punters off. "Once-loved", maybe. You have someone specific in mind?'

'A man called Jennings.'

'Never heard of him,' Sid said. 'But if the police are interested in him I'd say not having anything to do with him would be a good thing.'

'You could be right,' I said as we reached the top of the stairs. 'I'll see you, Sid.'

A shop on the next street along was being raided, police officers in LDNPD tactical gear dragging a man and woman out in their pyjamas, slamming them against the police car bonnet. A crowd was gathering, an angry murmur replacing the singing of earlier. I hurried back to the checkpoint. The officer with the machine gun shouted down that they'd almost given up on me. I smiled, pretending to laugh along. Then I got in my car and drove back towards the lights of London proper, happy to be on the right side of the fence and eager to put as much distance between me and the refugee sector as possible.

9

Sacred Things

The streets were wet and the walls were wet and the guttering was black and shiny with the cascading rain. I knocked again on the door of Harrington & Sons. The shutters were closed and there was no light inside. Half a mile away the bells of St Mary-le-Bow sounded six. I knocked a third time, pressing myself against the door in an attempt to avoid the rain already working its way through my coat. I was about to give up when the door opened and a thin old man stepped back to let me inside.

'Hello, I'm...' I began.

'You're a copper. The fifth one to come see me this week,' he said.

Time had not been kind to Harold Jennings; his cheeks were shrunken tight as though from illness, and the stubble that grew there was flecked with white.

'You'll be here about my murdered child, I expect.'

I tried to formulate a response as he retreated into the shop.

'Don't just stand there, dripping on the doorstep,' he said. 'Come and drip inside, all over my lovely things.'

I followed him in. The shop was a small, rectangular room and with the curtains drawn, only a faint yellow light seeped in from the yard at the back. Overhead, the ceiling was hung with a hundred dead lamps and chandeliers, intricately carved and jewelled, each dangling a white price tag. Shelves and tables occupied the rest of the space, holding pottery elephants, dolls' houses, stuffed teddy bears covered in dust, polished brass candlesticks, two battered violins fixed with a patchwork of repairs. Almost every other surface was piled with untidy stacks of unwanted books with faded spines.

Jennings traced my eye. 'No market for new books. Everyone's reading the "classics". So now any bookshop is an antiques shop. You've got a nerve coming here, by the way. Do you know how much good stock I had to get rid of because of your Section A4000204?'

He asked the question like it had just happened yesterday.

'Right. Yes,' I said. 'Mr Jennings, I'm sorry to call on you so early. I'm very sorry for your loss; I'm the officer leading the investigation into your son's death and I promise you we will do everything we can to find his killer.'

'You're the second copper to say those exact words to me,' Jennings said, making his way behind the counter. There were no customers but I got the impression that this was the only place he felt safe, even in his own shop.

'What do you mean?'

'A young policeman with an old fashioned haircut came to see me the day after they found him and told me the exact same thing.'

Stohl. 'And who were the other police officers that came to see you?' I asked. 'You mentioned I was the fifth?'

'I don't see why it really matters when my son is dead. But if

73

you must know: there was a spotty kid in uniform came to tell me about his death, and a few others.'

'Then you may have answered some of my questions before, in which case please accept my apologies.'

'Get on with it,' he said, waving his hand. He glanced towards the door as though expecting a sudden surge of customers, despite the hour.

'Is there somewhere we'd be more comfortable?'

'I'm comfortable here.'

'Of course. Then I'll begin. You adopted Caleb when he was fifteen, is that right?'

He nodded.

'Why not take his sister, too?'

'You've done your research,' he said, clucking his tongue. He looked me up and down, as though sizing me up anew. 'What do you think an old man like me needs with two teenagers running around the place? One was trouble enough.'

'Then why take any? And why a teenager, instead of a younger child? As far as I can see you aren't married and have no close relatives. It can't have been easy.'

He waved the question away. 'I suppose, perhaps he was an investment.' He nodded at the bric-a-brac piled high on his shelves. 'Like the rest of this junk.'

'An investment in what?'

He took his glasses off and began polishing the lenses. 'In the future, I suppose. And it didn't matter to me how old he was. He was a child and he needed a home. But, like I told the first copper, I hadn't seen Caleb for nine years. We'd had a falling out. Well, what did he expect? He wanted to go on television again and sing those daft songs. He thought he could make a career out of it. In these times! He genuinely thought he was contributing to the culture. But how could he? By parroting the empty words of some no-brained songwriter? Never mind that it was illegal. Look around, detective, you can see that I'm only interested in things of real, *lasting* value. Things that make people think and feel and wonder about the world.' His chin dropped slightly. 'Or at least things that used to.'

'You fell out because of Caleb's singing career?'

'What career? I always told him he couldn't do it but he didn't listen. And here we are.'

I couldn't help but think that Jennings Sr and my father would have gotten on well.

'Do you blame him for what happened?'

He looked at me then like I was an idiot. 'Of course I don't blame him. He was my son. I loved him. No matter how different we were.'

'Is there anything you can tell me about where Caleb worked? Did he have friends, or a partner, perhaps?'

Jennings shook his head in a sharp, jerking motion. 'He never had time for friends. Or "partners". He was always too focused on his singing. And he didn't work, as far as I know. Maybe the odd job as a receptionist.'

'Where did he work?'

'Anywhere and everywhere. He never stayed anywhere for long. But I'm not really up to speed on the last few years. I told you, we had a falling out.'

'So there was no one else in his life? No one close?'

'He had no one else,' Jennings snapped. He looked away then back to me, his mouth narrow and brittle-looking. 'I should have kept him safe, but I'm the reason he's dead. I didn't do my job.'

'What do you mean?'

'I told the other coppers; he came to see me the day before he died. He tried to hide it, but I could tell he was scared. Said someone had been following him. Hadn't seen him in nine years but there he was on the doorstep. It was raining then, too.'

Pieces were beginning to fall into place. Caleb notices someone who may or may not turn out to be his killer following him. This goes on for a while. Eventually, seemingly having exhausted all other options and with no real friends to turn to, he goes back to ask his estranged old man for help. Either he knows about his policeman friend, or it's a coincidence. Either way, dad decides it's time to get in touch and calls his old pal, Bagby. Only, while he's filling in his old friend – most likely over a bottle – the bad guy gets to Caleb first and he's killed.

'Why didn't you take him in if you thought his life was in danger?' I asked.

Jennings looked at me. 'What would you have had me do? Drag him inside and lock the door? He was a thirty-year-old man. I tried. He wouldn't come home.'

'Had he reported his concerns to the police?'

'Not that I'm aware of.'

'What did this person look like? The one Caleb thought was following him?'

Jennings shrugged. 'A man... he didn't say much. Maybe middle-aged, white...'

'Think,' I said, with irritation. 'This is important.'

'He didn't say much about him,' Jennings said. 'Just "a man", like I said.'

I held my breath for a few moments then changed the subject.

'You mentioned that I'm the fifth police officer to come to see you. Myself, my partner, the uniformed officer on the day of Caleb's death... who was the first?' I could guess that the fourth had been our mutual acquaintance, Bagby.

'I don't know,' Jennings snapped again. 'I've had more important things on my mind.'

'If you're able to remember anything, anything at all… it might help,' I said.

He clicked his fingers at me. 'Suit yourself. The other guy was a short, boxy fellow in an oversized trench coat. Ex-military look to him. Wore gloves. I don't think he gave his name.'

'And what did he say?'

'It was after Caleb had been to see me. He said they'd had reports of a strange man following people around. They thought they knew who this guy was. They followed him and saw he was acting suspiciously. He said… he said there wasn't enough to charge this guy but if he could speak to Caleb at home, persuade him to come in, they might be able to put the guy away for good.'

My face twitched from the effort of keeping everything together. 'I see. He told you this here, in the shop?' There was more I wanted to talk to Jennings about. Better not reveal the extent of his mistake just yet.

'He came in, kept picking things up. Looked quite well off – for a bobby – so I didn't mind.' He put his glasses back on then looked back at me with something like defiance in his eyes. 'I hoped I'd make a sale, things were slow. I told him everything I could, everything I knew about Caleb, where I thought he was living, the best time to contact me if anything came up. He even asked about one of those old porcelain narwhales. But by the time I'd been downstairs to wrap it for him, he was gone. Anyway, that was the last I heard of you lot until… until they came to tell me he was dead. Not a bloody lot of good it did… I thought you lot were going to protect him. I thought he'd be safe.'

'Do you mind,' I asked as he trailed off, his attention elsewhere, 'if I use your bathroom?'

He didn't answer, so I made my way through a door marked 'private' then turned up the corridor and padded upstairs to the flat above. There was a bathroom and two small bedrooms over the shop. One bedroom was untouched, with an identical boy band poster to the one in Caleb's bedroom. The bed was covered in a blue duvet with musical notes and stars on it. I didn't go in.

The next bedroom was Jennings'. In contrast to the shop below it was surprisingly neat with a single bed pushed up against the wall and a stack of history books on the ancient Egyptians, Babylonians and the Cucuteni-Trypillians on the floor beside an empty mug. Facing the bed was a low shelf lined with prized knick-knacks that would not have looked out of place in the shop below, including a plate commemorating the last Queen's Golden Jubilee and another commemorating the King's funeral in 2031. I hadn't pegged Jennings for a Royalist but it was true that, post-revolution, nationalistic tat like this fetched a particularly high price. Next to these were more stacks of books, and a pair of tortoiseshell reading glasses. There was no picture of his son or of his old revolutionary companions, but there was a small ceramic Alsatian. The only indication of Jennings' past life was a cheap bust of the long-dead Bulgarian revolutionary Vasil Levski facing the bed. The expression was stern and the eyes were dark and hollow. But one was darker than the other. I took my pen from my pocket, inserted the end into the left eye socket and pushed upwards. The tiny bug fell out. The camera was small enough to avoid detection and, once set in position, long-lasting enough to run for years. I knew exactly who had put it there.

'Get the hell out of my house,' Jennings' voice said from behind me.

I turned slowly, my arms outstretched at my side, anticipating the gun.

I'd gotten sloppy. But with my back to the door Jennings' couldn't have seen me slip the tiny camera into my pocket.

'Does Bagby know you keep that gun?' I asked to break the ice.

'What?' he asked, squinting slightly as though this might help him understand the question. The gun – a small calibre revolver – hovered in his hand, pointed somewhere around my midriff.

'He's the real reason I came to speak to you,' I said. 'I'm his partner.' Then, deciding today was as good a day as any to croak it: 'Your name isn't Leslie Jennings, is it? It's Harold Jennings. You and Bagby were revolutionary brothers in arms. And when your son came back to see you after all those years it was him you called for help.'

'You're Internal Affairs,' Jennings said, raising the gun at my heart. 'You've come digging around for dirt on him. You think because my son is dead I'll roll over on my old comrade without thinking. Shame on you. He chose the police force over us – you know that, you bastard – and he's been out of the game for fifteen years now.'

'I'm his partner,' I repeated. 'He and I are on the same side. I know you called Bagby first – or rather, you called him after this mystery policeman had been to question you. Perhaps it was because you didn't quite trust the first man?'

My arms were getting heavy now. I lowered them slowly to my sides. Jennings didn't shoot me.

'He was a copper. I trusted him as much as I trusted any of you.'

'Why did you call Bagby?'

'Because… because I thought he could help. He might have

joined the enemy, but I know there's still a good man in there somewhere.'

'You knew Caleb was dead before the police came to tell you, didn't you?'

He opened his mouth then closed it again and said, 'Yes. He called me that night to tell me he thought that maybe he'd imagined the whole thing. He sounded relieved, as happy as he ever had. He even mentioned that he and I might go for a cup of tea sometime... Then he went to answer the door. A man's voice asked his name – don't ask me what he sounded like, he was just a man – then there was a slap and a crash. Then... then it went quiet for a moment and then Caleb's song came on, the one he did on television. It was very loud. I don't know what happened, he must have been knocked unconscious and come round again because what happened next sounded like one hell of a fight.' His hand trembled as he lowered the gun. 'One hell of a fight.'

He looked at the gun then put it down on the dressing table. 'Someone hung up the phone and that was that. It was all over with a click and a dead line. I rang Bagby straight away but I knew it was too late. I asked him to come here and when he arrived I told him my son was dead.'

'Why didn't you tell this to the other police officers?'

'Because the police didn't do anything to stop it, so why would they find his killer?' he snapped. 'And why should you be any different?'

He reached for the gun again and slid it into his pocket. 'Anyway, I told you to get out. Didn't I?'

'It's OK, I'm leaving,' I said, easing past him with my hands held up again. 'If anything comes to mind... please let myself or Bagby know.'

I stopped when I reached the top of the stairs. 'Caleb had one of those, you know,' I said. 'The ceramic Alsatian, the same as yours. He kept it by his bed.'

I thought I heard something like a sob. But I didn't look back as I made my way down the stairs, and out into the rain.

There was no answer at Bagby's place. I called his name then tried the door. It swung open. I took out my .45, made sure there was a round in the chamber, and stepped inside. Then I put the gun away again. I sat down on the sofa in the middle of an obliterated living room. Vinyl records had been pulled from their sleeves and shattered, books had had their pages torn out, sofa cushions had been sliced open, spilling their insides, and the bouquet of lilies had been stamped into the carpet. The person behind this had been fired by a different, more methodical passion than whoever had smashed up Caleb's sticks of furniture. It was a textbook case of someone searching for something they had no business possessing. I thought again of the Kid in White, no doubt still carrying the mark of Bagby's bullet. If the Kid wasn't dead already, this might well have been his work. But whoever had been there was long gone, and so was Bagby. There was no sign of a struggle. No bloody table corners or blunt objects matted with bits of scalp. And it was unlikely Bagby had come home to this destruction and fled. No, someone had most likely picked him up elsewhere, then come here afterwards to toss the flat at their leisure.

Once, when he had slipped off the wagon a few years back, I had brought Bagby home and lowered his wine-soaked bones onto the sofa. I went to fetch him water. When I returned I found him with a coffee table book on floriculture in his lap, opened sideways as if he were looking at a landscape photograph. He snapped it shut when he saw me and threw it under the table. Flowers, I knew, had never been his thing but bugs – surveillance cameras, listening devices – had been his biggest obsession ever since that day under the bridge.

The book was untouched on the shelf among with a few faded Penguins in their orange jackets. The cover read: *The Field Guide to Floriculture: 2027 Edition* by Jasper Farhang. Inside, the pages had been cut away, and in their place was a small, ancient laptop that turned itself on automatically. I lifted it out and set it on the table. The desktop was littered with video files labelled 'Jennings', dating back close to fifteen years. I opened a file at random. There was Jennings and a teenage Caleb, arguing silently in his bedroom as he held up a packet of cigarettes. I picked another. There were Jennings and Caleb some years later, sitting idly and reading magazines, glancing up every now and then in case a customer was about to appear. There they were eating spaghetti in the kitchen. There was Caleb smoking in the shop, then stubbing the cigarette out on a dusty vase. Apart from the bathroom and Caleb's room, Bagby had the entire shop bugged. As far as I could tell he had the cameras on a random timer. I opened another and another. Each showed domestic scenes of a normal, dysfunctional family. Then, one day, the videos stopped as Caleb walked out of the door, a bag over his shoulder. He shouted something back into the gloomy depths of the shop but as per the other videos there was no sound. Afterwards, Jennings sat behind the counter staring at the closed door. His shoulders began to shake and his head pitched forward into his hands. He stayed like that for a very long time before the tape ended.

There was no sign of any visiting police officers, nor anyone claiming to be police officers. Nor were there any video files depicting Bagby's own flat. Whether out of hubris or distrust of even his own observation system, at home Bagby had remained hidden and alone.

There was only one actual folder on the desktop, hidden

in plain sight among the loose files. Inside was another batch of videos. I opened the first one and saw Jennings' bedroom again. A shadow fell across the bed, then Jennings sat down. He was talking, silently, to someone off camera. Then a second person came and sat beside him; Professor Faron. She was saying something to Jennings, then she reached out a hand and brought his head down to rest on her shoulder while she stroked his hair. The video was nine years old, dated the same day Caleb had walked out. The remaining videos in the folder were all from the last eighteen months. There were twelve in total and each had the same narrative: Jennings appeared on camera, led by the Professor. He took his shirt off while she undressed herself, her back to the camera, then they slid under the covers. Each time the tape cut out before anything could happen.

I realised then that the white lilies trampled into Bagby's carpet were the same as the single lily on the Professor's desk. Was there something between them, too? Was that why Bagby had never mentioned Professor Rachael Faron, and appeared to have distanced himself from Jennings? Was there more between them than revolutionary hangovers and long-fermenting grudges?

For whatever reason, the Professor and Jennings had agreed to adopt Caleb and Kate, but to keep them separate. Whether Bagby agreed with this decision or even knew about it, he was still the only person Jennings could turn to when he thought his son might be in danger.

I closed the computer and tucked it away inside my jacket, wondering what Bagby's disappearance meant, how much he knew, and how much more there was to Caleb's death than a simple Vigilante Hit.

Knowing what I had to do next, I found a roll of bin bags and began bagging up as much contraband from Bagby's flat as I could. Before I left, I slipped the photograph of Bagby and his revolutionary pals – Professor Faron, Jennings and RZ – into my pocket. There was no point leaving it lying about for Stohl and his cronies to find. Then I called Mercer and left a message explaining the situation, leaving out my visit to Jennings and Bagby's hidden cameras. Whatever Bagby had got himself into, the best chance of finding him alive and well was to pursue this through the official channels. I performed a last sweep of the flat, looking for anything that might get Bagby in trouble. Stohl might show up, of course, but Section A4000204 had nothing to do with his job.

There was a chance I might have missed something but, despite her frustrated attitude towards him, I knew Mercer didn't really want to see Bagby in trouble and hoped she'd do her best to hush up any finding of illegal material.

I went downstairs, hid the bin bags full of illegal books and records somewhere they wouldn't get damaged, and stood looking up at the sky, waiting for the police to arrive.

10

Ancient Histories

I was waiting in the Professor's office when she arrived. She raised an eyebrow. Then, instead of greeting me or asking what I was doing there, she walked to the window and pressed her right index finger to the glass.

'If you don't get out of here now I'll call campus security,' she said. 'Now, if you'll excuse me, I'm late for class.' And with that, she scooped up a stack of books from the desk and left.

Alone again, I peered at her smudged fingerprint on the windowpane. I crouched slightly to match the Professor's height, and closed one eye. A small patch of garden was just visible behind an old and crumbling faculty building. The fingerprint marked a wooden bench half-lost among the undergrowth.

No one seemed to take much notice as I crossed the campus. I found the entrance to the garden down the side of an ancient science lab, test tubes and conical jars showing behind dusty windows. The overgrown grass was heavy with dew and shrubbery kept the outside world out. There was no one around. I found the bench. There was a rusted inscription on a tarnished brass plate. It read: 'Dr Edward Faron 1994 – 2039'. Then, in italics: '*All that I know about my life, it seems, I have learned in books.*'

More Sartre.

'He would have liked this,' the Professor said, appearing behind me. 'The mess, I mean. Nature free to do what it wants. And the privacy, too. He would have thought it was somewhere he could smoke unseen.'

The circular window of her office looked down onto the bench, but other than that, we were safely obscured by various university buildings.

We sat down together.

I went first. 'How did he die, your husband?'

'It was an accident. A fire. We had a research facility out of the city. Whitstable. There was no one else around.' She smiled sadly. 'They told me it would have been quick.'

'I'm sorry. That must have been hard.'

The Professor retrieved a vape pen from her breast pocket. She puffed away for a moment, then laughed a mouthful of steam. 'We were working for the government, if you believe that,' she said. 'Only it didn't go to plan. And now...'

'And now you're here, teaching undergraduates. It must have been quite the comedown from having your own lab.'

The Professor shrugged.

'I've been thinking more about my mother lately,' I said. 'She died when I was a child. A car accident. My father took it badly. The HAF virus killed him, later. But my mother, she would have loved this garden too, I think.'

'Is this how you get people to open up to you?' the Professor asked.

'Not quite,' I said. 'I read about you more thoroughly after our last meeting. You're no longer allowed to carry out research. Why? Who did you piss off?'

'Everyone, I think,' she said. 'Or everyone that mattered.'

I decided to chance my luck. 'How much does Bagby know about your work?'

The Professor gave me the side-eye, as if she'd been waiting for me to bring him up. As though everything so far had been a test.

'Bagby knew a little,' she said warily. 'Never enough to make a difference. He was never around long enough to learn more.'

It was likely, from the way her hand rested loosely and relaxed on her knee and how her eyes didn't try to hold mine, that she was telling the truth about Bagby's role in her past. It was also very unlikely that she would be this calm if she knew about Bagby's surveillance cameras or his current MIA status.

'He's missing,' I said. 'Bagby, I mean. His flat had been turned over. But something wasn't quite right... You've known him longer than I have... Any idea where he could have gone? Any old revolutionary boltholes we don't know about?'

The Professor laughed again, for real this time. 'You think he's gone to ground? Reverting to old revolutionary discipline? We were protestors, not anarchists. After my husband died... for a few brief months... Bagby and I... he was a help. But he chose the police force over the revolution. I wasn't able to speak to him after that. And I haven't spoken to him since.'

I almost believed her.

'Bagby aside, what about another old friend of yours, Harold Jennings? Did he tell you I'd be coming to see you?'

She tapped her vape pen on the arm of the bench. 'So many ex-comrades coming out of the woodwork. And no, Jennings didn't tell me anything. Which is to be expected of him.'

I didn't push it. If Bagby had felt the need to install his security cameras, it was because the Professor and Jennings' relationship was being conducted sub rosa. Any mention to the Professor would tip her off that her liaisons weren't as secret as she had presumably hoped.

'What about RZ? Has he been in touch?'

The Professor twisted around to face me, frowning as if I'd just asked her if Anne McLaren had been in touch. 'RZ? Why on earth would he have been to see me? *How* would he have come to see me? From what I hear, there's nothing left of him. I'm sure you know more about that than me. They've had him locked away in that... that place for fifteen years. The man we once knew is dead.'

This wasn't quite what the official records said. 'How so?' I asked. 'He gave himself up voluntarily after the Black Week riots. After the deaths. He went to Downing Street to negotiate the peace talks when the conflict was at its worst. He saved lives. He helped shape the country as we know it. If his mental faculties suffered afterwards, well that's understandable, the strain he was under.'

The Professor shook her head. 'A true believer. I didn't think they made them any more.'

'Excuse me?'

'RZ certainly did all of that. But you don't honestly believe that after months – *years*, even – of unrest and destruction the government would just let him go? That he just happened to quietly have this devastating breakdown after peace was announced? It was Descartes who said, "*It is very certain that, when it is not in our power to determine what is true, we ought to act according to what is most probable.*" Don't you agree? No, RZ was one of the most brilliant people I knew. They prodded and threatened him exactly where they knew it would hurt him most. And, when he finally called a truce and went in to negotiate with them, they just couldn't risk allowing him to go free. So they pumped him full of chemicals in an attempt to wring every last bit of information out of him. They co-opted his policies – like his belief in low culture rotting the brain – and used them to show the people they were on their side. When really they were twisting his words to suit their own purposes.

'Then they locked him away and declared the revolution a success. The next day one of the biggest re-branding exercises in history began. They told us all that they were emerging from the ashes as a new and enlightened government. Bullshit. All the Reformation did was give them the perfect opportunity to horde even more power and ruin even more people's lives. Nothing changed for any of us, except that we'd all lost a lot of good people. On both sides. The Reformation just cleared the air, gave them a clean slate to continue fucking us all over, that's all.'

The enlightened, post-Reformation government did not believe in capital punishment but nevertheless, since the events of 2039 three people had been executed. One, a woman, for setting off a bomb in a Sheffield shopping centre, and, two years ago, a brother and sister from Nottingham were given the zap for attempting to kidnap the Prime Minister. Their plan, they had said, was to make her admit on live television that the revolution had failed. The Professor's words were in no danger of getting her executed but, uttered around less sympathetic ears, she might have found herself joining a growing number of vocal dissenters currently languishing in deep dark holes across the country.

'You must trust Bagby, still, to talk to his partner like that.'

The Professor shrugged again. 'Not many police officers would bother trying to interview the same person twice, these days. Even in a murder case. Or go out looking for their missing partner, for that matter.'

I changed the subject. 'You said they threatened RZ With what? His history was well known. The drugs, the promiscuities. They could hardly have dug up anything new on him. And he had no family, unless you believe the rumours about an illegitimate son?'

The implant in my wrist buzzed. A voice in my ear told me DI Stohl was calling. I pressed my thumb to my forearm to decline the call.

'RZ was like a monk after he left all of that celebrity nonsense behind,' the Professor said. 'He would have been the last person to father an illegitimate son. But he's ancient history. He may not even be still alive. Even if he was, last I heard there was nothing left inside that shell of a mind of his.'

'What about the people setting off bombs? They must think there's hope of reigniting the fuse. They must be looking for a leader…'

The Professor shrugged. 'You overestimate the role we played last time around. Why should they give a shit about RZ? Or me? Or Bagby? We're old news. Fifteen years is a long time to forget. And they don't exactly teach what happened in schools. The Class of '39 means nothing to them. Whoever they are, they've got new things to be pissed off about, I'm sure. And plenty of people to point them in the right direction.'

Despite all the talk of revolution the garden was almost peaceful with butterflies dancing among the long grass. Then a bus rumbled by on Euston Road, shattering the illusion.

'Well,' I said. 'If you do hear anything from Bagby – however that information might come your way – tell him that I've been checking in on him.'

'Did you really come here to talk about revolution, detective? Or did you come to talk about murder victims?'

'I'm sorry; you're right. Here's a question that's been bothering me: why didn't Kate and Caleb ever know the other existed? Why not adopt them together?'

'Because after the revolution, after what they did to RZ, and after the death of my husband, after Bagby abandoned us, we didn't feel safe. If one of us had taken both of them and then been arrested for something, the children would have gone back into care. This way, we split the odds. Plus they never even knew the other existed. They were separated at birth. And we couldn't tell them about the other because then they'd want to meet, and then they'd start digging into a past that was better left buried. It was simpler for everyone that way.'

'But why adopt them at all?'

'Because a lot of good people died in the revolution. They fought for change but never got to see how close we came. How could we, as the survivors, let their children go uncared for?'

We both fell silent then. A student was standing at the edge of the garden, puffing on a vape pen.

'Out of bounds...' the Professor mumbled. She stretched out her legs and something popped. 'Well, detective... as invigorating as this conversation has been I have to get back.'

'Professor, one last thing. Jennings said that Caleb thought that he was being followed. Your daughter claims she hasn't noticed anything similar herself. But what about you? Perhaps a tall, thin boy? Possibly dressed in white. Most likely wearing a sling on one arm? A student, perhaps?'

The Professor stood and dusted down her coat. 'No. Nothing. And there's no one like that here, I'm afraid.'

My wrist buzzed again. Another thread presented itself. 'You said you and your husband worked for the government. Which company? Was it Vangelis, by any chance?'

'Good guess,' the Professor said, 'but hardly ground breaking detective work. Every scientist in the country works for them. Although, if we're being pedantic they're not strictly the government, just its best friend. When they kicked all the corporates out for not paying tax after the Reformation, Vangelis was the only one left. No wonder they run everything now. Now, I really have to get back. I trust you'll keep our conversation to yourself?'

'Of course,' I said. 'Thank you for your time. If anything comes to mind – about anything we've discussed – you can find me at the station.'

'Fine. Before you go, I have a question for *you*,' the Professor said. 'How did they know where Caleb lived? His killers? It was Jennings, wasn't it? He tipped them off somehow?'

'It would be wrong of me to speculate at this time,' I said, falling back on one of the force's most used get-out clauses. 'We're still exploring what may have happened. But I'll let you know when we know. Thank you for your time, Professor.'

I give her a good headstart then got up and re-traced my steps back across the quads. The sun had come out but there didn't seem to be anyone around to enjoy it. Except for an unexpected visitor in the form of Stohl, leaning against his car by the entrance.

'Come on,' he said as I drew level. 'Let's take a ride.'

11

Stuffed Animals

'You've been avoiding me, partner,' Stohl said as we drove through the city. 'A more sensitive man would think you didn't want to work with me. I know you're keen to solve this case. Something to do with your mother's death, possibly. She was a singer too, right?'

'I want to solve this case because a man is dead and I am a police officer,' I said. Then, changing the subject: 'How did you know where I was?'

'They've turned on the tracking beacons. Another bomb went off last night. In Grimsby. The powers that be thought it important to put police officers online first so they can ensure their safety at all times.'

He held up his wrist. A tiny blue light blinked beneath the skin. 'Me too, of course. And if you're thinking of using this to find Bagby, think again. We already tried and it turns out that he's been turned off. Perhaps he hasn't been paying off his CashPlant^{TM} ... the folly of combining everything into one device.'

'You think he did it himself?'

'Removed his beacon? I didn't say that. But yes, definitely.'

Perhaps Stohl knew Bagby better than I thought. 'Perhaps he did. But that doesn't mean anything. You still think he's involved in Caleb's death?'

'Of course he's involved. Just like you and I are involved.'

I let that hang as we cut through Marylebone and came out onto Oxford Street.

'What did uniform turn up at Caleb's last job?' I asked.

'Absolutely nothing. He was a good, quiet worker. No one had any idea he was pursuing an illegal singing career. It seems most of them didn't really know anything about him, for that matter. A dead end, all in all.'

We followed the border of Hyde Park. In a few weeks they would be setting up the Christmas fair. We slid down into the station's underground carpark and sat with the engine idling.

'Are you still trying to prove Bagby did it?' I asked.

I sensed, rather than saw Stohl tense under the security lights. 'I never thought he did it. I was simply exploring options. Besides, the OU tape has been wiped, so we may never know what DCI Bagby got up to the day Caleb Jennings died.'

He killed the engine. We got out of the car.

'That said,' he continued, 'what we're about to see should clear it up. Come on.'

We caught the elevator up and stopped at the morgue.

'We aren't going to see Mercer?'

'Mercer doesn't know about this,' Stohl said. 'Follow me.'

He led the way inside. There was Kavinsky, bent over the body of a young boy, Pink Floyd playing on an ancient record player in the corner. 'Ah, gentlemen,' he said, throwing a sheet over the body as we entered. 'Punctual as ever, I see.'

'Good to see you again,' Stohl said. 'Now, I want you to tell my disbelieving partner what you told me.'

Kavinksy eyed me then rubbed his hands together in anticipation. 'Well, as I explained this morning; after your partner forced me to perform a completely illegal advanced toxicology report, I spent all night working on various samples. I tested our guest for ricin, strychnine, hydrofluoric acid, polonium, dimethylmercury, and more. You name it, he doesn't have it in his system.'

'And what *did* you find?' Stohl asked.

'Absolutely nothing,' Kavinsky said with glee. He tapped an index finger on his desk to illustrate the point, and to make sure that I was listening. 'I ran every test we're capable of and I can reliably say that this man was not injected with anything.'

'How thorough are these tests? Is there anything it could miss?' I asked.

Kavinsky laughed a high, sharp laugh with little humour in it. 'You mean like some secret new toxin? That sort of thing is usually reserved for cheap sci-fi paperbacks. Also illegal, as I'm sure you're aware,' he said flatly.

'Tell him what you found,' Stohl said. 'Or rather, what you didn't.'

Kavinsky sighed, perhaps irritated that his game was over. 'OK, listen very carefully so you don't miss anything. Ready? So, the average human body contains anywhere from five to five and a half litres of blood. Now, allowing for his size and the wounds sustained in his death, he's still missing, at my best guess, exactly half a litre.'

'He couldn't have lost that much in the fight,' I said. 'And the odds of losing such a precise amount must be... minuscule to say the least.'

'Give him a prize. He is a detective after all,' Kavinsky said flatly. 'Yes, it is very unlikely that he lost that much blood in the fight. The bullet wound was almost dry when you brought him in, and the technician's spray sealed his wounds nicely.'

'So what you're saying…'

'Is that whoever killed him took a blood sample from his arm while he was still alive. Possibly unconscious.'

'Then he woke up and fought back,' I said.

'Exactly. They weren't trying to inject him with anything. He already had what they wanted. They were trying to get it back,' Stohl said.

'I'm glad you've caught on,' Kavinsky said. 'Now, do remember who helped you here. Perhaps there's something you can do for me…'

'We owe you,' Stohl said. 'But right now my partner and I have to follow up some leads.'

Before Kavinsky could reply, Stohl was driving me by the elbow, leading me out of the morgue and back into the elevator.

'Good spot. The needle bruise on the arm,' he said when we were out of earshot. 'I'm sure Kavinsky's too proud to admit he missed it the first time.'

'Thank you. But if Kavinsky can't tell us what it means, we're somewhat stuck,' I said.

'Not necessarily; there's a man who works for my uncle. A scientist. He should be able to tell us why someone wanted to take a blood sample.'

The doors opened. I followed Stohl out into the lobby.

'When do we meet him?' I asked.

'Tonight,' Stohl said. 'There's a family engagement. I'll introduce you and we'll go from there.' He tapped something on his watch and an address flashed up on my own device. 'Meet me there at 9pm. Don't be late.'

I watched him disappear down the steps and out into the day, sunlight glinting on the glass doors like the flash of an atom bomb.

The party was taking place near Waterloo Bridge in an old converted warehouse on the edge of the river. I was late but far from the last to arrive. I joined the mingling crowd of black suits, red flower lapels and silver and green and blue evening gowns as we waited to be granted passage inside. It was hot and a faint, unpleasant scent came off the river. Anywhere else, I would have badged my way to the front but this was not that sort of party. Eventually, the doorman took my badge from me and stared at it for a long time before handing it back.

'Go right in,' he said with an American inflection.

Inside, tuxedoed security guards manned a metal detector. 'We'll need your weapon, sir,' the nearest one said. 'You can get it back when you leave.'

'He's fine,' a voice called. Stohl was waiting on the other side of the scanners in a midnight blue dinner jacket with black lapels over a black shirt and bowtie.

'Right you are,' the guard said, waving me through.

'You're dressed for a party,' I said.

Stohl looked me up and down, perhaps wondering if my worn old suit counted as Bad Taste or not. 'Well, this *is* a party. It's also my uncle's party so I'm afraid tonight I can't quite get away with the police officer's usual sartorial indifference.'

He led me through a set of doors into the main room. We entered into the large, rectangular belly of the warehouse. Arranged among the guests were huge glass tanks filled with the pickled remains of a Malayan tiger, a mako shark, a blue elephant, a stingray, and more; the works of the latest artist to imitate his favourite canonical master. The exhibition was called 'Extinction Party' and it had been colleagues within my unit that had vetted it A1 – appropriate for public consumption. Unlike Hirst's originals, however, this new artist plunged his fauna into the formaldehyde heavily sedated, but alive. A lamb was frozen in a tank only slightly larger than my bathroom. Its eyes registered a sort of dumb terror and its hoofs suggested the message to run had not quite found its way down from its motor cortex in time. Cute livestock aside, the rest were animals I'd seen on television as a child. Now, one extinct or endangered animal per tank, they formed a maze of alleyways and passages, forcing the crowd to weave among them as the animals stared emptily out at the dominant species. Elsewhere, the ceiling had been made to mimic the stars and the walls were hung with navy blue drapes giving an overall impression of comfort and wealth.

Stohl took two flutes of champagne from a tray. It fizzed like the real thing. It was a nice, retro touch.

'I'm sure you're aware of my upbringing,' he began. 'How I was adopted by my mother's brother after my parents died. Adopted into... all of this. But, in case you have any doubts, you should know that I'm a police officer first and foremost. This,' he said, gesturing around the room, 'isn't for me.'

'I was never in doubt,' I said. I took a sip of champagne. It was real. I palmed the glass off on a passing waiter. 'There's something you should know about *me*. I don't drink. I didn't think anyone did anymore.'

Stohl made a clucking noise with his tongue then raised his glass. 'How the other half live.'

'So, what's the idea behind all of this?'

'My uncle has invented a machine that can artificially replicate the ideal temperature of an animal's habitat in the wild – at present up to an area of 20km^2, apparently. He's had the fantastic idea that global warming is destroying their territory and he's decided to do something about it. He's throwing this party to emphasise the risks to his pals in the government. He's certain that if we act now the remaining seven per cent of living animal species can still be saved. He'll also make a hell of a lot of money out of it.'

I looked at what was possibly the last silverback gorilla on the planet, captured forever in its tank of chemical goo. 'Well, everything deserves a chance to live.'

Stohl drained his glass and put it down on the floor next to the gorilla. 'You're right; "*Ever since we arrived on this planet as a species, we've cut them down, dug them up, burnt them and poisoned them.*" David Attenborough said that. My uncle wants to be seen to be giving something back. You know how it is with rich people. They accumulate all the money they can then have a sudden revelation that perhaps their pursuit of it hasn't benefitted everyone else in quite the same way.'

'Apart from their adopted nephews, of course.'

Stohl met my eyes in the great ape's reflection. His expression could have gone either way for a second. Then he smiled. 'Of course.'

We made our way through the maze of animals and emerged into a large central space with a microphone waiting at one end and a glistening bar along one side. The Police Commissioner and Chief Superintendent Ormsby, commander of the Unit – and, as such, Stohl's de facto direct superior – stood nearby. The Commissioner was dressed in her formal attire but Ormsby was in a simple black suit with a white shirt and black tie. He held a glass of champagne but didn't seem to be drinking from it. The Commissioner was in her seventies, and clearly still physically fit. Ormsby was somewhere in his fifties and looked like his health could go either way. On the rare occasion I had been in his company he had always looked slightly bored by whatever was happening around him. Both had a reputation as people not to be crossed.

The Commissioner turned to acknowledge another guest. Ormsby scanned the room, giving the slightest nod as Stohl passed through his field of vision. Stohl tipped his glass then our attention was pulled away as a tall, broad shouldered man of about sixty passed through the crowd. He wore a white dinner jacket over black trousers and his bowtie looked like it had been put on with a spirit level. I recognised Elliot Wallace from Vangelis' promotional material. If anything, he looked younger than in the company's latest video. The suntan and the blond-grey hair swept back from his forehead complemented the effect. By his side was a shorter, middle-aged man with square shoulders who limped along on an artificial leg. His eyes picked faces out of the crowd with a bodyguard's precision as Wallace greeted his guests. The scars on the bodyguard's face suggested a long and illustrious career in Her Majesty's Armed Brigade. Judging by the bulge under his sleeve, most of his left arm appeared to have been upgraded along with the right leg. It was difficult to focus on him, however, beside the glow emanating from Wallace.

'Your uncle could be a poster boy for clean living,' I said.

'One has to stay in shape if one insists on starring in all of the company's promotional material,' Stohl replied. 'Now come on, I'll introduce you to Cadmus Fomalhaut, Head of Futurism and Efficiencies. He's the brain behind my uncle's looks.'

We made our way through the crowd towards a man comfortably in his seventies. He was dressed in a white tuxedo with a red flower in the lapel, standing slightly bent. *Health*span, rather than lifespan, was now the dominant pursuit in medical science, but unlike Wallace – and to some extent the police Commissioner – it looked like Fomalhaut had started his health regiment a little late in life. Two women in their forties gripped his arm and bent over in faux mirth as he spoke. He looked up, saw us approaching, and with a quiet word the women departed.

'My boy,' Fomalhaut said, taking Stohl's face in his hands and kissing him on each cheek dramatically.

'Hello, Cadmus. I suppose I should be flattered that you're always so pleased to see me,' Stohl said, with a hint of discomfort. 'Although, I'm afraid I'm here on official business.' He turned to me. 'I'd like you to meet my partner. There's something we were hoping you could help us with.'

Fomalhaut turned to me and held out his thin wrists. They looked like blue ropes wrapped in mottled paper.

'I knew you'd come for me in the end,' he sighed. 'It's OK, arrest me, I won't complain. And at a party, too!'

I laughed out of politeness, but also because I couldn't help but like the old man. I assured him he was in the clear as I shook his hand.

'Pleased to meet you,' he said. 'Stohl, I've just been speaking to your colleague, CS Ormsby. I asked him if I could steal you away to come and work with me and your uncle. He says you're a crucial cog in an important machine.' He held up his palms in surrender. 'What can you do?' he asked me.

'We were hoping you might be able to lend your expertise to a case we're working on,' Stohl said, clearly trying to steer him back in the right direction.

'Of course he can,' a booming voice said. Elliot Wallace swam through the throng towards us. He had ditched the bodyguard but looked like he could look after himself, if it came to it.

'I didn't get your RSVP, otherwise I would have made special arrangements,' he said, embracing his nephew. 'And this is your new partner.' He offered me a hand. 'Pleased to meet you, Ormsby has been telling me all about you.'

'Really?' I had never been properly introduced to Ormsby and was unaware that he even knew who I was, unless Mercer had told him. But then, if he'd inserted Stohl into our squad to keep tabs on Bagby, he would have done his homework.

'Well, it's an honour to meet you, sir,' I continued.

Wallace smiled and spread his hands. 'What do you think of my exhibition? Some of the finest beasts on this planet, gathered in one room. All of them now either sadly extinct or on their way. With more to follow if we don't do anything about it. The world is only getting smaller. There are twelve billion humans on this planet who have to eat, live, shit somewhere. There simply is not enough liveable habitat left for our apex predators. It's a sad fact that the majority of our wildlife has simply grown too big to sustain itself. Restoring their natural habitats is a small gesture, but it may eventually prove significant if we can get enough governments onboard.'

'Perhaps it's us that have grown too big to sustain ourselves,' I said.

'He makes a good point, Elliot,' Fomalhaut said. 'Much of our work is about limiting the damage we humans inflict, in one way or another.'

Wallace pursed his lips. 'You've always been so moralistic, Cadmus. That's why you make a brilliant scientist.'

'So brilliant that these boys have some questions for me,' he said. 'Apparently, there's something I can help them with.'

'My ex-partner, Bagby, agreed with your point. About the damage humans inflict being limitless,' I said.

'Then he's a wise man,' Fomalhaut said without a flicker of recognition. If Stohl had been sent to keep tabs on Bagby, it was strictly a work affair and nothing to do with his uncle's interests.

'If you're interested in all of that – nothing less than the evolution of the human race, I mean – then you must both come to the laboratory tomorrow,' Fomalhaut said, signalling a waiter then handing around a glass of champagne each. 'A party is no place to talk police work. Or politics.'

I was about to insist that it wouldn't take long when Stohl interrupted. 'Tomorrow sounds fine. How about nine?'

'Make it eleven,' Wallace said. 'This is a party, after all.'

I kept my small talk to a minimum and was able to get away ten minutes later. As I searched for the exit among the representatives from species of the dead and dying Stohl caught up with me, catching my sleeve.

'There's a certain way to play this game,' he said. 'People like this won't just be questioned outright, you have to court them first.'

I snatched my arm away. 'I've been a police officer for fifteen years… I haven't had any major setbacks yet.'

'And I've been doing this for seven years. I think I have an idea of how this works, too.'

It was the first time I'd seen him agitated. I was making progress. 'OK. All right, you could be right. Fomalhaut seems keen, at least.'

'I told you he'd help us. Quizzical mind, and all that. I don't have the luxury of sneaking out early like you, so I have to go back. But wherever you're going now, try to get some sleep, yes? And meet me at the station tomorrow at nine. It'll take us a few hours to get to the lab.'

I waved him off without offering much in the way of reply and set off in search of an exit.

A few minutes later I was yet to locate a way out when I spotted Fomalhaut standing by himself on the edge of the party, a large white rhino separating us. I couldn't pass up the chance to get him alone, away from Stohl and his uncle. I rounded the rhino's case and found myself alone. I realised it had been a trick of the light; Fomalhaut had been standing behind where I had just been. I retraced my steps, boxed in by animals leering with glassy eyes, tusks and teeth bearing down, hoofs suspended in midair.

I spotted Fomalhaut again, through a box housing an ostrich in full charge, its wings spread, its neck curved, its beak about to strike. Fomalhaut was no longer alone, but leaning in close to listen to a tall young man in a white dinner jacket with his left arm in a sling. Under the jacket he wore white jeans and tennis trainers. I couldn't hear them, but the boy seemed to be threatening Fomalhaut, leaning in close, one hand squeezing the scientist's arm. Here was Bagby's Kid in White. I'd seen it all before, on the OU tapes: the way the Kid shielded his injured arm, the way he walked, with a loose, bouncing shuffle, the way his eyes shone with arrogance. Fomalhaut gestured animatedly. Then, his business complete, the Kid turned and moved quickly away among the animals. I traced the row of display cases, following the Kid's progress. Somewhere off in the centre of the room Wallace was delivering his pitch, the laughter of the gathered guests booming like a series of subterranean explosions.

I came to a dead-end among the cases and ran to retrace my steps, feeling along for some gap to slip through. I found one and reached the back of the room. An emergency exit door swung closed. I ran to it, pulled my gun from my shoulder holster, checked the safety catch, then pushed through. Metal stairs descended in a breeze block shaft wet with mould. I hurried down, gun first, hoping I wouldn't have to use it. There was no sign of the Kid, only the drip of water coming from either high above or down below.

Then came the sound of a door slamming. I hurried down the remaining steps. At the bottom was another door. I listened against it for a moment, then pushed through, the .45 held high. I emerged under Waterloo Bridge, the Thames rushing past flecked with reflected light, tower blocks sparkling white and silver against the night. I shoved the gun in my pocket as a couple walked past, arm in arm, the footpath lit by powerful sodium lights. There was no sign of the Kid in White.

12

Icarus

I woke up at 5am and couldn't get back to sleep. I'd been having this feeling, lately, like I'd slipped out of myself and was watching my body move without my mind telling it to. It often happened as I walked along the street, and I had the same feeling then as I lay there trying to sleep. Eventually, I gave up and watched television instead. There had been another mass shooting, this time in Bournemouth. Elsewhere, UK forces had scored a great victory in Roskilde, with only twenty fatalities. They didn't say on which side. In extraterrestrial news the debris from the STAR rockets had caused a ring of garbage to gather around the moon. Tonight, for the first time, we would be able to see its shadow, a faint black band hanging over the lunar surface like an erased pencil mark in a favourite book. On and on the news went and on the other channel a re-run of a documentary on Basquiat. On the third and final channel, an exercise programme for the over-seventies. Bagby always said sitting like this in the glow of the screen helped him think. Helped the pieces slide into place. But I was no closer to knowing where Bagby might have gone, or even if he might be in danger. Nor had I much hope of finding the Kid in White without Bagby's help. Or Bagby without the Kid.

I turned off the television as the sun came up. I showered, took my Wellness Pills and left the flat. Stohl was waiting outside, leaning against his car, a recyclable polystyrene cup on the bonnet.

'Green tea,' he said, handing it to me.

'I thought we were meeting at the station?'

'We've got a long drive, and the station's in the opposite direction.'

I nodded as I slipped into the passenger seat, hoping I might be able to make up a few lost hours on the drive.

The roads were emptier than usual, even accounting for the new petrol allowance. Stohl moved easily among what little traffic there was. Fuel might have become a luxury, but police and government vehicles were for the most part unaffected. We tore along, heading north and then west until London was behind us and grey satellite towns spread out in front of us. After an hour of this we were into green country lanes watched over by bare-branched trees and the odd empty house, their windows boarded up or broken. An hour and a half after we set off we turned off the main road and took a narrow second turning uphill through a dense pine wood. Ten minutes later we came to a smooth, black wall reaching eight feet overhead and stretching away into the woods on either side. Its surface was unblemished, with no light or shadow falling across it, like dulled obsidian. Stohl stopped the car beside it. A red light appeared from somewhere among tree branches still wet with last night's rain and soundlessly scanned his face. Apparently satisfied, the light blinked off and the gate slid open.

We passed through onto a smooth, dark driveway which drew us among yet more fir trees. I was certain, at the driveway's conclusion, that we would come to a stately home, old and gutted, its interiors replaced with the best and shiniest of high-tech laboratories – Vangelis' secretive and sweeping countryside nerve centre. In actuality, we emerged from the trees to be confronted with a long, low building seemingly carved out of a single piece of the same black material, its walls sloping gently upwards so that the entire structure appeared to be rising up out of the fog like a futuristic ark.

'That isn't imposing at all,' I said as Stohl stopped the car in a carpark of which we were the only occupants.

'I used to call it "Carfax" as a boy,' Stohl said. 'It used to terrify me. But don't worry. There are no vampires here.'

We got out of the car and Stohl shivered despite the November heat. 'Let's get this over with and get back to London.'

We stepped forward. The blackness opened up with a whoosh of automatic doors. Light spilled out. We found ourselves in a bright, glass-sided atrium that reached all the way up to a skylight in the very highest part of the building, perhaps five storeys up. Before us on the other side of a soundproof glass panel automated machines worked endlessly to construct something out of metal sheets and circuit boards. Apart from the quiet hum of Schubert and the efficient air conditioning we were alone.

'Space rockets,' a voice said, taking me, at least, by surprise.

Stohl and I turned as one to find Wallace standing there, dressed in loose-fitting trousers, a white t-shirt under a midnight blue blazer and a white pocket square, looking every inch the hung-over CEO. He seemed to beam with pride as he directed our attention to the construction taking place on the other side of the glass screen. 'If you'd told me when I was five,' he said, 'that I'd be building rocket ships for a living, do you know what I would have thought?'

'That you were crazy?' I said.

'Ha. No, I would have thought you were exactly right. I've always thought that there's too much going on in the world, from war to famine to constant injustice. We need a little bit of a distraction. We need to look to the skies again, with hope in our hearts.' He paused for a moment and I thought he was about to wipe his eyes. Either that, or go full JFK. 'We're going to do it, you know, put a human in Venus' orbit in the next five years. Nuclear fuel is the answer. We'll be able to make the journey there in days, instead of weeks. Maybe even hours. What? Don't look so perturbed, we don't carry out our nuclear tests *here*. That's all done far away. Safe in the North.'

'Uncle,' Stohl began.

Wallace clapped his hands. 'I'm sorry. My apologies. It was a late night and an early morning. I'm rambling. You wanted to speak to Fomalhaut. He's in the middle of something at the moment, but why don't I give you the tour?'

Before we could respond, he was ushering us through a door that had appeared in the side of the glass wall. I caught Stohl's eyes. He sighed as we followed on. We passed down a long corridor with windows on either side. Behind them were coders seated at humming computer screens, engineers tinkering with drones, scientists in face masks tinkering with chemical formulae, every facet of Vangelis' mission laid out for visitors to take in.

'Do you know what we make here?' Wallace asked, turning to me.

'Delivery drones, surveillance drones, military and police drones, prosthetic limbs, computer hardware, software, inner-city surveillance systems, outer city surveillance systems, waste disposal rockets, military exosuits, weapons and medical equipment, televisions, railway infrastructure, pharmaceuticals, in vitro meat, Wellness Pills... in short, everything.'

'Ha!' he laughed again. 'Not quite everything, but I admit we're close. You could say we make the future here. And we were born out of the future, too; the Reformation was the best thing that happened to us. We're lucky in that, post-Reformation we've just about handled every tech contract in the country, allowing us – and Britain – to make great leaps and bounds forwards. The protestors were right: consolidate the government, consolidate industry, and things move along much more quickly.'

We came to a cafeteria, one hundred empty tables stretching to the back of the room, the floor, furnishings and fittings a brilliant white with only a service hatch and a stack of black trays to indicate what the room was used for.

'This is really all I can show you without revealing our secrets,' Wallace said. 'The majority of our space is given over to workshops and testing stations and unless you want to get kitted out in lab coats and protective eyeglasses it's probably not worth your time, I'm afraid.'

He indicated that we should take a seat beside an expensive-looking and finely engineered coffee machine. 'I'm glad I had chance to show you around,' he said without a hint of irony. 'Fomalhaut will meet you here in a moment. If you'll excuse me I've a press release to sign off regarding last night's event. Have some coffee if you need it and I'll see you again before you go.' He retraced his steps, heading back to the labs, leaving us alone in the centre of the room.

'How much did you raise?' I called after him.

He paused with a hand cupped to his ear. 'What's that?'

'How much did you raise, to get the new habitat tech off the ground?'

'Oh, not nearly enough. But it's a start!'

Stohl and I sat quietly, both waiting for something to happen. Then came the distant sound of a door opening and the tap of slow, ponderous feet making their way across the expanse of the canteen.

'Well,' Fomalhaut said when he eventually reached the table, holding on to its edges as if the exertion of crossing the room might cause him to topple over at any moment. Out of his suit and in linen trousers, a white-shirt and a lab coat, he looked in his element. 'It's nice to see you both again. I hope you didn't enjoy too much of the festivities last night? Even the Bad Taste police must let their hair down eventually, eh? What's the point in us all living so long if we can't enjoy ourselves?'

'Very true,' I said, for the sake of easing things along.

'You'll forgive me for getting to the point, Cadmus,' Stohl said, 'but we've had a fair journey out here and now that we're all settled we were hoping we could ask you some questions.'

Fomalhaut smiled at each of us then placed his hands palm-down on the tabletop. 'Of course. Ask away.'

'This may sound bizarre,' I began. 'But hypothetically speaking, if you were a killer, why would you take a blood sample from your victim before you killed them?'

'You have a body that is missing some blood?' Fomalhaut asked, rapping his fingers on the table in thought.

'Precisely half a litre,' I said. 'Why might that be?'

'Well, it's obvious,' he replied, evidently intrigued. 'Your killer required a blood sample. In one way or another it was valuable to him. Or her. Granted, that is rather a large sample, but maybe that tells us something too. Two hypotheses arise from this. The first is that the blood itself was useful; perhaps they wanted it to frame this person for a crime. Of course, that is unlikely if the person is now deceased. Unless, of course, they didn't mean to kill them. The second hypothesis is that there was something *in* the blood that was of value. A germ or a rare genetic strain that might be of monetary value or...' he swallowed then smiled, 'something dangerous that could be used as a threat to extort money from someone. Perhaps a single private citizen, or a larger group, like a government.'

Stohl and I sat silently for a moment. Then I asked, 'This is your speciality, disease, yes?'

Fomalhaut smiled. 'My department specialises in curing the incurable. In the last fifteen years we've been able to expand the lifespan of stage four cancer patients by up to five years. HIV and many types of orthocoronavirinae have been all but obliterated and the *health*span of the entire population has risen incrementally, as I am sure you're aware. A woman in this country will now happily see her ninety-sixth birthday, while her husband may well get to blow out the candles on his ninetieth. We can't take all of the credit for this, of course, but it's a fact that the human lifespan has been advanced by an average of ten years, and in the next decade we believe everyone today under the age of sixty will celebrate a century of existence.'

'Impressive,' I said. 'But to cure these diseases – to cure death – you have to study them, right? Say our victim had a "disease" in their blood, as you suggest. Surely that would have killed them?'

'I like him,' Fomalhaut said to Stohl. 'He's thinking like a scientist.' He turned to me again. 'Well, the answer is obvious, isn't it? If that were the case, your victim was likely immune to whatever they carried. It's quite possible, you know, that a person's blood can carry the genetic make-up for a disease long after their body has fought off any infection.'

'How recently would this person have had to have been ill for this illness to be present in their blood?'

'As far as all of our tests have shown, our victim wasn't ill at the time of their death or at any point during their life,' Stohl clarified. He turned to me. 'Kavinsky confirmed it; Caleb didn't show any signs of any longterm or terminal illness. He was in every way, a perfectly healthy young man.'

'Ahhh, but that's it!' Fomalhaut said, clapping his hands in what I felt was misplaced glee. 'He, your victim, that is, needn't have developed any symptoms. Some people can incubate a disease without ever getting ill. In most instances a virus is passed from our body after time, but certain… things, leave a permanent imprint on our DNA, which can be undetectable unless you happen to know exactly what you're looking for.'

'It sounds like you should look over our body,' Stohl said.

Eager to maintain protocol, I cut in, 'This was the sort of thing Edward Faron was working on, yes, before his death?'

Fomalhaut leaned back in his seat. It squeaked beneath him. 'I haven't heard that name in some time. Which is a shame, because we should all know Edward Faron's name. He was a genius, and he would have changed this world for the better. I still to this day don't understand why he did it.'

'Did what?' I asked.

'Took his own life, of course. His research was far beyond anything I've ever…'

'He killed himself? I was told… I heard he died in an accident.'

'Yes, it was reported as an accident. Only his closest friends knew what happened.'

'And what did happen?' I asked, starting to think Professor Faron hadn't been entirely honest in her account of her late husband's last weeks.

'As I say,' Fomalhaut continued, 'unfortunately, Edward Faron killed himself shortly after the end of the Reformation. Killed himself and torched his lab. A decade of research was lost, chewed up in the flames. Something about that time must have pushed him over the edge. It was a trying time for us all. His wife still refuses to admit it was a suicide. I send her a bouquet of chrysanthemums every year on the anniversary of Edward's death. Four years ago she returned them. When I opened the box they'd started to decay. There was a note, asking that I don't send her any more. A note and the faint, sickly-sweet smell of rot. Of course, I don't bother anymore.' Fomalhaut paused, wrung his hands. 'She was working with him on the research too, you know. But I think she scrapped it all and took a rather low paid job as a school teacher. She's vastly overqualified in my opinion.'

'But why did he kill himself?' I asked. 'If you were close to him you must have an inkling of why what happened happened. People don't just snap.'

Stohl stood up. 'I'm not sure how this is pertinent to our case,' he said. Then: 'Thank you for your time, Cadmus, but we must be getting back to London. You've given us plenty to follow up on.'

I hesitated in my seat, but it was evident from Stohl's demeanour that the interview was over.

'Not at all, not at all,' Fomalhaut said. 'By the way, if you're interested in Edward Faron, you might like to know… and I don't lend any credence to this at all… but there was a rumour that his wife was having an affair at the time of his death. But as I say, I regard that as nothing more than gossip.'

'Thank you for your help,' Stohl said, re-adjusting the badge on his belt.

'Glad to help, and all that,' Fomalhaut said, climbing to his feet with a clear effort. 'If anything else comes to mind or if you do want me to have a look at the body you know where I am.'

We shook hands and I followed Stohl towards the exit. Fomalhaut watched us, still leaning against the table.

Just as we were about to leave, I stopped and called back. 'Sorry. One more question. What were they researching?'

'Why,' Fomalhaut called back. 'With everything we work on here it's almost embarrassing to say, but they were working on a cure for the HAF virus. They never had any luck. The Swedes developed a cure before the Farons could. Maybe that's why he took his life? Vital work. But hardly worth dying over, if you ask me.'

We made our way back to the reception unguided. I assumed Wallace's schedule must have stolen him away. Just as we were about to step back out into the atrium I made a show of patting down my pockets.

'I don't believe it. I've left my keys behind.'

Stohl looked at me but said nothing.

'I won't be a moment.' I left him there and hurried back along the corridor.

The canteen was empty but a door at the far side led out into another corridor at the end of which was another set of doors. I passed through and found Fomalhaut turning into an office. He had moved at an exceptional pace for such a frail old man.

'Did you forget something?' he asked, with a smile.

'I lost my keys,' I said, taking them from my pocket and holding them out for him to see. 'But they're here now.'

'Oh, that's lucky,' he said. 'Was there something else I could help you with?'

'There was, actually,' I said, glancing over my shoulder as Stohl appeared at the far end of the corridor. 'Last night at the party a boy dressed all in white accosted you, out of sight of the other guests. Who is he? I think he may be of interest to our case.'

Fomalhaut appeared to shudder before he spoke. 'Oh, I didn't realise anyone had seen us. As far as I was aware he had wandered in off the streets. I told him there was a guest-list, but he could use the bathroom facilities if he desired. He became quite agitated at the suggestion. A scene which it appears you had the misfortune to witness...'

'All right,' Stohl said, reaching us. 'Sorry, Cadmus, but we have to go.'

'He was threatening you,' I said, pushing the point. 'Why? What did he want?'

'Oh, just the usual. You know what youngsters are like these days – the ones that didn't make the military, at least. All pent-up anger at the older generation that supposedly ruined everything for them. Ha. It's as if they've forgotten what happened fifteen years ago. Then again, I suppose most of them were only children at the time.'

'We should get back to the capital,' Stohl said. I glanced at him out of my peripheral. He was doing his best to keep his cool, but there was no point in pushing him.

'Oh by the way, detective,' Fomalhaut said just as Stohl and I had turned to retrace our steps. 'I thought your name seemed familiar last night, so I looked into you. I was a big fan of your mother's, back in the day.'

'Erm, thank you,' I said.

'*On oceans we float, away from it all, and birds they soar, like my heart at your door*, and all that,' Fomalhaut sang, finishing with a little smile.

'It's... nice to hear that. I'm sure my mother would have appreciated it. Thank you for your time,' I said, taking Fomalhaut's hand again.

'Not at all. Safe journey home,' he said. 'Always nice to see you, Stohl,' he called as we made our way back towards the entrance.

There was no sign of Wallace in the foyer, and Stohl didn't seem particularly anxious to see him so we hurried outside through the newly arrived rain and ducked into the car.

'Look, it only just occurred to me,' I said.

'He's an old man and he'd already been incredibly generous with his time.'

'But I was right,' I said. 'He was scared of this boy. He even shook as he told us about it.'

Stohl stared at the rain coming down the windscreen, the grey clouds and black edifice of the offices draining the colour from the day. 'Let's just get back and write up what we know for Mercer.'

I don't claim to know cars, but for one reason or another ours wouldn't start. Stohl tried again, then again. Then came a knock on the windscreen and there was Wallace.

'Car problems?' he asked as Stohl lowered the window. 'Come inside, have lunch with us and we'll get someone to fix it. We're having wakame soup, I believe.'

'Thank you but we have to get back, Uncle,' Stohl said, raising his voice slightly over the drumming of the rain. He inclined his head towards me. 'My partner here has another appointment.'

Wallace slapped the roof of the car. 'Then Koch can take him back, and you I and will catch up over lunch.' He leaned closer as if conspiring with me. 'Fomalhaut and I do look forward to these catch-ups with my nephew. I hope you'll excuse him for an hour, or so.'

There was nothing for it. Stohl turned off the engine and we got out of the car. The same short, squat assistant from the party was holding an umbrella over his employer, his metallic fingers curved around the leather handle. In his black suit and tie he almost blended in against the wall of the building. I guessed that this was Koch.

'Wait here,' Wallace said to me. 'Koch will bring the car around.'

They left me, then – Stohl without a backwards glance –

and disappeared back inside the vast, granite-like laboratory-cum-headquarters. Three minutes later, Koch reappeared at the wheel of a pristinely maintained '98 Mercedes-Benz SL600. If I'd been waiting for him to come and collect me under the cover of an umbrella I would have been waiting a long time. I introduced myself to the backseat instead and we set off, Koch driving fast through the rain and with evident experience, his robotic hand accosting the wheel.

'What did you want with the boss?' he asked abruptly as we reached the parameter wall.

'Pardon?' I asked, leaning forward in my seat. When he didn't say anything else I said, 'It actually wasn't him we wanted to see. It was Fomalhaut. We had a few... technical questions about an ongoing case.'

'That's what I meant,' Koch said, his eyes on the road. 'A little joke. Implying that Fomalhaut is the boss. He gets everything done around here. The real innovations, as it were.'

'Right,' I said, sitting back in my seat.

'You weren't in the military,' he said – a statement, rather than a question.

'I joined the police force just before the Reformation. They've kept me there ever since.' It was clear what he wanted me to ask, so I obliged him. 'And how long did you serve?'

'Almost thirty years altogether,' he said. 'Lincolnshire Harriers. A few years here, a few there. The usual spots.' He met my eyes in the mirror as though we might share some common understanding of what the 'usual spots' were. Up close he looked older than I had imagined at the party, the grey hair combed back from his forehead revealing a web of lines and scars reaching up to his temples.

'And they invalided you out?' I asked, nodding to where his mechanical hand rested easily on the gearstick.

'Drone strike. One of theirs, not one of ours. Took my left

118

arm up to the elbow and my right leg to the groin.' He lifted his hand for me to inspect and flexed the fingers like clothes pegs. 'Fomalhaut saved me.' He sighed and seemed to go off elsewhere for a moment. 'Next gen. Back then there was a shortage of willing volunteers.'

If only Mercer had been so lucky.

'He can't have much shortage of them now, with all the fighting going on,' I ventured.

I thought he might stop the car there and then. 'You don't approve of the wars?'

'I understand why they're necessary,' I said. 'But wouldn't it be nicer to live in peace?'

'You're a man after my own heart,' Koch said. 'The world would be a better place without war. But we're too far in now to back out. Too heavily invested. The only safe option is to keep moving forward. Fight until we're the last ones left. That will be true peace. There are twelve billion people in the world. We cannot sustain these numbers. There isn't enough food, or space. The only option is to cull ourselves. Fight until we have reduced this number by half. Fight on towards peace.'

'You're talking about sanctioned mass extermination through warfare,' I said.

'Don't pretend it isn't already happening. It's a shame that it can't be done sooner, logistically. But everybody has A-bombs now, and who knows what kind of restrictions are sufficient to stop these wallah countries utilising these new types of biological warfare? How does a virus know its enemy from its friend? No, only a soldier knows that. Or a drone. But a virus or a missile that could tell you that would change the world.'

'It's an interesting thought,' I said.

'We're overcrowded. You only have to walk down the street. All these soldiers living rough in doorways and parks. Veterans don't deserve that. And people don't deserve to see it.'

Bagby had a theory that technology was at least partly to blame for the Reformation. It was a fact that upwards of sixty per cent of all ex-servicepeople ended up living on the streets. Once we all started wearing headphones we didn't hear them asking for change. Once we stopped carrying cash, we had nothing to give them even if we wanted to. Their options then were to join the revolution or starve. The result was that thousands of ex-army personnel across the country threw their weight behind RZ's cause; a ready-made revolutionary army.

'Isn't there a chance you might have ended up doing the same had Wallace not taken you in?' I asked.

'I might have,' Koch said as we slid out onto an A road. 'But I like to think that I would have had the honour to do the right thing.'

I didn't ask what the 'right thing' was. I let the conversation die and we lapsed into silence as London loomed on the horizon. By the time we were speeding over the river the sun was setting and the tower blocks were coming alive with electric lights. Koch dropped me at the station then got out to see me off. He moved quickly despite his prosthetic leg but when he shook my hand with his metal appendage he was surprisingly gentle.

'Be seeing you, I'm sure,' he said as he got back into the car.

'I hope so,' I said. I lingered, watching him drive away. Only when the car and its singular driver had passed out of sight did I venture down into the tube.

13

Nocturnal Creatures

There was time, before I went home, to stop by the Diamond Club and ask Cindy if Bagby had been by. I found her outside in the patio area, the orange embers of a real cigarette aglow in the darkness. Tonight her outfit resembled a see-through rain mac with a shaggy black brassiere protecting her modesty beneath it.

'Looks good, right?' She called, indicating the newly-remodelled patio area.

All traces of the shootout had disappeared, scrubbed away as though it had never happened. As though Bagby had never been there.

'It does. Have you seen him, by the way? Bagby?'

'He hasn't been back here since that night,' Cindy said, her eyes bright with concern. 'It's not like him at all. Recently he's been hitting a visit a week. At least.' She jumped down from the table she was perched on, a sudden idea lighting up her face. 'I know Mr Macelleria has... dealings with the police. I could ask him if he can put the word out.'

'I wouldn't get him involved. I think it's best if he doesn't find out about what happened here. I don't think he'd be too pleased.'

'But he already knows,' Cindy said. 'He came round the night after it happened. To inspect the damage.'

'I told him you paid for it all, though,' she added quickly. 'He was pleased.'

'And did you mention Bagby?'

'He knew all about it, he must have found out before he came. One of the other girls, maybe. He has his favourites.' She glanced towards the doorway. Soft, muffled jazz seeped out from inside like chocolate oozing from a cake.

'And what about the kid in white clothes? The one Bagby shot. Has he been back?'

Cindy flicked the cigarette end away and squared up to some imaginary foe. 'Here? He wouldn't dare show his face around here again. No way. Mr Macelleria has put the word out that it wouldn't end well.'

'OK, well be careful anyway. And tell the others to keep an eye out.'

I left her to it then and headed home. I thought of stopping by Bagby's flat to see if anything had changed, but bet against it. It wasn't quite time to give up hope but I could see it on the horizon. By the time I was trudging along the street to my sixth-floor flat, a takeaway bag of ghormeh sabzi growing cold in my hand, I had all but exhausted myself turning the possibilities of Bagby's disappearance and Caleb's death over in my mind.

But then, leads always turn up when you least expect them. There, sitting on my doorstep with her sunglasses on, was Kate Faron.

I called out a cautious greeting. She looked up in surprise. In the glow of the streetlight I saw the black rivulets of mascara still running from under her glasses and down her cheeks.

'You'd better come in,' I offered. It wasn't strictly policy but there didn't seem to be much else I could do.

I tapped the code into the front door and she followed me inside with a murmured 'Thanks.'

'Don't thank me yet,' I said. 'The lift's broken.'

We made it to the sixth floor, eventually, and I let her in. We hadn't spoken on the way up. I'd barely closed the door when Kate steadied herself against the kitchen counter then slowly slid to the floor. It was as though, in that moment, the full weight of her brother's death had landed upon her.

'They cremated him today,' she said, her sunglasses discarded as she wiped her eyes with the back of her hands. 'My brother's gone and they cremated him without even telling me.'

'I'm sorry,' I said. 'That's news to me, too. Someone should have told you.'

Kate sniffed, then shook her head. 'It's not your fault.' She looked around, as if only just realising where she was, then started to push herself to her feet.

'Here, let me help you.'

She shrugged my hand away before it could reach her. 'I'm fine.' She straightened her collar and brushed the hair out of her face. 'I'm sorry. I shouldn't have come here. I wasn't quite sure what to do when I found out. It's funny, that he only became real to me once he had been turned to ash, isn't it? Sorry. I'll go.'

The reserved and suspicious Kate I had encountered in the museum was returning, all vulnerability in the process of being packaged away into a box.

'You don't have much here,' she said, looking around at the empty walls, the expectant shelves.

'I'm not here much,' I said, by way of excuse. 'Can I get you something to drink?'

She nodded and I filled two glasses with tonic and lime and took them across. The glasses didn't quite match, and for some reason I felt embarrassed about this. I sat on a stool by the kitchen counter, cradling my drink.

Kate sipped her tonic water and shrugged slightly as though still not quite sure why she had sought me out.

'Excuse this next question,' I began, 'but if memory serves my card carries my address at the station?'

Of course I'd encountered witnesses and persons of interest outside of the station before, but never here, in my home. Even Bagby had only been here once or twice.

Kate put her glass down on the coffee table, then faced me over the side of the sofa. 'I'm sorry; you're in the database,' she said. 'I should have called. Or come to you at the station.'

I'd almost forgotten about the database. Introduced nearly a decade ago in the interests of complete transparency between the public and law enforcement, it listed the telephone numbers and home addresses of every member of the police force. I'd thought the whole thing had been shut down after a young PC was attacked on her doorstep by a crazed 'fan'. Seemingly, I was out of the loop. I'd have to speak to Mercer about getting my name removed.

'Don't worry, I'm not here to shoot you,' Kate said. She followed it up with a forced laugh. 'That was a joke, sorry.' She took another hurried sip of her drink. 'I suppose we shouldn't make those sort of jokes, not after all of this. But then I'm not really sure what I'm supposed to feel. Or do. No one warns you about how it feels when your secret sibling is murdered.'

'I'm glad you aren't here to shoot me,' I said. 'And I can't even imagine what you must be going through. If you want to talk about it…'

Kate shook her head. She leaned forward and in the dull light her mis-matched eyes were dark, flat ovals. At thirty years old, Kate possessed none of the youthful naivety of Caleb's teenage headshot. There was none of Caleb's hopelessness, either; only a measured and informed resolve. 'That isn't why I came,' she continued. 'I came because I want to know how close you are to catching his killer.'

It was late and an evening spent in search of Bagby had exhausted me. I didn't have the energy for stonewalling. 'We're following up some leads,' I said. 'Usually not a lot of pressure is put on solving cases like these. But I told you I'll do my best to find Caleb's killer.'

I don't know why I told her the next part, 'And to complicate matters, my partner has disappeared.'

'I'm sorry,' she replied, with something genuine in her voice.

'I'm sorry; that's not relevant to Caleb's case,' I said.

Kate shrugged. 'It must be hard, nevertheless.' She examined her hands before she looked back at me. 'Why do you think Caleb was killed?'

'I'm not sure,' I said. 'Sometimes people are just killed for no reason.'

Kate nodded, although we both knew that wasn't true.

To divert the conversation I pointed to the takeaway bag I had left on the counter. 'There's more than enough food, if you think it would help to eat something?'

She shook her head. Her hair swung with it, like a curtain. 'I don't think I have an appetite. A man is dead. That I never met him doesn't seem to make that less sad.'

'You're right,' I said. 'Look, it's late and I've had a long day. If you like, I can escort you home, or call for a car to pick you up?'

'My brother's death hasn't made me an invalid,' Kate said, standing up and pocketing her glasses. She took a card from her pocket and placed it on the table. 'From now on I'd appreciate you letting me know about any new developments directly.'

'Of course,' I said.

She moved towards the door. 'Thanks for the drink,' she said, then she was gone and the flat was quiet and empty again.

Half an hour later I lay in bed going over the events of the day. A streetlight shone through my bedroom window and fell across my pillow. But it was OK; I wouldn't be able to sleep anyway.

14

The Kid in White

I called the station as soon as I woke up and enquired about yesterday's call to Kate. A lowly grunt from the admin pool had called her to tell her about the cremation – but only after the fact. It was a routine courtesy but the officer had hung up when Kate had voiced her displeasure. For some reason this made me especially angry. I felt like I owed Kate another apology. I dialled her number without thinking and she answered after ten or so rings.

'I'm sorry to call you so early,' I said. 'I just wanted to apologise again for yesterday. The officer that called you was in the wrong. I'll make sure it won't happen again.'

'I appreciate that,' Kate said. Then, 'What are you doing now? I could use a lift to work.'

'I'm not sure that's protocol,' I said. Then, realising the museum wasn't much of a detour from the station anyway, 'But I don't see why not.'

'Great,' she said. 'I'll be waiting.'

I arrived outside Professor Faron's house half an hour later.

Kate answered the door looking bright and fresh, as though the upset of the previous evening had been scrubbed away with cold water.

'I appreciate this,' she said as she got into the car. 'It's my last day today. Now that the museum is closing it seems I'm surplus to requirements. Once I've finished packing everything up, that's it.'

'I'm sorry,' I said.

'Don't be. I'm not the only one losing my job. It's the same at every gallery, every museum in the Capital.'

'Still, I'm sorry.'

We drove to the museum in silence. I'd been half-expecting Kate to fill me in on some secret titbit of information that would suddenly make everything with her brother – with Bagby – that much clearer, but she didn't. Instead we rode along saying nothing and the quiet was not uncomfortable.

'Here we are,' I said, stating the obvious as I pulled up at a side door of the museum.

Kate got out of the car and for some reason I did too.

'Thank you again for the lift,' she said. 'And for checking up on who called me yesterday.'

'Any time,' I said over the distance of the car roof. 'Just doing my job.'

In films, soon-to-be murder victims see their assailants sneaking up behind them in the reflection of the car bonnet, or a shadow looming over the windscreen. All I had to warn me was Kate's small intake of breath and the tearing sound as the knife slipped through my jacket.

I stepped aside at the last moment and felt the tug as the knife was pulled away. By luck rather than skill I managed to grab the boy's wrist. Up close he was just as skinny as he had looked at the party but, with his sling gone, he was free to demonstrate that strength came in all sorts of packages. Before I could force the knife away, he headbutted me and I fell back against the car. I blinked and my head felt heavy. The boy laughed and licked the corner of his mouth. He tossed the knife to his other hand and made to step around me, towards Kate. I had enough sense left to reach for my gun. Before the Kid could get to her, Kate threw her handbag in his face and he was hit by a flying mess of lipsticks and vitamin pills and wellness bars.

I slid off the bonnet, gun in hand. The boy turned, saw it, and ran.

'Stay here,' I said to Kate. I staggered across the road, my ripped jacket flapping like a sail, the Colt held out beside me.

The boy ran along the street towards Hyde Park. I hurried after him, keeping my head low in case he had a gun he wanted to use on me too. He looked back over his shoulder, checking I was still playing his game. I followed him all the way along the street, my stamina being put to the test. Then the Kid jumped up and white t-shirt, jeans and trainers disappeared over the park wall. I put the gun away and hauled myself up after him. In the time it took to hoist myself up, the Kid had managed to scale a tree by the wall. To prove it, he jumped out and kicked me in the face just as I'd mastered my ascent. I fell the eight or so feet to the ground and landed on my back. A jogger stopped and tried to help me up. I pushed him away and clambered back up onto the wall. This time I made it over, and half dropped, half fell to the ground. I pulled the gun from my holster again, then pulled myself up and stumbled through the mud.

The Kid was watching and waiting from a copse of bare trees, ten yards away. He didn't even appear to be sweating. He looked like he was in no hurry to get away, as though the whole thing really was a game and he wanted to waste as much of my time as possible. As if he wanted to distract me from something else. I thought of Kate, left alone by the car. I swore loudly. The Kid seemed to be laughing, leaning back against his tree with his arms crossed against his chest.

I shoved the gun in my waistband and jumped back up onto the wall, feeling chipped stone push up under my fingernails. I hauled myself over and landed only slightly more successfully than the first time. The jogger had gone. I hurried back towards the museum. My car stood alone in the street. I sprinted up to it, feeling air drag itself into my lungs as my head imploded. Kate wasn't there.

I collapsed against the bonnet, feeling lightheaded. A voice from the doorway said, 'I guess you didn't get him, then?' and there was Kate sitting on the steps, looking like a vision sent to save me.

'You need to see the medic,' Mercer was saying, leaning over her desk as I propped myself up in a chair. 'It's my neck if you fall down dead the minute you leave this office.'

'I will,' I said, a wet towel pressed to the slapped-steak bruise that was forming above my eye. 'See the medic, that is. But first we need to find this kid. He could have killed Kate. He might have killed Bagby.'

Mercer banged the desk. 'Don't be so wet behind the ears. A less understanding superior might think you're purposefully trying to inherit Bagby's problems. Sadly, I can't spare you to go running around playing cowboys just now. What you're going to do instead is put a call out on this kid. He's bound to be on our files, a rugrat like that, so find him and get uniform to go pick him up.' She waved a dismissive hand. '"Advised: suspect is armed and dangerous." All of that.'

'He's not on the system,' I said. 'I checked after Bagby's run-in with him.'

'Then he bloody will be soon,' Mercer said. 'And another

thing, you're supposed to be finding this dead man's killer, not trying to sleep with the sister.' She pointed through the window to where Kate was sitting by my desk. 'Or did you miss that part of your training? "Don't shag persons of interest."'

'There's nothing…' I began.

'That doesn't matter!' Mercer cut in. 'The Board only has to get a hint of this sort of thing and that's us with a scandal on our hands. Take her home and leave her there. Leave your romantic intentions until after we've found the person who shot her brother in the head. In the meantime, have uniform find this boy and we'll deal with him as and when.'

'OK?' she said when I didn't make a move. 'Now would be a good time to start!'

'She didn't sound sympathetic,' Kate said when I reached my desk.

'She wasn't. I've got to take you home. She doesn't think this is related to your brother's killer.'

Kate shot a look over my shoulder. Clearly Mercer wasn't watching or she'd have dragged Kate out of there by her hair. 'Of course it's related. Did you see the way he came towards me with that knife? He was after both of us.'

'I know,' I said, steering her towards the door. 'I saw what you saw. But if we're going to make any progress we'll have to play it Mercer's way. At least for a while.'

'Did you forget to hit him back?' Stohl called as he came in from the elevator.

'This is my partner,' I said to Kate. Then, 'Stohl, I'd like you to meet…'

'I know who she is,' he said, his eyes fixed on her face. 'She's the ghost of our dead singer. Almost the mirror image. And you say the two of you had never met?' he asked her.

'If we have met, I don't remember it,' Kate said. 'Nice to

meet you, detective, but your partner was about to give me a lift home.'

'Well, that's a coincidence because I was just heading out myself. Let's take the stairs.' He walked along with us, directing us towards the rarely used staircase in the far corner of the office. The door swung closed behind us as we began our ascent towards the light.

'It was a good job you were there to protect him,' Stohl said.

'I think it was a pretty even match,' Kate said without looking back at him.

'My partner's face doesn't agree.' Stohl turned to me. 'You should have shot him.'

I gripped the banister, wondering how much longer Stohl would be my problem. 'Not all of us are so trigger happy.'

'The benefits of a military career,' Stohl commented.

We reached street level. Kate pushed open the door. Light and air came flooding in. Just as I was about to follow her through, Stohl caught my arm, holding me back.

'Partner,' he whispered. 'Go home and rest up. You and I have a busy night ahead. I know who he is. I know where we can find your boy in white.'

15

Nightclubbing

That evening found Stohl and me sitting in the dark cockpit of his car, cold green teas standing on the dashboard. Across the street stood the Cat's Eyes club – the jewel in Macelleria's crown. It occupied a grand old Victorian building that from the outside looked like a shoebox hung with fairy lights, on the edge of a de-gentrified housing estate in Stockwell. Unlike the Diamond Club, the Cat's Eyes was one hundred per cent above board; there were no dancers here, just rich customers letting off steam over a glass of fake booze. As an imitation of what a real bar had been, it was seen as a key social hub, and thereby a vital component of our emotional wellbeing.

During the uprising the estate had been a hotbed of insurgent activity and more than one activist had lost their life battling against police in its winding alleys or attempting an escape through the wide expanse of the club's now defunct car park. In other words, it was the perfect location for a club looking to cash in on the gritty austerity aesthetic.

'His name is Billy Kader. We brought him in two years ago,'

Stohl was saying, the club backlit by the white glints of the tower blocks. 'A whole litany of unsavoury offences. A few of us wanted to throw him down a hole then and there. Disappear him. But "saner" heads prevailed.'

'Brought him in for what?' I asked. 'And why haven't you been keeping track of him?'

'Classified,' Stohl said (with a straight face, no less). 'And do you really think we can keep track of everyone who crosses our paths? We have to let some go or we'd spend most of our time filling out forms and looking for places to put them.'

'Why was there no record of his arrest?'

'I told you, it was classified,' Stohl said. He shrugged, his eyes on the club. 'Sorry, that's just the way it is.'

'He threatened Fomalhaut, he attacked Bagby, and only this morning he attacked the sister of a murder victim. I think it's safe to say your department dropped the ball on this one.'

'Then take it up with Ormsby,' Stohl said coolly. 'And by "your department" I hope you mean "ex-department", because I'm working with you now, as I've explained. Remember that it was me who informed you that Kader – alias your boy in white – is an up-and-coming stooge of Macelleria. A rising star of the criminal underworld.'

'And sitting here isn't getting us any closer to finding him,' I said. 'What makes you think he'll show up?'

'It's called a "stakeout",' Stohl said. 'I'm sure with all of your experience you've heard of them?'

'We don't have time for a stakeout,' I said. 'Whether the Kid is in there or not, Bagby might be. And if Macelleria did take him, this would be the perfect place to hide him away. It's hiding in plain sight. The largest private club in the city, and it has police protection.'

'Allegedly.'

I pulled my gun from my holster and placed it on the dashboard.

'What are you doing?'

'I'm going in to talk to Macelleria,' I said. 'I'll scope the place out and we'll see if Bagby is there. If the Kid turns up, that's a bonus.'

'If this place really is under police protection that would piss a lot of people off.'

'I'm trying to protect a member of the police force right now, as well as apprehend a suspect.'

'Then why no gun?'

'Because I don't want to give them an excuse to start anything. If Bagby is in here I'll drag him out with my bare hands if I have to. The Kid, too.'

'You don't really think the Kid had anything to do with Caleb's murder?'

'Let's find him and find out,' I said.

It had grown stuffy in the car. I didn't like the atmosphere. I reached for the door handle and felt Stohl's hand on my elbow. 'I meant it, earlier on. You really should have shot him. When it's him or you, it has to be him.'

'Maybe it doesn't have to be either of us.'

I got out of the car and crossed the vast, empty expanse of the car park before I could talk myself out of it.

Even from a distance the doorman looked big enough to cuddle me to death. He didn't get any smaller the closer I got. Before I could pull my badge he laughed quietly to himself and stepped aside, gesturing with a sweep of his arm that I should show myself inside. I pushed through a red velvet curtain, ignoring the cloakroom assistant. No one looked up as I entered, except for the barman, who pursed his lips then went back to polishing the glassware. It was still early, but a few suited patrons stood leaning against the zinc-topped bar, or lounging in one of the fist-shaped chairs that skirted the first room. Soft, dreamlike jazz played in the background. The walls were decorated with imitation prints: Warhol's Skulls alongside some Georgia O'Keefe and Edward Hopper. Chinese lanterns hung from the ceiling.

I took a space at the bar. The barman looked over.

'I'm here to speak to your boss.'

'Drink?' the barman asked, as if I hadn't spoken.

'Maybe later. Where is he?'

'You have to be a member to drink here,' the barman said, running a wet cloth around the rim of a martini glass. 'Do you have a membership chip?'

I was about to embarrass myself by pulling out my police badge again when I became aware of a figure emerging from behind a second curtain in a corner of the room. It was Macelleria, leaning heavily on his cane, teeth glinting, his body wrapped up in a velvet dinner jacket. A green polka dot cravat was the only thing keeping his chins in place, his head resting atop it like a fleshy bowling ball adorned with greased-back hair.

'All right, Ted,' he said to the barman. 'Dial down the tough guy routine. Our friend here's just come in for a chinwag. Look, he's not even carrying a weapon. Although his jacket has seen better days.'

'I'm here to –'

'I know why you're here,' Macelleria said, his voice east end gangster by way of a cement mixer. 'Follow me, we'll talk.'

He disappeared back through the curtain. I followed him. As I stepped into the darkness I pulled a small metallic sphere from my pocket, held down a button on the top for half a second, then dropped it to the floor. The Scope would hover inches from the ground, moving slowly under its own power from room to room. It worked by sending out an invisible pulse

136

that relayed a three-dimensional plan of any building back to whoever had the visual unit. In this case, the one I'd stashed in Stohl's car. Designed to avoid detection and automatically take advantage of the nearest egress once finished; for police work at least, the Scope might have just been the single most advantageous invention of the last ten years. Without a warrant they were of course highly illegal. But sometimes, I reasoned, the end justifies the means. Bagby would have approved. My father would have reported me to my superior officer, then disowned me.

'We'll be comfortable in the lounge,' Macelleria said. He slid a Japanese-style wooden door open to reveal a small room with red walls and four low tables arranged at random. A narrow stream ran diagonally across the room before slipping away to somewhere else. Small mechanical goldfish swam in pre-programmed loops in its artificial pools.

'My architect got carried away,' Macelleria said with a shrug. 'You give them a brief and they throw it out the window. What can you do?'

Two women in trouser suits sat at one of the tables, talking quietly but forcefully about a business matter.

'My apologies, ladies,' Macelleria said. 'Would you mind giving myself and my associate here a moment? There'll be a fresh bottle of Champsynth waiting for you upon your return.'

The women left without acknowledging us or pausing their conversation.

When we were alone, Macelleria indicated that we should sit at a table in the corner. I did so and watched as he slowly, awkwardly, lowered himself down opposite me.

'You've come galloping in here to rescue your partner,' he said before I could get a word out. 'Well, he ain't here.'

'Which is exactly what you'd be expected to say, in this situation,' I countered.

'Well,' he said, emitting a hollow, monosyllabic laugh before poking at something in his teeth with the tip of his tongue. 'Say we are in this situation you refer to – I'm being polite here, of course, for the sake of brevity. Say we are in this situation, and say I've reminded you of my relationship with certain key figures within the police force. Say we've said all that. Well, there wouldn't be much left to say, would there?'

'Your boy attacked my partner before he went missing. He attacked me this morning. The evidence all points a certain way.'

Macelleria drew himself up, pulling his dinner jacket even tighter about him with his meaty hands. 'If you're referring to Billy Kader, well, it fills me with sorrow to have to inform you that we decided to end our mutual association some time ago.'

'You're saying he no longer works for you?'

'Regrettably. Although his dress sense alone was enough to get him kicked out. All that bright white sports gear? That's bad taste enough, isn't it? That is your department, yes? Bad taste?' He continued before I had chance to add anything. 'Still, I remember when taste used to be subjective. Although I imagine you're too young for that. Not too young to remember what Bagby did that day, though, during the big scrap outside parliament, I'd bet. You know, under the bridge. A dead boy. A dead copper. What? Didn't think anyone else knew about that? You don't think Bagby comes to my club, my bars, my cabarets so often without spilling some secrets? You don't think I've other friends who know everything about him? About you? About your new girlfriend…'

Confrontation was the quickest path to flat out denial. I tried a different tack. 'If Kader no longer works for you, who does he work for now?'

Marcelleria shrugged, his head sinking as his shoulders rose to meet his ears. 'Search me.'

I didn't believe him, but the Kid was only a shortcut to finding Bagby. 'OK, let's forget the kid for a while. I'll give you one chance to help me find DCI Bagby,' I said, aware that I'd just thrown my own rulebook out the window. Bagby would be proud.

'One chance is all I need,' Macelleria said adjusting his cravat. 'And I've already taken it. I told you: I don't know where your partner is. And if I did, it would be in my interests to tell you, believe me.'

'Then how about Vasily Popov?' I asked, intentionally withholding news of his death.

'Popov?' Marcelleria asked, his eyes widening momentarily with what could only have been amusement. He chuckled. 'I heard poor Vasily doesn't work for anyone anymore.'

'Not that you'd know anything about that?'

Marcelleria shook his head. 'No, I know everything about it. Some dago vagabonds from the International Zone cut his throat and booted him in the Thames. Apparently he cheated them at a game of virtual Cheat. Which is ironic, to say the least.' He clapped his fleshy hands. It sounded like two bulls rutting. 'Good riddance, I say. Popov was a thorn in my side from the moment I took him on. No appreciation for the managerial structure. Didn't value the tier-system of reward and advancement we've got going on here. In short: he had not one fucking iota of respect.'

'So –' I said.

'Nope, despite your accusatory tone, and despite Popov being a useless halfwit, I didn't have him killed,' Marcelleria said, finishing my sentence.

We were getting off topic. Marcelleria was right; Popov's death didn't matter. 'Let's return to my wayward partner,' I said. 'When was the last time he was here?'

Marcellaria spread his hands. 'Search me. A week, two weeks ago?'

'Gambling?'

'Detective, you know we don't endorse that. But no.'

The almost bored tone in which he delivered his reply indicated that he was telling the truth about that at least.

'So, you've absolutely no idea where DCI Bagby might be?'

Marcelleria sighed. 'It takes a while to get through to you, doesn't it? No, I don't know where Bagby is. That's the very final time I'll say that.'

I let that hang, then nodded. 'I hope we don't have to have this conversation again,' I said.

Macelleria laughed. 'We might. We might, but not tonight. I'm about to receive my first important customers – couple of big-paying finance-flippers – so do excuse me.'

He laboured to his feet and stepped lightly over the miniature stream. 'You don't need me to show you out, do you?'

Two heavies appeared in the doorway. I stood up.

'We'll speak again, I'm sure,' I said.

Macelleria moved away down the corridor, swinging his cane before him with each step. 'I'd like that,' he called over his shoulder.

I sized up the two heavies, expecting a back alley exit accompanied by a goodbye slap, but they only smiled then turned and followed after their boss. Left to my own devices I made my way back through the bar. The barman was still polishing glasses.

'Drink?' he called as I made for the door. 'We've got some good French brandy. The real stuff.'

I stopped and turned back to him. 'What did you say?'

He shrugged, the cloth still in his hand. 'Armagnac.' He winked. 'Come on, even coppers deserve a night off.'

Whether purposefully tipping me off, or brazenly offering me a glass of Bagby's favourite tipple in a two-fingered salute to the police force, he had made up my mind.

Stohl started the car when I was only halfway across the carpark, the lights like searchlights reaching through the darkness.

'Anything?' I asked as I climbed inside.

'Take a look for yourself,' he said as the car pulled away quickly gathering speed.

He handed me a tablet computer with a live display of the Scope's journey through a three dimensional rendering of the club, the image constructed in an architect's blue lines. The Scope had almost completed its scan of all four floors but it was the basement I was interested in. I tapped the screen. A small room in the far north-east of the building was empty apart from a chair in the very centre. Directly in front of this was a drain with a pool of some sort of liquid running down into it from beneath the chair. The chair itself was empty but the rough outline of handcuffs attached to either arm showed it had until recently been occupied by someone who likely wished they were anywhere else.

'We've got him,' I said. I filled Stohl in on what had happened inside. Outside, the Oval slid past. 'Where are we going? The station's that way.'

'We're not going to the station,' Stohl said. 'If Bagby's in Macelleria's club, we need to get in there ASAP, right? Armed response, the whole shebang.'

'Right. But Mercer will never sign it off.'

'She won't,' Stohl agreed. 'But Ormsby will.'

We stopped near Vauxhall Bridge and pulled up outside an inconspicuous all-night cafe bathed in the glare of lights from a nearby building site.

'Let me handle this,' Stohl said, getting out of the car.

Inside the cafe the air was steamy with grease. A hearty clientele of workmen in neon jackets dined on fare without healthspan at the forefront of its considerations. In the corner, his back to the wall with a mug of tea and a copy of *The Times* spread out before him, sat Ormsby.

'My decades of police training tell me something is afoot,' Ormsby said, looking up from his paper before either myself or Stohl could speak. He was dressed in a black coat, his black hair swept across his forehead.

'Sir, this is…' Stohl began.

'I know who this is,' Ormsby said. 'Sit down, both of you.' He sighed and shuffled the paper with agitation, like a man who has accepted he won't be enjoying the comforts of home tonight. 'I'm assuming this is about your missing partner, Bagby?'

'We think we've found him, sir,' I said.

'We think he may be being held in the Cat's Eyes club,' Stohl added.

Orsmby took a sip of his tea. He smiled before swallowing. Inside his jacket I could see two Glock pistols hanging in opposite shoulder holsters.

'And how did you obtain this information?'

'From a Scope, dropped about…' Stohl checked his watch. 'Twenty-six minutes ago. We found a chair with cuffs and possibly blood running into a drain. It looks like an interrogation room, Sir. And it looks like it's been used recently.'

Ormsby sat back. 'You have a warrant for this?'

'We were hoping you may be able to help with that, sir.'

'You think this is linked to your murder case?' he asked, addressing me.

'I think so, sir. The deceased reported a man following him

and this morning a low-level thug associated with Macelleria attacked myself and the victim's sister. It can't be coincidental.'

Stohl shifted from one foot to the other. It was obvious to both of us that the Kid didn't match the description of Caleb's stalker but however tenuous, the connection might be enough to persuade Ormsby to act.

'Plus,' I continued, feeling Stohl's admonishing side-eye burning into me, 'Marcelleria all but admitted to having Vasily Popov killed – another thug who attacked Bagby. I believe his intention was to silence Popov so he couldn't discuss his role in the attack on Bagby.'

Ormsby contemplated us both for a moment then leaned forward in his seat, pushing his tea away. 'Hardly a smoking gun…'

Stohl and I stayed quiet.

'So, you're requesting a top-tier raid? Tactical support. Drones. The lot?' Ormsby asked.

I did as he'd asked and let Stohl do the talking.

'Yes, sir, but the Commissioner won't like it.'

'The Commissioner is dining with the Prime Minister tonight,' Ormsby said. 'I doubt either of them would want to be disturbed. I'm going to need a lift back to the station. We'll call ahead and get things moving.' He stood up. A light flashed on his wrist and the bill was paid automatically. He left the newspaper where it was.

'Let's get moving, gentlemen,' he said, straightening his jacket, 'DCI Bagby won't locate himself.'

16

The Raid

'Have you lost your mind?' Mercer was saying as I strapped on a tactical vest.

We occupied the shadows on the edge of The Cat's Eyes' carpark, facing down the brightly lit club from a bank of police cars, tactical officers checking their weapons and fixing their helmets.

Mercer had arrived at the last moment, a red shirt under an open coat, no weapon or hint of wanting to take part. Her breath coiled away in the night air. 'Do you realise what engaging in a full scale gun battle in the middle of London – with Macelleria of all people – will do to this department?'

'Ormsby gave the go-ahead,' I said. 'Any blowback will be on him.'

'He only gave the go-ahead because an officer from *my* department has gone missing, and two others convinced him this is a good idea. And now we're going to have a bloodbath. Oh, for God's sake.' She took hold of my vest and roughly pulled the straps into place. 'You're losing control of this situation. I hope you know what you're doing.'

'Everything will be fine,' I said. 'He's in there – Bagby. We have to get him out.'

Across the carpark, the club waited beneath the spotlights of the police drones. Adapted for surveillance and 'urban conflict resolution', these small nimble aerial units had more in common with the type of drones you'd buy your father for Christmas than the sleek, hovering leviathans of desert warfare. Most were equipped with spotlights but their cargo could be adapted depending on our needs and I knew that tonight some among them carried machine guns and others laser-guided rockets. During the post-Reformation clean-up, it was not uncommon for the full, explosive capabilities of our drones to be used in the middle of Brixton or Chalk Farm against a final nest of those who would seek to return the country to the old order. But nothing like that had happened for a long, long time.

The club was by now full of customers, and although Macelleria had seemingly been clued in ahead of mine and Stohl's earlier visit, there was no sign of any preparatory activity taking place inside. No goons cradling machine guns appeared in the windows. No customers shrieked as they were repurposed as human shields. The surrounding tower blocks made up for this lack of activity: lights flickered on, figures appearing on balconies even as our snipers hurried to rooftops and vantage points surrounding the club.

'Here they come,' Mercer said, nodding over my shoulder.

Ormsby and Stohl were making their way along the line of police cars towards us, two black coats swishing in the dim light. Behind them was the tactical captain, walking slow and erect with 'LDNPD' printed in white letters across his chest.

Ormsby made the introductions. 'Mercer, you know Brendan?'

Mercer nodded. 'This has escalated quickly. I don't suppose the Commissioner is going to be overly enthusiastic when she hears about this.'

'Dealing with the Commissioner is my job,' Ormsby said. 'And we've got the best team on the force to make sure this goes off without a hitch.'

Brendan agreed. 'We'll get the job done. Whoever's in there, standing between us and one of our own, is going to wish they'd called in sick today.'

'OK, Brendan, thank you,' Ormsby said, a hand on his shoulder.

Brendan nodded and set off back along the line, shouting into the radio attached to his chest. 'Move those civilians back from the balcony. We won't be responsible for collateral damage.'

As if on cue five or six new drones were launched from a police vehicle down the line. They flew together like a flock of metallic birds, rotors whirring. When they reached the towers they broke off and positioned themselves at different floors, powerful searchlights shining into front rooms. As one, they boomed out a crackled message: 'Police business. For your own safety please retreat to your homes. Police business…'

'Well if they didn't know we were here before…' Mercer said.

'With all respect, Ma'am, they know we're coming for them,' Stohl said.

'All right,' Ormsby snapped. 'We're all here to do a job so we may as well get on with it. We've got sniper cover from the towers, drone cover overhead and A, B and C teams going in three entrances. You two,' he said, pointing to me and Stohl, 'will go in the front, after A team. It's your circus, after all.'

'Sir,' Stohl said, pulling his Sig Sauer from his shoulder holster and checking the breech.

I took out my Colt .45 and did the same.

'Safety's off,' Mercer whispered.

'Ready?' Ormsby asked. 'OK, do it,' he said into his radio.

Two rows of tactical officers in dark blue fatigues with the same LDNPD motif across their kevlar helmets hurried from behind the police cars, their boots moving silently across the tarmac, Heckler & Koch submachine guns cradled against chests, carabiners, plastic hand ties and flash grenades clacking lightly on their belts.

'That's us,' Stohl whispered, and then he and I were hurrying after them, running fast and low with our pistols out, our fingers on the trigger guards and my heart thumping.

'Hold it!' Brendan called from somewhere ahead and both teams slid to a dead stop and dropped to their knees, weapons trained on the windows, doors and roof of the club.

Stohl and I crouched at the back of the group, keeping our weapons to ourselves and out of the way. Three drones had converged on the entrance to the club, overlapping spotlights illuminating the scene like a stage. The door opened and after a second or two the doorman and the two stooges from earlier walked out, followed by at least six more men in the same dark suits. They spread out in a line, revealing the submachine guns and pistols held in their hands.

'Steady!' Brendan shouted.

The men knelt together and placed the guns at their feet then stood up with their hands raised overhead. Macelleria emerged, leaning on his cane as he stepped out into the night, the drone spotlights readjusting to keep him in a pool of light.

'Gentlemen,' he called over the steady whir of rotor-blades. 'If you wanted to come in, all you had to do was knock...'

Stohl and I leaned over the video monitors, scanning the club's surveillance tapes while the crime scene geeks swept the basement room. Stohl and I had led the charge, kicking in the door to find a room outfitted with a video tripod, shelves stacked with rubber bondage equipment and the MP for Lambeth handcuffed to the chair. By this point I don't think either of us held high hopes that the substance on the floor would be blood, or belong to Bagby.

'Nothing,' Stohl said now, as the previous night's OU footage sped across the screen.

'We'll go through it again,' I said, 'back at the station in the morning.'

'Someone tipped them off. They knew we were coming – even before you paid Macelleria a visit.'

Ormsby appeared in the doorway, Macelleria behind him. 'It's time to pack it up, gentlemen. We've wasted quite enough of Mr Macelleria's time.'

'Nonsense,' Macelleria said, his large, ringed hand on Ormsby's shoulder. 'Do take as long as you need. I just wish you had called ahead; we could have assisted you more thoroughly,' he said, his eyes on mine.

Stohl and I trudged back upstairs to the bar. A group of whispering guests sat corralled in a corner. This would be little more than an amusing story for them to tell tomorrow. After this interruption, the drinks were sure to be free all night. At the expense of the police department, of course.

The same barman from earlier looked up as we approached. Mercer sat at the bar, a tomato juice in her metallic hand, her other pushing its knuckles into the corners of her eyes.

'Ma'am.'

'Don't you "Ma'am" me. My office, first thing tomorrow. You've really fucked us over here, gents. The brains of the century! A sex dungeon! You thought your partner was being held in a sex dungeon...'

Stohl led me outside before I could say anything else. The last of the tactical teams were packing up before hurrying back to the station.

'We nearly had him, I'm sure of it,' he said. 'All this means is that someone talked to Macelleria first, not that we were wrong.'

I mumbled something noncommittal in response. It didn't really matter who had tipped Macelleria off; the trail had gone cold.

'Need a lift?' Stohl asked.

'I'll walk to the tube,' I said. I pulled off my raid vest and dropped it into the backseat of his car. 'Helps me think. Or try to.'

Stohl nodded. I left him there and set off, jeers echoing from the tower blocks at my back. I was tired and it would take a long time to get home. I wondered whether I would find Kate there again, waiting.

17

Antiques

Kate wasn't waiting for me when I got home. I let myself in, threw off my torn coat and pistol holster, and poured myself a sparkling water. Then I sat by the window in the dark, looking out over the still and empty street outside.

Caleb Jennings' headshot poked out from under the book Bagby had given me. I pulled the photo out and studied it for the hundredth time. I could count the decent leads on one finger; Fomalhaut had suggested that there was something valuable in Caleb's blood. But what meaning that might hold I didn't know, and I was becoming less and less certain of how Billy Kader – alias the Kid in White – tied into it all. My eyes ached. My head didn't feel much better. I closed the blind and laid down on the sofa. Mercer was right; instead of looking for Bagby, I should be looking for the man who had followed Caleb. I fell asleep thinking that by allowing myself to become distracted I had failed a dead man and also, wherever he was, Bagby was big enough and ugly enough to look after himself.

I woke to a banging at the door. I sat up, confused at

finding myself on the sofa instead of in bed. Sunlight crept in under the blinds. The banging persisted. Thinking it might be Stohl come to try and place the blame for the previous night's debacle literally at my door, I got up and flung the door open, ready for a confrontation. But it was only Kate, standing there looking like she hadn't slept much, either.

'Kate… Is everything all right? Come in.'

'My mother didn't come home last night,' she said, ignoring the steaming mug of tea I'd just provided. 'I haven't seen her in twenty-four hours. She didn't leave a note and she isn't at the university, either.'

This was not good, but I didn't want Kate to know I thought that. That wouldn't help anyone. 'Don't worry,' I said. 'We'll find her.' Then, because somehow that didn't feel adequate, I added 'I'm sure she hasn't gone far.'

I thought about Bagby's videos. The Professor and Jennings captured *in flagrante*. That the Professor would leave her daughter to shack up in Jennings' bolthole seemed unlikely, but it was the only idea I had. There was a risk that taking Kate to the shop might reveal more than she wanted to know, of course, but, if I went in first, made a lot of noise, it might be passed off as two concerned parents catching up. If the Professor wasn't there, and I could avoid facing Jennings' gun again, there was a chance that I might be able to retrieve the rest of Bagby's sub rosa surveillance cameras. That Jennings hadn't already discovered any of them over the years was a miracle.

Thirty minutes later I stopped the car at the top of the lane leading down to Harrington & Sons. It was raining again.

'Why would my mother be here?' Kate asked beside me.

'A friend lives here who might have seen her,' I explained. I scanned the streets. No one was about. 'It might be best if you wait here. I'll only be a minute.'

She didn't argue. I set off towards the shop. It was still early and as far as I could see the blinds were still drawn over the various windows lining the road. I knocked on Jennings' door. It opened inwards of its own accord. The gloom inside spilled out to mingle with the morning. I listened for a moment before stepping inside. Usually, in a situation like this, you're supposed to call out and announce yourself. The idea being that it scares the assailant/attacker/burglar away. Either that, or they come out shooting and you have a lawful excuse to put them down. But the antiques shop was silent; whatever had happened here had finished happening a long time ago.

I moved through the shop, treading heel-toe, heel-toe. Everything was as I remembered, except for two cups and a china teapot left on a table top. One of the cups had fallen over onto its side. Flies buzzed around the whole set-up. I dipped a finger into the tea and tasted it. It was cold and there was no indication of any poison I recognised. I searched what nooks and crannies there were and found no one. The door to the overgrown back yard was locked, which just left upstairs. I went up.

As I stepped into the room, my hand, which had strayed to the gun in my holster, slowly relaxed. Jennings was lying on the bed, on top of the covers. He was fully clothed, his head resting on a pillow. I crossed the room and felt for a pulse. I could have waited all day if I had the time. Harold Jennings was dead.

Sitting beside him like a nurse watching over her patient was Professor Faron. Even with her back to me I could tell that she was somewhere far away from the dingy bedroom at the end of a crumbling lane. Her head had slumped sideways onto her shoulder and her hair was dry, like a neglected bouquet of flowers left on a window ledge.

I felt for her pulse, just to make sure. But her wrist was cool and lifeless.

The Professor had closed Jennings' eyes post-mortem, but the rigid mask of pain was still engraved on his face and, when I turned to the Professor, I was met by the same constricted lips, the same taut skin stretched across the forehead. Clenched between her fingers was a single duck egg-coloured pill – a back-up in case the first failed to take effect. In her pocket was an empty gelatine capsule belonging to the pill that she had poured into Jennings' tea before leading him upstairs to bed. The official report would call it a murder-suicide and no capable police officer would argue otherwise. I was sure, however, that the Professor believed her actions to have been justified, no matter how drastic they were. She had been too rational to act on a whim. But of course I needed to know why. I patted down her pockets. She had made no effort to conceal the evidence. Inside the front pocket of her jacket was a small video drive with my initials on it. I slid it into my pocket then touched my palm to the Professor's cold cheek.

'I'm sorry,' I said.

The sound of Kate's empty cry came from behind me. She pushed me aside and held her mother's head to her breast, her fingers entwined with the Professor's hair as though somehow she could pass on her own life force, if only she held on for a little bit longer.

There was nothing to gain from being discovered there, but any number of ways we – or Bagby – might be tied into it. When it came to closing cases, the most obvious explanation wasn't always the most convenient. With Bagby linked to both of the deceased – and still missing – it was clear how this crime scene could be manipulated to someone else's benefit.

The Professor had left me the video drive for a reason, and until I had chance to find out what that reason was, what had happened here had to stay a secret.

I touched Kate's shoulder. 'I'm sorry. But we have to go. Kate. We have to go.'

She turned and slapped me across the cheek. Her eyes were full of anger, nothing else. 'How... who?'

I took her hand and pulled her towards the door. 'Later,' I said. 'We'll find out later. I promise.'

We made it downstairs. I hurried us towards the rectangle of bright sunlight let in by the open door. We didn't stop to lock the door, I only pulled it shut as we stumbled out into the street.

'We have to call an ambulance...' Kate was saying. 'She might...'

'She isn't,' I said. 'Walk normally. Slow down.'

I glanced at the buildings overlooking the lane. No one seemed to be awake yet. As long as they hadn't heard our commotion we still had some time. I forced Kate into the car then raced around to the other side before she could get out. If anyone had been watching it might have looked like an abduction. Kate sat there in a state of shellshocked silence, eyes fixed and unblinking.

I started the car. 'I'm sorry,' I said again, failing to find other words.

'Where are we going? Why aren't we calling for help? Why—'

I didn't get chance to respond. Before I could, a car smashed head-on into our driver's side, sending us skidding into a roundabout in a slow-motion cacophony of broken glass, flying hair and tiny ruby droplets of blood. We came to a stop against the side of a parked butcher's van, the impact sending us pitching forward in our seats.

Kate sat back with blood trickling down over her eye. She murmured, a hand pressed to her head. She turned to me. Her lips moved. Her voice was distant and dim.

'Are you all right?' she repeated.

I was aware, somewhere in the back of my consciousness, of a car revving its engine. But I was having trouble turning away from Kate who, as if in answer to her own question, raised a familiar handgun and fired two booming shots through the driver's side window, the rounds passing my chest in a rushing suck of air.

The sound brought me back to my body. I snatched the gun by the barrel, the heat searing my hand, and yelled 'Give me that!'

My ears were bruised and everything sounded like my head had been wrapped in bandages. I shoved the gun into my pocket then tried to open my door, but the entire side of the car was crumpled in on itself like a drinks can stomped underfoot. Kate was leaning across me, shaking my arm, her mouth forming urgent words I couldn't hear. She pointed past me, out of the shattered window and I got the hint; the Kid in White was facing us from behind the wheel of his white 1990s Peugeot, its front end crumpled up like a broken nose. I could pick out each gleaming tooth as he smiled at his quarry. For all her good intentions, Kate's shots had missed their target.

Someone punched my arm, then sound came rushing back as Kate screamed '–ing move!'

I ground the gearstick into first and the car lurched forward, the engine whining as we jumped over a flower bed. The steering wheel was sticky. I spun it, trying to get behind the Kid. We scraped alongside him, the jolt of metal on metal grinding through us. The car shot forward, shearing off his windscreen and sending it bouncing across our bonnet. The Kid accelerated. We inched ahead and our back-end shot out.

I gripped the wheel as the momentum pulled us around behind him. Then we were free, following his broken tail lights as he shot away along the empty street and under the viaduct.

My only thought was that he was here, and he was mine. Whatever the cost, I was going to beat, if not answers, then some sort of satisfaction out of him.

'There!' Kate yelled, pointing to the entrance to a multi-storey carpark rising like a concrete temple from the street.

I wrestled with the wheel and the car just about made it inside. There were no barriers ahead, only the brake lights of the Kid's car as he swung around a column and mounted the concrete ramp leading upward. Our car struggled after him. We swung out onto the next floor and stopped dead. The Kid's car was gone. The carpark was almost empty, and the cars that remained looked like they hadn't moved in a long time. We crawled forward, scanning the parked vehicles.

'Do you see him?'

'Sssh!' Kate hissed.

A car reversed at speed swinging its rear around, aiming for our bonnet. I was faster and we shot backwards before the Kid could hit us. I sped up and got alongside him, metal screeching as the cars collided. We rounded a corner together and approached the next ramp. The Kid took the up ramp. We took the down ramp but in the wrong direction. At the top we swung after him again. Then, some luck; the Kid took the next turn too quickly, and instead of going where he had intended, his car skidded sideways, thudding into a concrete support column, the impact lifting the right side wheels off the ground where they spun freely, uselessly, for a moment before crashing back down.

I stopped the car ten metres short. No one was moving in the other car. I felt Kate's hand dip into my pocket, reaching for the gun again. I grabbed her wrist.

'We're going to arrest him. Question him.'

'He killed my brother.'

'We don't know that. Stay here.'

I got out and hurried towards the crashed Peugeot. My right leg dragged. The ankle ignited in sudden pain. I clenched my fist and gritted my teeth. The Peugeot's door opened and the Kid jumped out, landing knees bent, his white sports clothes stained with blood. He shook himself off, then smiled at me and hobbled away, towards an empty parking space hemmed in between two people-carriers. A chest-high barricade separated him from a two-storey fall. The Kid reached the barrier and fell against it. I flung myself on top of him as he fumbled something from his pocket. The pistol spun away and out of sight among the foliage below. Then I had the Kid by the shoulders, lifting him against the barrier, blinking blood and sweat from my eyes.

Behind me Kate was saying my name. I looked back. She shook her head. I turned from the barrier and threw the Kid down on to the floor between us. My head spinning, I knelt on the small of his back, pulled out my handcuffs, and slapped them on him.

18

Adrift

'What do you hope to achieve in this life?'

The question was directed at me. If there was a correct answer, I didn't know it.

'Because you must be working towards something. Most of the officers here come to work to enforce the law. And then they go home again. We like to make this easier for them by assigning them to certain departments. Each department, you see, has a specific role within the police hierarchy and hence within the governance and, by extension, the protection of the populace. Maybe I'm not making myself clear. Think of an insect. If all of the legs are moving in the same direction the insect is able to live a successful life. The insect can find food, shelter and – if it's lucky – continue to procreate. If one leg becomes lame, the insect becomes handicapped and is easy prey for those that would wish to do it harm. The insect, in such a case, may be devoured before it gets chance to complete the job it has been put on this earth for, and that is not right. Do you understand this metaphor? Yes? Good, because we have not suffered through a revolution, all of us fighting bravely for change, only to have the new order sink into old, corrosive habits. Now, as I can see by your condition, you've learned some painful lessons today. What were they?'

'He's learned to bloody well follow my orders,' Mercer snapped. 'No one told you to go looking for this kid!' she said, advancing on me.

'That's enough, DSU Mercer, thank you,' Ormsby said calmly from behind his desk.

Mercer leaned back against the wall, arms crossed. The vein beneath her left eye throbbed at me. This was not good.

Ormsby's office was evidence of the extent to which he outranked Mercer. Up here on the eighth floor it was all white walls, sharp lines of monochrome furniture and high, bright windows looking out over Green Park. The office was sparse and free of decoration apart from a single picture hanging dead centre behind Ormsby's desk; a waterfall by Hiroshi Yoshida.

'Your job,' Ormsby said, turning to me again, 'is to investigate crimes against Section A4000204. You find and penalise those promoting "Bad Taste" in any and all areas of life. As the officer who found Mr Caleb Jennings' body, and due to the fact that he was once a contestant in a televised singing contest, it was decided that this crime fell under your remit, and DI Stohl would join you from my unit to assist in the investigation.' He sat back. His ergonomic chair creaked. 'Not only have you not done this within a satisfactory time period, you have apparently insinuated yourself into every aspect of the victim's life, including carrying out a relationship with his sister.'

He held up a hand, pre-empting my response. 'It is not in my interest to learn the nature of this relationship, but she has been seen entering your apartment block late at night. This alone would be enough to compromise the integrity of this investigation' – here Mercer kicked my shin sharply – 'without the collateral fracas you've pulled into your orbit. An assault at a members' club, a car chase through city streets, and last night's embarrassment at Macelleria's club. Now, I take full responsibility for the latter. I signed it off, after all. But Mercer is right. No one instructed you to go in search of your wayward partner. If we wanted him found we would have sent someone after him ourselves. And we did. Is that clear?'

'Yes, sir,' I said.

'As of now, the investigation into Caleb Jennings' death is closed. On the premises you found several pieces of paraphernalia illegal under Section A4000204, the so-called "Bad Taste Law", including signed photographs, a recording of a TV talent show appearance, and a poster of the former boy band known as "White Noise". As such, we have drawn the conclusion that the killing was carried out by a random upholder of the law, a so-called "Vigilante Hit". Is that clear?'

'And the actual killer?' I asked.

'Have you seen the news?' Ormsby asked. 'Have you heard about the bombing campaign being carried out across the country by thugs and domestic terrorists? We can't devote our resources to finding a lone killer of a man who was himself a criminal. Thousands of lives may be at risk if we don't stop these attacks. My advice would be to move on.'

He pressed a button on his desk. There was a buzzing sound and the door behind me opened. I could tell by his neat little footfall just who it was that had joined us even before he spoke.

'Ma'am. Sir.'

'Don't waste time, sit down,' Ormsby said.

Stohl sat in the chair beside mine without looking at me. Out of the corner of my eye I saw him calmly pull his trouser hems up and fold a leg across his knee.

'I've asked DI Stohl here to provide some additional insight

160

into certain recent extracurricular activities of yours,' Ormsby said. He looked blankly at Stohl. 'Stohl, how would you describe your partner's relationship with DCI Bagby?'

'I would describe Bagby as a mentor,' he said, without flinching. 'It is clear my partner looks up to him – is in awe, in fact – of some of DCI Bagby's achievements within the force.'

Mercer coughed, just loudly enough for me to hear.

'All right,' Ormsby said. 'And, in your own opinion and to the best of your knowledge, why would you say your partner has become fixated on locating DCI Bagby?'

'I believe...' Stohl began, his hands making the most minuscule of movements in his lap, 'that my partner believes DCI Bagby to be in danger.'

'How so?'

'Well, sir, Bagby was attacked at the Diamond Club shortly before he went missing.'

'You saw the attack take place yourself?'

'No, but my partner saw the aftermath. It's true that Bagby was in an inebriated state.'

'This is the evening that Caleb Jennings was murdered?'

'I believe so, sir. Yes.'

'OK,' Ormsby said, leaning back in his chair again.

'Sir, Bagby had nothing to do with the murder,' I said. 'I picked him up from the Diamond Club myself. A reliable waitress collaborated his story. He was there all night.'

'That's enough,' Ormsby said languidly. 'I don't have any questions for you at present.' He turned back to the class favourite. 'Stohl, you are of the belief that there is more to DCI Bagby's disappearance than meets the eye. Would you care to illuminate us all in the glow of this knowledge?'

Silence hung in the room. Even the birds in the park outside seemed to shut up.

'My partner has uncovered evidence that DCI Bagby has

been meeting with his old revolutionary associates. He has met with these people on a number of occasions, as has my partner in his search for Bagby. It is my belief that these ex-revolutionary members may somehow be linked to the recent spate of bombings and propaganda appearing across the country. As such, I believe that DCI Bagby has himself decided to forsake the forces of law and order and take up arms alongside his old revolutionary comrades once again. Their aim is nothing less than a complete and total second revolution.'

'You f–' I began.

'Sit down!' Ormsby yelled. Then, when the fog had cleared, 'DSU Mercer, I already know the answer to this because nothing of its sort gets off the ground without my knowledge, but have you in any way authorised or encouraged DCI Bagby to seek out his old friends in an undercover capacity? Perhaps with a view to ending these recent attacks?'

Mercer's response was as final as a rope being cut. Or a noose being fitted. 'No, sir, I have not.'

'In that case, DI Stohl, your secondment is over. You're being drafted back into the Unit – effective immediately. You're to find Bagby and bring him in for questioning, as well as any of his revolutionary colleagues that you might encounter.'

'Sir...' I cut in. 'You should know that this may all be connected somehow: the death of Caleb Jennings, the attack by Billy Kader, and Bagby's disappearance. I think... I think the simplest way to clear it up would be if I were able to speak with RZ. He was close with both Bagby and Caleb's adoptive mother. He's the strongest strand tying them both together. And he's sure to know about any revolutionary stirrings. He may be able to shed some vital light on the situation, and help exonerate Bagby. If you'd just grant me permission to see him, I'm sure…'

'Don't be so ridiculous!' Mercer snapped.

'I have to agree,' Ormsby said. 'It's absolutely out of the question, I'm afraid. No one has had access to RZ since the Reformation. The man's a… hero. And he deserves his rest.'

'… Just have twenty minutes, sir.'

'Impossible. Even if I wanted to help you, all requests have to go through the Prime Minister. It's above my pay-grade, and far, far above yours. I suggest you forget it, along with the name Caleb Jennings.'

'I can't just forget it, sir. I've been attacked. Twice.' I held up my banged hand and pointed to the sticking plasters on my forehead. 'Billy Kader almost killed myself and Caleb's sister today, and if he isn't working for Macelleria then he has to be working for someone else. RZ might be able to tell us who.'

'The only thing that man will be able to shine a light on is the fact that his brain has turned to mush,' Ormsby said. 'Sadly, the stories are true. When he turned himself in he was on the verge of mental collapse – exhausted from fighting the good fight – and he's only deteriorated since. As for this "Billy Kader"… Mercer, do you want to fill him in?'

'We've had to let him go,' she said, not quite meeting my eyes. 'The evidence is all circumstantial. We can't prove he attacked Bagby, and as far as today looks, you and him were involved in a traffic accident, during the course of which you chased him and beat him half to death, discharged your firearm in a public location, and caused him to crash his car. We're lucky he doesn't have any broken bones.'

'You can't just let him go!'

'We can and we did,' Ormsby said. 'Now, that's it. I've said everything I want to say. Go home, take a week to recover.

Then I'm sure there'll be a new case for you to work on when you return. Thank you.'

Mercer stood up. She glared at me. I stood up too, my injured ankle taking my weight.

'Stohl, stay here,' Ormsby said.

I don't know why I felt so disappointed that my one-time partner ignored my eyes as I walked past him and out into the corridor.

The bodies of the Professor and Jennings would be found as soon as the investigation into Bagby's associates began in earnest. Seeing as Ormsby had evidently already begun setting up the pieces, this was sure to be sooner rather than later.

Kate had disappeared as soon as we got Kader to the station. Either she was overcome with grief, or her late mother's distrust of the boys in blue was rubbing off on her. Either way, Bagby was the only person I could help right now. Police tape aside, his flat was just as it had been left: pictures, furniture and books tossed about the room. If Mercer had found anything she didn't like in there, I hadn't heard about it.

I stood in the centre of the lounge and knelt among the debris. The more time I spent among the detritus of Bagby's life, the more certain I became that wherever he was, Bagby was laughing at us. Pages had been torn from books, records trodden into little jagged pieces. But, here and there I spotted the odd book or record left intact, as though purposefully spared. They were the records he played for me late at night, the books he gave me copies of for my birthdays. They were artefacts, purposefully preserved in order to send a message. It was a code, a signal to me and me alone that he was all right. That he was simply off somewhere biding his time. Which made me equally relieved and annoyed that he'd kept me out of his plans. But I knew that unless I was imagining things, when he was ready, whenever the pieces of whatever game he was playing had fallen into place, Bagby would reveal all.

Ormsby was wrong about Bagby's revolutionary intentions, but at present there was little I could do to prove it.

I drove home, inserted the Professor's video drive into my computer, and watched as a shaky camera image appeared on-screen. The Professor had balanced the device on the window ledge in order to record herself, and I recognised the antique tat on the cabinet beside her as belonging to Jennings' bedroom. His body must already lay beside her, growing cold on top of the bed.

'Hello,' she said, greeting me by name. It was evening outside and the failing light cut across her face. 'So, this is my mea culpa. Or I suppose you might call it my confession from beyond the grave.'

She smiled and her burdens seemed to fall away, if only for a second.

'By now you know what I've done,' she continued, looking directly into the camera. 'If Bagby has been up to his old hidden camera tricks you might even think you know why I did it. But sex had nothing to do with this.' She chewed her bottom lip and a flush of anger lit her sunken cheeks. 'This had to be done. Jennings gave him away. His own son. He told me the story of that first "policeman" who came to see him. I don't know how he could have been so naive... I think he realised, after the fact, that this man meant Caleb harm but he was too cowardly to do anything about it. He called Bagby, yes, but too late. I can't forgive that. His stupidity or cowardice – or a mixture of both – was the end of Caleb. And now of him.'

She stared off-camera at something. I guessed it to be the trees outside, the gently swaying tops of the conifers.

'So, Harold deserved to be punished. But the real criminal

here is me. It was my late husband and I who said we'd keep the children safe after we found out who they were. It was Jennings' idea to take one each. They didn't know each other existed, anyway, and it would be safer like that. Between us we made a promise. And we let them down.'

She glanced down at her hands, then back at the camera. 'Fifteen years ago, at the height of the uprising, the HAF virus killed six million people worldwide. "Revolutionary Fever", some called it. You know all of this, of course. You lived through it. It killed your father. But indulge a dying woman as she sets down her last thoughts for posterity.

'None of us knew what to do about the HAF pandemic. The government certainly didn't. The planet was dying and it was taking us with it. It started in Canada, then spread into Russia and Asia. The British and American governments were glacially slow to close the borders. Naturally the virus got in. Naturally they blamed immigrants instead of their own inadequacies. Then they locked down hard. That was the original reason the borders were closed. And they've remained closed for fifteen years.

'The virus started with cold-like symptoms – runny nose, shortness of breath – then advanced to bleeding from the mouth and eyes, red blotches on the skin, rasping breath. Followed by death, the lungs slowly filling with liquid over 72 hours.'

I remembered. How could I not? I remembered my father clawing at his throat, trying to breathe, red sores all over his hands. I'd been happy, then, that my mother wasn't alive to catch it. God only knows how I managed not to. Certain tabloids had called it 'the Foreign Disease', laying the blame on immigrants, like the Professor said. The Professor was right; arising simultaneously with a national uprising, through incompetence or indifference, the government was ill-equipped to deal with such a pandemic. I don't remember a single colleague, newspaper or MP opposing the resulting immigration ban. It was a matter of national security. With the country under attack from within, Britain's interests had to come first. Post-Reformation the government refused to re-open the borders, naively envisioning Britain as some new, forward-thinking utopia.

'My husband and I were working with the government, trying to find a cure for the HAF virus at our lab in Whitstable,' the Professor continued. 'It was our first big contract. Well, in our search for the cure we discovered something amazing; by adding a bit of this, or taking away a bit of that, we could make the virus programmable. We managed to isolate a dormant state of it – one that wouldn't make you ill – one that we hoped could be programmed into a cure. We even believed that the cure could be programmed to work with a person's specific biology to work faster and more efficiently. A bespoke cure, if you will. You have to understand that we were never able to develop an actual, viable cure, just a framework that might have worked. Perhaps if we'd been free to carry on our work without being harassed... Before we could develop our work further, we reported our findings, just as a matter of protocol. Well, the government suddenly started showing a huge interest. Inspections at the lab at all hours. Secret policemen escorting us to and from work. Edward and I were fairly certain they had got an idea into their head – they even hinted at it a few times; they thought that if the virus could be programmed to help, it could also be programmed to do even more harm than nature had intended.

'The uprising had just ended and we were in the middle of the period of reforms that would imaginatively become known as the Reformation. Everything was supposed to have been fixed, but it quickly became apparent nothing had changed.

Who knew when another period of unrest might arise? Imagine a single virus programmed to kill certain groups, and certain groups only. Protestors, dissidents, for example. Imagine having the ability to wipe out the millions of people rising up across the country – or our enemies abroad – with a single infection.

'It was pure science fiction, of course; there is no way to program an infectious agent to affect people based on belief, race or religion. All we'd been able to do was focus it to work more efficiently on different blood types. But they didn't listen, and when it became clear we wouldn't do what they wanted, the threats began. The men standing outside our house in the middle of the night. The slashed tyres on the car. Edward and I talked about escaping, leaving the capital, but we had Kate and she was just beginning to settle in. She didn't eat or speak for a fortnight after we took her out of the system the previous year. I'm not sure she ever really recovered. It was important we provided some stability. Plus, the HAF virus was still spreading, and finding a cure was more urgent than ever. We couldn't abandon our work. And then, just like that, Swedish researchers found the cure and HAF was over. The Reformation was finalised and a cure for the pandemic found within a month of each other. The country celebrated. But that same night my husband got word that they were coming to raid the lab. We didn't have time to finish our research. Edward knew we couldn't let the virus fall into their hands. Even if they couldn't use it exactly how they imagined, it wouldn't have taken much to create an advanced strain that could have wiped out the entire country. We knew they were just incompetent – or malicious – enough to do it. Edward stopped them. Hoping his death would bring an end to our harassment, that Kate and I would be able to live in peace, he hanged himself and burned down the lab.'

I paused the video, wishing for the first time in a long time that I kept a strong drink in the flat.

'Cadmus Fomalhaut came to see me, after Edward's death,' the Professor began when I started it again. 'Wallace didn't know about the visit, he said. Evidently, Fomalhaut didn't trust his employer. It was a blow to Vangelis, being beaten to the cure – they weren't then the global giants they've become today. Fomalhaut said he was worried what Wallace might do if he got hold of our "cure" and offered to help me destroy any remaining samples. Of course, I told him there weren't any samples left. I told him Edward had destroyed them all, along with all of our data when he torched the lab. That wasn't entirely true.'

'Before he... died, my husband did make a copy of our viral code. There was still a chance that it might be adapted into a cure, should the Swedish cure be proved defective, or should the virus mutate. He did this the only way possible, by injecting it into a living host. By injecting it into our daughter.' She wiped a tear from a sharp cheek. 'It was the only way of preserving the specimen. Kate didn't know what it was – she was only fifteen at the time. Edward told her it was just a flu jab. She still doesn't know anything about it, a decade and a half later. Probably has no memory of it. But she still carries the genetic code. Caleb had nothing to do with it. Neither did Harold Jennings. But whoever is after this code now didn't know that when they killed Caleb. And it will only be a matter of time before they come for my daughter. And it will all be because of me.'

She straightened up and sniffed. 'She'll never leave London as long as I'm alive, but getting away is her only hope. They're still watching me, I know it. They've been watching me for fifteen years, and for fifteen years I never so much as whispered anything about Edward's and my work, hoping they would go away. Now, *you* have to get Kate away from them. It would only be more dangerous if I went with her. I'm the one who did this to her, I contributed to the virus that made her a target, so it's me that has to pay the price. She trusts you and if Bagby does too, that's enough for me. Take her far away from London, far away from this country. It's the only way she can be safe.' She held the pill in the palm of her hand. 'You can promise me that, at least.

'I've done all I can for Kate. And I wouldn't be much help soon, anyway. I've managed to hide it from her. From my students, maybe I even hid it from Jennings... but it's Alzheimers. Early onset. Like my mother. We can cure a global pandemic, but we can't stop our brains turning in on themselves. They gave me six months to a year. Soon I won't remember anything, which is why I had to record all of this now. Why I had to act while I still could. No, it's better if Kate remembers me as I was. And if I can save her in the process, well. Tell her, tell her that raising her has been the proudest accomplishment of my life. Tell her that she is my life's work, and that she must carry on.'

She leaned towards the camera and attempted a smile. 'Bagby is fond of quotes. So here's one for him. We thought we could change the world for the better, but Joseph Heller had it right all along, "*Peace on earth would mean the end of civilisation as we know it.*" Turns out he might be right.'

She smiled, then tossed the pill into her mouth. She must have flicked a switch because the video died in a fuzz of static. I pictured her slipping the video drive into her pocket even as the pill began to blur the edges. I sat there for a long time then rewound the video and watched it again, trying to take everything in.

So that was that. I stood up, walked a few steps, then gripped the kitchen counter to stop myself falling over. I filled a glass with water and swallowed some painkillers to kill the thoughts churning in my head. Then I splashed water on my face and sat down heavily at the counter. I'd left the photograph of Caleb there and I turned it over and stared at it. Even though they were twins, there was very little resemblance between him and Kate. Apart, of course, from the eyes. I slipped the photograph into my pocket as a knock sounded at the door. I slid off the kitchen stool, pulled the Colt from its holster and cocked the hammer. I opened the door slowly, keeping the gun out of sight behind it.

Stohl stood there, his collar pulled up around his face, his hair wet from the rain. It might have been a trick of the light or my frazzled brain but bags seemed to have formed under his eyes.

I stepped forward, blocking his view of the flat.

'Take it easy,' he said, his voice betraying his fatigue. 'I don't want to come in. I only wanted to tell you that I've spoken to my uncle. He made a few calls and, if you still want to, we can go and see RZ tomorrow. We have an hour from 11am. I'll meet you there, but you can speak to him alone.'

'Why?' I asked.

'Because I want to find Caleb's killer, too,' he said. 'And if you have an uncle that controls everything from the culture we consume to the hospitals, it pays to take advantage of him every once in a while.'

Whatever angle he was playing, I couldn't turn down a chance to question RZ. Then again, just maybe speaking to his uncle was his form of olive branch.

'Thank you,' I said.

Stohl nodded. He pulled his rain-wilted collar up, then, with nothing left to say, turned and walked away down the corridor. I let the hammer down on the gun then shut the door. Alone in my flat again I took the Professor's video file and ground it into tiny broken bits beneath my heel.

19

The Messiah

'OK, so all you have to do is throw the ball through the hoop and you'll avoid the slime! Sound fair? Well, we couldn't get much fairer than that, could we, ladies and gentlemen? No, of course we couldn't. Sound good to you, Minister?'

The minister for the economy – a slim man in a slim suit – nodded. His grin said, *Sure, let's do it!* His eyes said *I'm going to fire my fucking publicist after this.*

'Right, then let's get on with it!' RZ said. 'Strong arm, now...'

The minister threw the ball, missed, and was dunked into a vat of slime.

'Oh, unlucky, Minister!' RZ said with overblown glee from beside the vat. 'Well, you can't have everything, ladies and gentlemen, can you? Where would you put it? Now, like the rest of the country, perhaps the minister for the economy knows what it feels like to be dunked in crap!'

I would have been in my late teens when that episode aired.

Too old to be watching that sort of thing, really. My father must have been at work, or he never would have allowed it.

I remember hearing about the complaints the show received after RZ's swipe at the government, though. Looking back during the uprising, the few journalists who wrote about RZ pinpointed that episode as the beginning of his political stand. Not long after the Reformation of course, writing about RZ was banned along with all re-runs of his shows, stand-up routines, and political speeches. Already well into middle age, he had still been handsome then, and very charismatic. Superficial but essential qualities for a leader.

I hadn't thought about that show in years. Probably not since I'd first watched it as a teenager. But riding beside Stohl, en route to see its former host, it all came back to me.

The facility was on Fulham Road, set back out of the way inside what had once been the Chelsea and Westminster Hospital. Stohl parked by a shady copse at the side of the building, the boughs covering a graveyard of moss-covered Victorian headstones.

'You know the Stones used to live down that street back there?' he said. Post-Reformation, both the Stones and The Beatles, of course, were very much allowed.

'Did you want to stop for a photograph?'

'One decrepit old man is enough for me,' Stohl said lazily, his hands lingering lightly on the steering wheel as the engine died.

The hospital had been shut down shortly after the Reformation when the NHS was centralised. Now the wooden boards covering the windows were distorted with rain and the brickwork was black with patches of damp.

'Over there.'

A shiny black door under a clean stone archway was the only indication that any part of the building was still in use. I followed Stohl to it. The retina scanner slid over his face then I took my turn. The door slid open. His uncle must have called ahead. Inside, a long, sterile and featureless corridor led us into the hospital. At the end was an octagonal room with seven doors, with a series of seemingly random numbers on them. There were no signs but somehow Stohl knew where we were going. On the other side of our door was a low, black-topped counter. A middle-aged nurse sat behind it in a white matron's apron, a square box hat on her head.

'Yes?' she said, looking up.

Stohl gave his name. The nurse looked from him to me then back again with suspicion. Evidently RZ didn't get too many visitors.

'I'll have to ring through.' The nurse picked up the phone and dialled someone. After a few moments she said, 'Yes... yes... yes... but why?... OK.' then hung up and smiled up at us bitterly. 'The doctor will be right with you.'

A door opened and a tall, thin doctor of about thirty-five entered. He wore a green flannel shirt and had a pen stuck in his lab-coat pocket. He shook our hands enthusiastically, fixing us with round, unblinking eyes.

'Hello, hello, I'm Dr Daniels. Do come through.'

'Thanks,' I said as he led us down another long white corridor. 'I don't imagine you get many visitors. Not to see him, anyway.'

'Oh,' Daniels said, addressing me over his shoulder. 'You're the first visitors he's had in fifteen years.'

The door was painted a peeling aquamarine. Ten metres down the corridor was another exactly like it, and a third further on.

'This is it,' Daniels said. He pulled a heavy iron key from his pocket and slipped it into the lock. 'I'm afraid we do things the old fashioned way here.' He turned the key and the door clicked open. 'Right,' he said, reclaiming the key. 'He's all yours. You have an hour. But please, try not to agitate him, he can be touchy.' With that he turned and hurried back down the corridor, his body swaying slightly on his legs.

When he was gone I pulled open the door to RZ's cell and stood back, indicating with a swipe of my hand that Stohl should go first.

'Oh, not me,' he said. 'I'm sitting this one out. He's your interviewee. It's your partner you're searching for, after all.'

'Already got the room bugged, have you?'

'There's no need for that,' Stohl said with an expression of false injury on his face. 'I want to find Bagby just as much as you do. And I hope to God he's had nothing to do with these rebels.' He nodded at the open door. 'Fill me in later.'

There was a shoebox sized window high up on the wall at the end of the corridor. Stohl walked towards it, whistling. I slipped into the cell and pulled the door shut behind me. The room was rectangular and furnished with a deep Persian carpet, a high if narrow bed along one wall, a cracked and comfortable-looking leather sofa, and books – thousands of them, stacked in piles against the walls. Watercolour paintings hung in the spaces. Two windows, criss-crossed by black blinds and iron bars, faced the door I had entered through. Beyond them was an almost perfect rendering of a sunlit meadow. Only the occasional electronic blip gave away the fact that in actuality, the windows most likely faced out onto a disused and abandoned hospital corridor.

In the centre of the room, naked apart from a pair of yellow Adidas running shorts, was RZ. He was somehow holding his body off the ground, using only the palm of his right hand, the rest of his body suspended horizontally, parallel to the carpet. He was sixty-six years old but – despite the average human healthspan having been greatly improved – he looked twenty years older. The lines in his skin looked deeply etched and his eyes – both the same cloudy grey – peered out from under heavy hoods.

His overly aged appearance may have been deceptive. Long-term hospitalisation did not seem to have interfered with his fitness routine. As I stepped further into the room RZ lowered himself back down to earth then stood up with only the slightest quickening of the breath to indicate he'd been doing any form of exercise. His chest hairs shone with the efforts of his exertion and his torso looked like it was made of a bunch of white cigars bound tightly together with twine.

'I can usually do that for longer,' he said in greeting.

I had expected a long white beard, hair down to the shoulders and a crazed, dislocated wander to his eyes. He had cultivated a more youthful version of this aesthetic throughout his careers as first a stand-up comedian, then light entertainment presenter, and eventually as the revolutionary prince of Great Britain. Now, he stood with a shaved head marked by scars and a faint sheen of white growth. His chin, too, was clean, although a knife-like scar ran from the right corner of his jaw down to his Adam's apple.

'You were expecting some withered old man? A rabbiting sensei jabbering on about a long-dead revolution. No? Or Obi-Wan Kenobi, perhaps? Take a seat, come on. I'm knackered.' He gestured to the rug then plopped himself down and sat cross-legged. I couldn't help but notice the bottoms of his bare feet, worn soft and brown from fifteen years of pacing back and forth on the same stained rug.

'You're a policeman and you've come to ask me questions,' he surmised.

'I am,' I said, introducing myself.

He smiled and spread his hands. 'Ask and the Oracle shall answer.'

Caught off-guard, I spoke without thinking. 'Do you like it here?'

His shrug told me it wasn't a question with a simple answer.

'Where else would I be? There's nothing left for me to do on the outside.'

'Not everyone would agree with that, I'm sure. Don't you miss it?'

'The television presenting or the stand-up comedy? I'm told there's not much call for either, and hasn't been for a while. We stick to what we know now, don't we?'

'Told by whom?'

'By the voices in my head,' he said, pointing towards the door. 'No, Daniels is a good man. We enjoy the odd conversation. He's teaching me to paint.'

I looked again at the paintings on the walls, bright panoramas of sunsets and cloud-filled skies. I'd once painted similar scenes with my mother at the kitchen table. I couldn't help but feel their creator was holding on to a sliver of optimism.

'Daniels painted these?'

'Heavens, no. I did. And they're awful. I don't suppose they pass your Bad Taste law, do they? I think that's what it's called? The "Bad Taste" law?'

'Not in so many words. But it is referred to as such, sometimes. I think you'll be all right with these anyway.'

'I was wrong, you know,' he said. 'High or low are such arbitrary definitions when it comes to culture, aren't they? All of it is a distraction. All of it is essential. Guess it's too late to pass that message on to the Prime Minister, right?'

'It might be,' I said. 'You seem to know a lot about the outside world. Does Daniels keep you informed?'

'He has to,' RZ said. 'You're the only other visitor I've ever had, apart from some police officers and the old Prime Minister, way back at the beginning.'

'No other visitors? No family?'

'I never had any family,' he sighed. 'I'm sure you've heard about it, but Daniels informs me I'm rumoured to have a long-lost son. Well, he hasn't sent me a single fucking birthday card, if so.' He laughed quickly and sharply. 'Or maybe you're too young to have heard about that? Time passes in here and everything stays much the same, but I forget that out there things are moving rapidly, gaining momentum every day.'

'Just the opposite, actually,' I said, warming to him. 'In times of unrest innovation is too unpredictable,' I said, thinking of the Professor's breakthrough.

'Then you and your friends have a lot to answer for,' RZ said, arching an eyebrow. 'But what do you mean, "times of unrest"? Surely all of that is in the past? I'm locked away in here, after all.'

It was obvious from the glint in his eye that he didn't believe a word he was saying, and knew I didn't either.

'It must be a busy time for you, detective. Tell me, you look just old enough to have been a police officer during the Reformation. Never been tempted to switch sides?'

'No,' I said, fully aware I was being baited. 'I want to protect people.'

'Then wouldn't you be better off joining the call for change, joining the call to protect people from this government?'

'Let's talk about something else,' I said.

I took the photograph of him, the Professor, Jennings and Bagby from my pocket and put it face up on the rug between us.

A thin smile was his only tell. 'Old faces,' he said. 'We were friends. Good friends who wanted to change things.'

'You did. You brought about the country's biggest social upheaval since the Second World War.'

'And for that they lock me in here and once every fifteen years they bring me photographs of people I used to know.'

'You can keep it. I took it from Bagby's apartment. Do you still count him as someone you used to know?'

'Or have I seen him recently, do you mean? Gone for a little wander has he? Well unless they've been lacing my food again, I can't say I've seen him sneaking in here at night to whisper messages in my ears, no.'

'You were close once – do you have any idea where he might go if he was in trouble?'

'You mean do I know if he's gone off to join these new revolutionaries? The people behind the bombs from Tynemouth to Boscastle? I don't think so, no. Why should this new generation want old hands like us involved? It doesn't take a genius to put together a spark bomb or sign a petition, you know.'

I glanced at the door, imagining Daniels or Stohl listening in. 'Perhaps they feel like the job wasn't quite finished last time and want him to help make sure it goes to plan now.'

RZ sat forward, narrowing his eyes at me. 'Which are you more afraid of, that he's gone to join up as a revolutionary, or that he's hunting them down as a cop?'

I smiled and decided to change tack. I took Caleb's headshot from my pocket and placed it on the carpet beside the other photograph. 'And him? Is he familiar?'

RZ leaned forward and peered at the photograph. After a moment he straightened up and smiled. 'I haven't a clue. But he's very handsome.'

'He may have looked a little different last time you saw him,' I said. 'Around fifteen years younger. Or more. Perhaps you last saw him as a baby. Or maybe you've never seen him. I'm not quite sure of the details. His sister, too.'

RZ pursed his lips and looked me over.

'He's dead now. Caleb,' I said, tapping the photograph. 'He was murdered by someone searching for something. But he didn't have it, his sister did, and now the bad people know that and they're going to come for her.'

'I don't know what you're talking about, sorry,' RZ said. 'Unfortunately I know nothing about this.'

But his face was falling to pieces even as he spoke. My instincts told me that he knew where Bagby was, and he knew who had killed Caleb. If he wouldn't talk he deserved to be spared no pain.

'I think you know more than you're letting on. Tell me, who's after them? Who wants to kill your children?'

'I haven't…' he began.

I could see it now, the family resemblance. They all shared the same nose, the same brows.

'If no one has been to see you that means they still don't know that they're yours. Professor Rachel Faron and Harold Jennings hid them for you. Took them out of the care system when the revolution was at its height. A year later, Edward Faron injected your daughter Kate with something. Something valuable and dangerous. I suppose that's enough of a revolutionary link. Whatever Kate knows or doesn't know, this is your chance to help me protect her. Bagby knew what was going on but he decided to try and handle it on his own instead of trusting me. You can help me help both of them. Help me find Bagby, and I'll find Caleb's killer and protect Kate, too.'

I glanced around the room at the bars on the window, the dented mattress, the paintings peeling off the walls. With one visitor in fifteen years it was unlikely the room was bugged.

'You're powerless in here,' I said. 'I'm your only hope. But I can't do it without you.'

RZ was staring through me at the wall behind my head. 'Did they tell you how I came to be in here?'

'You turned yourself in, at the height of the revolution. You saved lives and negotiated peace.'

RZ laughed, tilting his head back. It was a dry and empty laugh. 'Ha. That's what the history books say, I suppose.' He met my eyes. 'I turned myself in because they were this close' – he held his hand up, thumb and forefinger millimetres apart – 'to finding out about my kids. I'd only just found out about them myself. I didn't recall sleeping with their mother. Maybe I could have helped her but for some reason she gave them up, separately, after they were born. Shortly afterwards she overdosed, and that was that. Fifteen years later they were still in the system. Someone inside the system and sympathetic to the cause got word to me that they were mine. I didn't believe it at first, but when I saw pictures of them as small children, I knew. I wanted to take them out, forget the revolution and live with my children. It was ego, everything I'd tried to eradicate in myself; the desire to put my own needs before the greater good of the nation. Rachael and her husband explained to me how dangerous it would be if I took custody of the children. How this would make them a target. They came up with the idea of taking the children on, to hide what the government would perceive as a weakness. It was Jennings' idea to keep them separate. After fifteen years apart, I suppose it was a good one. I never met them, I couldn't bring myself to go near them. The Farons were right; it would have been too dangerous with the government sniffing about. I thought if I handed myself in, ended the so-called Reformation, they would stop looking. I'd let them down their whole lives, it was the least I could do for them.'

'So they took you in and they tortured you,' I said. I had to get the facts straight, if only for myself. 'They fed you pills to dissolve your mind. They made sure you'd never be able to resist them again and called it a breakdown. Don't tell me they didn't ask about your family.'

'No,' RZ said, swatting at the air as though imaginary bats were swirling around him. 'I didn't tell them anything. I ate their pills and I kept quiet. It was my only option. They would have found my children otherwise. The things they would have done to them…'

'They're doing them now,' I said through gritted teeth. 'Who's behind this, and where's Bagby?'

RZ got up. He paced back and forth, pulling his paintings from the walls. 'He's where he always is. One step ahead. Of you. Of me. He's the one with the answers.'

'So tell me where he is,' I said, standing and crossing the room towards him, wanting to shake the information from him.

Just then the door opened and Daniels entered, one hand closed around something in his pocket.

'Well, we seem to be getting excited in here. Time for a break, perhaps.'

I wasn't sure which of us he was addressing. When neither of us replied he said, as though to himself, 'Yes, a nice quiet rest will do us all good.'

RZ didn't seem to notice that Daniels was there. He carried on tearing the paintings from the wall. Whether it was all an act or whether he was genuinely distressed, it didn't seem like I would get anything else from him.

'It's OK, Doctor,' I said. 'I seem to have tired him out. Maybe I'll come back and speak with him another time, if that's convenient for you, of course?'

'Of course, of course,' Daniels echoed. 'Whenever you'd like to. As I say, visitors are so rare. It would be a pleasure to have you with us again.' His hand relaxed around whatever he held in his pocket as I joined him at the door.

'Goodbye, RZ,' he said as he guided me out into the corridor. Then, with the door closed, 'I'm sorry if he was difficult, detective. We do try to keep the patients calm, but sometimes it's necessary to sedate them. I'm afraid that sometimes this can only add to their confusion.'

'I understand,' I said. 'Modern life can be taxing for the best of us.'

'Quite,' he said.

I scanned the corridor. Stohl wasn't there. 'Is my partner waiting outside?'

'Yes, he's down in reception,' Daniels said as we made our way back along the corridor.

'Can you tell him, please, that I've stopped to use the bathroom? I won't be a minute.'

'Of course. There's one through that door there, then just down the corridor.'

'Thank you, Doctor.'

I shook his hand then slipped through the door and continued past the toilet.

Down there in the depths of the hospital the paint was peeling from the walls and the damp was creeping in. I turned down another corridor and found a screened-off entrance to the old hospital. It was the work of a moment to slip through into the gutted bowels of the old theatre wing, and after a few moments I found a door that led out into a small, overgrown garden. A short walk through the undergrowth and a climb over a fence later, and I was retracing my steps to the front of the hospital. Stohl's car was still parked outside. I bounced his keys in my pocket, thankful that he hadn't noticed me take them. I got in the car and started the engine, glad to be leaving him behind.

20

Future Perfect

Soon the car was hurrying through the string of satellite towns wound tightly about London before spilling out into the countryside. The drive seemed shorter without Stohl beside me. The traffic was as sparse as usual and the air hung low and heavy over the fields. I reached Vangelis in the early afternoon. The obsidian gate opened automatically. I drove up to the monolithic building as rain clouds broke overhead.

If he hadn't guessed where I was headed, Stohl could turn on the car's tracker and find out for certain. But even if he had set off immediately, I would still have time enough to do what I came to do.

'We always have the worst weather,' Fomalhaut said, greeting me from the doorway. 'Come on inside. And welcome back.'

'You were expecting me?' I asked as we stepped into the atrium, a blast of warm air drying my clothes.

'My dear boy, we spotted you outside Bletchley. Come on in.' He took me through into the bowels of the laboratory.

A young man in a white lab-coat hurried by with a clipboard. He entered a room, joining other workers around a television bank showing the news.

'You'll have to excuse my staff,' Fomalhaut said, gesturing towards the window. 'It's a big day for us. Our colleagues in Bangalore have intercepted a signal being transmitted from Saturn's rings – likely just some sort of refracted solar flare, of course, but nevertheless, there's always the slim chance that we may be one step closer to finding out what it's really all about!'

He reached out and gripped my hand. I had a sudden vision of a solitary old man, working alone in the lab after dark long after everyone else had gone home to their families or children. Willy Wonka in his chocolate factory.

We paused on a walkway, looking down through a high glass window onto a small gym below.

'Not everyone seems to share our enthusiasm, unfortunately.'

Wallace was down there, pounding away on a treadmill. He was wearing a blue tracksuit, a VO2 Max mask covering his mouth and nose, like a space-age fighter pilot, wires trailing to a machine. He spotted us and waved dopily. Clearly, he wasn't surprised to find me there unannounced, either.

We moved on down the corridor. In the next room a squadron of drones hovered at chest height, facing a row of paper targets about ten metres away. The room flashed red as a spinning warning light washed over the walls. Then, with a muted sound like a champagne bottle being opened in another room, the drones fired, punching melon-sized holes in the targets.

'Not my proudest work,' Fomalhaut said, shaking his head. 'But there has been an increasing demand for drones with Final Authority capabilities recently. Both at home and abroad. We try to balance it with as much humanitarian work as we can, of course.'

'Like saving the animals?'

'Exactly that.'

We turned abruptly into a familiar corridor and I was led into a conservatively furnished office. I almost hadn't seen the door, a white panel hidden in the wall.

'Take a seat,' Fomalhaut said, pointing to a black Ludwig Mies van der Rohe and Lily Reich chair.

Beside the chair, an L-shaped couch and a low coffee table formed a small lounge area. The far side of the room was taken up by a large desk spread with papers, blueprints, an empty vase, reference books, a half-filled water carafe shaped like a leaf, and a collection of used glasses. It seemed a disorderly environment for one of the most brilliant minds in the country. But then I remembered another of Bagby's favourite maxims, this one from Picasso, '*The urge to destroy is also a creative urge.*'

'On the subject of humanitarian work,' I said, taking the indicated seat opposite Fomalhaut. 'During my last visit you touched upon Vangelis' work on the HAF virus. Specifically the role of Professors Rachael and Edward Faron.'

Fomalhaut sat back and sighed. 'Ah yes, you'll remember we called it "Revolutionary Fever". Hubris, of course. This little power struggle of ours made no odds to anyone outside of the UK, whereas the HAF virus took six million souls across the globe. A hangover from colonialism, perhaps – the idea that Britain sneezes and the world holds its breath.'

'Or catches its cold. You commissioned a team to find a cure.'

Fomalhaut nodded. 'Yes. But so did every lab across the country. Across the world. It was the Swiss, I believe, who got there in the end.'

'Forgive me, but wasn't it the Swedes?' I asked.

Fomalhaut smiled, as if he'd been testing me. 'Yes, you're right of course. It was the Swedes.'

'The search for a cure was the last thing Edward Faron worked on before his death. His suicide,' I said. 'How close did he and his wife get?'

'To finding a cure?' Fomalhaut fell quiet for a moment. Of course, I had the answers from the Professor. I just wanted to see if the official story matched up. When he spoke again, his voice sounded like it belonged to a man of his age for the first time since I'd met him. 'Edward very nearly did it. He was one of the best we had. Such an utter, utter shame.'

'Was your employer, Wallace, keen to extrapolate from his research? To carry on his work?'

'There was no point. The virus was cured. Even if we wanted to…' Fomalhaut trailed off. He exhaled. 'Even if we wanted to, I told you how he took his own life. The tragedy. The fire… he and all of his research were lost. Had he lived… the world would have been better off in many, many ways. He and his wife were a formidable team. Perhaps one of these days I can coax her back to research.'

There was nothing to be gleaned from a softly-softly approach. If Vangelis really was the all-knowing, omnipotent corporate deity everyone believed it was, it was likely that Fomalhaut would know about Professor Faron's death as soon as the police did, if not before.

'I don't think so. She's dead,' I said.

I thought he hadn't heard me at first, then his shoulders sagged and he slumped forward, his fingers tracing ghostly piano keys on the edge of the table. 'I'm… I'm sorry to hear that. How did it happen? First Edward, and now Rachael. What a damned waste. What a…' He seemed lost for words. 'What a waste,' he said again, finally and quietly.

He looked up and met my eyes. 'How did it happen?'

'The same way as her husband. Suicide.' I had to keep a few cards close to my chest. 'Although we're not yet sure what the reasons behind it were.'

'I see. What a… waste. And how is their daughter coping?'

'She's doing as well as can be expected. Oh, and incidentally, she happens to be the estranged twin sister of the murdered man I spoke to you about before. I don't suppose you have any idea why anyone would want to hurt her, or her brother, Caleb?'

Fomalhaut sat up straight and alert, like a bird that finds its nest slipping from its bough. 'I have no idea. I never met their children. I didn't know they had *two*. Edward certainly never mentioned it. And no, I don't have the faintest idea why someone would want to harm either one of them. It's the last thing on earth I can imagine. Rachael and Edward were brilliant people. Brilliant. I can only imagine their children must have grown up as considerate and intelligent as their parents.'

'Actually, the children never met. They were adopted separately. Kate didn't know about Caleb until he turned up dead. So, as someone who had known her for a long time, I wanted to ask you if Professor Faron had any enemies? Rivals, anything like that?'

Fomalhaut looked taken aback. 'Enemies? Not in this company. Not to my knowledge. And rivals? Her husband aside, I've never met anyone as brilliant as Rachel Faron is. Was.'

'No one who was envious of the research carried out by her and her husband, perhaps?'

Fomalhaut frowned. His forehead was all liver spots and creases. 'There are branches of this company from Seoul to St Kilda, each specialising in its own unique field. But, no; no one has any enemies at Vangelis. We succeed at all times in encouraging one another.'

'OK. Did Wallace know them, Edward and Rachael?'

Fomalhaut spread his hands. 'Of course, this is his company. But as I said, we employ so many brilliant people that I'm not certain that he would remember them to any great degree.'

'And do you think I might ask him about this myself?'

Fomalhaut smiled. 'I'm afraid he's rather busy this afternoon, meeting with the Prime Minister.'

'Tomorrow, then?'

'I'll have to see if his schedule permits. Finding a hole in it is torturous. I've been trying to meet with him myself for a week. I'm happy, of course, to answer any questions on his behalf.' He smiled again. 'We really don't mind a friend of Stohl's stopping by, but you must understand, we work every hour of the day and it can often be impossible to take time out for interviews such as these.'

'I'm not a friend of Stohl's,' I said, rising from the chair. 'I'm a police officer investigating a murder. Thank you for your time. But I'd appreciate it if you could let Wallace know that I'd like to speak to him. As soon as is convenient.'

'Of course,' Fomalhaut said. 'I hope I've been of use to you, detective. Although, it does seem to me that this line of enquiry may have hit a dead end.'

'Well,' I said. 'I'll let you know if anything else comes up.'

He followed me out into the corridor then made a show of checking his watch. 'You'll have to excuse me – there's a procedure I need to check in on. Solar flares, and all that. Time is of the essence! Miki can show you out.'

A young woman in a trouser suit appeared at the end of the corridor, inviting me to follow her with a smile. As we reached the reception I heard the dull boom of raised voices. I looked up to the raised walkway on the other side of the glass vault. There was Wallace, still in his tracksuit, storming along the corridor followed closely by the bodyguard Koch who was nodding his head and pumping his legs as he tried to keep up. Perhaps he was running late for the Prime Minister. Wallace glanced down into the atrium. I was certain he caught my eye, and scowled at seeing me there.

The announcement went out while I was driving back to London. Special notice, all departments: Professor Rachael Faron and Mr Harold Jennings, two former revolutionaries, have been found dead, and DCI Bagby is wanted for their murders.

I swore loudly and put my foot down. That it had been a murder-suicide instigated by the Professor was obvious, even in the absence of her confessional tape. It was difficult to see what anyone would have to gain by framing it otherwise but I was certain that someone stood to benefit. Mercer, at least, must have known that Bagby was innocent. But all of that was academic; whatever the powers that be knew or didn't know, an A1 search and arrest warrant had been put out on Bagby, authorising the use of deadly force in his capture if necessary. With his old revolutionary affiliations, no one would ask too many questions if he was killed while being detained.

The rain started in earnest just outside of the city. I drove east through a thick black soup. I parked at the top of the lane leading to Harrington & Sons then hit the dashboard with my hand.

The lane was wound up in blue crime-scene tape, a handful of uniformed coppers sprinkled about for good luck. Stohl met me as I walked towards the antiques shop. The rain had stopped but his shoulders and hair were wet.

'Had a nice day?' he asked.

'An exhausting one. Thanks for the loan of the car. Sorry I had to dash off without you, something urgent came up.'

'Well,' he said, turning back to the shop where they were wheeling out a black-bagged shape on a stretcher, 'something urgent has come up here now, too.'

'And how long are you going to pretend Bagby had anything to do with it?' I asked, well aware that I was taking the bait.

'For as long as it takes for him to turn himself in and prove us wrong,' Stohl answered in a tone that suggested the whole thing was a game he was rapidly growing tired of playing. 'Follow me, take a look.'

Inside, the crime scene geeks were busy dusting things down and dropping things into plastic bags. The shop was such a jumble of junk that finding evidence against Bagby in there really would be like looking for a needle in a haystack – never mind that the crime was fabricated to begin with.

'Careful,' Stohl shouted as a junior officer backed into the table holding the untouched cups of cold tea. They rattled in their saucers as the officer's face turned the colour of sour milk.

'So, Bagby stopped by for a cup of tea before he did it?' I asked, playing my part.

'Why not? They were friends, after all,' Stohl shrugged.

'And what did he use to kill them?'

'That I cannot tell you,' Stohl said with a grimace. 'Not yet, anyway. Now, if you'll excuse me, I've a search team to organise.'

His words triggered something in the back of my mind; in the excitement of the Professor and Jennings' deaths, and my and Kate's run-in with the Kid in White, I had forgotten about the secret security cameras Bagby had littered throughout the shop. The recollection felt like lowering myself into a cold bath, fully clothed and feet first. Of course, apart from the videos taken in Jennings' bedroom, the most recent video depicting the shop was nine years old, and showed Caleb walking out. I hadn't seen anything on his computer to indicate that Bagby was still recording the shop, or that if I did find a camera, what was on it might help clear his name. Then again, if Bagby hadn't removed his cameras in the intervening years, there had to be a reason why; maybe he was still using them, perhaps via a second secret computer. There was also the possibility that any cameras contained their own internal hard-drives that could be accessed via the actual camera itself. With the full facilities of the Unit behind him, it wouldn't be long before Stohl was able to connect any remaining units to Bagby. There was also the slight concern that any overlooked cameras might have captured me visiting the scene of the crime and removing vital evidence. Whichever way you looked at it, if any of Bagby's cameras remained, better I found them than one of my colleagues.

The shop was crowded at the best of times. Even if I could work out from my memory of Bagby's videos where the cameras might be located, it was unlikely I could retrieve all of them without being noticed. It was then that I saw it, a camera winking at me from the space between the frame of an old watercolour and a Grecian bust. Stohl had gone back outside and the crime scene geeks had plenty to occupy them. I looked around quickly, then, seeing the coast was clear, reached out and retrieved the camera, stuffing it into my pocket as I headed towards the door. One would have to do.

'Don't you want to see upstairs?' Stohl called as I passed him.

'I've seen enough,' I said, without looking back. He didn't stop me.

I hurried home, eager to find out what, if anything, Bagby's camera had captured. Judging by its location in the shop, any footage on it should be enough to prove Bagby's innocence, even if that meant incriminating the Professor. It wasn't ideal, but it couldn't be helped. My door, when I reached it, was ajar, a faint light spilling through the crack. I didn't know how Kate had got inside, but I was glad that she was somewhere safe. I called out in greeting, but when I entered the flat it was Koch I found sitting on my sofa pointing his pistol at me instead.

21

The Bull

'Have you come to give me a lift somewhere?' I asked from the door.

Koch smiled as he cradled the gun in his lap. He must have hurried there as soon as I left Vangelis, but he didn't look put out. He was sitting back on the sofa, dressed in a brown three-piece suit. It looked like he was having a comfortable evening.

'Sit down,' he said, watching me lazily, like a person who knows they're in charge of a situation.

I couldn't help but look at the gun again. From this range he'd be able to cut me down even as I reached the top of the stairs, even through the wooden front door. My own pistol was firmly in its shoulder holster. There was no chance of getting to it in time. I'd have to win him over.

'How about a drink? I've got a bottle of that new quinoa imitation-vodka. It's absolutely disgusting.'

'Take a seat first,' Koch said.

There wasn't much to be done, so I sat down opposite him. He shifted along the sofa ever so slightly to give himself a clearer shot. There was no silencer on his pistol; either he was planning to very publicly shoot a policeman – I assumed I had neighbours and that they'd start at the shot – or he wanted to get me outside and do the job away from prying eyes. Vaguely, somewhere deep down in my stomach, I hoped that there was a third option, that he didn't really want to kill me at all, that it was all some sort of misunderstanding.

'We used to do a hell of a lot of work to stay in shape, in the forces,' Koch said as his opening gambit. 'Up and down windswept hills, crawling through tunnels flooded with icy mud, carrying bodies through assault courses…'

'I thought you boys just piloted the drones these days?'

He riled at that, shifting the gun from his real hand to his mechanical one in irritation. Perhaps I could get him angry enough to crush it between those metallic fingers.

'We've lost the art of soldiering, somewhat, with these drones,' he opined. 'Fifty years ago it used to be men who took all the risk, men who gained the respect of the nation for their heroic endeavours.'

'I suppose it's hard to know who to thank first when our wars are never-ending.'

'Thank the men who are working to bring about the future. The end of war. The end of death,' he said, sitting up straighter with each word, the fire of conviction burning in his eyes.

'So, your boss has been racing to get back what he lost. His cure for war, which ironically works by killing off everyone who's opposed to it – or anyone opposed to more or less anything else he believes in. I take it those allowed to live will be given a round of strategic immunisations well in advance?' I asked. 'That's the point of something like this, right? Making sure the right people make it through to the other side? What I don't understand is, why wait fifteen years to dig it out of the toy box again? Or is that question beyond your pay-grade?'

'My boss is a great man. He's configured the future of this planet long beyond the lifespans of you or I. And unlike the pair of us, he'll be alive to see it. He'll live forever. Until then, a time and a place for everything,' Koch said, nodding his head as if proudly remembering a rhyme that his mother had taught him as a boy.

'And everything in its place? Where does that leave me?'

Koch raised the gun and shrugged. 'Collateral damage. Although I don't think anyone will miss you, not anymore. It looks like you're all but finished in the police force anyway. No one will question what you've done.'

'And just what have I done?'

For an answer he slid his free hand into his pocket and pulled out a clear capsule, the pill no larger than an aspirin. 'Take this,' he said holding it up between his thumb and forefinger. 'Get yourself a glass of water, if you like.'

'I don't think I want to take that.'

'It will save you a lot of pain if you do.'

'I suppose you've arranged a note. Or will it be a video confession?'

'That can be arranged afterwards.' He held the pill towards me. 'There's really nothing left to live for. We know where the girl is. We'll pick her up in the morning, just as your bosses are trying to work out how best to hush this up.'

'Will it be quick for her, too? Quicker than her brother, at least?'

'Oh, we don't need to kill her. It's much easier to take blood samples if she's left alive. Her brother brought what happened on himself. I asked him not to fight back.'

I looked at his hands. He held the pistol in one and the pill in the other and was waiting to see which I'd choose. From the way the corner of his mouth twitched in expectation I could see that he was enjoying this, like a Rottweiler waiting to be let off the leash.

'Pass me the pill,' I said.

Koch hesitated a moment, clucking his tongue in his mouth as though trying to size up my intentions, then he leaned forward and passed the pill across. I took it between my thumb and forefinger and held it up to eye-level, examining it in the light. The capsule was a dirty translucent white. Inside were crushed black pellets of death that may as well have carried a skull and crossbones on them.

'Bottoms up,' I said, giving Koch a wink as I tossed the pill towards my open mouth.

At the last moment I leaned forwards and the pill bounced off my chin and away under the table. I swore. As Koch got to his feet I got down on my knees, reached beneath the table and, with my shoulder wedged beneath it, heaved for my life. The table flipped over with a flurry of old newspapers and magazines.

Koch fired once as he fell back onto the sofa with the broken table on top of him. The round skimmed my arm. I fell to the floor then stood again and vaulted over the back of the sofa, fumbling for my gun. Before I could reach it, Koch landed on top of me, knocking me to the ground. Like an ape messing about with a toy, he turned me onto my back, then hit me in the face with his metallic hand. I'd never felt pain like it, and when I blinked again the room was covered in dark spots. Koch's hands were around my throat. Slowly, the black dots grew until they began to merge at the edges. I swung a fist into his side but he laughed it away and bashed the back of my head against the carpet in return.

His gun was lying there, off to my side.

Koch went for it first, lurching off me towards it. I sat up and gasped for air like a man emerging from the bottom of a river.

Koch was on his knees beside the kitchen counter, his hands fiddling with the gun. I stood as best I could and ran into him. We collapsed together and somewhere in the whirlpool of my mind I heard the gun thud to the floor. I kicked out and made contact, sending it sliding away. Koch hit me between the legs. I gasped again and felt bile rising from my stomach. I reached up to the counter. My hand closed around something, the edge of a chopping board. I swiped it off the counter as Koch tried to claw his way up my body, his metallic fingers pulling at my legs.

The chopping board spun away across the room. I touched the edge of a glass water bottle. Before I could grasp it, Koch threw me down onto my back, thumping the air from me. Stooped and breathing heavily, he jumped towards me. I kicked out with both feet at once and he shot back against the counter. The glass bottle fell and shattered harmlessly beside him.

The door wasn't too far away. I rolled onto my front, and, dribbling blood, pushed myself up and hobbled towards it. There was a shot and a cloud of dust billowed from the doorframe. Then came the click of a jammed weapon. My hand touched the door handle. Then Koch's arms were around my chest, lifting me from the ground in a great big bearhug that was slowly crushing the last of the oxygen from my lungs.

'The pill would have been simpler,' he whispered in my ear. 'But less fun.' He squeezed extra tight. 'I had fun with Caleb, too. Although he put up more of a fight than you.'

I stomped on his toe and he laughed. I kicked at his knees and he howled in amusement.

'You can't even die according to plan. Never mind, though, after what you've done to your boss it won't matter. They'll cover it up. They'll be glad you're dead.'

I thought of Mercer but couldn't connect the wires. Koch

squeezed again and I heard something snap. We were close enough to the door that I could get a foot up on to it and kick away, but Koch simply stepped back, holding on. The black dots in front of my eyes were spreading like an ink stain on blotting paper, leading me towards the end credits. Then the wires connected momentarily and something came to mind. I let my legs go loose and Koch adjusted his weight to keep me upright. He shifted his arms slightly as I dropped, just enough for me to reach across my body, inching my right hand towards my left armpit. And then he was crushing me again, my lights slowly being turned out.

I tried to say something but spittle and air fizzed out of my mouth without meaning. And then my fingers touched the butt of the Colt .45 still in its shoulder holster and then they were dragging themselves along the grip and under the holster. And there was the hammer and there was the trigger and there was my finger squeezing it with everything I had left.

From that range, the blast sounded like a barrage gun erupting. I stumbled and fell against the wall, my hands against my ears. Koch had disappeared. One moment he was there, the next he was gone. In that empty, senseless world I held a hand to my eyes and wiped away something wet and warm. I could smell a pungent mixture of cordite and meat and body odour. I blinked and gasped and blinked a bit more as the black dots burst like balloons. Something was searing into my side and, with my head clearing, I realised it was the hot gun barrel pressing against my ribs. With shaking hands I tore my jacket off and threw it on the counter then unhooked the holster and threw that away too, the gun with it.

Freed, I made my way to the sink, a hand grasping the counter to steady myself. I doused my head and hair in water from the tap. I drank some in my cupped palms, tasting blood. Koch was lying on the floor, face-up with his arms and legs stuck out at odd angles, moving slowly like an insect stuck with a pin. The front of his suit was a red bloom with a darker hole at its centre where the flesh was all chewed up like mincemeat. At that range the exit wound on his back would resemble a watermelon trampled underfoot – both in size and appearance. I knelt down beside him. He was trying to speak. I watched his red-stained teeth and then, just like that, he expired, the life going out of his eyes like a dimmer switch. I shook myself off and leaned against the counter. I had never killed a man before.

The lights were out at Mercer's house and the street was dark and quiet. I hurried up the steps and knocked on the door.

Bagby's camera had been crushed to bits in the scuffle with Koch. Wallace's henchman had succeeded, at least, in destroying the evidence; if any of the footage showed Koch questioning Jennings about Caleb's whereabouts, we'd never see it. With it, I also lost any slight chance of proving that Bagby was innocent of the Professor and Jennings' deaths. Without unequivocal proof of Bagby's innocence, and with Stohl's uncle siccing his goons on me, Mercer was the only police officer left in the city that I could trust.

I knocked again. Still there was no answer. Mercer was old school, I knew, and the door still worked with a key. I dug the spare out from under the ceramic toad on the path and let myself in. The light switch was broken. I called Mercer's name in the darkness. I felt my way along, through the open double doors into the lounge. It was only when I saw Mercer's bloody and broken body propped up in the wicker chair, framed by the moonlight streaming through the window behind her, that I remembered Koch's words, 'After what you've done to your boss it won't matter… They'll be glad you're dead.'

He was right. I had just lost my only ally.

22

Flight

'Mercer,' I said, kneeling beside her.

Her head lolled forwards. A murmur sounded in the darkness. She was still alive. I stumbled into a lamp. I switched it on. Light bled out on to a horror-show of a crime scene. Mercer was slouched in the chair. Her face was a fleshy mess of bruises. Her eyes had almost swollen shut and her shirt was stained with blood. Her good arm dangled by her side and her metallic arm looked like it had been crushed at the elbow.

I took her good hand in mine. 'Mercer...'

She raised her head slowly. 'Short... brown suit...'

'It's OK. I got him. I... I shot him. He's dead.'

The bruises around her mouth twitched in imitation of a smile.

I pressed the implant in my wrist. A robotic voice answered in my ear. I gave my name and unit number, then requested an ambulance. 'We need help. We need an ambulance,' I said, speaking to the empty room. 'It's DSU Mercer, she's –'

'No,' Mercer said, with difficulty. 'You need to… get away. It's a… frame job.'

Her chin indicated something on the floor. A blood-smeared sheet of paper was facedown among bits of broken glass and furniture. I turned it over and saw a headshot of Caleb, the same picture I had in my flat. In fact, as far as I could tell from the coffee rings marking it, it was the *exact* photograph from my flat. So, Koch had been poking around before paying me a visit.

'Go,' Mercer gasped. 'North. Out of London.'

'I'm sorry, Ma'am. I wish I could.' I lifted her and carried her across to the sofa. 'You'll be more comfortable over here. Until the ambulance arrives.'

I propped a cushion behind her head. She had fallen silent and still, her eyes closed, her cheeks rapidly losing heat. I felt for a pulse then wiped some of the blood from her neck with my sleeve and tried again. I couldn't feel anything. I placed an ear to her chest but any faint murmur was drowned beneath the approaching swell of sirens. Then, a wash of bright light flooded the room as Medi-Drones whirred outside.

There was a bang and a human voice shouted 'Hello? Medic!' from the front door.

'In here!' I yelled.

But Mercer and Koch were right; under the current circumstances being caught over Mercer's body was as good as admitting I'd killed her. It would be the end of everything. The end of finding Bagby. The end of finding Caleb's killer. The end of keeping Kate alive.

'I'm sorry, Ma'am,' I whispered, a hand on her forehead. Then, as the paramedic arrived, I ran out through the back door, and into the night.

I made it to the house without being stopped. Kate opened the door and pulled me inside. She sat me down on a bench in the hallway.

'What the hell happened to you?' she asked, concern lending an unexpected edge to her voice.

'Doesn't matter, I'm OK,' I gasped as I tried to regain my breath.

'Sure you are. Here, drink this.' She handed me a glass of non-synth vodka. I drank it back while she drank from the bottle. Her eyes were red, and a cut above her eyebrow sustained during our automobile escapade had turned purple and swollen. She looked like she'd been having trouble sleeping, too.

She touched my jacket. 'Whose blood is this?'

'I'm not sure,' I said, the vodka spreading its warmth to my brain. 'It doesn't matter. Listen, you're not safe here; the people that killed your brother are coming for you. They may already be on their way. They're serious. They attacked Mercer, they tried to kill me.'

Kate crossed to the door and peered out through a small glass panel. 'Who's coming? And why are they coming for me? Because of something I did? Something Caleb did?'

'Vangelis. And neither of you did anything. I'll explain later, once we're on our way somewhere else.'

'The tech company?' Kate asked. She returned from the door and knelt beside me. Her fingers moved aside the ripped flap of jacket where Koch's bullet had grazed my arm. 'You're bleeding. Come on, you're not OK.'

'I'll live. They wanted to make it look like I'd killed Mercer, then taken my own life. I fought the guy off. He... he killed Caleb. But I killed him. I've never killed anyone before.'

Kate weighed the vodka bottle in her hands. She laughed,

bitterly, then took a swig. 'Well... at least that's something. But surely all you have to do is show Stohl the body? That's all the evidence you need that you're innocent.'

I shook my head. 'Vangelis will get rid of the body. They probably already have. And I... I don't think Mercer's going to make it. To everyone on the police force, it looks like I killed her then ran off to join the resistance with Bagby. In their eyes we're both guilty. And they think he killed your mother, too. They don't care about anything else. They don't want to hear anything else,' I said, with a sinking realisation that this last part was true. 'It's easier for them this way.'

Kate looked at me over the lip of the vodka bottle. 'I know. But that isn't how it happened. My mother killed the antiques dealer. I don't know why she did it, but I know she must have had a good reason. The police are lying. They don't care about my mother. Or my brother.'

She grasped my knee. I couldn't avoid her eyes. 'If I come with you, you have to help me find the people responsible,' she said. 'You killed the man who killed Caleb, but I want to know *why*. I want to know exactly who's behind it – some faceless corporation isn't enough.'

A bag was packed and waiting in the hallway. She had evidently been waiting for something, or someone, to arrive. I realised it was me.

'We will. We'll get them. I have a good idea of who to start with.'

'Then we have to hurry.' She pulled what looked like a crumpled white envelope from her shirt pocket. 'Luckily, I know exactly where we're going.'

'What's that?'

'It came this morning. Some friendly advice.'

I could just make out the handwritten address on the front.

The post drones would deliver anything, but there were only two people I knew who still wrote letters: Mercer and Bagby.

'Here,' Kate said, pressing it into my hands.

I slid out the single sheet of paper from inside the envelope. It read: *'What's taking so long?'* with a set of coordinates.

The unbelievable, presumptuous bastard.

'It's from Bagby,' I explained. 'These are coordinates. We have to find out where…'

'Already found it.' Kate pulled an ancient and creased road atlas from her bag. 'My mother hung on to everything,' she said. 'Even this.'

She took the empty glass from me, and pulled me to my feet.

'Bring that bag, will you?'

'Wait,' I said. 'They turned on the tracking beacons when Grimsby got bombed. They're in the CashPlants™. If we don't get rid of them, we may as well draw them a map.'

Kate held up her wrist. 'Don't have one. You forget I'm the daughter of a former revolutionary. Why would I have something injected into my arm that can help the government keep tabs on me?'

'Good point. Paranoia pays off for once. Just me, then.' I thumbed the hard, oval lump under the skin of my left wrist. 'If we can hit it with electromagnetic radiation it might knock it out. I don't suppose you still use a microwave?'

Kate shook her head. 'No. And no time. Come.' She grabbed my wrist and pulled me through to the kitchen. Her fingers probed my wrist. 'Got it.'

'What are you doing?'

'Taking care of this.' She poured vodka on my wrist, then pulled a kitchen knife from a knife block and poured the remainder of the bottle on the blade.

'Wait…'

'Don't worry, it's sharp.'

Before I could protest, the blade sank into my skin and sliced down vertically. Kate pulled it out again just as quickly, then her fingers found either side of the wound, and squeezed. The narrow, inch-long chip emerged, with its shiny film of blood. Kate pinched it away and snapped it in half.

'OK?' she asked, wrapping my wrist in a cloth.

'Got any more vodka?'

'You'll be fine. It's a shallow cut and it isn't bleeding much. Just like squeezing a spot. Or removing a splinter.'

I wrapped the cloth tighter around my wrist and tried not to think about the pain. Or the blood.

I followed Kate to the front door. 'That doesn't mean we're in the clear. Just that we have a head start. They'll find us eventually,' I said.

'Then let's make the most of it.' She picked up her bag and we stepped out into the street.

'Wait,' I said. Kate paused on the threshold. I scanned the streets. No one was around. But that didn't mean much.

'Satisfied? Then let's go,' Kate said, taking the last few steps in one.

I followed after her. 'Right behind you,' I said. 'But do you mind telling me exactly where we're going?'

'To join your partner in the North, of course,' she said, as she hurried briskly along the street, away from her mother's house. Away from her life. 'To find out who killed my brother. To join the resistance.'

23

Chlorophyll

We stole the car at random from beneath a broken streetlight at the end of a quiet road, then headed north out of the city. We must have passed a thousand surveillance cameras. Every light overhead took the shape of security drones patrolling, lenses penetrating through the smog, searching out renegade bombers and AWOL police officers wanted for murder.

Despite my paranoia it seemed that the checkpoints had not yet been updated with orders to look out for a man and a woman in their thirties travelling out of the city. We slid through with ease – lovers heading for an illicit weekend in the countryside, guards smiling knowingly as they waved us on.

With the effects of the vodka wearing off, Kate rode beside me in silence as the lights of London were peeled back to reveal dark stretches of countryside and, beyond, quiet motorways with the blinking lights of service stations like outposts, or lighthouses in the darkness. Kate came alive again as we reached unfamiliar roads, squinting at the map and tracing our way over its illustrated lines. My wrist throbbed as I drove.

Hoping for the best, we inched ever closer to Bagby's rendezvous point, our headlights pushing the darkness away before it sprung back into place behind us.

An hour or so outside of London, travelling along a long, narrow road leading through a pine forest, we saw the blast of a STAR rocket overhead, trailing red jet fuel as it raced towards the stratosphere.

'Look,' I said, but Kate was asleep, her head resting on her shoulder.

With my guide out for the count, I followed the map as best I could, driving with it folded around the steering wheel. The car made interesting noises as I drove, but I tried not to worry about it. I was just happy to be putting distance between us and the capital. Between us and Wallace, between us and Mercer's broken body. Koch's corpse. The ghost of Caleb Jennings that had started all of this.

Each turn in the road revealed yet another empty expanse, each dark road looking much the same as the last one. A few miles more and the petrol light blinked its angry red eye. I consulted the map, then turned off towards a main road in search of fuel. The first petrol station we came to was closed, the windows boarded up. The next was open and near-deserted, a lone teenage assistant staring out from the office at the empty forecourt. I bought fuel and food with some ancient and gummed up coins and faded paper money I found in the glove box. The teenager took no special interest in us, or the real-life cash I handed him. But the cameras at each corner of the forecourt and the two behind the counter would already be relaying my image to the central database even as I returned to Kate.

The car took a while to start then whined unhealthily and eventually kicked into life. Kate, awake now, rummaged through the carrier bag of assorted foodstuffs and held up a squashed chicken sandwich that looked like it might survive a nuclear fallout. 'We're not in the capital anymore,' she said.

'That's true,' I replied, my eyes on the white lines in the centre of the road leading us onwards. I didn't tell her that I'd never been this far from home before, either.

'There's something I should tell you,' I said. 'Before she died...' I stopped myself. Telling Kate about her mother's video confession would only cause more hurt. If the Professor had had time to dictate something to me, why not record something for her daughter, also?

'Before who died?' Kate asked.

'Before your mother died,' I continued, 'we spoke a few times. About the case. Naturally enough the conversation turned to you once or twice. She told me then that raising you was the proudest accomplishment of her life.'

At first I thought Kate hadn't heard me, but when I chanced a glance at her in the mirror I caught her wiping something from her cheek. I left her with her thoughts.

After a while she said: 'I don't really remember it, you know. Those fifteen years in the system. Her and my father were the only life I really knew. Even if I only knew my father for a short time. I don't even think I was aware then – I mean really aware – that there was a revolution taking place. We were out there in Whitstable, by the sea. My parents had their work, and I suppose it was easy enough to pretend the outside world couldn't touch us. Looking around at everything that's going on now, I wish I'd been more involved back then. Do you think it would have saved my father's life?'

'I have no idea,' I said truthfully. 'But I think what happened then was probably out of your control. You were just a child, after all.'

'Well, what about my mother's life? If I'd been more

involved in what's going on now, do you think she might still be alive?'

'Kate,' I said. 'Your mother's death had nothing to do with you,' I lied. 'Once a person has made up their mind to... to do that, it can be impossible to change it. There's nothing you could have done.'

'I know it's your job to uphold the laws of the land and all that, but nothing's really changed, has it?' she said. 'If anything, things are worse than ever before. Immigrants are treated like third, fourth, class citizens. That's when we actually let them in. More people than ever before are sleeping rough. It isn't just food banks anymore. Do you know how many of my colleagues have actually lost their homes – their *lives* – because the government has shut their jobs down because of some arbitrary culture rule set out fifteen years ago? Unless you're born rich your only real options are to work in menial jobs, or join the military. Why are we fighting so many wars? When did we all agree to that? And what happened to freedom of speech? Of expression? Did they ever exist? I know they must have from old stories my mother told. But not for as long as I can remember. We cured the HAF virus, but the Reformation just let another virus grow and grow. Corruption. Inequality. The desire for complete control over everything and everyone. It's everywhere. No wonder people want... no wonder people want things to change.'

Even after everything I couldn't shift my paranoid notion that every conversation was being listened to. Out of habit, I said nothing. For the first time, this made me feel ashamed.

'It's OK, you can admit it,' Kate said, as though reading my thoughts. 'There isn't another soul for miles and we're as far away from the capital as can be.'

I shrugged, keeping my eyes on the road. I don't know why I felt like I could talk to her. Maybe it was because we were so far away from everything – farther from London than I'd ever been in my life. Maybe it was because my life had been steered so far off course that I wasn't sure what to believe in any more. Maybe it was because she was her mother's daughter. Or maybe it was because right then, cocooned in this car in the middle of nowhere, we were the only people that existed in the world.

'I suppose it's easy to look back and wonder if your life might have gone a different way,' I said. 'Sometimes I… My mother died when I was young, a child. Sometimes I wonder where I would be now if my father had died instead.'

'Do you remember her?' Kate asked.

I nodded. 'She was a singer. Nothing major. Pubs and social clubs. But she did have a hit song, once. My father thought we'd become rich and famous, but it wasn't meant to be. She died coming back from a gig in a pub. My father was at work so he couldn't pick her up. He was a policeman, too. It was a drunk driver who did it. For some reason my father blamed my mother. Blamed her singing. Blamed music and books and art and everything like that for putting the idea that she could be successful in her head in the first place. For some reason, I didn't question him. I was only a child, but I just grew up believing what he said was true. He didn't like books in the house, didn't let me listen to my mother's music. I can't remember there ever being another option for me other than being a police officer. So here I am. He died from the HAF virus. I remember thinking I was free then, to do what I wanted to. But by then I'd already joined the force and I suppose it felt good to have some stability in the middle of the Reformation. So I stuck with it. Fifteen years later, here we are. Had my mother lived and my father died, I don't know. Maybe I would have joined the revolution too.'

This conclusion came as surprise to me. I shut my mouth and focused on the road again.

'There's still time for all of that,' Kate said. I couldn't tell if she was being facetious or deadly serious. I let it lie. Slowly, the miles slipped by. But I couldn't shift the uncomfortable feeling that Kate was right about everything.

A few hours later we crossed an old suspension bridge over a slow-moving river. Kate pointed to our approximate position on the map. We were closing in on Bagby's location. I hadn't given any real thought to what would happen when we arrived but knowing Bagby, whatever he was planning, he had been planning it for some time.

'Do you really think Bagby can help us?' Kate asked.

'If anyone can, it's Bagby,' I said. 'He'll be able to tell us what this is all about. He's been through a lot.'

'We all have,' Kate said, her eyes on the window.

The sun was a flat band of gold rising among the trees as we left the river behind. The car had begun to make some deeply unsettling sounds. It was getting difficult to ignore, but I knew next to nothing about cars so the only option was to keep going.

'Kate, it might not be my place but... I'm sorry for everything that's happened to you. You deserved a better life than this.'

'I've had a good life,' Kate said. 'And it isn't over yet.'

Soon, we were among arable fields, beyond which lay row after row of long metallic huts, stretching out beside the road. Signs on the huts read 'Artemis Agriculture', and I realised that we were passing through one of the in-vitro meat processing plants owned by a subsidiary of Vangelis.

Faintly, under the sounds of our dying car, we could hear the sound of cows milling about in their enclosures, waiting for another DNA sample to be taken then multiplied in the lab to form a thousand synthetic-meat burgers.

'They'll see us,' Kate said. 'We should get off the road, away from cameras.'

But there was nowhere to turn so we carried on, flanked on either side by the sprawling facility until, ten minutes later, the woods took over again and swallowed us up. We turned onto a B road and managed another twenty miles before the car spluttered, the engine died and the lights of the dashboard went out. Kate and I looked at each other. Evidently, we had both surpassed the extent of our automobile expertise. The car shuddered and slowed and then we were coasting down the side of the road. Another few metres and we came to a dead stop.

'That's that, then,' Kate said.

We got out of the car.

'We're not too far away,' I said. 'We can walk.'

'Someone will see the car,' Kate said. 'But then, they've probably been watching us since London, anyway.'

'Maybe,' I said. 'Either way, let's get away from here, quickly.'

We set off into the trees. After a few minutes the car disappeared behind us. The woods were much the same as woods had always been in Autumn; silence, bare trees, brambles clinging to our trousers. We pushed forward, heading in what I hoped was a generally north-easterly direction towards the black circle on the map. Towards Bagby and answers. A group of large black birds flapped up from a bare ash tree as we passed. I squinted after them in the morning light, looking for wires or blinking LED eyes. The drones up here, Bagby used to joke, had all gone off-grid and turned feral. Now they roamed the northern skylines in flocks, migrating on the air currents like metallic crows.

We carried on, crossing a dried-up stream turned to mud then scrambling up the opposite bank. The sky above was grey and featureless. A short while later we came to a tumble-down wall of old stones, overgrown with moss.

'This could be it,' Kate said.

'Keep an eye out – we don't know what to expect,' I said as we climbed over.

We'd only gone a few steps further when a woman appeared from the trees ahead of us, carrying a shotgun. 'You're right there,' she said.

Before Kate or I could react, she was joined by others, men and women emerging from the trees all around us, hunting rifles and battered old shotguns in their hands. The first woman was tall and dressed in dark trousers and a bomber jacket. Her red hair was shaved close to the sides of her angular head with a short crop on top. An angry scar ran from her eyebrow to her ear.

I tried to make eye-contact. 'Look,' I began.

Before I could come up with something to say, Kate took the initiative. 'Lower your guns, please. We don't want trouble. We're just looking for a friend,' she said, taking a step past me towards the woman.

'Kate,' I said.

The strangers eyed us, some through the eye holes in their balaclavas. All handled their weapons easily and with expertise. We had stumbled into – I hoped – a faction of the revolutionary army thought to be biding its time in the woodlands of the north. If that was the case then there was a good chance that Bagby was among them, perhaps waiting back at a base camp. If I was wrong, it would have been difficult to persuade these armed strangers that we should be allowed to pass through alive. Even if by some miracle we had been able to fight our way out, there would have been nowhere for us to go except onwards into the trees.

'She's right... we're looking for a friend,' I offered, but the woman held a fist up for silence and my words died between us.

She took a step forwards and looked us up and down. 'I think it's time you met the boss.'

She reached out to take Kate by the arm. I reached for my weapon instinctively, before I remembered that I'd left it back in London, beside a dead man. The woman, very much alive, stepped forward and cracked me across the forehead with the butt of her own gun. I fell down among the leaves as the world turned dark.

24

The Farmhouse

I woke up with my heels dragging through leaves, men holding me under the arms. 'Lift him,' a voice said, then my arms were lifted up and hooked around shoulders as we pressed on through the trees. Directly, we emerged from the tree line onto open fields bisected by a winding dirt road leading to an old, three-storeyed farmhouse. Outbuildings, various four-wheel drives and more armed men and women stood about outside. The main building had been added to over the years and seemed to be spreading haphazardly over the land. I tried to memorise as much as possible as a dark and deep chasm opened up in the middle of my head. An Alsatian came running out to meet us. Before I lost consciousness again, I watched it bound up and lick Kate's hand.

There was a knock at the door. I managed to call out. The woman who had hit me came in with a pile of folded clothes. She laid them on a wooden dresser: a pair of trousers and a dark, flannel shirt. In her other hand she carried a pair of old, military-style leather boots, scrubbed clean.

'If this lot doesn't fit you that's tough luck,' she said.

Her index and middle fingers, I noticed, had been replaced by metal prosthetics, and under the dark collar of her bomber jacket I could just about make out a regimental tattoo.

'You've been out all day,' she continued, 'but we didn't want to disturb you. It isn't often we get policemen wandering through the woods to visit us.'

I sat up sharply in bed. My bruised head made its protests known. I realised that my wounded arm had been cleaned and dressed.

'Don't worry,' she said, glancing at me as she busied herself laying out the clothes. 'We know all about you, and you're safe enough here.'

When I didn't respond she offered a now empty hand. 'I'm Sarah.'

I took it and told her my name, trying to project an image of a calm and rational man.

'Where's Kate?' I asked.

'Downstairs. Helping with dinner.' Sarah checked her watch. 'Give it an hour and we should be ready for you. We cleaned you up as best we could, but you should take a bath. It's just down the corridor.' A glass of water and a china saucer with two yellow pills in it stood on the bedside table. 'They'll make you feel better. You're black and blue.'

I realised then that I was lying naked in the bed. 'Thank you for the clothes. But where are *my* clothes?'

'The incinerator. Covered in mud, blood and who knows what else.' She nodded to the pile. 'Put those on. And relax, you're safe here.'

When I was alone, I got out of bed and pulled a towel around my shoulders. Bruises left by Sarah's shotgun and

218

Koch's hands competed for my attention. A small, oval window let light into the room. I rubbed the grime from it with a corner of the towel. Down in the yard, men and women were unloading a small lorry, carrying sacks and long black boxes marked with military stamps into the barn. Two men joined them from the direction of the long, muddy driveway, shaking their heads. Work stopped momentarily as the newcomers pointed back in the direction they had come from, shrugged, then walked towards the house, leaving the others to their tasks.

Squinting through the dirty glass, it was difficult to tell if any of them had been the ones who had found us in the woods. If they were different people, that would make seven people below and five in the woods for a total of twelve – not counting any others I hadn't yet met. Like Sarah, I suspected they had all been professional soldiers at one time or another. Fifteen years as a police officer had taught me that it was dangerous to make assumptions, but their weapons all but confirmed my suspicion that these ex-soldiers now belonged to the revolution. Something, or someone, had alerted them to the fact that Kate and I were on our way. Yet even though Sarah claimed to know who I was, I was almost certain that Bagby wasn't here. If he was, he would have brought the clothes to me in bed, or sent word that he'd had to go away and would return soon. And, if the revolutionaries weren't affiliated with Bagby, Kate and I might be in trouble. For now, it was better to stick closely to Kate than trust her safety to others.

I dressed and left the room. Light filtered in from windows on either side of a narrow corridor. Straight ahead was a staircase. Cooking smells and laughter came from below. If they were feeding us it was unlikely that they meant to do us any immediate harm. Kate would be safe enough while I worked out what to do next. The corridor led away from the stairs and around a corner. The floorboards were old and warped and creaked underfoot. Threadbare patches of assorted rugs had been laid over them to warm the toes. Wooden cabinets stood against the walls, holding old photographs, a vintage oil lamp, lace doilies. The house was like a museum; there were few signs here that the revolution had ever happened. The door at the end of the corridor opened. A young man of about twenty with a crew cut emerged, nodding to me as he passed. Whoever the farm's original owners had been, it didn't seem likely that they were still here now. Now, the house had the air of a requisitioned army barracks in occupied territory.

I found the bathroom and locked myself in. A fluffy pink bathmat had been soiled by countless pairs of muddy boots. I turned on the bath taps then sat on the toilet seat. I examined the pills Sarah had left and thought of that other pill that Koch had supplied just for me. I got up and flushed the pills down the toilet. Then I sat back down and took stock. It had been easy, in London, to view the national situation with an air of detachment, focusing on the day to day of life in the capital, and thinking no further than the edges of the M25. It might have been the blow to the head, but out here in the country I felt as though my face had been thrust into the mud, a boot pressing down on the back of my neck.

When I came down for dinner the kitchen was full of steam and the smell of stew and the clatter of plates and cutlery and glasses being pulled from cupboards. Kate was in the middle of it all, directing her troops. They'd outfitted her with a new getup as well – a forest green shirt over blue corduroy trousers.

'Lazarus rises,' she said, seeing me. 'How's the head?' She passed me a loaf of bread and a bread knife. 'Nothing's happened yet, but I don't trust them,' she whispered.

I nodded. 'Me neither.'

'Now cut this loaf,' she said, raising her voice for the benefit of those busying themselves around us.

I took the bread and the knife and went through into the next room. An old and chipped dining table stood at its centre, surrounded by a collection of mismatched chairs. Outside, through the large bay windows, the sky was the colour of a bruised plum. There were two others in the room who I thought I recognised from the woods. They paid me no attention as they set out our plates. Without warning, an alarm sounded from somewhere in the house; three short, high-pitched blasts. I gripped the bread knife. The other two seemed not to care. The door opened and the men and women I'd met before or seen from the bedroom window trudged inside, chatting as they pulled off their hats and gloves, stomped the mud from their boots, and set down their rifles and shotguns in a pile by the door like umbrellas. Including the two with Kate in the kitchen, I counted thirteen altogether. Not accounting for any left outside on guard duty, I had almost got it right.

Sarah came in last and directed all of us to the table. 'Policeman, sit down.'

Kate moved around the table, serving us from a large saucepan of stew before taking the seat beside me. Ingratiating herself into the group was a good tactic, a way of letting them know that they needn't expect any trouble from her. Should our situation change, I knew she would be ready to do what was required.

'I'm Kamal,' a short, unshaven guy with a Scottish accent said, taking the seat beside me. 'Sorry about the whack on the head there, pal, but we can't be too careful out here.' He turned to me and smiled, and I saw the electro-eyeball that had replaced his homegrown original, a web of scars marking his nose, check and eye socket like directions drawn on a map, all leading to the missing eye – the epicentre of his re-imagined appearance.

'Don't mention it,' I said, shifting my gaze to the bridge of his nose. 'But, if you don't mind my asking, what exactly are you all doing out here?'

Out of the corner of my eye I saw Sarah shoot Kamal a warning look across the table.

'Ah, fighting the good fight,' Kamal said, with a wink from his good eye. He turned to speak to his neighbour, a short woman with dark, shoulder length hair and a horizontal scar across her cheek.

I left him to it and turned my attention to my food. Kate was speaking to the man to her left. A convivial but brittle air had settled around the table. No one had started eating. Sarah had said we were due to meet 'the boss'. I guessed that the empty chair at the head of the table was for him or her.

'When can we expect our dear leader?' I asked across the table.

Sarah looked at me quizzically. Before she could respond, someone shouted 'Attenshun!' and the soldiers sprang to their feet, standing in rigid formation. Kate pulled me up to stand alongside them. Bagby would get a kick out of seeing me like that, I thought.

The door opened and two more soldiers came in, carrying automatic rifles. Then, to cheers and applause, came Vangelis' Head of Futurism & Efficiencies, the scientist, Cadmus Fomalhaut, dressed in old trousers and a farmer's jumper.

'Comrades. Please. Enough, enough,' he said, holding up a hand. He addressed the room as one, his eyes flitting over me with a glimmer of acknowledgement. 'Let us eat,' he said, taking the empty seat at the head of the table, all eyes on him. 'Please sit, sit. Our guests are hungry. They have come a long way to join our struggle.'

25

Visitors

Kate inclined her body towards mine under the pretence of passing the salt. 'What is it?' she whispered.

'I think your friend is surprised,' Fomalhaut said, demonstrating remarkable hearing for a man of his years. 'Surprised to find me here,' he continued, 'and sitting at the head of the table, no less. In fact I imagine I'm near enough the last person he would expect to find leading this so called "resistance".' He raised his glass in my direction. 'Is that about right?'

Sarah's eyes flitted between us. The others were too busy eating to pay us any attention.

'I can't argue with that,' I said, aware that as far as Kate was concerned Fomalhaut and I had never met.

'Don't worry,' he said. 'We'll sit down after dinner and all will become clear.'

The meal continued. Fomalhaut was right; he was the last person I had expected to find here. Especially since I had seen him less than twenty-four hours before, in his office. Like Koch, he must have moved quickly once I'd left.

His evidently having thrown in with a bunch of anarchists did not fit with the world-conquering vision of Vangelis, or any impression of its frail old head scientist that I had formed. Presumably, Wallace was unaware of his extracurricular activities. It seemed that what Fomalhaut had to offer the revolutionaries was technology, least of all the soldiers' high-end replacement limbs, digits and eyes. It was possible too that some of the weapons I'd seen outside came unofficial care of Vangelis. And, knowing that company, I suspected that all sorts of technological measures were in place to hide the farmhouse and all those inside it from the outside world. If that was the case it meant that Kate and I were now completely on our own.

While I mulled this over, the table emptied and the troops trudged back to their posts. Before I could pull Kate aside to explain just who Fomalhaut was Sarah appeared in the doorway.

'You've been summoned,' she said. 'Our exalted leader will see you now.'

We followed her up a flight of stairs leading to a self-contained collection of rooms at the back of the house. Sarah knocked once on a green door then left us.

'Come,' a voice called from inside.

We entered to find Fomalhaut sitting in the middle of a wide room beneath a narrow, sloping ceiling held up by ancient beams. Once upon a time it might have been the master bedroom. Now it was a command centre with a row of monitors set up along one wall and an old-fashioned telescope angled towards a round, portal-like window that looked out over the tree tops.

'This used to belong to my parents,' Fomalhaut said, touching the arm of his chair, a curved red mod relic of the

1960s that looked strangely out of place in this ramshackle old farm building.

'The farm, I mean, not just this chair. I inherited it after they died. It had taken up so much of their time and I was always so busy trying to make something of myself that I had long since fallen out of contact with them. When I came to clear this place out I was surprised to find this chair hidden away up here; evidence of a mild flirtation with a counterculture movement that had passed them by so long ago. It got me thinking. About who we are and about who we might have become, given half a chance.' His hand fluttered across his brow. He smiled. 'My apologies, do sit down.'

He motioned to two less fussy chairs. Kate and I sat in them.

'You've had a tough journey. I myself only arrived last night, after finally managing to sneak away from under Wallace's watchful eye. Work to be done, and all that.' He smiled to himself then changed the subject. 'How's the arm?'

It took me a second to realise he was talking to me. I held up my bandaged wrist. 'On the mend, thank you.'

Fomalhaut chuckled. 'There are easier ways of disabling a CashPlant™, you know.'

'And Ms Faron, you look like you've been in the wars too,' he said, full of concern.

'I'm sorry,' Kate interjected. 'But who are you?'

'Ah,' Fomalhaut said, clapping his hands. 'My apologies; you were expecting DCI Bagby. I'm told he's around. Perhaps tomorrow he'll grace us with his presence.' He met my eyes. 'Please accept my apologies on his behalf, detective. I'm sure he didn't mean to keep you waiting. In the meantime, I hope we can keep you comfortable. As for who I am, Ms Faron, my name is Cadmus Fomalhaut, and I am Head of Futurism & Efficiencies at Vangelis. Regrettably, I first met your chaperone here over the course of his investigation into the tragic death of your brother, Caleb Jennings.'

Kate shifted in her seat. '"Tragic"? It wasn't some accident. He was murdered.'

Fomalhaut bowed his head. 'I'm well aware. And I'm very sorry for your loss.' His face brightened. 'As to why you now find me hiding out in the countryside at the head of a resurgent revolutionary army, that is a more complicated story. It begins many decades ago, when I joined Vangelis as a junior research assistant. Slowly, slowly, slowly, I worked my way up the corporate ladder. In many ways I owe everything to that company. I've won awards, been lauded by my peers and even helped to influence the course of history.' He sighed. 'But one isn't always able to shape history in the way one would like. In recent years I've become increasingly concerned by the direction Elliot Wallace has been taking the company in. Over the past eighteen months there has been an influx of governmental contracts for all sorts of unsavoury things. New weapons. Surveillance. Data implementation. A narrowing of the culture laws you work so hard to uphold… Of course, it *is* his company. But, to put it briefly, after a long and fruitful collaboration I now feel our visions are no longer aligned. Quite simply, I cannot in good conscience allow these projects to continue.'

'And viruses,' I asked. 'What about viruses?'

'Yes,' Fomalhaut said, smiling patiently. 'And viruses, too. In fact, my dear, there is one particularly nasty virus that the detective here is referring to.'

'And what does it do, this virus?' Kate asked.

Fomalhaut looked at me. I nodded.

He sighed, then continued. 'The detective is referring to the HAF virus of 2039. You don't need me to talk you through the impact that virus had. What you might not know is that your parents were this country's best chance at formulating a cure. Well, they were so talented that of course they came close. Sadly they were never able to manufacture an actual, workable cure. But along the way they did discover a way to program the virus to only affect certain genetic codes, the idea being that the same technology could be applied to the cure, making it one hundred per cent effective in any host. This data would be extremely valuable today, just as a precautionary measure. My employer certainly thinks so.'

'We had believed all traces of your parents' data around this work to have been destroyed in an act of sabotage; a fire. But we were wrong. It seems that before he died, your father injected you with a dormant form of this programmable virus strain which you still carry in your blood. It didn't affect you, of course, but it did mean your parents' work would live on in secret. As I say, to certain people this virus would be extremely valuable. Our detective friend here believes this is why your brother was killed. A case of mistaken identity.'

Kate stood up. She paced to the window and back. I reached out to her but she pulled her hand away.

'What are you telling me?'

Fomalhaut held a hand across his brow, as if shielding himself from her glare. 'I'm afraid that what I'm about to say isn't pleasant. I'm ashamed to say that, after fifteen years of tinkering – attempting to rediscover the formula – my employer has become desperate. A new revolution is on the way, you see, and if he can provide the government with a way of defeating the protestors without a repeat of what happened fifteen years ago, well, he would be the most powerful man in the country. If not the world. All he needs to complete his work is a sample of the original material. This would allow him to not only kill those of a susceptible genetic make-up but also, essentially, whomever he so chooses. For obvious reasons, this cannot be allowed to happen. All it would require is a DNA sample from which to tailor the virus to that person, and that person only. And of course, through our CashPlant™ technology, Vangelis has whole data banks of DNA samples from everyone in the country. The world, even.'

'You're insane,' Kate said. 'Deranged. You and your boss. Who dreams up something like this?'

'Your parents,' Fomalhaut said without missing a beat. 'They believed that given the chance their accidental discovery could be used for good. To halt another pandemic, for example. I am of the same mind.'

'Quite a blackmail tool in the wrong hands,' I said. 'Forget revolutionaries – if one had foreign armies or political opponents one wanted to keep in check, this would make them unstoppable...'

'No, it's more than that,' Kate said. 'What he's describing is a tool for genocide. Social cleansing. Whole areas could be infected. Through the water supply. The air. Attack drones carrying cans of the virus, spritzing it on the people below. Whole countries could be affected.'

'Or controlled,' I said, looking at Fomalhaut. 'This isn't about revolution at all, is it? It's about population control. It's about keeping people in check and threatening to kill them if they step out of line.'

'But why should people need to step out of line? What could they possibly have to complain about? The Reformation is over. We won,' Fomalhaut said, a smile revealing him as devil's advocate.

'How about the fact that we have a government that treats people like insects, distracting us through a make-believe obsession with culture and wellbeing and war?' Kate asked. 'We're told we deserve only the best, that demanding only the highest, most nourishing standards for body and mind will make us better people. People who'll want to talk our grievances through instead of fighting again. But it isn't a real choice. About how to live, what to wear, what music to listen to. It's a choice between A, B and C, where D really does stand for "Death". They want us to believe that if we want to survive the only real option is to remain docile and pacified.' As she spoke I saw Professor Faron sitting there in her place, her form grown suddenly incandescent.

Silence filled the room like the pressure that builds before a thunderhead breaks.

'Now you see,' Fomalhaut said, tapping his fingers on the chair arm. 'Now you see why not only must those planning to weaponise this virus be stopped, but the government must be stopped as well. The rumours about what they did in Šibenik, Pogradec, and Hebden Bridge are true. I know this for a fact; this supposedly peaceful, just and enlightened society we live in is a facade. You only have to look at the growing support these revolutionary cells are attracting to realise that. No, the virus' potential is too great. Neither Wallace nor the government could pass up a weapon like this. It is up to us to intervene. To take their power away and by doing so, finally make things fairer for all. We stand at a pivotal moment in history. Now is the time – the only chance – to act in good conscience.'

'You aren't suggesting that your tin pot revolutionary army use the virus against the government and Wallace instead?' I asked. 'That's no solution. Neither is this bombing campaign your so-called "revolutionaries" have been carrying out. Or people fighting in the streets. I can remember how that goes.'

Fomalhaut bowed his head. 'We all can. And, of course not. The virus must be hidden away until we know how to use it for good and only for good. Think of it as a preventative. But, as is often the case, I'm afraid that things must get worse before they can get better.'

I stared at him for a moment, taking in the lines on his face. He would have been an old man back when the first Reformation rolled around. And here he was, calling for another.

'Say, for the sake of conversation, that a second revolution goes ahead. How does that benefit you?' I asked. 'You said yourself that you have the best job you could ever wish for. You live a charmed life. You work with the government on a daily basis and have the ability to shape the trajectory of the most powerful corporation in the world – anything you dream up in your head today changes the course of the world tomorrow. As far as I can see, you're already holding a winning ticket.'

'Because,' Fomalhaut said, 'a person's life shouldn't benefit just that person and that person alone. Sometimes my innovations have helped others. Often they haven't. After a lifetime of making weapons I want to wash some of the blood off my hands. Something has to change. Or when I die my name will go down in the records next to Oppenheimer in terms of the destruction I've caused.'

'And bombs are the solution? Killing innocent people in provincial towns? In London?'

Fomalhaut winced. 'As I said, things must get worse before there can be any improvement. But don't lay the blame for these explosions solely at my door; there are revolutionary factions like this one all over the country. Hundreds of them, largely staffed by ex-servicepeople and each following a different leader. These people are used to conflict. They understand that a short, hard battle is preferable to a prolonged campaign and that spilling blood now will eventually lead to a longer-lasting peace. It's true that some among the revolutionary ranks believe that ever since the government exported violence to its permanent foreign war zones the public has grown numb. They believe that the nation needs to see violence up close and personal again. That it needs to be woken from this "death of affect", as Ballard has it. In short, that people need to get angry and stay angry and have this anger guided to where it could do us all some good.'

'And to do this you have to mobilise a nation before Wallace learns how to weaponise this anti-revolutionary virus. Bring about a revolution before your employer can kill the revolutionaries,' I summarised. 'Cadmus – this is insanity. We should be working to stop the revolution. And Wallace. Come back to London with me, testify against Wallace and we'll end it that way. We'll put him away for a long, long time.'

Fomalhaut looked at me with something like disappointment in his eyes. 'You don't really believe that would work, do you? That there's any chance of putting Elliot Wallace behind bars – revolution or no revolution?'

'Make it public,' Kate said. 'Make the blueprint for the virus public. No one can use it if everyone has it.'

'The government would never allow it,' Fomalhaut sighed. 'Wallace would never allow it. It's too valuable to them both.'

Silence returned. After a minute or two Kate broke it. 'My mother always insisted that my father's death had been an accident. But even back then I knew something was off. I knew that that wasn't the case.' She paused, cleared her throat. 'The day my father... killed himself, he gave me an injection. Before he left for work. He said it was a flu jab. And all along they thought it was my brother who had this thing swimming inside of him. My brother that I'd never met, who was murdered instead of me... I never asked for this.'

'Your father was a brilliant man,' Fomalhaut said. 'He and your mother were two of the very finest in their field. I'm sure they didn't mean to burden you with this. Only to entrust the virus to you as its guardian. Your father gave it to you because

231

he loved you. Because he saw you as a symbol of hope. He had run out of options. But I'm sure he believed that, given more time, a universal antidote could eventually be engineered from your blood. There are still HAF epidemics in Africa and many parts of Russia, after all. You were his hope for what came next, even as he learned that there were those who sought to abuse his research, and use it to solidify their own power. Passing the virus to you demonstrated his belief that there could be a better tomorrow.'

Night had long since fallen. Outside, the darkness hung heavy and complete. Kate got up and went across to the sideboard. There was a bottle of real gin there. She poured herself a drink, finished it off, then poured another.

'People have died for what's in my blood. You're saying more people *will* die because of it. That I'm effectively a walking weapon.' She spoke with her back to us, her shoulders a rigid shape against the darkness. 'I can't allow anyone else to die.'

'My dear,' Fomalhaut said, shifting around in his seat to better address her. 'In the right hands you're a *cure*. The whole world could be immunised, if only we were able to develop what is in your blood. This virus is a gift. A gift from you to the world.'

'She isn't a lab rat to be experimented on,' I said, standing up. 'Find another way to wipe out the HAF virus. Or let it kill Africans and Russians. But either way, leave her alone. She's been through enough.' I sat down again, feeling all energy drain from me. 'Can't she just –'

Kate finished my sentence. 'Go back to living a normal life? Both my parents are dead. My mother killed herself and murdered someone else in the process. My brother has been murdered. Oh – and this pales in comparison to all of that – but I've also lost my job. What have I got to go back to?'

'Your father,' Fomalhaut said.

I shook my head, but it was too late.

'Your real father is still alive,' Fomalhaut continued. 'And despite my reputation as a man of science, I believe it is no less than fate that brought you here to continue his work.'

Kate put her glass down. 'My "real" father didn't want to know us. My mother told me all about him. As it happens she sat me down on the day before she died. In hindsight it seems she wanted to leave this world with a clear conscience. I know all about "RZ". What kind of a hero leaves his children to be raised by strangers? What kind of a hero has his children separated at birth? My life was better before I knew anything about him.'

'He didn't know about you,' Fomalhaut said. 'Your birth mother didn't tell him. When your father found out that you existed he was in too precarious a position to take you on. He wanted to, of course, but his friends – chiefly, your mother and Harold Jennings – advised him against it. They decided to take the two of you instead, to keep you safe. Your real father would have loved you – both of you – had he only been given the chance. He still would. He is a great man. If you don't believe me ask the detective here – he met him, only yesterday.'

I could feel Fomalhaut manoeuvring me into position like a chess piece. Of course Fomalhaut knew that Wallace had arranged the visit. Had one or both of them ran the numbers on what I'd do next? Configured an algorithm of best possibilities, coming to the conclusion that letting me meet RZ would eventually and inevitably lead me here, delivering Kate to his revolutionaries?

'It's true,' I said, faced with Kate's expectant stare. 'He's alive.'

She looked at me, or through me, as if seeing me for the first time.

'You'll meet him, I'm sure,' Fomalhaut continued. 'He would be proud of what you're doing.'

'And what about the fifteen years before the revolution?' she asked. 'Fifteen years in the care system. The same for my brother. Where was he then? Why didn't anyone tell him about us? Why didn't anyone do anything?' Her voice shrank as she spoke, and the room seemed to shrink too in response.

'Your father's enemies would have used you against him,' Fomalhaut said quietly. 'If you come with us now, as his heir and daughter, people will rally to the cause.'

Kate had turned from the window while Fomalhaut spoke. She crossed to the door and stood with a hand on the handle. 'Your revolution might change things for the better. It probably will. But I don't want a part in it,' she said. 'Not like this; I'm not a weapon. Or a marketing tool. And I'm not RZ's daughter. My parents were called Rachael and Edward Faron, and they were great people.'

'Kate, don't…' I began.

'Make the virus public. Take away its power,' she said with a finality that killed any objections dead in our throats. She left the room in the silence that followed. The door closed quietly behind her, and that was that.

'Well.' Fomalhaut raised his hands then let them fall helplessly back into his lap. 'I hadn't even considered… that we would use her as some sort of mascot is just… just…'

'It is,' I said. 'Why didn't you tell me any of this when we met before? You had plenty of chance.'

'How could I?' Fomalhaut asked. 'You were a police officer, then. I wasn't sure where your loyalties lay. In fact, I'd be willing to bet that you're not so sure yourself, even now.'

I ignored him. 'Your friend, Koch, killed Caleb Jennings,' I said. 'He tried to kill my boss. For all I know, he may have succeeded. He tried to kill me.' It was my turn to cross to the window. Outside, pine tops stood still and stoic against the night. I couldn't stop a revolution on my own. I thought for a long moment before making up my mind about what had to be done. 'I'll help you take down Wallace. But I won't fight the government, or the police. They're still good people, for the most part.'

'That's all I can ask,' Fomalhaut said.

'Then that's settled. But here's another question: when did you spot us? In the woods?'

This elicited a laugh. 'My dear man, we've had eyes on you since the police checkpoint, even if the police haven't. Don't forget,' he added with obvious pride, 'that I designed this country's eyes. I gave it sight. I built the infrastructure. Even now, while our men and women patrol outside, we have eyes in the sky, in the forest. Checkpoints and tripwires everywhere.'

He swept an arm towards the bank of television screens. Night-vision visions of empty forests and soldiers looping around outbuildings flickered back at us. 'We're entirely safe here because of the measures I personally have put in place. And that is the same reason why our revolution will be a success. As soon as we have the manpower we won't need bombs – or even a virus. We'll be able to shut the cities down with a click of a button. Vangelis was the vehicle I needed to help me develop the technology. Now it is time to take my gifts away from Wallace and use them against him, re-purpose them towards good, and a better tomorrow.' He clasped his hands together and shook them as if in prayer. 'You can feel the energy, detective. Just look at what we've achieved here, already.'

He joined me by the window and grasped my wrist. His grip was unexpectedly firm. 'Real change is coming. Make no mistake,' he said. 'This revolution will succeed where the last one faltered. I'd give my life to make it so. It will happen. It must.' He let go of my wrist and smiled, the old man creeping back into his face as what was left of his sudden burst of energy dissipated. 'But for now,' he said, 'this old man is in need of a rest.'

I nodded. 'Of course.' I made my way to the door. 'One last thing. Where's my partner?'

'Ah! The big question! DCI Bagby is out rendezvousing with another group. He will be back tomorrow,' Fomalhaut said.

There was something off about the ease with which he delivered this line. A pre-prepared lie always arrives faster than the truth. But, it was late and there was more to discover before I felt up to making a move against the status quo. 'OK,' I said instead. 'If you see him before I do, tell him he owes me an explanation.'

Fomalhaut smiled, saying nothing. I said goodnight and went in search of my bed.

26

Reinforcements

I waited for two hours, lying in the dark, then got up and put my ear to the bedroom door. Muffled, drunken voices came from downstairs but the hallway outside seemed quiet. I eased the door open and slid out. Kate was in the next room along. I had checked on her after our meeting with Fomalhaut, but she had sworn at me and sent me away. She had promised, however, not to go anywhere or do anything until morning. I hadn't heard anything from her since and all was silent now.

I was certain that there was more to Fomalhaut's strange farmhouse menagerie than he was letting on and his interest in Kate was far too similar to the malevolent and ignoble plans he claimed of Wallace for my liking. Even if Fomalhaut truly believed that he was acting in the nation's best interests and that Wallace was the real threat, in my mind one crackpot old man was as bad as another. The seemingly frail and brittle Fomalhaut had already proved that he possessed a unique measure of cunning – he couldn't have maintained his position at Vangelis, all the while secretly planning a revolution, otherwise. Outnumbered and outgunned, I had to find out for certain what Fomalhaut's intentions were before Kate and I could work out how to stop him, or – as seemed more likely – slip away and call for help.

A window at the top of the stairs looked out on an outbuilding. A lone woman standing hunched and smoking solidly against the drizzle looked to be the only sentry. Those who weren't warming themselves with a drink downstairs would most likely be sleeping before later patrols. Baring the odd bathroom trip, it was unlikely I would bump into any of them.

The stairs creaked but I got down them eventually. The party was in the dining room. I crept through a low archway into a small sitting room that looked out from the other side of the house. The lights were out and the view outside was one of endless dark fields stretching away to a darker line of trees on the horizon. From somewhere nearby a toilet flushed and a door-handle turned. From under a piano in the corner I watched an unsteady pair of legs in muddy jeans cross the room. Then came the sound of battered sofa springs taking weight, followed by snoring. After a minute I crawled out from under the piano and retraced my steps towards the door. A car engine sounded from outside. Headlights washed across the window and along the wall. The snoring man woke with a start and hurried to investigate the new arrivals. I just had time to climb the first few steps back towards the bedrooms before he passed by, then I snuck down behind him and back through the small lounge.

Voices met me from the dining room.

'More reinforcements from the capital.'

'Oh thank Jesus, they've come to save us from these lonely fields.'

'We need people,' Sarah's unmistakable voice said.

'You're telling me,' the first man said. 'Six fucking hours we were scouring those woods today. No sign. And yesterday. I'm telling you, no one's out there. The old man's seeing ghosts.'

'Careful…' Sarah replied.

'At ease soldier!' one of the men said.

'Pass me the bottle then go fuck yourself.'

I ducked as someone came into the kitchen and, with his back to me, reached for the bottle on the counter. The kitchen door was on a latch. I waited until I was alone then slipped outside onto a muddy path and traced the wall towards the back of the building. I didn't see any electronic eyes watching. Which only meant that the cameras were as well hidden as Fomalhaut had claimed. I would have to take my chances; if more soldiers were arriving it was vital I got a look at them so that Kate and I knew what we were facing. I edged towards the back of the house and peered around the corner. A grey cat jumped out and shot away into the fields. I followed his lead and ran to cover, finding myself kneeling in a cold puddle behind a parked jeep.

The newly arrived car sat idling beneath a spotlight. The smoking sentry and Sarah had come to greet it. Two men dressed much like the others were pulling duffel bags from the back seat. The third newcomer was familiar – even in his Barbour jacket and Hunter wellingtons I recognised Billy Kader – the Kid in White.

In an instant, my worst fears were confirmed. Far from finding a safe haven, Kate and I had unwittingly stumbled into the viper's nest.

Sarah greeted the Kid as an old friend.

'We're about to go out searching for our friends again,' she said. 'Want to join us?'

Kader shook his head. 'Too tired. But don't let that stop you.

Before you go, tell me, which is his room?' His voice was much more mellifluous than I'd imagined it would be.

'The old man's asleep,' Sarah answered.

'He won't mind,' the Kid said. He winked at her then strode away towards the house.

I thought back to Wallace's save-the-animals gala and how the Kid and Fomalhaut had appeared to be arguing. How the Kid had seemed to always know where to find me. It had been right there in front of me the entire time.

The lights went out as I was halfway up the stairs and the alarm sounded a few seconds after that. A melee of voices followed me up from below. The only word I could make out was 'raid', called and answered again and again, spreading like a fire through the compound. So, the LDNPD had caught up to their revolutionary quarry. Kader, it seemed, had inadvertently led them straight to us and his beloved scientist. Ormsby and Co were only interested in the revolutionaries, but finding Kate and me here wouldn't do my current standing any good. That was if Kate and I were able to stay out of the way long enough to survive the firefight.

Time to go.

In the darkness I bumped into a shape that sounded like Kate, all elbows and shoulders with a revolver in her hand.

'Kate. Time to go. Fomalhaut's not quite the benevolent old grandfather he paints himself as; the kid who attacked us has just arrived downstairs. They've been on the same side all along. We have to get out of here before either his soldiers or the police shoot us.'

'No,' she said, her voice dominating the dark corridor. 'Fomalhaut killed my brother and drove my parents to suicide. Does he think I'm an idiot? If he wants to use my blood as a weapon I'll see his on the walls first.' Even in the darkness I could feel the words hissing through her teeth.

'There'll be time for that later.' I whispered. 'If we try something now we'll never get out of here alive.'

'Fine by me –' she began.

Just then the lights came on, flickering to life with the power of an emergency generator.

'Kate – whatever's happening, they'll kill me and take you away,' I said. 'We have to get away before that happens.'

Footsteps sounded on the stairs. I flattened myself against the wall, snatched a vase from a chest of drawers, and swung it full force into the face of whoever was coming to kill me. The vase shattered in a cloud of powder and blood. The man fell into me, then stumbled backwards, blood trickling down his forehead into his eyes even as he tried to level his pistol at my head. I kneed him in the stomach and pushed him against the window. It didn't bother him much. He levelled the gun at me when a loud report from outside became even louder as a bullet broke through the window and entered the back of his head. My adversary went cross-eyed for a split second then crumpled to the floor.

'Get down!' I yelled, pulling Kate to the carpet.

Another rifle shot sounded from far away and then another. Automatic fire answered from downstairs, punctuated by the odd pistol shot.

The revolver hung uselessly in Kate's fingers. 'Leave that,' I said. 'Maybe we can get out via the roof.'

I picked up the dead man's pistol and edged towards the window, chancing a look. The soldiers were running back and forth in the yard, taking up positions behind the outbuildings and farm vehicles. They were firing off into the woods, spent shell casings falling to the muddy ground. I couldn't see any LDNPD vehicles, personnel, or drones. A man who looked a lot like Kamal fell down as he ran towards the barn and didn't get up again. This told me that wherever the attackers were hidden they were more than capable. So much for Fomalhaut's security systems.

A fleet of Vangelis drones buzzed skywards from the yard, heaving heavy machine guns beneath them. Through the cracked window they appeared as a kaleidoscopic swarm of death. The latest, pre-market models, they made the LDNPD's inner-city drones look like toys. A stray round thudded into the window ledge. I ducked away, registering the heavy throb of the drones' guns over the automatic rifle fire.

Kate had found her feet again. It was her turn to drag me along. We rounded the corner as the door at the far end of the corridor swung open. I fired automatically, once, twice, and only vaguely felt my stomach sink as the young soldier I'd encountered earlier fell forward to lie dead on the carpet. Before I could do much more Kate took me by the shoulder and pulled me through the open sash window onto the sloped roof outside.

The tiles were wet and slippery. The cold hit me and I shivered.

'This isn't a police raid,' Kate yelled, gesturing to the tree line with the revolver she still held in her hand. There were no spotlights, no loudspeakers, just dark and quiet trees and the crack and whoosh of rifle fire.

'Who are they?'

'We're better off not finding out,' I said.

Without warning a drone appeared overhead and began strafing the nearest copse. The shells clattered down onto the roof and rolled down into the guttering. Kate grabbed my hand and between us we managed to stay upright.

'It isn't shooting at us!' Kate shouted over the noise.

A flash of yellow, then another, erupted from the nearby

field and then the drone was spiralling, spinning out of the air, its gun spraying the house, the empty window, the space where our bodies had been before we jumped from the roof. It crashed off into the field as Kate and I rolled away from the farmhouse.

'This way,' I said, pulling Kate back towards the house. 'We don't know who's out there. We should get to the barn at the front of the farm, see if we can get to a car.'

We ran past the lounge windows, ducking low as shapes and shadows flickered about inside, gathering ammo and supplies. There was no sign of Fomalhaut – or Billy the kid. It didn't take much of a stretch of the imagination to guess that they were already well on their way out of there.

'Here,' Kate said, steering me towards a jeep parked a little way away from the main building.

We ran behind it as bullets pocked the ancient walls behind us. We lay against the cold ground, pressed together as broken chips of brick rained down on us. Then the torrent of bullets passed, sweeping away to another target. There was no time to waste. Kate crouched and tried the jeep's door handle.

'It's open,' she said, her face a pattern of mud and sweat. 'Get in, I'll drive.'

'Not so fast,' a voice shouted in reply.

We looked up as one, surprised to find Sarah staggering towards us with an M16 cradled in her arms, a metallic finger on the trigger. Beneath her open jacket her t-shirt was stained red and her eyes seemed to focus somewhere over our heads before switching back to us, like a projectionist trying to find the right aperture. 'You're needed here,' she said, swinging the gun around to face Kate as bullets kicked up the mud around her feet. 'You're vital to our success, you're–'.

She didn't finish what she was saying. A burst of machine gun fire knocked her down instead, sending her sprawling back in the mud, her eyes forever on the stars overhead, without seeing a single one.

'Hurry up, for fuck's sake!' another voice called.

Something, somewhere, must have communicated through the fog clouding my mind to prevent me shooting the figure lumbering out of the field with a rifle slung across its shoulder.

'We can't hold them off forever, not with these drones,' the figure yelled as it coalesced into the shape of a man. 'Let's move. *Now*!'

I nodded to Kate.

'Fuck it,' she yelled as something exploded somewhere behind us.

We pulled each other to our feet and ran, bent low as we followed our saviour into the field, leaving the farmhouse behind.

With my breath ragged in my lungs and my heart in my throat, I made the introductions. 'Kate, I want you to meet my partner, DCI Bagby.'

27

Alliance

We ran towards the tree line with heads and shoulders and bodies ducked low, Kate and I hurrying to keep up with Bagby, my injured leg doing its best to slow us down. The shooting at our backs had subsided to a sporadic pop accompanied by bursts of machine gun fire.

'Where are we going?' Kate shouted as we reached the trees.

Bagby waved us into cover. 'Keep going. They'll be here in a second,' he gasped, visibly unfit for a man in his early sixties.

We passed between dark trunks. A camera lay smashed to pieces on the ground. Fomalhaut would have other eyes elsewhere. As if reasserting this a drone buzzed overhead, its searchlight cutting through the trees.

'Here!' Bagby said, pulling us back against a dead, hollow trunk.

Our bodies were pressed close, and I could feel Kate shivering through her clothes. The searchlight passed. Shouts of men and the bark of dogs crossing the fields came towards us.

Bagby led us off again. 'Let's go.'

I stumbled and he caught me by the arm. 'We can't outrun dogs,' I said, gasping myself.

'We don't need to.'

We slid down a bank of dry earth, coming to a rough road cut through the trees. An engine coughed nearby.

'They're coming,' Kate said. She knelt behind a fallen log, her pistol aimed back along the road.

'No need for that,' Bagby said as a small blue van rumbled into sight. 'He's a friend.'

'Another revolutionary?'

'To the core,' Bagby said as the van trundled past then came to a stand-still with its engine running.

Torchlight swung through the trees behind us as the dogs' whines grew in pitch and excitement.

'In the back, quickly,' Bagby instructed.

Kate and I did as we were told. Bagby climbed in behind us and the van lurched off again. We went over a bump and Kate and I almost hit the ceiling. The driver's cab was open and Bagby climbed into the front seat, cradling his rifle on his lap.

'Introducing your two-man rescue squad,' Bagby said.

The driver eyed us in the mirror. 'Hello partner,' Stohl said.

We stopped outside an old, run-down cabin on a rise about five miles down the road and piled out of the van. Stohl shut the driver's door, a sniper's rifle slung over his shoulder. He had swapped his suit for a woollen sweater under a dark wax jacket, the collar turned up around his chin. A black smear of cordite marked his right cheek – blowback from his high-powered rifle. I remembered Bagby's mention of his military experience and guessed it had been Stohl shooting from the trees, drawing fire while we made our escape. It had been these two, not the LDNPD that had saved our lives.

'Happy to see me?' Stohl asked, with something like weariness in his voice.

I ignored him and turned to Bagby. 'What's going on? Where have you been? Why are you here with *Stohl*? He wanted to bring you in!'

'Let's get inside,' Bagby said. He scratched his chin then peered up at the sky as though weighing up what he saw there. 'We're safe for now, but we don't have long.'

'He's working for Ormsby,' I continued. 'He's been trying to bring you in for treason the entire time!'

Stohl leaned towards Bagby. 'I'll take a look around,' he said, excusing himself before slipping off between the trees, carrying his rifle.

I watched him go. The sun was beginning to rise. With it, the world was coming back into focus. We were on the side of a valley stubbled with broken and jagged tree trunks, the leftovers of years of intensive logging. Looking down on it all was like looking down at the end of the world. I turned my back on the scenery and followed Kate and Bagby into the cabin. Inside was a single room with two rolled up sleeping bags on the floor and stacks of tinned food on the counter. A grey plastic box with an aerial sticking out of it stood by the window, its red light blinking.

It was far from the full-force police raid I had envisioned back at the farmhouse.

'A scanner,' Bagby said, nodding towards the jury-rigged contraption on the window ledge. 'Blocks their search systems. It's not just Fomalhaut who can cobble this stuff together. Stohl learned a thing or two from his uncle. But it's only a matter of time before they go old school, pull out a map and spot this cabin.'

'Then let's leave. Now,' I said. 'Preferably before he comes back.'

'He's a good man,' Bagby continued. 'He's been helping me out for longer than you know.' Time playing out in the woods had stripped some of the weight from Bagby and although the lines had deepened around his eyes, freed from the city dust, the eyes themselves seemed to shine brighter, and with fresh purpose.

'Why do you trust him?'

Bagby smiled. 'Because he has the revolutionary spirit. He's an orphan, remember? His uncle didn't care about him. Both he and Kate have spent their lives watching from the outside, learning to ask questions about the system. Stohl thought he could make a difference to the world by joining the police force but the apple was rotten long before he took a bite. Instead, for the last two years he's been quietly funnelling his allowance from his uncle – Vangelis dividends, no less – to the resistance. That was how we met. He'd read my file, even found out about what happened that day under the bridge. For a long time I thought he was trying to entrap me. Internal Affairs, that sort of thing. The role he's been playing now, in fact. But then I saw him, getting out of a car with his uncle at a charity function. Wallace was all expensive suits, flashy watch, polished shoes. Stohl got out and walked straight past the cameras. It was the look in his eye that convinced me. It wasn't disgust. It was hopelessness. I knew then that there was something there that I could work with. A glimmer of potential. I hoped that he might, eventually, be persuaded to join the cause. And he has. He told me on our first meeting that for the longest time he didn't know when or if a world like this could ever come to an end. I told him I might be able to help.'

'So where's the rest of you? The other police officers?' Kate asked.

Bagby shook his head. 'This is it, just me and Stohl. And this has nothing to do with the law. We both left that behind a long time ago, even if Stohl is forced to pretend otherwise.'

Bagby turned to me. 'I'm sorry we couldn't have had you in on it but we needed his cover to seem realistic. And we needed your focus to be on Kate,' he said. 'She's the most important thing in all of this.'

He sighed and didn't quite meet my eye.

'We only learned afterwards that Fomalhaut had sent Koch to kill you,' he said. 'I'm sorry we couldn't do anything to stop it. And Mercer, too. That was their insurance plan, in case you escaped Koch. If he couldn't have you dead, Fomalhaut wanted to force you out of the city, into his hands.'

'Don't give us that,' Kate said. 'You sent me that letter with the farmhouse coordinates. You knew Fomalhaut was there, and what he wanted to do with us. You delivered us to him, then waited to see what would happen. What would you have done if he'd killed us?'

Her pistol was on the table, within reach. For a moment I thought she might turn it on Bagby.

'She's right,' I said. 'He knew we were coming. They met us in the woods. You knew he'd intercept any messages going to Professor Faron's house. And when he saw that you'd directed us right to him, he could see that you were watching him, too. He knew you were out here all along, his soldiers had been out searching the woods for you. What if they'd killed you then overpowered Kate and me before we'd realised what was going on?'

'All valid points,' Bagby said. 'But I can't apologise. We were watching them watching us the entire time. More importantly, we were watching *you* the entire time. Nothing would have happened. Not with Stohl's shooting skills. You saw that yourself; he saved your life just now at the top of the stairs, didn't he? Look, I'm sorry we couldn't tell you more. Either of you,' he said. 'But we weren't even certain Fomalhaut was behind it all until he sent Koch after you. For the longest time I thought it was the uncle. So did the kid. That's why it had to be you, not Stohl, who stayed in the dark. He couldn't very well investigate his own family without giving the game away.'

I looked at Bagby, no longer sure how well the word 'partner' fitted our relationship.

'And what exactly have you been doing?' I asked. 'We thought you'd been abducted.'

'Pfft. I taught you better than that. Come on, you saw how I left the flat; all your favourite albums were intact. Don't tell me you missed that? As for what I've been doing, mostly just staying out of the way. Meeting people. Setting things in motion. Waiting for you two to arrive.'

'Setting what in motion?'

'Come on,' he said. 'You know what's going on. The bombings, the protests – the government are on the back foot and running scared. I know Ormsby is. The revolutionaries are rising again. It's only a matter of time before the government responds, starts cracking down and locking people up. That'll be all we need to bring all of the revolutionary groups together under one flag – to mobilise the people, make them see what a crock of crooks the government is. Then we'll finally have the society we deserve. The one we fought for fifteen years ago.' He glanced at Kate. 'The one that, in one way or another, claimed some of the bravest people I ever knew.'

'The bombings were to provoke the government into a response? To make them crack down on innocent people?' I asked, the bitter taste of disgust in my mouth.

'That's right,' Bagby said. 'Prod the snake and it'll show you its fangs. That's what the people needed to encourage them to wake up. Before you give me a lecture, know that

Stohl and I had nothing to do with any bombings. There are a hundred different revolutionary groups across the country, tens of thousands of people waiting to strike. Some are more militant than others. Blame them.'

It was the same line Fomalhaut had spun me. Hearing it come from Bagby's mouth instead didn't make it any more palatable. Or believable.

'Ever since I "disappeared", I've been travelling around the country, trying to unite the groups together into one cohesive force,' he continued. 'The old revolutionary networks are still in place and our numbers have been bolstered by a new generation waiting to strike. They're ready to act. They just need a leader.'

'And that's you?' I asked.

Bagby looked surprised. 'God, no. Too much responsibility. Leave the groups to argue about that. My job is just to get them all in the same room, talking to each other about how to carry off a productive coup, instead of spending all their time blowing up shopping centres in Guildford. It took some doing, I can tell you that. Meanwhile, Stohl's been keeping an eye on you two and reporting back to me when he could. It was him who found Koch's body in your apartment. He made contact with me straight away, then hightailed it out here so that we could be ready by the time you arrived.'

'How is this any different to what Fomalhaut wants?' Kate cut in. 'He talked the same shite, about bringing together revolutionary factions for a better tomorrow. How do we know which of you to trust?'

'Because he and I,' Bagby said, pointing at me, 'have been working together for fifteen years. There's no one I trust more than him. And he, me.'

I wasn't quite ready to endorse this.

'Fix your friendship later,' Kate said. 'And answer my question.'

Bagby rubbed at his cheeks in exasperation. 'Think about it; Fomalhaut is essentially a tech mogul. He's been labouring under Elliot Wallace for decades with Wallace taking all the credit. Now Fomalhaut wants what he thinks he's earned: power. Not just being able to cosy up to the government and influence policy like Wallace can, but the ability to make his own policies, run this country as he sees fit. He's the only one with the know-how to use the virus in Kate's blood. If he can encourage a revolution to mask what he's really up to, Fomalhaut can use the virus to take out all of his opponents while the country is in chaos, emerging victorious and unstoppable once it's all over.'

'Why not just take over tomorrow? Why waste time stringing these ex-soldiers along?' I asked.

'Because even though he controls enough of the country's infrastructure that he could probably shut it all down and seize power tomorrow, it'll still help to have soldiers loyal to him – boots on the street and all that,' Bagby said. 'The human soldier can still hold his own against drones when it comes to finding and torturing undesirables. That group he has at the farm house are a fraction – a *fraction* – of the people ready to rise up and demand change. They've just chosen the wrong messiah. Whether through prosthetic limbs requiring constant and expensive updates or Wellness Pill addiction, Fomalhaut has his teeth in them, and the only way for them to survive is to serve him, help him achieve his ends. The others want real change, not just the illusion of it. They're ready to succeed where we failed before.'

'And what about me?' Kate asked. She banged a hand on the table. A food can fell off and came to rest at Bagby's feet. 'Is it really true that I'm carrying some sort of virus in my blood? Or is that old man just delusional?'

Bagby looked down at the can then back up at Kate. 'I wish it wasn't true,' he said. 'But it is. Fomalhaut thinks this virus is the quickest way to wipe out those who stand in his way – including the real revolutionaries. But the virus was meant as a cure. I knew your mother and father. And your real father, too, for all that he matters. Rachael and Edward Faron, though, they loved you. Ted wouldn't have done it unless he thought there was no other option. He'd chanced upon something he thought could help people, but others wanted to use it to cause hurt. He thought the only way to ensure that it survived, that no more questions would be asked, was to... to do what he did, leaving the only sample of the virus in the safest hands he knew; yours.'

'He could have fucking told me about it,' Kate said. 'He could have said goodbye. He just vanished. One morning he was in our lives, and then he wasn't.' She closed her eyes and exhaled slowly. 'He didn't have to leave us like that. My mother... me. Now my brother is gone, too,' she said. 'These people don't have the right to do that...'

'They don't,' Bagby said. 'Your brother was supposed to be in safe hands. Jennings and I... we both have to share the blame for what happened to Caleb. But Jennings never knew about the virus. He just wanted to protect you both from being used as political weapons – as blackmail tools against your real father. In the end, I was too late to help your brother, and I'm sorry for that Kate, I really am.'

Kate crossed to the window and leaned her head against the dirty glass. Outside the sun was sending its first rays out into the day. 'You did what you could,' she said after a minute. 'You didn't take him away. Or my mother.'

'I could have done more,' Bagby said, quietly. 'But now

we have a chance to strike back. I was there alongside your mother and father when this happened before and I've lived with the guilt of our failure for fifteen years. This is my last chance to do something meaningful but this could change your future for the better. It will change the *country* for the better. For good this time.' He shook his head. 'No more corruption, ethnic segregation, restrictions of personal freedoms. No more perpetual war. No more policemen beating young boys to death in tunnels.'

His eyes found mine. 'Partner, it's now or never.'

'I can't just let this happen,' I said. 'Whatever the reason behind it, a revolution means more dead bodies on the streets. On both sides. I agree that things are far from ideal but think of what happened before. Remember the boy in the tunnel, Bagby! Fomalhaut justifies the bombing campaigns as necessary – collateral damage – but that can't be who we are! There has to be a better way. It didn't work before,' I said. 'They sold us a lie, then essentially told us to shut up and get on with things, even as everything slid back to how it had been before the Reformation. Worse than it had been. All of those people died for nothing. Why the hell would it work now? The fact is, people don't want change, they want things to go on as they always have. If they allow themselves to believe some politician, or TV presenter, cares about how they feel every now and then – really sees into their soul and empathises with their daily struggle – well, that's all the revolution they need. What does the average person have to gain from revolution when the last one changed so little and cost so much? We have to arrest these people and campaign for change through the proper channels. And we have to arrest Fomalhaut, too.'

Bagby kicked the can by his foot. It shot away and hit the wall with a bang. 'Don't be so narrow-sighted! You know we'd

avoid killing if we could. You saw what I did in that tunnel…
But this isn't about you or me living with a clean conscience;
it's about shouldering the burden of revolution so that the next
generation, and the one after that, and the one after that, don't
have to. And besides, have you forgotten that we've been at
war for five decades? Are you saying you don't mind men
dying, just as long as the fighting is in foreign fields and it's
only on the news when we win?'

'Of course I'm not. I just think there has to be an easier way.
We go back to London, arrest Fomalhaut, expose what he's
done, and force real, political, reform.'

Bagby spat. 'As for Fomalhaut, he's the very embodiment
of everything we're fighting to stop: rich, corrupt, a murderer
without a conscience or morals. He deserves to die. It's the only
way.' The fury dropped form his voice. He seemed suddenly
worn out. 'Partner, please forgive me if I sound patronising,
but over a long career – much longer than yours – I have come
to believe that, as the Bard said, like life, justice is "*a tale told
by an idiot, full of sound and fury; signifying nothing*,"' he said.
'What we're doing *will* bring about political reform. It's already
begun. Now we have the numbers to do it. There needn't even
be *any* conflict. We're prepared to do this peacefully, so long
as the government is. So long as they recognise the will of the
people.'

'But that's –' I began, exasperated.

'Shut up!' Kate yelled. Bagby and I started then fell silent.
'He's right,' she said. 'Things have to change. None of us can
go on living like this.'

'Then join us, Kate,' Bagby said. 'People will follow you
because you're RZ's daughter. And the virus in your blood will
make you an invaluable weapon. We'd never use it, but just
the threat of it would make the government stop and listen.

This revolution is going to happen, and we all want it to be as bloodless as possible. The government won't want to fight if they know you're on our side, and what you have in you. We could save thousands of lives.'

'So I'm a walking biological bomb?' Kate asked. 'You're saying, threaten them with me and it will all be over quickly?'

'Bagby, are you mad?' I asked. 'Do you know how many government departments and private organisations there are that would want to keep her locked up in a laboratory for what's in her blood? Wallace might not be involved in Fomalhaut's plans, but regardless, Vangelis will be the least of it!'

'It isn't your decision,' Kate replied. 'It isn't a decision for either of you. Or Fomalhaut. Or anyone else. My father did this to me, and now more men are arguing over how to use me. I'm not a pawn in your games. I'm a person. I'm not this virus. I'm me. And I'll decide what should be done.'

I said nothing, feeling ashamed.

Bagby turned away. He stared quietly out of the window. His lips moved as he mumbled, debating back and forth with himself.

'I'll help you, but under my own conditions,' Kate said eventually. 'Something has to change, I agree. I agree with every fibre of my being. And if change means holding those who killed my family to account, then all the better. I don't like it, but I am RZ's daughter. His last surviving child. You say the revolutionaries will respect that. Well, if that helps bring everyone together, then so be it. I'll do it. I'll help you bring the revolutionaries together, on condition that this is a peaceful revolution. That no one else dies.'

'It could work,' Bagby said. 'She might be able to bring the groups together. Stop the violence, on both sides.'

I shot a warning look at him.

'What, you think I'd let her come to harm?' he said. 'After what her mother meant to me? Kate's right, this could be a way to end things peacefully.' His shoulders drooped and his face fell. For a moment he looked like an old man, lost in the woods. 'I want to fight, partner,' he said. 'But I've had enough of killing.'

'The other condition is that no one finds out about this virus. You honestly think that some revolutionary won't want to weaponise me? They're blowing up shopping centres, for god's sake. No, if you want my help, that part remains a secret. I'll join you, but I won't be a pawn. I'll be a leader, like my mother was. And I'll help make sure this revolution actually works.'

Bagby was watching her with tears in his eyes. 'It's a deal,' he said.

'Then let's get on with it,' Kate replied.

Before we could argue any more, before I could voice my objections, the door banged open and Stohl came in. 'Time to go.'

'We'll talk more,' Bagby said, touching my arm. 'We can't rush into this, Kate. But, for now, we should take our friend's advice. Otherwise, should Fomalhaut find us, none of us will live to see this revolution through.'

He bent to retrieve a bag from the floor and I saw pain jolt through the wires of his face.

So did Kate. 'You've been shot…'

He straightened up and held a hand to his shoulder. 'Flesh wound.' He wiped his bloody hand on his trousers. 'Now, let's get going.'

'Hang on, let me,' Kate said.

Stohl and I gathered up their bags while she wrapped a length of bandage around Bagby's shoulder.

'Fomalhaut will be heading back to London now that his cover out here is blown,' Stohl said to me as we loaded up the van. 'He'll hole up at the Vangelis headquarters and re-group from there. He doesn't know I'm involved in this yet; I can get in close and take him out.'

'We'll come back with you,' I said. 'It isn't safe for any of us out here. At least in the city we stand a chance of stopping him. After that I'll worry about the revolution. But for now, stopping Fomalhaut is the priority. You get me close to him and we'll arrest him, together. I'm sorry, but I'm still not prepared to kill an old man – or anyone for that matter – no matter what they've done.'

Stohl's eyebrow twitched – his only tell. 'OK,' he said, 'Have it your way. But if that doesn't work I'll do what has to be done.'

'It's me he wants, not you two,' Kate said as she tightened Bagby's bandage. 'Let me go on my own. He killed Caleb... my mother and father. I can do it. I can kill him.'

'You don't mean that,' I said. 'You aren't a killer, Kate. It's something you can't come back from. It will ruin your life.'

Kate smiled at me as if I was a child about to learn that the world wasn't quite what I thought it was. 'I lied to you in the car on the way down here,' she said. 'My life is already ruined. But at least I have a chance to decide what happens next.'

'He's right, Kate,' Stohl said. 'It's too dangerous. We stand a better chance of stopping Fomalhaut if we come at this from different angles. That way we'll have more than one chance to do what we need to. I'll return to my unit and try to get Ormsby on board. Give me twenty four hours to work on him. I'll fill him in on the situation – only him – and he'll help us, I'm sure. You saw how he wanted to help Bagby, back at the club. If I can send the right people off into the countryside looking for bad guys, instead of whispering in Ormsby's ear, Ormsby should be receptive to some common sense. Then who knows, maybe Fomalhaut dies in a police raid. In the meantime, you two lie low.'

'OK,' I said. I had my doubts but thought it better to go along with Stohl's plan for the time being, get back to London *tout suite* and come up with a better plan while he was busy trying to convince Ormsby that the bogeyman was real.

'All agreed? Then let's get going,' Stohl said.

Kate had finished wrapping Bagby's shoulder. I helped him ease his jacket on.

'Round went through,' he said, trying to hide the fact that he was not, in fact, superhuman.

I caught his eyes. 'You'll be OK… For a brief minute back there, I really thought you'd kicked the bucket,' I said, to cheer him up.

'Oh no,' he replied. 'Not me.' He grasped my arm. 'It's good to see you again, partner. I'm sorry I had to leave you in the dark.'

'You can work on your apology on the way back to London.'

Bagby shook his head. 'Not I; I can't go too far with a clipped wing. Besides, every copper in the big smoke is looking for me. I'll draw too much attention. If they get you, you can just claim you got caught up trying to help out your old and foolish partner. But I've been swimming out of my depth for years. They've been watching and waiting for me to flounder all along.' He sighed. 'What can you do?'

'We can help you,' Kate said.

'No,' Bagby shook his head. 'I'll help you. Like I should have helped Caleb. There's a large group, up the coast a few hours north from here. If I can get through to them we'll have a decent sized force to come and back you up. Or finish the job if you don't make it. If I can't get through to them I can at least cause some trouble for the rest of Fomalhaut's men out here. I may not have Stohl's sharpshooter credentials but I won't make it pleasant for them.'

'Bagby…' I began.

'Don't worry about me, partner,' he said with a wink. 'I might just make it.' He took my hand and squeezed it. 'I'll see you soon, back in the capital.'

He clasped my wrist and in his eyes I saw the sunlight casting shadows among the tree stumps, dark lines crisscrossing the hillside.

'I killed someone,' I said, feeling a sudden rush of bereavement. 'Two people. Koch and a boy back at the farmhouse. They were going to kill me, but…'

'You had to… But it's not a bad thing to hold onto a little bit of what came before,' Bagby said quietly. 'This isn't the end. Remember that. No matter what they throw at you, you'll always come out the other side.'

He let go of my hand.

'Take care of her,' Bagby said. 'She's the future.'

'We will,' Stohl replied as he climbed into the van. 'It's been a pleasure fighting alongside you, sir. Now, go find the others. Tell them we're waiting. Tell them the time for action has arrived.'

Bagby nodded. He embraced Kate. Her shoulders stiffened, then softened. I thought I heard her say something like, 'Thanks for trying,' before they broke apart.

She and I climbed into the back of the van. Stohl started the engine and we set off along the wooded trail, leaving Bagby and the little cabin behind.

28

Home Again

We split into two cars, requisitioned from the car park of a National Trust site on the edge of the forest; an old 2035 BMW for Stohl, a banged-up Vauxhall for Kate and myself. I prayed it was in better condition than our last stolen car, but we didn't really have a choice; it was this or nothing.

As we drove south, Bagby hung at the periphery of my thoughts; wherever he headed now he was travelling into an uncertain and violent future. Then again, we all were. Whether Bagby made it or not, the old order was fading and it was either up to us or Fomalhaut to decide what happened next.

'You don't have to go through with this, you know,' I said to Kate. 'Joining the revolution. It'll happen with or without you.'

'I want to join them,' Kate said. 'Not just because I really think I can save lives. Because I'm angry. At everything. I have all of this fury boiling up inside me, and I'm going to use it for good. You can't stop that. I can't just sit this out. None of us can.'

The Professor would have been proud, I thought. And Kate was right, it wasn't up to me or anyone else to try and protect her. I left her to her thoughts and went back to mine as we followed the dark and empty motorway towards the capital. Grey clouds unfurled around us, closing off the north in a shroud that sank down to meet the asphalt like a veil, dim patches of sunlight burning through. The roads were deserted; even the sparse traffic we had encountered on the way up had disappeared.

'Something's happening,' I said. 'The roads are too quiet… '

'A curfew?'

'Maybe. Or maybe some sort of Executive Order. The government closing the roads… they've done it before but only in exceptional circumstances.'

'Our trip to the country can't have made that much of a splash, surely?'

'Let's see.' I tried the radio but all channels were either adverts or wellness workouts on loop. 'No news.'

'Is good news?' Kate finished, dryly.

'Probably not in this instance.'

A helicopter flew overhead as we neared the outskirts of the city.

'Maybe Bagby's new pals have struck sooner than he anticipated,' Kate said, peering up at the helicopter through her window.

I thought for a moment. Fomalhaut had the technical ability to shut down the country's power supply, but no actual power to order a shutdown of the roads. This had to have come from the Prime Minister's office. I tried to remember the protocol. A significant attack in London was enough to implement a nation-wide lockdown.

We didn't have to wait long before we found out more. A police checkpoint had been set up along the slip-road leading to the North Circular Road, the red rubies of taillights from the few cars there guiding us in. We joined the back of the queue.

'We should have gone to Greys… to the military camps. We might have been able to get on to a supply vessel coming up the river… we could have said we were journalists from the *Mail*, supporting the war effort…' I said, thinking out loud.

'Well, we didn't, and now we're here,' Kate said. 'At least it's not raining,' she added sarcastically.

A pair of police officers were working their way along the line of cars, rain running from their caps.

'Flash your badge,' Kate suggested. 'Tell them I'm the leader of the resistance. Say you've arrested me and you're bringing me in.'

'Very funny. We'll both be shot.'

The officers drew nearer. I reached for my badge out of habit, but of course it wasn't there. And of course, in our muddied and torn country garments we looked every inch the dubious out-of-towners.

The butt of a torch tapped against the window. The shape of a police officer was visible through the rain. I wound the window down. The officer peered into the car. The wearable OU device on her chest would be recording everything. I tried to ignore the possibility that Fomalhaut could have hacked into the system and installed some advanced form of facial-recognition software programmed to send word to him whenever Kate and I reared our heads. But it was too late to worry about that now; we just had to keep moving.

The officer opened her mouth to speak then whipped her head away and sneezed violently. Once, twice. She swore, coughed, then turned back to us.

'Apologies.' Rain was running down her forehead and her

eyes were heavy with flu; budget cuts had eaten into junior officers' Wellness Pills allowance.

She peered into the car again then said, 'Be on your way,' and waved us through, evidently wishing to get her job done and get out of the rain as quickly as possible.

I re-started the engine and we crept forward, into the capital. As we moved away, I noticed Kate's hand formed a bulge in her pocket, holding what could only have been a pistol. We were in dire straits, but I hoped that neither of us had the inclination nor the nerve to shoot a police officer in cold blood. The situation was not yet that desperate.

I tried the radio again as we wound through North London. The evening news was just beginning. Since we had left there had been another bombing, just a few hours ago, in Stoke Newington, a shooting in Highgate, and a protest had turned violent outside Downing Street. The exact death toll hadn't been released but the newsreader called these events a 'significant attack on our liberties and way of life.' The Prime Minister promised 'real and resounding retribution,' her voice quivering with rapt fury. The united government, she said, would no longer stand for this sort of thing and the culprits should prepare to face her wrath and that of every decent soul in the nation. Once again, firing lines were being drawn outside Parliament. That explained the curfew.

'It's beginning again,' Kate said, looking out of the window as we navigated the near-empty streets, the odd car speeding past us on its way to somewhere else, others hurriedly parked and abandoned by the side of the road. 'They think they can stop this revolution before it happens, don't they?'

I didn't answer. Black LDNPD vans were parked around Marble Arch. Brendan's men cradled automatic rifles and stared after the car as we crept past.

'Wherever we're going we'd better get there soon,' Kate said.

Further along the road a police officer had a middle-aged woman bent over a bench as he fitted his cuffs. Next to them a toddler cried in its pram. Elsewhere, a group of foreign exchange students were being made to empty out their pockets by a small military squadron as its commanding officer leaned back against her armoured car, smoking a vape pen. A row of youths had been lined up against a wall outside a kebab shop by Victoria Station, officers pointing pistols at them.

'This is insanity,' Kate said. 'This is how it all started before. Paranoia. Brutality.'

I had nothing to add. Last time scenes like this had been seen on the streets of the capital, I was one of the men doing the searching.

'Look,' Kate said, pointing across the car as another helicopter buzzed low over the Thames following the path of the river, kicking up white foam in its wake. 'Stohl was right; we should deal with Fomalhaut while the police are distracted. No one will be looking for us with all of this going on.'

'Getting rid of Fomalhaut won't stop this,' I said. 'For now, we need to find a safe place to hide.'

We left the car outside the tube entrance and took the train three stops in the wrong direction before changing and coming back the other way, changing again to another line after five stops. Finally, we got off a stop early and ran the rest of the way in the rain. If they were looking for us, they'd see us. There was no way around that, but our convoluted trail would keep them busy for a while. We crossed the road. The rain was giving up and the streets were shining. I led us down the side of a DIY wholesalers. We skirted a vacant yard behind it, overgrown with dead grass. The wall of the International Zone rose up before us, a black, dull barrier of painted brick.

A rusted-out van stood in the corner of the yard. Behind it, a mouldy mattress leaned against the wall.

'Give me a hand with this,' I said.

Kate grabbed the mattress and together we heaved it out of the way and let it fall to the ground, revealing a strip of blue tarp hung over a section of wall. I pulled the tarp aside, uncovering the person-sized hole in the bricks.

'Smugglers' route,' I said. 'Bagby showed me it. A small detail like the fact that he's supposed to be upholding the law couldn't keep my partner from his contraband. After you.'

Kate ducked and crawled through. I followed, letting the tarp fall into place behind us. We emerged behind a disused newsstand, road-soaked posters advertising ancient editions of *The Spectator* and *The Guardian* peeling from its walls. The street was a parade of dark and silent facades.

'Where now?' Kate asked.

'Now, we find a friend. Follow me and stay in the shadows. Don't talk to anyone, and we should be all right.'

Kate nodded, keeping her hand in her pocket. 'Lead the way.'

There was roughly a mile between where we were and Sid's bookshop. It would have been a difficult journey at the best of times but now smoke was rising over the International Zone, the glow of fires climbing the sides of its buildings. Groups gathered on street corners, sharing news of bombings and police activity in a mish-mash of animated accents. Kate and I kept to ourselves.

Kate's hand touched my chest, stopping me. 'Look.'

She motioned across the street. A squadron of uniformed officers were dragging a family – an old woman, an old man, a man of about thirty and three children of varying ages – out into the street, the door to their house hanging open. A cry came from a second storey window, then a cabinet toppled and crashed to the ground, exploding into broken wood and loose sheets of paper. One of the officers went over to the mess and picked up a book from among the debris. He held it up to his colleagues. I couldn't hear what he was saying, but I didn't need to. With a nod, the entire family was led into the back of a van, the door slammed shut behind them. That this family had anything to do with bombs or shootings was laughable. That this was plain for everyone to see didn't seem to deter the police officers.

'Keep moving,' I said.

Three streets later we came across a crowd chanting disparate slogans in the middle of a grass square. Some held broken chair legs aloft, some cricket bats or baseball bats. A woman climbed up onto a lamppost, shouted something and then the crowd cheered as one and followed her off into the streets. Kate hung back, staring after the group as though torn between our task, and following along on whatever futile protest they were involved in.

'We should be with them now. We should be going after Fomalhaut, not hiding.'

'Kate,' I hissed. 'We're close. Let's keep going.'

Headlights shone in the street behind her accompanied by the rumble of a truck engine.

'Come on, Kate.'

She hesitated, glanced back at the approaching LDNPD truck, then swore and followed after me. 'Fine, lead the way.'

The lights went out two streets later. It wasn't citywide; we could see the skyscrapers of Tower Hamlets glowing in the distance. It was only the International Zone that was plunged into darkness, like a black hole in the middle of London.

'Perfect timing,' Kate said.

'We're nearly there. It's here.' We'd reached the bookshop.

Sid emerged from the door, dressed in an overly long grey

trench-coat that collected around her shoes. Beneath it I could see at least two other coats – no doubt high mark-up units from her inventory of illegal garments. Her back was hunched under the weight of two suitcases. The two security guards I'd encountered before lumbered after her, carrying torches and their own large suitcases.

'If it isn't my favourite police officer,' she said. 'And dressed so… *country chic*.'

'Sid. A word.'

She put the suitcases down and stretched her neck. It cracked loudly. Sid winced. 'All right. But hurry up, we're going on a trip.'

'Go wait over there,' she added to the two bodyguards.

I waited until they were out of earshot before I made my request. 'Sid, we need somewhere to stay. Somewhere out of the way.'

She glanced at Kate. 'Romantic getaway is it? I think I might have some garments you can borrow if you want to smarten up a bit, darling. No charge. Any friend of his is a friend of mine. And I won't be needing them back, anyway.'

'I'm fine, thanks,' Kate replied dryly.

Sid ignored her. She turned to me and sighed. 'It's gone too far this time. What happened to the common decency of warning crooks before a raid?'

'Look, Sid,' I cut in, 'we need to get off the streets for a few days, it's complicated –'

'They think you killed your boss and that you're tied up in a new revolution,' Sid said. 'I hear things,' she explained for Kate's benefit. She shrugged. 'We've all been there.' She pulled a scrap of paper from her pocket. 'Pen?' She found one herself while Kate and I searched our own pockets. 'Go to this address. The building is empty. You'll be alone. Just for a few days, mind. Actually, fuck it, move in there for all I care.'

'Thanks, Sid,' I said, taking the piece of paper. 'I owe you one, when this is all over.'

'Not me,' she said, picking up her cases again. 'I'm leaving. The Capital's too heavy. It's a life by the sea for Sid. Suntan and sardines. Margate. Brighton, perhaps.'

'Well, good luck, then.'

'You too,' she said. She turned to Kate. 'And don't pay attention to me; you look stunning.'

It was Kate's turn to sigh.

'We didn't see each other, OK?' Sid asked.

I nodded.

She turned to Kate and raised an eyebrow questioningly. 'OK?'

'Fine by me,' Kate replied.

'Oh, and by the way,' Sid said, turning to me, 'You know your "Bad Taste" laws make no fucking sense, right?'

I nodded, but Sid was already limping away towards her waiting heavies.

The address was the last rundown terraced house in a long row by Earl's Court. The white paint had long since started to peel and rain-streaked damp marked the windows as if they were crying. The front door was open. Ours was the top floor flat. By the time we'd climbed the stairs up there I was too exhausted to worry that the flat door was already open.

'Wait here.'

I left Kate on the landing and went inside to survey the rooms. The lights flickered back on as I entered, went out again, then returned. There were two bedrooms with their thin curtains drawn, yellow streetlights throbbing outside. A small bathroom, a kitchenette and the hallway completed the lodgings. 'It's OK; it's empty,' I called.

Kate and I had been awake for over twenty-four hours, running on adrenaline. Now exhaustion tugged at my bones. My clothes were starting to smell, and my body felt like someone had pulled it up out of the ground. I turned on the spluttering kitchen tap and splashed freezing water over my face. My hands were a mess of scratches and cuts. Kate's would likely be in the same state.

'Glass of water?' I called.

'No,' Kate answered, her voice behind me in the room.

I turned around in surprise. She stood in the doorway, her features drenched in shadow.

'You made me jump,' I said. 'This place seems good enough. We'll be OK here for a few days. Until we come up with a plan.'

'I'm sorry,' she said, reaching into her pocket. 'I already have; I've earned the right to kill him. And I want my revenge.'

She shot me once in the stomach then turned and left as the lights went out again.

29

The Bridge

It was still dark when I woke up. Somehow, the stars had slipped through a crack in the window and were dancing overhead as waves crashed against the building. The sound was quiet and calming and even though I knew that the water would soon rise and wash me away I was too comfortable lying there in that warm pool to move. Instead, I flipped over onto my stomach and closed my eyes again and felt the stars burning into me as they dropped from the sky.

When I woke up a second time it was light. I was alone, lying on the floor. Now the stars were fizzing and searing inside of me. It came back to me then, how Kate had pulled the small Walther from her pocket and shot me through the stomach. We had argued about killing Fomalhaut. Of course that was it. I was the straight-edge policeman standing between her and retribution for the death of a brother she never knew and a mother that was almost her entire world. I might have done the same thing in her place.

I rolled over onto my back. Something not quite dry had

stuck my shirt to the floor. As it tore away from my skin I felt white flashes of pain shudder inside my stomach, jumping from cell to cell like sparks of dancing electricity. It was all I could do to stay conscious. I studied every inch of the bare lightbulb hanging from the ceiling and hoped for an epiphany. After a while, when no epiphany came, I pushed myself up onto my knees and crawled out into the hallway. There, on the mat by the front door was a crumpled piece of paper. I picked it up and smoothed out the pages with stiff fingers. Eyes swimming I read: '*Ormsby will meet you at Albert Bridge at midnight. You're in good hands – Stohl.*'

The writing was untidy and rushed, and not Stohl's own. So, he had known I'd go to Sid and managed to get word to me that way. Perhaps Sid had sent a runner as she prepared to leave the city. The message must have arrived sometime in the night, while I was out cold. I held on to the note and slowly pulled myself up against the doorframe. Dreams of water came back to me. My head throbbed and my mouth felt hot and sour. My stomach felt like it had been kicked by a horse with a shotgun attached to its hoof. I needed a doctor, but until help materialised water would have to do. I staggered back into the kitchen, a sweaty hand steadying me against the wall. The sink was a few hundred metres away. The lightbulb was still hanging overhead and, as I wobbled across the room, the epiphany finally arrived. It came in the form of the lights crashing out around me as I realised I'd done too much too soon.

It was dark again when I came to. The pain in my stomach had sunk down to a sharp, persistent throb that spread through my veins whenever I tried something ambitious, like breathing. Sitting up, I noticed a small kitchen clock on the counter. It read: 22:58. There was still time to meet Ormsby on the bridge, if I hurried.

I grabbed the edge of the sink, then hauled myself up. The bullet wound tugged at my skin but the dried blood seemed to hold me together. With difficulty and much pain, I pulled off my shirt. The bullet hole was in my lower left side. The little finger-sized hole on the other side was almost identically lined up, meaning the bullet had gone all the way through. The small calibre meant that there was little chance of the bullet breaking up inside me and there was no bone down there to stop it. Provided I was treated soon, it wouldn't kill me, but it would be painful. I washed the wound with handfuls of cold water from the sink. The kitchen drawers yielded an old roll of masking tape. I wound this round and round my middle, watery blood trickling down my side as I bit off the end. The pain was every bit as torturous as I'd expected. A 35cl bottle of gin had been left in a drawer. It was fourteen years out of date. I'd poured half of it over the wound and drank the rest before I realised it was alcohol-free Ginsynth, and useless. Then, I put my clothes back on and headed outside, down the stairs and out into the streets where everything remained quiet and empty.

I reached Albert Bridge just after midnight. There were few cars on the roads and none at all on the bridge. The lights – like fairy lights – shone overhead, fuzzy against the night. To my left and right was the murky blackness of the Thames. I took my hands out of my pockets as I neared the middle of the bridge, showing whoever was certainly watching that I was unarmed and ready to negotiate. Ormsby was waiting for me, leaning on the railings and peering down at the water as though he'd just happened to pause there on his evening's stroll. I stopped a few feet short, keeping some distance between us.

'Not even that late,' Ormsby said. 'You get around well for a wanted man.'

'I try my best.'

Ormsby turned to face me. He looked fed up, as though even the sight of the river below had bored him. Or he had other things on his mind. He loomed out of the darkness like Harry Lime, dressed in a long black coat buttoned up to the throat and a black trilby rested low on his head. He pulled his leather gloves off one by one and slipped them into his pocket.

'Stohl has filled me in,' he began. 'It all sounds reasonable enough. We know you had nothing to do with what happened to DSU Mercer. And that man Albert Koch... well no one is going to miss him. As far as I'm concerned, you're in the clear. There are, however, a few things I'd like to clear up about your partner. Stohl says he drew you out to the countryside but once you arrived there DCI Bagby was nowhere to be found. Now, I wonder why he'd do that? Why don't you and I go back and discuss this at the station? I want to get this whole episode squared away. Plus, it's cold out here.'

Usually, I would have credited Ormsby with a more inventive, less direct ploy to get me back to the station but the hour was late and there were bombers abroad, after all. Better to get this business dealt with quickly, and for good. It was inevitable, of course, that he would try to take me in – especially as I was in no condition to run. Before that happened I judged I had ninety seconds or less to convince him that Fomalhaut was the real enemy, not myself or Bagby.

'If Stohl told you everything, then you know that we have to arrest Cadmus Fomalhaut. Koch worked for him. They're after Kate Faron. They killed the wrong sibling, thinking Caleb had the virus in his blood. We have to make sure they can't hurt anyone else. Tonight. Before it's too late.'

'Ah yes, Cadmus Fomalhaut,' Ormsby said. 'Stohl fancies him the leader of the new revolution. Do you agree?'

'Forget the revolution,' I said. 'Fomalhaut isn't interested in any revolution. It's just a ploy, a distraction. He wants to be in control, that's all, and thinks this virus is the way to get it. The revolution doesn't matter compared to that. Fomalhaut could kill millions.'

Ormsby took off his hat. He smiled quickly, the smile disappearing as he turned to look out over the river again. 'And where is the girl now?'

'Safe.' It wasn't a lie; the pain in my side proved that Kate could look after herself.

'Either you don't trust me and decided to leave her at home – which is reasonable, I suppose under the circumstances – or, she's responsible for that wound you're trying to disguise and the truth is that you're not quite sure where she is.' Ormsby smiled again, grimly and without pleasure. 'If you were me, which would you believe?'

'It doesn't matter where she is,' I said, feeling the tape pulling at my middle. I took a step towards Ormsby then stopped, conscious that there were gun barrels poised somewhere nearby, waiting for an excuse to put me out of my misery. 'Fomalhaut is the one we have to focus on.'

Ormsby put his hat back on. It may have been the shadow that fell across his face, but he looked suddenly exhausted. 'And what do you expect me to do?' he asked. He lowered his voice. 'There are processes that have to be followed. Other than the word of a police officer wanted in connection with a murder, what actual evidence do we have? Where are the witnesses? Where are the bodies with Fomalhaut bent over them, smoking gun in hand? I can't just go around arresting people like that on suspicion of a crime I'm not even sure they've committed, or ever will.' He slid his gloves back on, one hand at a time. 'No, I'm sorry,' he said. 'I trusted your wild theories once before and it almost cost me my career. It won't happen again.'

He raised a hand to his left ear, an obvious signal to whoever was waiting just off stage. In seconds the sky was filled with a whirring flock of police drones, their spotlights dissecting the inky blackness, gun barrels trained on the fugitive on the bridge.

'I'm sorry,' Ormsby said, meeting my eye. 'I really am.'

'So am I,' a voice said from behind me.

I turned to find Stohl standing there in a fresh suit, a pistol in hand, the dangerous end aimed at me.

'Put the cuffs on him, and take him to Station B,' Ormsby said, fatigue draining his voice of any enthusiasm. 'Call me when they've found something out.'

He turned away. The drones buzzed to one side to let him pass before falling back into place like a swarm of automated bees.

'I wish it didn't have to be this way, partner,' Stohl said as he put the cuffs on me, 'but some things just cannot be avoided.'

Four minutes later I found myself in the back of Stohl's car, heading south over the bridge and through Battersea. So, my new partner was rotten after all. Was this a triple bluff, or a quadruple bluff? I was losing count.

'Why?' I asked, trying to meet Stohl's eyes in the rear-view mirror, my handcuffed hands pulling my shoulders back painfully.

'Because Ormsby is right,' he said, his eyes on the road. 'We can't arrest Fomalhaut. What evidence do we have? I mean, *real* evidence? All we can do is monitor the situation. Besides, he won't have a chance to do anything while my uncle is there keeping an eye on him.' The car swung left down a street of Georgian houses. Rain spattered half-heartedly at the windshield. 'We have to put all of this aside,' he continued. 'Today's events have shown that there is now a real and pressing danger facing us all. Stopping Bagby and his revolutionary friends is priority. With your help we'll find them.'

'He trusted you,' I said. Then, with surprise, 'I trusted you.'

Stohl's eyebrows lifted, like a shrug. 'Then you were both fools. You've been around long enough to know that you should never trust anyone.'

He was right – Kate's going away present proved that, too. I had been caught off guard and unprepared and now here I was.

We drove in silence for a while, turning down streets I didn't recognise, through run-down areas that a police officer had no business being in. 'Where are we going? Where is this "Station B"? I've never heard of it.'

'It isn't a nice place,' Stohl said. 'But don't worry. I don't think your stay there will be very long.'

We took a left turn and a tunnel loomed out of the darkness ahead.

'I'd still like to know where we're going,' I said.

Stohl ignored me as the tunnel swallowed us.

'Bloody tunnel,' he said, slapping his hand against the Observation Unit on the dashboard. 'Always interfering with the video system.' He hit the box again, then gave it a thump with a clenched fist. The noise of wires unspooling told me the device was dead.

There was silence for a heartbeat then Stohl said quite calmly, 'We haven't much time. You're going to make your escape and lie low while I find Kate. You and I are going to put an end to whatever nonsense she's planning, then kill Fomalhaut.' He turned and looked back at me. If he registered my surprise he didn't show

277

it. 'Once we stop, you're going to get out of the car and take the first left. Then you're going to take the next two rights, and the third left. Knock on number 182. It's a friend. Someone who can look after that gunshot wound.'

Bagby had been right; my new partner had come through in the end after all.

'I – Thank you,' I said. 'But if you're looking for Kate I'm coming with you.'

'Well, you see, you're the one in handcuffs so it seems that you're not really in a position to tell me how things are going to go,' Stohl said. 'We're running out of time,' he continued, 'so I want you to listen carefully. This next part is very important; you're going to strangle me with the cuffs then I'm going to crash the car. Don't argue. We have to make this look real. You can get your hands out from under your back, can't you? Don't worry about pulling your wound open, you'll be fixed up again soon enough.'

We left the tunnel and sped out into the night. A park occupied the darkness to our right, a row of houses to the left.

'Do it now,' Stohl said.

I lay down on the back seat and pulled my wrists as far apart as the cuffs would allow. Already, I could feel the bullet wound reopening. I brought my knees up close to my chest and brought my hands forward, feeling like my shoulders were about to dislocate as I slid the cuffs up and over the bottom of my shoes. I held my cuffed hands out before me, my wrists bleeding.

'Strangle me. Now,' Stohl said.

I reached over the seat and looped the handcuff chain over Stohl's head, then pulled it back against his windpipe.

'Harder,' he gasped. 'Leave a mark.'

I thought of Koch attacking Caleb. I thought of Mercer lying broken in her home. I thought of Kate finding her mother dead. I pulled back on the cuffs, then Stohl was tapping at my arm. I let him go.

'Hold on,' he said, his voice rasping.

He grabbed the wheel and swung the car. We mounted the kerb and collided with the nearest tree. I shot forward then back onto my seat. Stohl went forward into the airbag and lay there unconscious. Dazed, I leaned forward and tilted his head to one side so that he could breathe. Then I took the handcuff key from his pocket. Freed, I got out of the car and ran around to him. I put my ear to his mouth. He was still breathing.

I left the car behind and limped as fast as I could in the direction Stohl had described. My legs moved of their own accord, bowing at odd angles as my body recalibrated itself post-crash. I had bitten my cheek and blood pooled in my mouth. Something like a broken rib stung every time I inhaled and my shirt was heavy with blood from my re-opened wound. If Stohl's 'friend' wasn't at home, I'd probably be dead before morning.

After taking the first of the two rights I slowed to a walk, holding on to the black iron railings of front gardens. I was sweating now and feeling as likely to keel over as to ever see this case through. Eventually, I made it to a miserable-looking house on a quiet street of miserable-looking houses with dreary palm trees in their front gardens. I double-checked the number then climbed the wide steps. I leaned my weight against the door and pressed the buzzer until it was ringing in my ears. A light went on inside then the door swung inwards. Unable to stand any longer I fell forward into a strong pair of hands.

'For goodness sake,' a voice said. Its owner shut the door and turned out the light. 'Do you want the whole street to see you arriving here in the middle of the night? Not only a fugitive, but also well on your way to bleeding to death?'

Even in the darkness I recognised the mortician, Kavinsky.

30

The Factory

I woke up on a tattered chaise longue with a drip in my arm, bandages wrapped tightly around my middle and wrist, electric lamplight suffusing the room in golden arcs of light. I propped myself up on an elbow, looking for Kate. It took me a moment to remember that she had left, and how she had left me. A clattering came from the corridor. The door banged open and Kavinsky entered, carrying a tray which he set down on the table beside me under the lamplight. The tray was patterned with yellow and brown flowers and looked old. On it were a roll of gauze and a syringe half-filled with a yellowish liquid.

Kavinsky sat down in a wicker-backed chair without greeting me. He was dressed in a dressing gown patterned with Japanese fish and looked utterly in despair.

'I thought you only dealt with the dead?' I said, although neither of us seemed in the mood for humour.

'Dead. Living,' he replied, his hand flittering by his chest like a moth. 'There's not much difference when it comes down to it, between taking people apart and putting them back together again.'

'I can see why you never became a doctor,' I said, trying to disguise my pain as I sat up. Kavinsky had dressed me in paisley pyjamas. A new outfit of trousers, a t-shirt and a jacket lay over a chair. 'Pass me those clothes, will you? Hurry.'

'Lie down,' Kavinsky said. 'The wound on your wrist was infected. Thank the heavens that you weren't awake when I pulled the bandage off. It wasn't pretty. It made a mess of my carpet.' He gestured at something on the floor but I didn't bother to look. In the gloom I doubted I would have been able to see anything anyway.

'Your stomach, however, will be fine. Now, it's time for an injection. Rabies. You never know.'

'I was shot, not bitten,' I said. 'Do it later, I'm leaving.'

'It will only take one second, and will only hurt a bit,' Kavinsky lied as he jabbed the needle into my stomach.

Afterwards, as I rubbed the small, bloody mark, I wondered how far Kavinsky's allegiance to Stohl went. 'I never took you for a revolutionary,' I said, easing my bruised body into the new clothes as quickly as I was able. 'Miserable and chronically unhappy, yes, but I didn't think it was bad enough to make you actually do something about it.'

He almost smiled as he rolled a cigarette with a steady, surgeon's precision. 'You forget my history. In my country we learned a long time ago that you cannot just sit by while the world goes to shit.'

It was a lesson I'd finally learned. My mother would have fought for change. Bagby and the Professor and Stohl and Kate and even Kavinsky were fighting. And so should I.

'Good, Stohl filled you in,' I said. I reached for the jacket. 'Come on, we have a woman to find and a mad scientist to arrest.'

Kavinsky nodded without urgency as he stubbed out the cigarette on his tray. 'I'm afraid your fight is over. You're too badly hurt to be of any use and, Stohl thinks, too invested in the girl. Even if you were well I'm not sure there's much that you could do...' he continued. 'It may be too late. You won't have heard, but after they found Stohl in the car they called an ambulance. The paramedics had the radio on and through his stupor, Stohl heard what it said, and what it said was that his uncle, that famous, guiding light of industry, a shining example of all that is good in this world, had died but thirty minutes previous of heart complications. They tried to revive him, of course, but he had suffered a total death experience. His nephew stopped the ambulance then and there, requisitioned a car, and headed off towards his uncle's offices. He fears, of course, that our friend Fomalhaut is behind his uncle's untimely passing. Either way, with Stohl's confirmed, lifelong commitment to the police force, Fomalhaut is now the de facto leader of the mighty technological behemoth that is Vangelis. In short, he is now free to do whatever he likes, without scrutiny from any employer, or indeed, the state.'

'When was this? How did you find out?'

'Stohl set off two hours ago, not long after you arrived here – which is exactly where Stohl told me to keep you, in fact.'

'And who went with him? Surely not Ormsby?'

Kavinsky laughed. 'No, of course not Orsmby. Stohl set off quite alone, and with the empty roads, he will have no doubt arrived there by now.' His eyes settled on the floor. 'No, Stohl is quite alone.'

'Then let's stop wasting time,' I said, guessing at what the mortician was getting at and wishing he would just come out and say it. 'The chief mortician is required to have a car, yes? It's down to us now, Kavinsky. Don't just sit there. You've stitched me up and I'm grateful, but this isn't over yet, for either of us.'

'Stohl needs us, yes?' Kazinsky said, his voice heavy with theatrical fatigue. 'If he isn't dead already.'

I pulled on my boots and crossed to the door. 'Jesus Christ; just give me the keys, I'll go on my own.'

'Wait, wait. There's no need for that,' Kavinsky said, standing up. 'We'll go together. Maybe I can make the journey easier. If there is a body at Vangelis it makes sense for the chief mortician to be in attendance, no? *It's the niceties that make the difference, fate gives us the hand, and we play the cards,* after all,' he quoted. 'You can't argue with Schopenhauer.'

Kavinsky was right. The journey out of the city was easy. With me rolling about in the boot, gripping my stomach to stop my insides falling out, and Kavinsky working his charm on the checkpoint officers, we made it past the barricades with ease. With the city behind us, Kavinksy stopped as soon as he dared to let me out and back into the passenger seat. Then, it was a long and hurried drive through dark country roads, the clock on the dashboard blinking 02:46, the car closing every second on what could potentially be the end of us both. Halfway there, we came to a gridlocked queue of cars. We passed by in the unobstructed middle lane, wondering why the drivers didn't do the same. But the cars were empty. The row of unmanned traffic cones and blinking orange lights at the head of the queue offered no clues as to where the drivers had gone. Later still, we passed a military convoy travelling in the other direction, towards London.

Then, we were turning off the main road, following the track through the pine woods towards Vangelis.

The gate stood open.

I turned to Kavinsky. 'Last chance to turn back.'

'Not on your life.'

We advanced along the driveway. In the darkness, the building had lost some of its lustre, appearing like a lump of coal dropped in the middle of the forest. Blueish spotlights came on as we neared and there, alone in the centre of the carpark, was a single empty car. It seemed that following the sudden demise of its CEO all Vangelis employees had been sent home. I wondered if Kate had managed to make her way out here, and hoped she hadn't.

'Nobody's home,' Kavinsky said, shutting off the car.

'Somebody's home. That must be Stohl's car. And he hasn't come out again.'

'So, we go in and find him?' Kazinsky asked, apprehension replacing his usual coldness.

'No,' I said. 'You wait here. Get hold of Ormsby if I'm not back in thirty minutes. Then, if I were you I'd get out of here. Ormsby won't be pleased when he finds out that you helped me.'

'You mean how you kidnapped me at gunpoint? No, I don't imagine he will be happy to hear that at all.' He smiled, and then there was the same, grim mortician. 'Take care,' he said, raising a finger from the wheel in farewell.

I left the car and headed towards the entrance. A wind was blowing dead leaves across the ground. Finally the cold weather had arrived. I knew it was here to last. I could feel it inside the little black hole in my stomach.

I let myself in. The entrance was bathed in darkness and the central atrium rising high overhead conjured an image of an empty cathedral viewed alone at night. In the absence of gunfire, screams, or the general indication of some sort of climactic showdown, I set off towards Fomalhaut's office. Lights flickered in quiet laboratories and complex machinery continued on its automated path as I made my way along, wondering if I should pretend to carry a gun. I needn't have worried about that, or getting lost. Like a spectre emerging from out of the ether, Kader appeared at the end of the corridor, once again outfitted in his signature pantone.

'It's so windy and confusing in here, isn't it?' he asked, his voice a sort of child-like shudder. I could see his eyes clearly, but only the gun in his hand glistened. 'I always get lost.' He smiled, holding the weapon like a toy. 'Here, follow me. I'll take you where we're going.'

I followed along behind him. A few moments later we arrived at Fomalhaut's office.

'Do come in,' Fomalhaut called. 'Only, close the door behind you won't you? Despite all of our fancy gadgetry there's a constant draft in here.'

Fomalhaut was sitting back comfortably in his fancy chair, dressed in his best lab coat. I had half-expected to see Elliot Wallace laid out on a trestle table surrounded by candles and anointed with fragrant oils. But not much had changed since I had last been there apart from the addition of Stohl's body lying slumped on the sofa. His throat was a grisly red ribbon, his face a bouquet of car crash-induced lacerations, his chest rising and falling at half time.

'What did you do?' I said, crossing the room to him.

'Nothing dramatic. I just gave him something to help him rest,' Fomalhaut said. 'He found himself understandably overcome with the news of his uncle's tragic and untimely death. And very agitated.' He shook his head. 'Who can blame him, really?'

The Kid busied himself pouring from a bottle of Krug champagne in a gold-trimmed ice bucket. 'Drink?'

'A bit early for me,' I said.

The Kid shrugged and put the tray down on the coffee

table. He passed a glass to his boss, letting a hand linger on Fomalhaut's shoulder.

'You're sure you won't have a drink?' Fomalhaut asked.

'It wouldn't make much difference, now,' the Kid said.

'Billy!' Fomalhaut scolded. 'Until he proves otherwise the police officer here is our friend. Yes, that business at the farmhouse was unpleasant, but our guest can hardly be blamed for that. Not when we have the guilty party here.' He looked towards the sofa and Stohl. 'And after all I did for him, too. I practically raised him while his uncle was off spending all of his money… Anyway, won't you have a seat, detective?'

I propped Stohl up and sat beside him. The Kid hadn't searched me, so they must have known I was unarmed. Either that, or they thought a gun couldn't save me from what was coming. The only option was to wait it out. Perhaps Kavinsky would have already called for backup. Or perhaps we'd make friends and laugh about it all afterwards.

Fomalhaut sighed apologetically. 'They won't let you arrest me, you know. The reality is that there are too many people depending on my technology to help run the country. Not to mention to keep their bank accounts full. To keep their enemies out of power. To help them clamber over the competition on their way to the top of the pile. What are you hoping for? That they'll put me in a prison cell? Something more secure? My technology single-handedly runs the prisons, the military, the transport systems, immigration centres, medical infrastructure, our country's food production…' He leaned forward as though having saved this next bit just for me. 'Perhaps you don't understand: I've already won.'

'Then why the need for the virus?'

He batted the suggestion away. The Kid laughed, squeezing Fomalhaut's shoulder in obvious admiration.

'The virus's strength isn't in its ability to consolidate power through threat of death, or by allowing me to kill off certain enemies,' Fomalhaut said. 'As you outlined back at the farmhouse, I already have the power to do anything I want. No, my aims are loftier. The virus' true power is in its potential to refine the customer field. Strengthen the sample. Face it, detective, this world is vastly overpopulated and competition for resources means less for all of us. A virus that can be programmed to remove certain genetic codes will be invaluable not just in thinning the herd, but in advancing the human race. Oh, don't look so surprised. I'm not talking about killing based on race, just on removing those who genetically don't offer as much promise as others. Forget this petty revolutionary struggle; this virus is a defining moment for our species. This is re-inventing the wheel, discovering fire all over again and purging our enemies in the flames.'

'You're talking about eugenics. About genocide. Who are you to decide who lives and dies? How could you even begin to presume –'

'My dear boy, I hope you won't accuse me of being patronising, but don't you think it's possible that someone who has dedicated their life to studying the human condition might just have a better grasp of this sort of thing than a police officer? Consider this: there are already twelve billion people on this earth. Many are living in poverty. We are farming meat in test tubes because if we continued to use cows we would exhaust this planet's resources in two years. The coral reefs are dead. Eighty per cent of the earth's fauna has become permanently extinct, and our government and others across the world employ a policy of permanent conflict simply in order to provide employment for the masses – and even then births outweigh deaths by roughly four to one, week on week. There is simply no future for humanity in its current guise. Something has to be done. A serious re-focusing of our efforts.

As a species we require a dynamic, universal undertaking to save us from extinction. I am the surgeon performing the amputation that will allow the body to live. This virus will do away with the weak and strengthen humanity's immune system once and for all. By delivering this gift I will transcend from mere tech genius to the saviour of the human race. I am only sorry that you won't live to see it.'

The Kid shifted the gun in his hands. He was growing restless. My only hope was that Kate had gotten away, slipped out of the city to join Bagby and the resistance. With a small army behind her she'd be safe for the time being and should anything happen to her, Bagby would make sure her body never fell into the wrong hands.

'You know, all of this could have been achieved much quicker if Rachael Faron had just given me what I needed after her husband died. That was my first mistake, believing she didn't know anything about what her husband had done. It took me a long time to work out that Edward had injected a sample of the virus into someone. But then, of course, when you think about it, it really is obvious. Of course he wanted his work to live on, no matter the cost – that man always did have an ego. Then it was a simple case of running RZ's DNA through the CashPlant^{TM} records to find the boy. Looking back, I am embarrassed that we got the wrong sibling. My mistake was in thinking that Edward Faron wouldn't risk his own daughter's life with his virus. I was certain he would have gone for the boy instead. I suppose she was disposable to him.'

'Or he saw her as his one true hope,' I said.

'Maybe, maybe,' Fomalhaut said, sounding bored.

'So what now?' I asked. 'You kill me and Stohl, then what? You don't have the virus. You just admitted that you got the wrong sibling – or Koch did. Kate is your only hope and by now she's far, far away. Even with all your cameras and drones you'll never find her. And she'll outlive you, too. And on your death bed, as you give your last, gasping breath, you'll know you've failed.'

'On the contrary,' Fomalhaut said. 'Kate Faron just entered the building.'

A screen appeared above the mock fireplace. Sure enough, there was Kate making her way through the labyrinth corridors of Vangelis.

'Billy, be a gentleman and show our last guest to the party,' Fomalhaut said. He turned to me. 'These corridors can be so difficult to navigate at night; a wrong turn and one may never leave.'

The Kid passed my chair. There was a moment when I could have gone for him but before I could Fomalhaut reached into his pocket and pulled out Stohl's gun. He didn't look too frail to empty two shots into me before I reached him.

'Such vulgar weapons,' he said with a small shrug. 'But sometimes one needs to employ the more primitive methods in tandem with the more complex.'

Beside me, Stohl gasped then sat up violently.

'Welcome back, "nephew",' Fomalhaut said. 'You're just in time.'

'My uncle...' Stohl said, looking around the room as if he'd just been teleported there.

'Was a boorish man who inherited a lot of money and happened to invest in the right sector,' Fomalhaut continued. 'But there are more imminent matters at hand than your uncle's recent and necessary departure. We are about to be joined by someone far more important than any one of us. Someone you've both gone to great lengths to protect.'

Stohl tried to stand. The gun in Fomalhaut's hand followed him as he collapsed back onto the sofa.

'Have to…' Stohl mumbled, his face flat and white beneath the bruises.

'It's OK,' I said.

A muffled bang sounded outside as if to prove otherwise. Fomalhaut's eyes darted to the door before returning to his guests. 'Sit back down,' he said. 'Don't worry, detective. Billy would never hurt her. She's far too important.'

The door opened. The Kid stood there. He took a step into the room, then his legs buckled and he fell, a red ink blot spreading from under his right arm, even as he reached towards Fomalhaut. Even as he lay dead on the floor. Without blinking, Fomalhaut turned and fired at the doorway. The bullet hit empty space. The distraction was all Stohl needed. He launched himself clumsily against Fomalhaut, dragging him to the ground. Fomalhaut's gun went off again. Stuffing burst from the sofa beside me. I pulled myself up and, grasping my bandaged stomach, hit Fomalhaut across the face with the champagne bucket. He fell backwards and lay stunned but conscious in a scattering of ice.

Stohl knelt beside him, trying to catch his breath. He smiled weakly. 'Good work, partner.'

I helped him up and sat him down again, pocketing his gun.

Kate appeared in the doorway. She hadn't grown any less fond of the gun she'd shot me with, and held it pointed at us now. She stepped over the Kid's body, ignoring us, then turned to face Fomalhaut, towering over him beautiful and full of raw fury.

'Murderer,' Fomalhaut said, through bloody lips.

'You ruined my parents' careers,' Kate said. 'You forced them to take their own lives. You forced my father to infect me with this… disease.' She pressed the gun to Fomalhaut's nose.

'Kate…' I said. 'Don't.'

'It isn't up to you,' she said without looking at me, apparently unsurprised to see me there, and alive.

'Your parents understood what they were doing,' Fomalhaut said. 'They were scientists. They would have sacrificed a daughter to save the human race. Especially an adopted one.'

The gun went off. Fomalhaut's hand flew to his shoulder as if it had been nailed there. Blood ran between his fingers.

'Don't,' Stohl said. 'My partner's right; this is all for nothing if we don't take him in. Your parents... your parents were already proud of you. This won't change that. '

Kate turned to him. 'Maybe. But the police have done what they can. Now it's time for something else.'

Stohl seemed about to protest, then something painful washed over his face. He sank back on the sofa and sighed. 'Do what you have to.'

'You killed my brother too,' Kate continued, turning back to Fomalhaut. 'I never knew him. But I can see now that he wasted his life. Trying to be famous? In a world like this? But I'll make enough change for both of us. For my mother and father, too. I've been given a chance to remake this country for the better, and it wouldn't be fair to them, or myself, if I let it go to waste.'

Fomalhaut lifted his hand from his shoulder and regarded the blood that glistened like oil on his fingers. He smiled. 'Then you may succeed where it appears I have failed. You are your father's daughter after all – your *real* father. He would be proud.'

I'm not sure Fomalhaut ever realised his mistake. I still wanted him alive. I dived for Kate as the gun went off. The bullet ricocheted somewhere overhead.

'Idiot!' Kate's fist hit my stomach, dropping me like a cattle prod.

From my new position on the ground I watched a section of

wall slide away to be replaced by the black of night. And there was Fomalhaut, scurrying out into the cold.

Kate fired, once, twice, then sprinted after him, escaping just as the door slid shut.

'Go,' Stohl said.

I felt under the arm of Fomalhaut's chair and my fingers found a button. I pressed it and the door opened a second time. I ran through and found myself wading through dew-wet grass underneath a grey sky hurrying towards dawn. The door closed behind me. The air was cold and damp and the sound of sirens throbbed nearby. Kazinsky had done his job. Soon Ormsby and his team would arrive and pretend that none of this had ever happened. To lock Kate away and subject her to a short, painful life as a lab rat. I couldn't let that happen.

A distant slash of firs marked the beginning of the woods. The white flutter of Fomalhaut's lab coat made its way towards the trees pursued, somewhere in the darkness, by Kate. A shot rang out, followed by the crack of metal thumping into wood. Fomalhaut ducked. I hurried towards him, the earth tilting, the stars twisting in the sky. And there was Kate, tracing Fomalhaut's movements along her gun barrel as he reached the trees. I couldn't catch up in time. There was nothing else I could do. With the stars spinning above me, I raised my gun, focused on the small patch of back, and fired.

31

Repercussions

If I got very close to the window and twisted my head at just the right angle I was able to see the tops of the ash trees and the sun shining overhead. And if I pressed my ear up against the bars I could almost imagine the sound of birds chirruping and bees buzzing over the backdrop of the traffic on the Fulham Road. Later, at lunchtimes, an orderly would come and bring me my food. A ham sandwich with a side of coleslaw. They don't much go in for wellness in hospitals, these days. As I ate, the orderly would stand in the corner with his arms crossed, watching. I would smile at him and focus on the thin black hairs laid across his arms. It would not be good to meet his eyes.

In the afternoons, I focused on my fitness. Two hundred laps of my room. Fifty press-ups. I can't do lunges anymore. The gunshot wound healed well, but I haven't been quite the same since the inquiry. I think it was the pills. But I can't remember much about any of that. I can only remember an old man spreading himself against the trunk of a pine tree then sliding slowly to the ground. Then lights. Lights and voices. Police officers and the deafening hum of rotor-blades. Everyone searching, searching. The back of a van and then the small, square room in the countryside. Chalky white tablets and scorching blue electrodes. Sharp needles and blunt questions. And then... and then sometime in the New Year, my own room in the former Chelsea and Westminster Hospital.

Dr Daniels came to see me most evenings. We would talk about the paintings I'd been working on.

'Flowers,' he'd exclaim warmly, marvelling at the exotic blooms of red and mauveine and phthalo blue. He thinks they're influenced by Warhol. Repetitions of repetitions. High culture. All the rage.

'Very good,' he would say. 'But how do they make you *feel*?'

'Oh, they make me feel calm,' I would reply, doing my best to hold my smile until he returned it. Then he would slowly stand and leave, the big orderly following behind him.

It was the nights that caused me trouble. Long periods of lying awake with the silence. The moulding on the ceiling showing me the faces of people I used to know. Mercer was gone and there was no news of Kate or Bagby. The revolution wasn't quite the success its supporters had thought it might be and most uprisings had been crushed before they could get started. Someone had tipped the police off. Now, only a handful of revolutionaries remained, hiding out in the countryside. Kate and Bagby, apparently, were among them.

Stohl – Daniels told me – was doing well. He was promoted for his part in bringing down Fomalhaut, just in time for Christmas. It didn't make the news. How could it? It never happened. He refused the ownership of his uncle's company, of course. He really is dedicated to the police force. Now, with his apparent blessing, Vangelis has been taken over by the state, with all profits feeding into its new National Wellbeing initiative. The building block of a brighter tomorrow. And in this brave new world we must all find new ways of caring for one another as part of a strong and stable society. Daniels discusses this with great enthusiasm. There's even talk, he tells me in hushed tones, of a position for him. There's exciting research afoot in exploring the limitations of the human mind via nootropics and, apparently, the right people consider him the right man for the job.

The wailing of the other inmate kept me awake, too. As far as I could tell, he and I were alone in the building, although Daniels evaded the question when I put it to him directly. Instead of answering he would glance over his shoulder at the orderly, swallow wetly and say, 'And just what is it about *flowers* that draws your imagination?'

He was usually quiet at night, RZ, but towards the end he would cry brokenly into the early hours. Like a dog locked inside without any company. I couldn't help but feel that his sadness heralded a change, that he was the harbinger of terrible news.

On the last day, as I stood with my face pressed up against the bars of the window, trying to entice a sparrow to return to the ledge with its worm, the cell door opened and four figures walked in. I recognised them all, and greeted them with a wave.

'What do you think?' Ormsby said.

'I told you, he won't be any trouble,' Dr Daniels replied. 'If he does change his tune, the orderly and I will be waiting just outside the door.'

'Better you wait down the corridor,' Ormsby said. He nodded to the orderly. 'Can you?'

The big man came and took me by the arms and led me to my chair in the middle of the room. I tried not to struggle as he attached the straps to my chest, wrists and ankles. So this was it, the final interrogation. My hands shook and tears sprang to my eyes with Pavlovian efficiency. But I knew I could handle it. I had done it all before, after all.

'That will be all, thank you,' Ormsby said. Daniels paused, caught my eye, then nodded and left, the orderly following him out.

'Thank you, Stohl,' Ormsby said as my old partner dragged my little wooden coffee table in front of the chair then set up a screen where I could see it. He didn't meet my eyes but he looked healthy; his features sharper, his eyes sharper. He wouldn't be visiting the Farm anytime soon.

He withdrew to a chair by the door and sat on the arm, giving Ormsby the floor.

'Do you remember why you're here?' Ormsby asked, bending at the waist as he brought his face close to mine.

I smiled back at him.

'Damn it,' Ormsby said. 'You're not doing yourself any favours. You could have ended all of this with one word when we picked you up. I don't understand why you persist in doing this to yourself. You only had to swear that she had shot Fomalhaut and to tell us where she had gone – or even where you thought she *might* have gone – but you refused. And don't bother telling me you don't know anything. Lives have been lost as a result of your refusal to cooperate. More every day.' He ran a hand over his face. His hair was thinning, I noticed, and bags had settled under his eyes as if to shore up his eyelids. 'Stohl and I know you were a good police officer,' he continued. 'We know you did everything in your power to stop what happened happening. We know you had nothing to do with what happened to Mercer. We know you only wanted to protect the girl – but surely you understand that your response to all of this has been blown far out of proportion?'

He stopped abruptly and looked at me, as though waiting

for me to speak. Then he sighed and tilted his head back. 'We didn't want to have to do this, but none of it mattered in the end. Your memory might have failed you at the crucial moment but someone else talked, you see – someone always talks.' He nodded to Stohl who came and turned on the screen beside me before returning to his chair arm.

'We found out where they were hiding, you see,' Ormsby said. 'The girl, Bagby and their merry band of treasonous ex-servicemen. There was no chance of us bringing them in peacefully – last week's shooting in Scunthorpe and the bombing in Hove proved that. No, the Prime Minister favoured a more complete approach. One that guaranteed this rebellion would never rear its head again. This video footage was taken three nights ago.'

He leaned forward and pressed 'play'. The screen filled with a roving bird's-eye view of a forest at night. The drone advanced over the tree tops. A small camp appeared below; cooking fires, tents, men and women milling about. There was a bang, a flash of yellow light, and then the clearing was reduced to a smoking black plume, ringed by flaming trees. Then the footage switched to a view of Fomalhaut's farmhouse as more drones flew overhead. The same thing happened. The viewpoint switched to a burning country skyline. Then came a mirage of destruction: explosions over old buildings in small towns, over caravans standing in empty car parks, over barges moored along quiet canals, over cars fleeing along forested roads. I sat and watched, understanding RZ's horror: they couldn't resist showing him how his daughter had met her end.

'Turn it off,' I said quietly. 'Please turn it off.'

Ormsby looked at me for a moment then signalled Stohl with a wave of his hand. Again, he avoided my eyes as he leaned forward and flicked off the screen, the images of burned-out towns and houses and hideouts scorched onto my retinas.

'We have confirmation,' Ormsby said from the door, 'of a double hit on Bagby and Kate Faron.' He looked me in the eye. 'Don't feel sentimental for them. They knew which side they were choosing. They knew what would happen to them if they persisted down that road. If they had been more sensible they might have been allowed the same treatment as you. They might be getting out soon. You never know.'

He left the room without another word, leaving Stohl to linger.

'There's a place for you on the force, now that this is all over,' my former partner said, speaking as though we'd never met. 'Down in the evidence room, cataloguing OU files. It isn't much but… it's the best that I could do.' He pulled something from his pocket then left without another word. The orderly came in and untied me.

I waited until his footsteps had receded along the corridor, then picked up the object from the table. It was my old police badge, only with a new unit signifier beside the same hopeful photograph of that fresh recruit newly promoted to the rank of detective. I closed the wallet and put it down. Keeping me in the force was the best way to keep tabs on me. Besides, I had nowhere else to go.

Across the corridor RZ had resumed his wailing. The last of the children he had never known was gone. Her limbs, hair, eyes, mouth, feet, ribcage, ground into dust by a white flash of death that brought everything to an instant end. Along with Kate, Bagby had martyred himself in an attempt to recapture his glory days, a sense of purpose. With them died any hope of a new revolution. All their efforts amounted to was a brief cry of protest, echoing across the country like the aftershock of the explosions that killed them, their chance to force real change blown away like smoke on the wind.

I crossed to the window and stood again with my face pressed against the cold bars. It was already dark outside and there was no sign of the sparrow. The small, dark shapes of the bushes below met my eyes like accusatory ghosts, like the remnants of the best people I had ever known. Along the corridor, RZ wailed on while out on the Fulham Road a siren sounded.

32

The Lion

The train pulled into the station. I closed the notebook and slid it into my rucksack. A man stood back to let me out into the aisle. I stood for a moment, holding onto a headrest as the train juddered to a stop. These days, even the exertion of standing up is dizzying. Outside, the freezing air slid inside my coat. I drew the coat closer around me and joined the few passengers hurrying along the platform towards the barriers. The wind was blowing directly up off the sea, buffeting the blue-grey waves. I checked my watch. I had been told that the A23 bus would take me where I needed to go. Behind me, a security camera looked down from the station wall. I glanced up at it, straightened the straps on my rucksack, and set off down the road.

The footpath curved down towards the sea. I had distant memories of coming here with my grandmother as a child; the sea a rippling brown slab waiting just beyond the expanse of tar-streaked sand. Sometimes, the shore would be so far out that we would have to walk for a mile through sink pools, often falling in up to our knees, distracted by the tracks and shapes of small sea creatures. Razor clams and crabs. Dried-out starfish and dead seaweed. And then we'd reach it, the freezing water that we could only stand for two minutes before hurrying back to shore, pale and alive.

All of that seemed a long, long time ago. As I walked along the shore to the bus stop, the sea seemed to hold these memories in its depths. Perhaps they would be mined by the cleaning units bobbing on the horizon as they sucked up plastics and polystyrene, filtering the water like an artificial kidney. Already, certain species of eel and mackerel shark were said to be returning to the area. The town, though, was even more dilapidated than I remembered. A new art gallery had opened and quickly closed down. Now no one visited anymore. Social decay was not good taste. Two years ago a bomb had torn the pier from its stilts, completing the effect.

The bus came and I rode it along the coast to a small estate a few miles out of town, the buildings becoming shabbier and less hopeful with each stop. I got off where the bridge crossed the harbour. The fishermen were returning early, and with empty nets. Opposite the harbour stood a cul-de-sac of bungalows. The one I wanted was at the far end. I stood reclaiming my breath against the doorframe before ringing the bell. Eventually the door opened and there was Mercer.

'It's me,' I said after a minute.

She squinted then nodded and led me inside. 'You've lost weight. It doesn't suit you.'

We went through into a lounge cluttered with coffee-table books and weighty tomes detailing conspiracy theories and famous police cases.

'Take a seat,' Mercer said as she shuffled out into the kitchen to make us tea. I sat staring out of the low bay window, looking at the shrubs being blown about in the wind, trying to glimpse the sea between them.

When she came back neither of us knew how to begin. The years hadn't been kind to Mercer, either. Koch's attack had left her blind in one eye and a milky white ball stared back at me now. Her bionic hand had been replaced by a simple, cheap hook which she used with a sort of reluctant expertise as she poured out the tea. Whoever had re-set the rest of her bones had done only a slightly better job than Kavinsky had done on me, and she was left with a subtle hunch and a noticeable limp. The scars criss-crossing her face, however, had faded somewhat, hidden among the more natural lines brought on by age, giving an overall impression of quiet, distinguished dignity.

'I hear they still have you down in the evidence room,' she said. 'Almost two and a half years after it all happened.' She passed me a chipped cup filled with Lapsang. 'Cheers. So they haven't driven you out yet.' She took a sip and swallowed. 'They will.'

'We'll see.'

Mercer eyed my luggage. 'Did you bring it?'

I pulled the rucksack up onto my lap, undid the drawstring and pulled out a cardboard box with a yellow evidence tag still on it. If they caught me, they caught me. At this stage, I didn't think there was much more they could do to me. The pills inside rattled. I opened the box, took a bottle out, opened that and passed one of the pills across to Mercer. She held it in her mouth then chased it down with tea. She shuddered as it went down. Then, slowly, her shoulders relaxed.

'There should be enough for six months,' I said.

Mercer nodded that I should put the box down on the table.

'It's the cold that does it,' she said. 'It's a sad state of affairs that a woman of my age has to resort to illicit measures to numb the pain of wounds attained in the line of duty.' She held up her tea and saw the last bit off with a jerk of her wrist. 'Cheers. Fuck them.'

With the transaction over, I was impatient to move on to the real reason I had come down to the sea.

'We're safe here?' I asked.

Mercer looked like she might hit me. She scowled, held up a finger, then got up and crossed the room to a record player where she put on a record I hadn't heard in a long time. Violins swelled through the room, building into a soaring wave cut with staccato piano and a slow, languid drumbeat. I closed my eyes, and smiled as my mother's voice came in, lifting the song up into the clouds. I couldn't help the tear that came. When I opened my eyes again, Mercer was smiling at me. So, she'd known who my mother was all along.

I cleared my throat and got back to business while the song continued in the background. Time was of the essence, and there were revolutionaries to find.

'So,' I said. 'When did you last see her?'

Mercer looked hard at me for a moment as my mother reached the chorus. She shook her head. 'If this really is a path you want to go down,' Mercer said, 'you need to think properly about what it will mean. These people are serious. They're angry – angrier than ever after the massacres.'

'If they're going to strike, if it's going to happen –'

'You have to be a part of it. I know. But remember, it may be too late to atone for the failings of the past.'

I pulled my police badge from my pocket and laid it on the table. 'I'm finished. One way or another,' I said, my voice muffled by the record. 'I may as well make it count for something.'

'Take that away,' Mercer said. 'And what if I told you that

it was all just rumour?' she said after a moment. 'That I hadn't actually seen her, that I didn't know anything about it at all?'

'Then I wouldn't believe you.' It was my turn to quote Sartre. '"*Freedom is what you do with what's been done to you*"'.

Mercer nodded, then silently she took up my police badge and weighed it in her hand. She stared at it in contemplation. 'But it's true. I haven't seen her. I only told you that because I needed you to bring the drugs. I'm sorry.'

'There are easier ways to get painkillers. Closer ways, less risky ways.'

Mercer walked across to the fire and leaned against the mantlepiece, using her hook for balance. 'There's nothing left for you here. For any of us. Go home. You're nearly three years too late.' With her back to me she held her remaining hand over the flames, then dropped my badge into them. She held my gaze, then looked up at the ceiling light overhead. 'They'll be here soon,' she said as the record died and my mother's voice faded. 'You'd better go.'

I followed her to a screen door leading out into a small patch of garden at the back of the house.

'Goodbye,' Mercer said. 'I'm sorry it didn't work out differently.'

'Goodbye,' I said, wanting to say more but failing.

The door slammed behind me and I stood alone in the frozen garden. Through the window I saw Mercer's shadow and the painkillers left on the table. Then, inside, my mother's record started again from the beginning, and that was that. There was no one there to meet me in the garden. Not even a note. I waited, glancing back at the window but the curtain had been drawn, the music growing louder behind it. I made a tour of the lawn, which took all of twenty seconds. There was nowhere for anyone to hide, and nowhere to conceal any indicator of what I should do next. So that was it. That was my answer.

There was no point in waiting around. I left by the gravel path at the side of the bungalow and walked to the main road without looking back, my hands thrust into my pockets, the sea wind stinging my face.

'On oceans we float, away from it all. And birds they soar, like my heart at your door,' I sang under my breath.

'Excuse me,' a woman's voice said.

I looked up, but it was only a young mother with a pram, asking me to step aside as we passed on the bridge. The bus to the train station was pulling away. I was in no rush to meet it, and let it go. I stood waiting for the next one, looking out over the sea as the waves rolled up against the sand, gaining a little ground each time. Further along the promenade children in wetsuits were jumping into the sea. They plunged beneath the freezing waves before surfacing in a burst of spray and pink faces, then swam back to the seaweed-slick steps leading upward to safety.

I looked back along the road. The woman with the pram had stopped in the middle of the bridge, watching the skiffs come in. She was dressed in a long houndstooth coat and black boots. She leaned out over the water, her face obscured by a dark bob. Apparently bored of the fishing boats, she turned and walked away, leaving the pram behind. There was no one else around to intervene, so I hurried back to the bridge, calling after her. But when I reached the pram I saw that there was no baby there at all, just empty space.

'Hey!' I called again.

The woman paused at the far side of the bridge. She turned and looked back at me. I smiled. The next bus was pulling in and the children were launching themselves into the sea again. Soon the evening train would be departing for London, speeding back towards the bright lights, towards Ormsby and rules and regulations and a life that made little sense. I turned away from them and followed Kate across the bridge. There was work to be done.

Acknowledgements

Thanks to Mum and Dad who have been more than generous with their support and encouragement, especially when it seemed this book might not get off the ground. Thanks to Amelia who was my first reader and biggest supporter. Thanks, always, to Ralphie for the distractions. Thanks to Russel McLean for the late edits that helped make this the best book it could be. Thanks to Philip for your editorial input. Thank you to Andrew, Anna and all at Unbound for giving this book a platform. Thank you to Dave Hillier for the generous and unexpected support. And thank you to everyone who's supported (and hopefully, enjoyed) my writing so far.

Unbound is the world's first crowdfunding publisher, established in 2011.

We believe that wonderful things can happen when you clear a path for people who share a passion. That's why we've built a platform that brings together readers and authors to crowdfund books they believe in – and give fresh ideas that don't fit the traditional mould the chance they deserve.

This book is in your hands because readers made it possible. Everyone who pledged their support is listed at the front of the book and below. Join them by visiting unbound.com and supporting a book today.

Caspar Addyman
Jane Allen
Lulu Allison
Billy Anderson
Anna & Ben
Jason Ballinger
Laura Barbato
Zena Barrie
Lisa Bernhardt
Alex Beveridge
Sinead Bianchi
Stephanie Bretherton
Lynn Broadhurst
Debra Broady
Barbara Brocklesby
Dan Brotzel, Martin Jenkins & Alex Woolf
Lily Brown
Richard Budgey

Louise Bull
Victoria Cadman
Sinead Camp
Davey Candlish
Ben Challis
Mark Ciccone
Gordon Clark
Sue Clark
Janice Coates
Jason Cobley
Paula Costello
Alison Cruz
Nick Davey
Matt Davies
Harli Dewar
Rachel DiBiaso
Matthew Doughty
Tom Dowse
Doreen Duckett

Tina Dyson
Joe Ellison
Scarlet Emanuelle Faro
Barry Featherston
Matthew Felton-Dimmack
Nigel Fish
Kerri Fletcher
Connor Fowler
Sammie Fowler
Sarah Gallagher
G.E. Gallas
Harry Gallon
Daniel Garnham
Alan Gillespie
GMarkC
Emma Grae
Josephine Greenland
Debbie Hampton
Ann Harris
Freya Harrison
Neil Harrison
Maximilian Hawker
Jack & Abbie
Sebastian Jaskiewicz
Siân Jay
Annie Jones
Roger Jones
Dan Kieran
Julien Kilbourg
Patrick Kincaid
Alizé Kocadag
Emily Koppit
Ewan Lawrie
Amy Lord
Jose Miguel Vicente Luna
Stuart MacBeath
Kate Maxwell
Conor Charles McAvoy
Kath Meadowcroft
Barbara Joan Meier
Steven Melvin
John Mitchinson
Dave Morgan
Fiona Morgan
Jen & Rose Moxi

Rhel ná DecVandé
Carlo Navato
Janet Phillips
Lisa Piercy
Kelsey Pitcairn
Justin Pollard
Laura Pugh
Tim Relf
Timothy Rickards
Nicola Rimmer
Jane Roberts
Abi Robinson
Cathy Robinson
Michelle Robinson
Rachel Robinson
Joe Robson
Alistair Rush
Dick Selwood
Mike Shaw
Kieran Sills
Spencer Sills
Colin Simpson
Grace Smith
Jesse Smith
Eamon Somers
Greg Spiro
Roasty Spud
Sally Tait
Christopher Trent
Anna Trueman
Imogen Usher
Sonja van Amelsfort
Mark Vent
Valerie Wallis
Andy Ward
Myrtle Ward
Ross Warren
Patrick Wendtland
Debbie Wheeler
Derek Wilson
Tom Wilson
Sarah Wolfe
Philip Womack
Scarlett Wrench
Helen Young